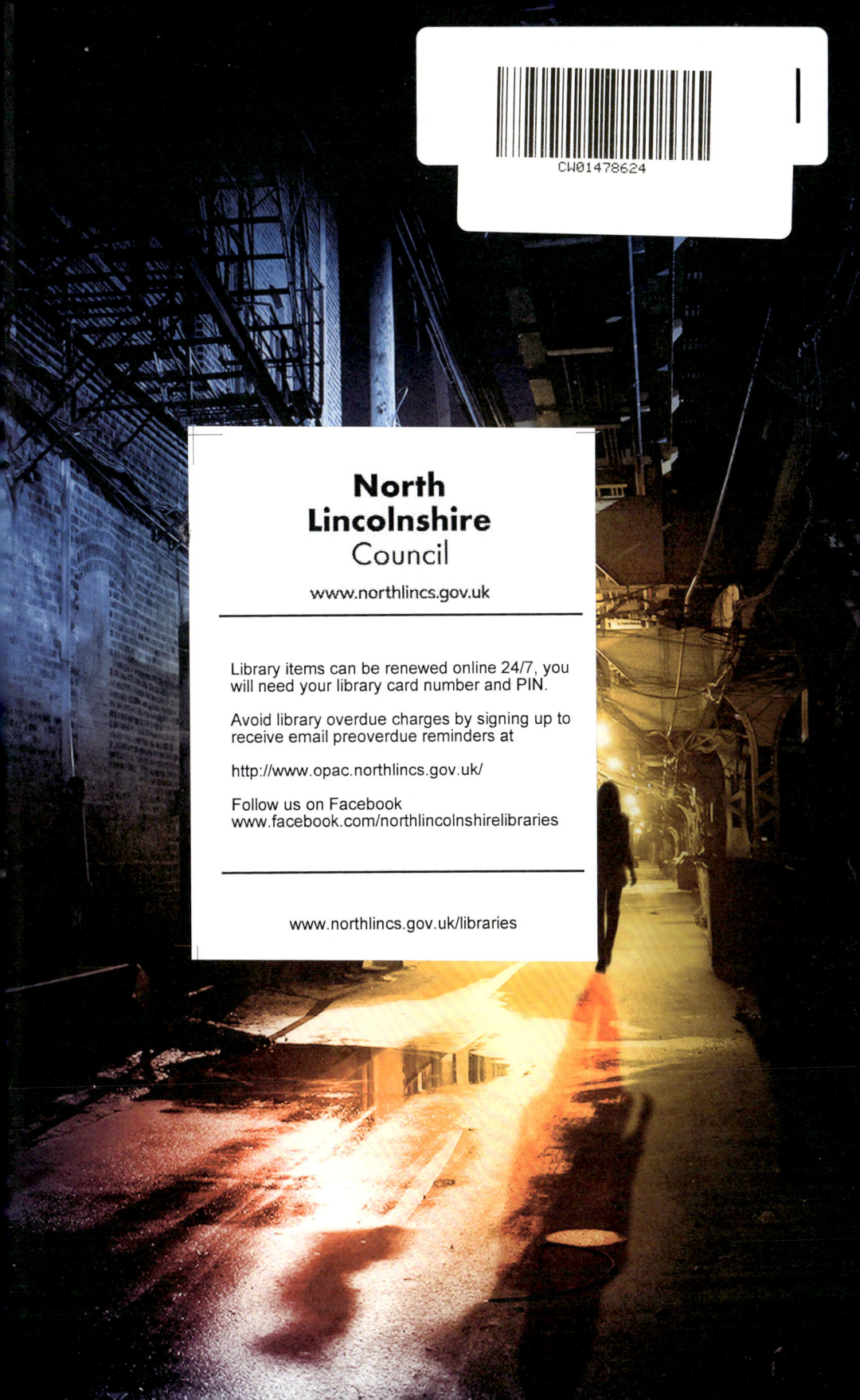

North
Lincolnshire
Council

www.northlincs.gov.uk

Library items can be renewed online 24/7, you will need your library card number and PIN.

Avoid library overdue charges by signing up to receive email preoverdue reminders at

http://www.opac.northlincs.gov.uk/

Follow us on Facebook
www.facebook.com/northlincolnshirelibraries

www.northlincs.gov.uk/libraries

CW01478624

NO REGRET

Martina Cole's bestsellers in order of publication.
All available from Headline.

Dangerous Lady (1992)
The Ladykiller: DI Kate Burrows 1 (1993)
Goodnight Lady (1994)
The Jump (1995)
The Runaway (1997)
Two Women (1999)
Broken: DI Kate Burrows 2 (2000)
Faceless (2001)
Maura's Game: Dangerous Lady 2 (2002)
The Know (2003)
The Graft (2004)
The Take (2005)
Close (2006)
Faces (2007)
The Business (2008)
Hard Girls: DI Kate Burrows 3 (2009)
The Family (2010)
The Faithless (2011)
The Life (2012)
Revenge (2013)
The Good Life (2014)
Get Even (2015)
Betrayal (2016)
Damaged: DI Kate Burrows 4 (2017)
No Mercy (2019)
Loyalty (2023)
Guilty (2024)
No Regret (2025)

On Screen:
Dangerous Lady (ITV 1995)
The Jump (ITV 1998)
Martina Cole's Lady Killers (ITV3 documentary 2008)
The Take (Sky 1 2009)
Martina Cole's Girl Gangs (Sky Factual documentary 2009)
The Runaway (Sky 1 2011)

MARTINA COLE

AND JACQUI ROSE

NO REGRET

HEADLINE

Copyright © 2025 Martina Cole

The right of Martina Cole to be identified as the
Author of the Work has been asserted by her in accordance with the
Copyright, Designs and Patents Act 1988.

First published in 2025 by Headline Publishing Group Limited

1

Apart from any use permitted under UK copyright law, this publication may
only be reproduced, stored, or transmitted, in any form, or by any means,
with prior permission in writing of the publishers or, in the case of reprographic production,
in accordance with the terms of licences issued by the Copyright Licensing Agency.

All characters in this publication are fictitious and any resemblance
to real persons, living or dead, is purely coincidental.

Cataloguing in Publication Data is available from the British Library

Hardback ISBN 978 1 4722 4955 5
Trade Paperback ISBN 978 1 4722 4956 2

Typeset in 12/16pt ITC Galliard Std by Six Red Marbles UK, Thetford, Norfolk

Printed and bound in Great Britain by Clays Ltd, Elcograf S.p.A.

FSC
www.fsc.org
MIX
Paper | Supporting
responsible forestry
FSC® C104740

Headline's policy is to use papers that are natural, renewable and recyclable
products and made from wood grown in well-managed forests and other
controlled sources. The logging and manufacturing processes are expected
to conform to the environmental regulations of the country of origin.

Headline Publishing Group Limited
An Hachette UK Company
Carmelite House
50 Victoria Embankment
London EC4Y 0DZ

The authorised representative in the EEA is Hachette Ireland,
8 Castlecourt Centre, Dublin 15, D15 XTP3, Ireland (email: info@hbgi.ie)

www.headline.co.uk
www.hachette.co.uk

For my best girls
Natalia and Loretta

Prologue

Margate, Kent

7 June 1977

All great things are preceded by chaos.

Deepak Chopra

Margaret Riley climbed aboard a Leyland coach decked out with bunting and photos of the Queen and claimed a window seat near the front. Given the choice of a street party or a trip to London to watch the parade, the residents of her little street in Margate had voted to hire a coach for the day. In holiday mood despite a northerly blowing in off the sea, they waited patiently for their turn to board, cheering on a latecomer who'd had to chase his plastic Union Jack bowler hat halfway down the esplanade after the wind ripped it from his head.

'Bleedin' hell, it's parky! You'd never know it was frigging summer.' Mavis Kirby, who lived next door but one to Margaret, hauled herself up the steep metal stairs and collapsed into the seat across the aisle. 'Good job I put me thermal knickers on. Mind you, they're pinching me fanny something chronic – it's like I've got a bloody lobster living down there. Let's hope it's warmer than this in London.'

Margaret gave her a weak smile but didn't say anything. When she'd left London, fourteen years ago, she'd been a different person, unrecognisable from the woman she was today. She hadn't set foot in the place since – she'd had no desire to try to reconnect with her past. Her focus had been on building a new life and forgetting the old one. But the memories were never far from the

3

surface and she was afraid the sight of those familiar streets would bring them flooding back. Now she was wishing she'd resisted all efforts to persuade her and stayed at home today.

'Room for a little one?' Shirley Green's voice cut through her thoughts. Without waiting for an answer, she squeezed her large frame into the seat next to Margaret and immediately began unpacking her striped nylon tote.

'I made these last night,' she said, pulling the lid off a Tupperware container and offering it to Margaret. 'Vols-au-vent – meat paste and egg.'

Shirley's teenage daughter, hovering in the aisle beside her, cast a longing eye at the pastries. 'Can I sit with you, Mum?'

'No, you bleeding can't! Young 'uns at the back,' Shirley said firmly. 'Go on, piss off, give us grown-ups a bit of peace.' As her daughter rolled her eyes and skulked off down the aisle to join the other teenagers, Shirley held out the box. 'Quick,' she said, 'grab one before that lot devours them all. Like bleedin' gannets, they are.'

Queasy with nerves, Margaret declined. 'Thanks, Shirley, but I've got a bit of a bellyache.'

'Nothing a vol-au-vent won't cure,' Shirley cackled, then proceeded to stuff a whole one in her mouth.

The roar of the coach's engine increased as it began to pull away from the kerb, and a cheer went up from the passengers, followed by a round of applause. Margaret clapped without enthusiasm, then tried to focus on the view. The streets of Margate were festooned with red-white-and-blue decorations. Balloons, many of them already deflated, hung from lamp posts, while flags had been draped over fences and dangled from guttering. Almost every window they passed displayed a photo of the Queen.

No Regret

Inside the coach, a cloud of smoke formed as passengers reached for their cigarettes and lit up. Paper plates of sandwiches were passed up and down the aisle as the neighbours engaged in good-natured banter, but Margaret couldn't bring herself to join in. She couldn't stop wondering what her Margate friends would think if they knew the truth. To them, she was the woman from number 37, respectable, nice tidy house, well-kept garden, always happy to help out when she could, never one to get into a barney . . .

But she hadn't always succeeded in steering well clear of trouble. If they'd had any inkling of the things she'd got up to in Camden Town back in the day, they would have formed a very different opinion of her.

Not that she was ashamed of the things she'd done. She hadn't exactly been blessed with a load of options, so it was a case of doing whatever it took to survive. No point beating herself up over it now.

Shirley, who'd been keeping up a non-stop monologue beside her, let out a cackle and gave Margaret a nudge in the ribs. '. . . then I said to him, "Listen, Arthur, I ain't missing seeing the Queen for nobody. Twenty-five years on the throne deserves a proper celebration. You don't want to come, fine. Suit yerself, ya miserable git."' Did you see them on the telly last night – the crowds lining the Mall? I said to my Julie . . .'

Margaret tuned out again, oblivious to the commentary. She was so lost in her thoughts that she barely registered the driver's assistant – a thin, pasty man with sweat marks under the armpits of his brown polyester shirt – getting to his feet and adjusting his paisley tie. Steadying himself against the front seat, he picked up a microphone and stood, swaying, as he waited for the passengers to notice him.

When they continued to ignore him, he tapped the microphone until the ear-splitting feedback had everyone wincing.

'Testing, testing . . . right then, ladies and gents.' His voice boomed through the speakers mounted on the dashboard of the coach. 'I'm Roger. Welcome to your Silver Jubilee special! God save the Queen! I hope you've all got your flags to wave . . .' He paused for them to wave flags before resuming: 'How about, to get us in the mood, we have a bit of a singsong.'

Shirley was waving her flag and sending vol-au-vent flakes all over Margaret's new outfit from C&A – white flared trousers and a red blouse and blue scarf – which she'd hoped would get her into a more patriotic spirit.

Gripping the microphone tightly, Roger launched into a rendition of 'Land of Hope and Glory', his voice surprisingly low. 'Come on, everyone – join in! Let's see if we can sing loud enough for them to hear us in Buckingham Palace.'

In the seat behind her, Brian from number 32 was belting out the chorus loud enough to wake the dead in Highgate Cemetery. Across the aisle, Mavis's husband was singing with his eyes closed and one hand pressed against his chest.

'Sing up!' Shirley paused between verses to give her a nudge. 'It's the Queen's special anniversary. No long faces today, love.'

Her heart hammering against her ribcage, Margaret pulled a cigarette from her bag, lit it with shaking hands and took a long drag. '*Get a grip,*' she muttered under her breath, trying desperately to summon the grit and determination that had got her out of London. After all, underneath the sensible clothes and good manners, she was still the same old Maggie Riley: didn't matter what anyone did to her, she'd never back down . . .

Book One

Camden

September 1962

The evil that men do lives after them.

William Shakespeare, *Julius Caesar*

Chapter One

'No dawdling, girl!' Kathleen Riley stood in the doorway of the laundrette, shaking her head as her daughter ambled away without a backward glance. 'Your da wants his beer money and there'll be trouble if you keep him waiting.'

Fifteen-year-old Maggie was used to her mother's nagging. It started the minute she got up, chivvying her to scrub this and clean that and tidy up her da's mess. And carried on all day as she worked alongside her mother in the steamy, stinking laundrette. She'd wanted to stay on at school, not least because it offered some respite from her parents, but they'd insisted she earn her keep.

'What's a girl need an education for?' her dad had grunted, slurping his potato soup like the pig he was. 'Leaving school never did your mammy any harm.'

If only Mammy had stayed on at school, Maggie thought. Maybe then she wouldn't have been so stupid as to fall pregnant and end up married to a bastard like Shamus Riley. But she'd kept her mouth shut. Backchat always resulted in black eyes and bruises.

'What's the craic, Maggie? How's your da?' Sean O'Brien, owner of the butcher's shop on the corner of Pratt Street, called as she passed by.

'He's good, thanks.'

Wiping his hands on a grimy blue-and-white striped apron stained with dried blood, Sean grinned. 'And your mammy? How's she?'

'She's good too.' Lately her mum had looked even more exhausted and downtrodden than usual, if that were possible, but it had been drummed into Maggie that their private business was never to be discussed in public. No matter who asked, the answer was always that things were good, all was well in the Riley household.

O'Brien nodded and scratched his bulbous red nose, which always seemed to have a large drip on the end of it. 'Will we be seeing her any time soon?'

'I don't think so,' she replied with a grin.

The butcher laughed good-humouredly. 'She's fierce proud that one. Salt of the earth.'

Maggie liked Sean O'Brien. He seemed decent, unlike most. While men like her father used their wives as punchbags and their children as skivvies, Mr O'Brien's family always seemed at ease in his company. She couldn't remember a single time she'd felt able to relax when her father was around.

Giving him a parting wave, she picked up her pace, darting across Bayman Street ahead of the rag-and-bone man as his horse plodded towards Camden High Street, head bowed low as it pulled the cart piled with scrap metal and junk.

As soon as she turned into the high street, Maggie caught the whiff of the fat fryer in Jo's fish and chip shop. Gripping the shillings her mother had given her, she peered through the glass shopfront, her mouth watering at the thought of a portion of chips and cod scraps with lashings of salt and vinegar. She could almost taste it, but the prospect of what her dad would do to her if she spent his beer money robbed her of her appetite. With a sigh, she walked on.

Ahead of her was the pub. As always, the sign on its battered blue door – NO BLACKS, NO DOGS, NO IRISH – made her think of Thomas. He'd come over with his family on the HMT *Empire Windrush* fourteen years ago. He couldn't remember much about Jamaica, being only two years old when they left, but like the rest of the Johnson family he longed to go back there. Their lives had been miserable since setting foot on English soil, but with his dad unable to work since suffering a heart attack last year, it was all they could do to pay the rent, let alone buy tickets to the Caribbean.

Though she'd never have said so to Thomas, Maggie was glad they wouldn't be leaving. He'd been her best friend ever since she could remember. He was the only one from school she'd stayed in touch with, apart from Pam Whelan who lived up the road, and she was a year older than Maggie.

Still, she could understand why the Johnsons hated London. Only last week, Thomas had taken a battering from a group of Italian Teddy boys. They'd dragged him out of a cafe on Delancey Street, hit him with an iron bar, then carried him to the canal like a prize trophy, before throwing him into the filthy water.

He might have died if it hadn't been for Rory Sheehan coming to his rescue. Rory playing the Good Samaritan had come as a surprise; everyone in Camden was afraid of him. Even her dad, who wasn't scared of anyone, was careful to keep on the right side of Rory.

It was beginning to get dark as she turned left by the lock. Music was playing – a song by some new group called the Bea-tles. She'd have liked to hang around and listen, but her da would probably be keeping an eye out for her. She could already see the warm lights of the Cow and Bull up ahead and a couple of figures on the pavement outside. It took a few more steps before she could make out who they were, and when she did, it stopped her dead in her tracks.

Her father was standing by the wall, trousers down to his knees, his hairy arse pumping away. She couldn't see the woman's face, but her skirt was hitched up and her knickers down.

And then the woman turned her head, the dim light catching her face.

Maggie covered her mouth to stifle a cry as she saw it was her friend Pam.

Chapter Two

Rory Sheehan looked down from his window at the Riley girl hiding in the shadows, watching her father fuck some tart. He squinted, trying to identify the tart in question. She wasn't much more than a kid, though that wouldn't bother Shamus. He'd fuck anything, young or old, provided they still had their own teeth and a pulse. Then again, knowing Riley, even that wouldn't stop him getting his leg over.

The old drunkard came in handy when Rory needed to bring in the heavy mob, deliver a beating. Built like a brick shithouse with fists the size of a Christmas ham, he'd rain down punches like he was swinging a sledgehammer. And he enjoyed it too.

But judging by the black eyes and bruises Rory had seen on the wife and daughter, Riley enjoyed knocking them around as well.

What went on between a man and his wife was none of Rory's business, but he took it as a personal affront when Shamus laid a hand on Maggie.

He watched her now, backing away into the shadows. He couldn't make out what she was wearing, probably some tat picked up from the church jumble sale his old mammy used to run, God rest her soul. But underneath that clobber her body would be soft and voluptuous. The thought of what lay hidden beneath the rags turned him on far more than the tarts with their beehive hairdos and heavy make-up, putting it all on display in figure-hugging dresses and stiletto heels. Maggie Riley was a diamond in the rough, and what made her all the more attractive was that she had no idea. She was pure. Innocent. A proper little virgin.

Feeling his erection growing, he turned away from the window and returned his attention to the man who lay sprawled on the floor. Above his expensive suit, the man's face was an unrecognisable mess of bruised, swollen flesh. His shirt had been ripped open, exposing deep burns and slashed skin. It was what Rory called a suitable punishment.

Without stopping to check whether the man was still breathing, he kicked aside a bloody tooth, stepped over the pool of blood and made his way to the door. He'd get his men to clean up later.

The Cow and Bull was one of three premises Rory owned. He'd started here in Camden, then branched out by opening a pub and club in Soho. Thanks to the success of the Raymond Revuebar, strip clubs were now all the rage and the place was heaving with punters. Only trouble was, it was proving attractive to rival gangs too. The Maltese, the Italians, as well as home-grown mobs like the Krays and the Richardsons – everyone wanted to get in on the action. Which meant Rory was having to plough a lot of his time and energy into protecting his assets and delivering warnings. The guy lying in the Cow and Bull's attic had failed to heed the warning; Rory didn't believe in second chances.

On reaching the foot of the stairs, he glanced down the dimly lit hallway that led to the bar before opening the side door. There was no light in the alley; taking a moment to let his eyes adjust to the darkness, he reached into his trouser pocket and wrapped his fingers round the flick knife he always carried. Seeing no one, he stepped out and silently made his way towards the place he'd last seen the Riley girl.

The sight of Pam and her da going at it had come as such a shock that Maggie had collapsed against the wall, unable to believe her eyes.

Pam. Pam with her da. Her first instinct had been to run up to them, pull her dad off, but then Pam had raised her head, looked over his shoulder and, seeing Maggie, she'd given her a big Cheshire Cat smile.

Da hadn't forced himself on Pam – she'd wanted it.

The thought of it made her sick. She bent over and vomited up the bread-and-dripping she'd eaten that morning.

'Maggie, are you all right?'

The voice was smooth and strong. She felt the gentle touch of a hand on her shoulder.

Wiping the bile from her mouth with her sleeve, Maggie stood up straight, embarrassed that whoever it was had seen her being sick. In the dim glow of the nearest street light she saw a handsome face with high cheekbones, a mop of hair slicked back with Brylcreem and a coy, boyish smile. It took her a moment to realise she was looking at Rory Sheehan. She'd never seen him up close before, and the gentle concern he was showing was completely at odds with the stories she'd heard about him. Except, she reminded herself, he was the one who'd saved Thomas after he got beaten up.

'Come in and get warm, love.'

'I . . . I . . . I can't . . .' She held up the two shillings clutched in her hand. 'My da will go mad if I don't give him his money.'

'Don't you worry about him. I'll sort him out.'

Maggie's heart raced. No one sorted out her da. If Rory said anything to him, she'd be in even more trouble. And her mum would probably give her a clout too, especially after she'd warned her not to dawdle. But when she tried to insist on going after her dad, Rory crouched to bring his piercing blue eyes level with hers.

'You look cold, darlin'. Come indoors and get warm . . .' He took her gently by the arm and ushered her down the alleyway, through the side door of the pub and into a large private lounge with a fire burning in the grate.

She'd never seen such a beautiful room. The smart red-and-gold wallpaper looked too good to put on a wall; it was the sort of thing you'd see wrapped round a present under a Christmas tree in one of those West End shop-window displays.

'Take a seat.' Rory pointed to one of the two leather armchairs.

Her cheeks burning with embarrassment, she stammered, 'Have you a newspaper for me to sit on? I wouldn't want to dirty your chairs.'

'You're fine, Maggie Riley. I'm sure the chairs will be delighted if you sit on them.'

Keenly aware of her tatty old shoes and threadbare coat, she sat down gingerly, keeping to the edge of the leather upholstery.

'Now, let me get you a drink.'

'I'm fine, thank you.'

As if she hadn't spoken, Rory walked across to a drinks trolley in the corner. He selected a cut-glass decanter, poured two large glasses of whisky and handed one to her.

'Thank you.' She placed it on the mahogany table next to her.

'Still seeing that boy of yours?'

'What boy?' Maggie blinked in confusion.

'That black boy you hang around with.'

A cold fear engulfed her. They'd kept their relationship secret, knowing what her dad would do to them both if he found out.

'Don't look so worried!' Rory laughed. 'I'm not going to tell your da.'

Afraid to meet his eye, Maggie stared fixedly at her hands, willing them not to tremble. The silence in the room was broken only by the crackle of the fire and the muffled hum of voices from the main bar.

'Drink up, girl – you've had a shock. It's not every day you find your old man shagging your mate.'

She knew her face must be red as a beetroot by now. It had come as a surprise that he knew her name, let alone that she was friends with Thomas and Pam.

As if reading her thoughts, Rory grinned. 'Running a pub means there's not a lot I don't know about round here.'

Rumour had it he did a lot more than run a pub, but Maggie knew better than to comment.

'You have my word, darlin'. Look at me.'

Shyly she raised her eyes.

'I won't utter a word to anyone. And, at the end of the day, my word is all you've got.'

She nodded. She believed him.

'Right then, drink up.'

She glanced nervously at the glass of whisky. Her mother would skin her alive if she found out she'd been drinking alcohol, but only a fool would say no to Rory.

Her hand shook as she reached for the glass and slowly brought it to her lips. She screwed up her face as she got a taste of the whisky.

'Not used to drinking?' He let out a bark of laughter.

Holding the glass in her lap, she shook her head.

'Next time, I'll open a bottle of champagne for you.'

She didn't want there to be a next time. No matter how kind he was being or how luxurious the room was, she just wanted to go home.

'Anyway, I was thinking, how would you like it if I asked your boy to come and work for me?'

Maggie's head shot up.

'I know how difficult it is for a black boy to get a job, and when I took him home last week after those eejits beat him up, it gave me a right shock to see the dump he's living in. It's just one room – the coldest, dampest room you've ever seen, mould on the walls and a leak in the ceiling – and him and his mum and dad have to share it. I couldn't believe it: the three of them have to eat, sleep, piss and shit in there!'

Maggie had never been to Thomas's house. He lived in King's Cross, but she had no idea where.

'They're obviously finding it a struggle to make ends meet,' he went on. 'And I was thinking I could help by giving the lad a job.'

'You'd do that?' Maggie looked up at him, once more aware of how handsome Rory Sheehan was.

He came over to kneel by her chair, then reached up and placed his hand under her chin so she'd meet his eyes. He brought his voice down to a whisper. 'Because he's your friend and it's the right thing to do. I'm a good Catholic boy, Maggie, and isn't that what Father Patrick teaches us every Sunday at Mass? That we should help the poor?'

She gave a small nod.

'And maybe, when he starts to work for me, you could come

18

with him from time to time.' He gave her a wink, then drew himself up to his full height and took the glass from her. 'Now off you go, darlin'. I'll see you soon.'

As she hurried away from the pub, Maggie knew she should be happy at the prospect of Thomas working at the Cow and Bull. But the nervous flutter in her stomach felt more like fear.

Chapter Three

'Oi, wake up!'

Maggie opened her eyes to see her mother looming over her. It was still dark outside. 'What time is it?'

'Never mind. I need you to come with me. Get dressed.'

When her mother stepped into the light, her face was a mask of pain. She was pale by nature, but now she was a ghostly white.

'What's happened? Is it Da?' Maggie hoped, as she so often did, that her dad had dropped down dead. She knew she should confess such wicked thoughts to Father Patrick but, given that her da and Father Patrick often went to the dogs in Walthamstow, drinking and gambling together, she kept her thoughts to herself.

'Maggie Riley.' Her mum pinched her arm. 'You weren't put on this earth to ask me questions. Get dressed, now! I'll be waiting downstairs – and don't make a noise. Your da is still asleep.'

As soon as her mother left the room, Maggie stumbled out of bed. She hadn't slept well, unable to get the image of her dad and Pam out of her head. The initial shock had now turned to anger. She couldn't wait to give Pam a piece of her mind. Who did she think she was? How would Pam like it if she were to find her dad having sex with Maggie? The very thought of it made

Maggie shudder. Pam's dad was like a walking lump of lard, beer gut spilling over the waistband of his trousers, always stinking of BO and, worst of all, those beady eyes that followed her every move whenever she called round.

Shivering, she pulled her clothes on and tiptoed down the bare wooden staircase.

Her mum was sitting at the kitchen table, clutching her rosary beads and muttering prayers to the Sorrowful Mother. As she made her way to the back door, Maggie noticed that the vegetables had been prepared and were already soaking for tonight's stew. Usually, it was her job to chop the veg as soon as she'd finished scrubbing the kitchen floor. Even when she'd been ill with mumps, Maggie had been expected to do her chores. Reaching for the toilet paper, she opened the back door and headed down the little patch of garden to the outside toilet.

The minute she was alone, her thoughts returned to Rory Sheehan and his offer of a job for Thomas. Though she'd never been to his home, she knew the Johnsons often went hungry because the rent took all the money they had. Last Sunday had been the harvest festival, and she'd crept back into church when the service was over to grab a loaf of bread, tinned kippers and a fine-looking Irish porter cake. She'd told herself it wasn't a sin to give the food to Thomas's family. It had been donated for distribution to the less fortunate, so she was just doing the Lord's bidding.

Suddenly, her stomach tightened. If Rory gave Thomas a job, he would start saving up to go back to Jamaica, and she'd be left here alone.

'Maggie!' Her mum banged a fist on the toilet door. 'Get a move on! We need to leave now.'

'Where are we going?' Maggie pulled the chain and opened the door. 'Are we leaving Da?'

'Maggie Riley, where did you get such an idea? I should wash your mouth out with soap for saying such a wicked thing. Under the eyes of God I'm a married woman, and I shall stay that way until my dying day. Now come on. No more talk.'

Together they returned to the house, put on their coats, and crept out of the front door. The streets were deserted at that hour. Lips pursed, her mother ignored her and they walked in silence past the church and the gasworks, only coming to a halt when they reached the bus stop on Euston Road.

When the bus came, she took the seat next to her mother. Head bowed, Kathleen Riley sat counting her rosary beads, only breaking off to pay the conductor.

Outside, a morning mist turned everything hazy, making it hard to track where they were going. It took two bus changes before they arrived in the East End. Although eighteen years had passed since the last wail of an air-raid siren, the bomb sites had yet to be redeveloped. Every terrace of redbrick houses seemed to have a gap in it where weeds sprouted from piles of rubble.

A milk float was trundling along behind them, crates rattling. Her mother paused, turning her face away as it passed. When it had gone, she grabbed Maggie's hands and looked her in the eye.

Her cracked lips spoke only three words: 'God forgive me.'

Then she stepped up to the front door of the end house and reached for the polished brass knocker.

Chapter Four

Thomas Johnson hadn't thought of himself as small since he turned twelve and suddenly found himself towering over the rest of his class, but standing in front of Rory Sheehan made him feel as if he were shrinking under the man's steely gaze.

'I see your wounds are healing up nicely,' said Rory.

Thomas's hand instinctively reached for the side of his face. He still had trouble seeing out of his left eye, although he counted himself lucky that he hadn't lost his eyelid completely. His cheekbone was fractured, and the deep split of his lip made it difficult to eat.

He had no idea why he'd been dragged out of bed by Rory's men and brought to a private lounge in the Cow and Bull at this hour in the morning. He tried to comfort himself with the thought that if they were planning on delivering a beating, he'd have been dragged off to the cellar or somewhere he wouldn't ruin the furnishings by bleeding all over them.

'I had a word with your girl yesterday, Thomas.'

'My girl?' It came out as a lisp, thanks to his torn mouth.

'Come on, Thomas. We both know who I'm talking about.'

'If you mean Maggie Riley, Mr Sheehan, I don't think she would want to be known as my girl.'

Thomas didn't add that he wished she were his girl, but at the same time the very thought of it frightened him. He'd seen what had happened when his father's friend, Michael Bennett, had courted a white woman. A gang of local lads gave him a kicking. No one saw anything, of course, and no one stepped in to help him. He was taken to Charing Cross Hospital but died from his injuries.

His family sold their few possessions to scrape together the money for a cremation, then paid for his ashes to be posted to his grandmother in Spanish Town, because Michael's last wish had been to return to Jamaica.

But somewhere between the smog of London and the sunshine of the Caribbean, the package containing all that remained of Michael Bennett got lost in the post. He never made it home.

'So you're not soft on each other, Thomas? Is that what you're saying?'

'No, sir,' Thomas lied.

The truth was the only time he felt happy was when he was with Maggie. With her, he could forget about all the bad stuff. The hunger, the squalid little flat, the Teddy boys who'd beaten him up. It was ironic, considering how dangerous it was to be seen out with a white woman, that in her company he could relax and feel safe for once.

Just being with her made Thomas feel better.

Rory took a step closer so he was just inches away. He tilted his head and observed him as if weighing up the truth of his statement. Finally, he spoke: 'That's good, Thomas, that's good, because Maggie Riley is not to be touched by you – or anyone else, for that matter.'

Then he stepped back, the menacing expression gone from his face. 'Anyway, that's not why I invited you here today . . .' He delved into his pocket, pulled out a packet of Capstan full-strength cigarettes and tapped two out, then offered one to Thomas.

'Thank you, but I don't smoke.'

Rory continued to hold out the cigarette for Thomas to take. The look on his face was a reminder that nobody in their right mind said no to Rory, so he took the cigarette, put it to his lips, and leaned in to Rory's cigarette lighter.

On his first draw of smoke, a cough ripped through Thomas, making his eyes water.

Rory roared with laughter. 'We'll make a smoker of you yet, lad. As me dear mother used to say, "A man that doesn't smoke is like a dog that doesn't bark – don't trust him."' He lit his own cigarette, narrowing his gaze at Thomas through the cloud of smoke. 'Right, let's get down to business, shall we? How would you like to come and work for me?'

'*You?*' Thomas blurted.

'You make it sound like that would be a bad thing?' Rory frowned.

'I . . . I . . .' This was the last thing Thomas had expected.

'Lost for words, Thomas?' Rory took another drag on his cigarette.

Thomas wasn't sure what he was supposed to say. He remembered the night Rory brought him home after he'd been beaten up. His mother had welcomed the stranger who'd saved her son, inviting him into her home, but when he gave his name her eyes had widened. Rory Sheehan's reputation as a hard man preceded him everywhere he went.

'When was the last time you ate a decent meal?' Rory asked.

Thomas thought of the tinned kippers and porter cake Maggie had given him last week, but knew better than to bring her name into the conversation.

He shrugged. 'I don't know, sir.'

'If you work for me, Thomas, you'll never be hungry again.' As if to prove his point, Rory drew a wad of five-pound notes from his pocket and threw it down on the table. 'Take it.'

Thomas's eyes skimmed the notes, his mind struggling to keep up. There must be at least a hundred pounds . . .

Rory nodded. 'Go on, take it.'

He'd never seen so much cash. Before the heart attack, when he was working all hours on the London Underground, his father's wages only came to eleven pounds a week. One hundred pounds would almost buy a ticket to Jamaica. If only tickets home were as cheap as the inbound voyage, all three of them could travel home for that money.

'I said, *take it*. And there'll be plenty more where that came from if you come and work for me.'

Whether it was a good idea or not – and his gut told him it wasn't – Thomas knew he had no choice but to accept the offer. He reached for the money; it still looked like a small fortune, but he suspected the price he'd have to pay would outweigh any benefit.

'Thank you, Mr Sheehan.'

'You've got good manners, Thomas. I like that. You'll do well in Soho.'

Soho?

Thomas had never been there, couldn't afford to visit the jazz clubs and coffee shops, much as he would have liked to. He'd also heard about Soho's seedier side: the strip joints and the women who hung around in doorways or posted signs offering 'French lessons'.

'You'll like it there, Thomas. It's not like Camden – no blacks, no Irish – you'll be able to mix with whoever you like. And, once word gets around that you work for me, no one will give you any bother. So what do you say?' He held out his hand to Thomas. 'Shall we shake on it?'

Thomas nodded and shook Rory's hand. As he was about to let go, the grip on his fingers suddenly tightened.

'If there's one thing I expect from the men who work for me, it's loyalty. I take it that won't be a problem?'

Thomas's mouth went dry. 'No, sir.'

'Good.' Rory released his hand and strode towards the thick velvet curtain that ran along the wall. He pulled it back to reveal a wooden door. Grinning at Thomas, he opened the door and waved for him to enter.

Fighting the urge to run, Thomas stepped into a room that at first glance looked as if it was waiting for the decorators to arrive. The furniture and the floor were covered by canvas dust sheets, but the man standing in the middle of the room was no decorator.

Malcolm was Rory's right-hand man, never far from his side. Like his boss, he was of Irish descent. Tall and imposing, his face was made up of hard angles, heavy brows and dark eyes. He was always well dressed and today was no different. But his immaculately tailored blue suit looked out of place alongside the three naked men huddled behind him, their hands tied behind their backs, gags across their mouths, sheer terror in their eyes.

'Do you recognise these men, Thomas?'

Rigid with fear, it was all he could do to shake his head in reply.

'Look again, lad.'

Trembling, he glanced at Rory. 'I don't know who they are, Mr Sheehan.'

'No matter.' Rory wrapped an arm round Thomas's shoulders and squeezed. He pointed at the men. 'These are the men who attacked you.'

Thomas's head shot round to face Rory.

'This lot need a taste of what they dish out,' Rory snarled. He pulled his flick knife from his pocket, pressed the button to expose the sharp, jagged blade, then handed it to Thomas. 'I won't have it said that Rory Sheehan allows people to get away with attacking his men.'

Thomas stared at the knife in his hand, his eyes filling with tears.

'Is there a problem?' Rory's voice was smooth.

'No . . . no.' Thomas blinked away the tears.

'Good. That's what I like to hear, because it wouldn't do for you to let me down. Not in front of people. That wouldn't do at all. So get stuck in, lad. It's a lovely knife, that – sharp enough for what you need to do. I always go for the stomach meself.'

The tallest of the three men lost control of his bladder and urine began to run down his leg, puddling at his feet.

Rory's eyes flashed. 'You filthy, fucking dog!' Snatching the knife from Thomas, he launched himself at the man, slashing down at his penis. He collapsed in a pool of blood, writhing in pain. Although the gag silenced his screams, Thomas could hear them loud and clear.

Rory handed him the knife. 'Right, now it's your turn.'

Thomas could barely see the knife, but he could feel the blood dripping down the blade onto his fingers.

'They said in the war, the first kill was always the hardest. After that' – he winked at Thomas – 'easy peasy. Because if they're not dealt with, next time it might be your mammy they hurt, and you wouldn't want that, would you?' The smile he gave didn't reach his eyes, which locked on Thomas with a dead stare. 'And I'm sure you wouldn't want anyone else to hurt her either.'

Thomas got the message. He raised his arm and plunged the knife into the man's stomach, again and again.

Chapter Five

Doris Turner stood on her doorstep, a roll-up dangling from her lips, her grey hair tightly wound in curlers. 'Kathleen, I'm sorry to be seeing you again. Still, these things happen.'

She was a small, round woman who'd seen both wars and hadn't thought much of either. Born and brought up in the East End, she had refused to evacuate from her two-up, two-down terrace off the Whitechapel Road even when the bombs dropped. 'If I'm going to be carried off in a coffin,' she'd told her husband, 'it's going to be from my own front door.'

Spotting Maggie standing behind her mother, Doris smiled, showing off an overcrowded mouth of teeth. 'I take it this is your girl.'

'It is.' Kathleen nodded.

'Fine-looking lass, you'll have to watch her.'

'When I need advice from you, Doris Turner, I'll ask for it.'

'Suit yourself.' Doris laughed, stooping to pick up the milk bottle on her doorstep. 'I suppose you'd best come in, then.'

As she followed her mother through the front door, Maggie's eyes darted around the hallway, taking in the brown wallpaper and the ceiling haphazardly daubed with green paint in an effort to cover the patches of mould.

'Come through to the kitchen – excuse the mess.'

She wasn't kidding about the mess. The torn net curtains were thick with grime, but what little light managed to penetrate revealed a rusty cooker coated with a thick layer of grease, a cracked and stained linoleum floor and greyish underwear dangling from a washing line that had been strung from the window to the door.

'Hold on, darlin', let me turn that down.' Doris limped over to the wireless, which was blasting out the Isley Brothers' 'Twist and Shout', and twiddled the volume knob. Then she flicked on the light.

Her brown eyes narrowed as she took a deep drag on her roll-up and studied Kathleen Riley. 'I didn't think I'd be seeing you here again. No offence, but you ain't no spring chicken any more, love.' Noticing the look on her visitors' faces as they spotted the bowl on the kitchen table overflowing with bloody rags, she added, 'Like I say, you'll have to excuse the mess. I didn't have time to clear up after me last guest.'

She moved the bowl to the draining board, then reached for the kettle. Glancing over her shoulder at Maggie, she nodded up at the shelf and said, 'Get them cups down for me, love. They're me best ones.'

But as Maggie picked up a sticky, cracked teacup, trying to avoid coming in contact with the filthy counter underneath, her mother snapped, 'I'd just like to get it over with, thank you, Doris.'

'Right you are. Let's get the business out of the way, then,' said Doris, holding out her palm.

Kathleen opened her battered faux leather handbag and began to fumble through the contents.

At a loss as to what business they could possibly have in a shit-hole like this, Maggie turned to her mother in alarm. 'Mum?'

'Be quiet, Maggie!' Kathleen snarled at her.

'Innocent as a lamb, ain't you, pet?' Doris shook her head. 'I'm sad to say, there may come a time when you'll be glad you've met me, darlin'.'

She took the envelope Kathleen had pulled from her handbag, opened it with a dirty fingernail, and peered inside.

'You're short, I'm afraid.'

Maggie watched in confusion as her mother raised her hands to the back of her neck, unfastened the cross of St Christopher that had belonged to her late mother, and dropped it into Doris's hand. 'That should cover it.'

Doris examined the gold cross and chain. 'I suppose it will have to do,' she sighed, slipping it into her pocket along with the envelope. 'Right, you know the drill: get yourself ready.'

'Mum?' Fear creeping up her spine, Maggie tugged at her mother's sleeve.

Face twisted with rage, Kathleen swung round and slapped her on the side of the head.

'Didn't I tell you to keep that mouth shut? Do as you're told for once.'

'Leave the poor child be, it's only natural she'd have questions.' Doris gave the girl a pitying look. 'Are you all right, love?'

'She's fine. I only brought her here because I'll need help to get home afterwards. I can do without her bloody questions.'

Not wanting her mother to see the tears welling in her eyes, Maggie turned her head away. It was then she noticed the bed on the far side of the kitchen table. As she took in the stained, damp-looking mattress, the smell hit her. Till then, she'd been trying not to breathe in the rancid stink of grease and sweat and mould, but now she was aware of something that reminded her of the slaughterhouses off Caledonian Road. Her eyes widened as she saw a tray next to the bed which held a bunch of knitting needles, their tips covered in a dried reddish-brown stain. Next to them lay crooked hooks, like the ones that her mother used when she crocheted and darned Da's socks.

'You should explain to her what's happening,' said Doris. 'She knows how babies come into the world; she needs to know how they go out of it—'

'I'll do no such thing,' huffed Kathleen. 'And I'll thank you to keep your nose out of it, Doris Turner.' Turning to her daughter, she snapped, 'Go wait in the hallway.'

Not wanting another clout round the head, Maggie did as she was told, but she left the door slightly ajar so she could hear what was going on.

'Come on, Kathleen, by the time you move your arse, we'll be christening the bloody baby! . . . Don't look at me like that, I'm only joking. You know me – I'd laugh at me own funeral. Now get a move on, take them knickers off and lay down on the bed.'

Maggie felt a wave of embarrassment wash over her. She'd never heard anyone speak to her mother like that. Putting her eye to the crack in the door, she saw her mother take off her coat, step out of her knickers and lie down on the mattress. Then she pulled out her rosary beads and once again started muttering the Seven Sorrows.

Doris cackled as she lit the stove under the kettle, and brought over a towel and the bowl full of dirty rags. She nodded to the beads. 'It's a bit late for that now. I reckon He's forgotten about the likes of us . . . Come on, open your legs . . . wider.' And in the dim light, she wiped her fingers on her stained apron while looking down at Maggie's mum, now motionless on the bed, only the sound of her shallow breathing giving away her fear.

Doris picked up a length of rubber tubing and a funnel, placing them by the bed next to the knitting needles. Next, she took the kettle off the flame before it began to boil, and placed it on the floor beside the bed. Then she reached into a cupboard and brought out a bottle. 'You want some gin to help you relax?'

Kathleen grabbed the bottle that Doris was holding out and gulped down several mouthfuls before handing it back.

'Right,' said Doris. 'I don't want this to hurt you any more than it has to, so take a deep breath, lie back and think of England, and let's get on with it.'

With that, she attached one end of the funnel to the tube, and inserted the other end between Kathleen's legs.

Maggie could see her mother's fingers gripping the side of the mattress as Doris poured warm water into the funnel. She heard a series of groans, followed by a scream, and then another.

On the fourth scream, unable to stand it any longer, Maggie flung open the door and rushed in.

'Get out!' Her mother's face was twisted in pain, drips of sweat beaded on her forehead. '*Oh Jesus! Oh Christ!*' Then she screamed again.

'What's happening? Why's she making that noise?'

Doris gave her a sympathetic glance. 'Your mum's pregnant, love . . . but not for much longer.'

Maggie's mouth opened and closed. She stared at her mother, who lay clasping her stomach. Then her eyes rolled back and her breathing grew ragged.

'Mammy? Oh my God!'

Blood was pooling on the mattress between her mother's legs. Her body writhed as she howled in agony.

'You need to help her . . . YOU NEED TO DO SOMETHING!' Maggie shouted.

Doris's face suddenly turned ashen. 'What do you expect me to do, love? I only know how to get the thing out, I ain't a doctor.'

'I'm going to call an ambulance.' Maggie scrambled for the door but Doris gripped her arm.

'Do you want us all to go to prison? Because that's what will happen if you go spouting your mouth off.'

'What do you mean?' Maggie looked from the woman to her mother, now whimpering on the bed.

'It's a crime, love. Surely, you know that much?'

'Then what are we going to do?'

Doris let go of her arm. 'Run to number 23 – it's the yellow front door halfway along. Ask for Bea. Tell her that Doris needs her help . . . and quick.'

Maggie raced up the street and hammered on the door. Too desperate to wait, she turned the doorknob and when it opened she burst in, running down the hallway and into the kitchen.

'What the hell—' A woman in a quilted lilac dressing gown spun round as if she'd just been given the fright of her life. Seeing Maggie's blood-soaked clothes, she blurted, 'Holy Mother of God, what's happened – and more to the point, who the fuck are you?'

'Doris sent me. It's my mum, she needs your help.'

Her panic forgotten, Bea picked up her fag from the ashtray and followed Maggie out of the house.

The moment they entered Doris's kitchen, Bea strode across to the bed where Kathleen lay motionless, her eyes closed, her legs spreadeagled, the pool of blood on the mattress spreading beneath her. Muttering to herself, she turned to look at Doris, who was standing by the kitchen table, pouring herself a large mug of gin. 'You need to get her some help or get her out of here.

34

She's dying.' And then she turned on her heel, making straight for the door.

'Where are you going?' cried Maggie. 'You're supposed to help her.'

'No, darlin',' Bea called over her shoulder, 'I don't need this kind of trouble. I ain't getting nicked by the Old Bill for anyone.'

Terror surging through her, Maggie dashed to her mother's handbag, took out her purse and ran back out into the road. She kept running until she saw a phone box. Yanking open the heavy door, she picked up the receiver and dialled O.

Between gasping for breath and fighting back the tears, she struggled to get out the words. 'Operator? Hello, *Operator* . . . I need . . . I need to get a number . . . and be put through to it.'

She gave the name and address and waited for what seemed like hours until finally she heard the ringing tone. As soon as she heard the voice on the other end, she took a coin from her mother's purse and pushed it into the slot.

'*Hello?*'

'It's me, Maggie – Maggie Riley. I need your help—'

Chapter Six

Luca Romano had a lot on his mind as he sat at the window table of his coffee bar in St Martin's Lane. Not least of his worries was a nasty dose of the clap. His penis was on fire, and the blisters under his foreskin were itching so much it was making it hard to concentrate on anything else. And as if that wasn't bad enough, Sofia wouldn't stop nagging him about their forthcoming wedding. The way she was going, it would end up costing more than Princess Margaret's do a couple of years back. And it wasn't as if he even wanted to marry the miserable bitch his parents had selected for him.

Like so many Italian parents, the Romanos wanted their son to marry a nice Catholic virgin from back home. That part Luca hadn't minded; in the West End, finding a virgin was like finding a chicken supping a pint – it was never going to happen. So he'd been happy enough for them to choose a bride from a good family, someone who'd be a proper Italian wife and give him proper Italian sons to carry on the Romano name.

He'd been less happy when Sofia was sent to London to stay with him and his parents until the wedding. To say she was a disappointment would be putting it mildly. Worst of all, she just wouldn't shut up. Always bending his ear about something else she wanted him to buy for her. It was driving him to distraction at a time when he needed to be focusing on more important matters, such as how he was going to deal with Rory Sheehan.

During the years his father had spent grooming him to take over as head of the family business, Luca had been taught the art of running a protection racket. The secret was to make it seem like a mutually beneficial arrangement where, provided payments were made on time, there was nothing to fear. Vincent Romano had been respected by the businesses he protected because he never demanded more than they could afford to pay, only putting up prices when profits increased.

Word had it that Rory Sheehan was bleeding his clients dry. And, when they failed to pay, the retribution he delivered was sadistic. The only thing keeping them from looking elsewhere for protection was their terror of what Sheehan would do when he found out. And that was making it difficult for Luca to gain a bigger share of the Soho market. He'd tried to come to some sort of agreement with Rory, but the guy wouldn't listen. If Luca wanted a slice of Soho action, there was only one way to get it: war.

Taking another sip of his coffee, Luca turned his gaze from the Mods standing next to their Lambrettas across the street to the bustling activity inside the cafe. Trade was good; the place was packed with office workers and typing-pool girls, chatting away to the accompaniment of the coffee machine pumping out steam on the counter, the aroma of espresso mingling with cigarette smoke. And unlike the pubs, which were curbed by licensing laws, the coffee bars could stay open for the late-night crowds.

At that moment, a group of men entered the coffee bar, their suits cut from the finest Italian cloth. Though his Romano cousins had embraced the English lifestyle a little too eagerly in

Luca's opinion – three of them hadn't even bothered showing up today, probably still sleeping it off after partying all night – he knew he could count on them to lay down their lives if it came to it.

No words were spoken, just an exchange of nods before Luca stood up, knocked back the last of his coffee, brushed down his pinstriped suit, then marched out the door with his men.

A minute later, they piled into the waiting black Jaguars and set off for Dean Street.

Chapter Seven

Maggie had been waiting for the knock on the front door. She flung it open and immediately burst into tears. 'I . . . I . . . I didn't know who else to call. I'm sorry.'

'You did the right thing.' Rory Sheehan smiled and cupped his hands around her face. 'I'm glad you called.'

Looking over his shoulder, he nodded for Malcolm to follow him. 'Where is she?'

'Through here.' Maggie led them down the hallway into the kitchen where her mum lay motionless on the rusty bed. Only the slightest movement in her chest showed she was still alive.

Rory took one look at her, then turned to Doris. 'Still butchering women, I see. When will you learn?'

'I was helping her.'

'*Helping?* Look at her. My mother would turn in her grave if she saw this. You're scum, Doris. I've a mind to sort you out once and for all.'

The menace in Rory's tone made Doris back away, but he'd already turned to give Malcolm his instructions.

'We'll take her home and then get my doctor to have a look at her.'

'She can't go home,' Maggie protested. 'I don't think my da

knows. He mustn't find out. You won't tell him, will you? Please don't tell him.'

'Maggie . . .' Rory gently wiped the tears from her face with his thumb. 'What did I tell you yesterday about me being a man of my word? Your secrets are safe with me.'

He took off his jacket and wrapped it round her trembling shoulders before turning back to Malcolm. 'We'll take her to the Murphys. They'll look after her.'

Kathleen's head lolled back as Malcolm lifted her from the bed. Blood dripped onto his shoes and left a trail along the linoleum.

'Maggie, go to the car with Malcolm – I'll be out in a minute. I just need a word with Doris.'

Hearing this, Doris shrank back against the wall next to the gas cooker. Rory waited until he heard the front door shut, then moved in closer to her. He lifted the kettle from the stove and, finding it lukewarm, struck a match and lit the burner. 'Now then, Doris, I've told you before not to do this' – he indicated the bloodstained knitting needles lying next to the bed – 'because, being a good Catholic boy, I see it as a mortal sin.'

Doris swallowed hard. 'I only do it because these women need me. They've got nowhere else to go. They come here cos they ain't got no other choice.'

Rory laughed, a sound with no humour in it. 'So you take their last money to butcher them. Don't pretend you care what happens to them – we all know you're only in it for the money.'

'That's not true – I do care. I've been there meself, so I know how it is when you're desperate. Yes, I charge, but we all need to earn a crust. That doesn't make me a wrong 'un.'

'Save it, Doris.'

Steam billowed in the dim light as the kettle came to the boil.

He picked up one of the bloody rags and used it to lift the kettle, holding it out in front of him.

'We both know you won't stop your sinful ways unless I make you . . . So put your hands out.'

'No, Mr Sheehan, please—'

'I said, hands out . . . or we can always find another, more permanent, way to make you stop.'

Sitting in the back of the car, with her mum's head in her lap, Maggie heard a piercing scream. A moment later, Rory came out smiling. When he got to the car, he crouched down so he was level with the open window next to her.

'Hold your hands out,' he said, reaching into his trouser pocket while laughing at some private joke. Then he dropped the gold St Christopher necklace into her palm. 'I'm sure your mammy will want that back.'

Maggie looked at it in wonder, then at him. 'I don't know what I can do to thank you.'

Getting into the front passenger seat, Rory flicked down the vanity mirror and looked at her in the reflection. 'Oh, I'm sure I can think of something.'

Chapter Eight

The smell of fried eggs and greasy bacon hit Luca as he walked into the cafe on Dean Street. The walls were stained yellow from years of cigarette smoke, and the square clock above the counter ran fifteen minutes slow. Behind the scratched glass of the display cabinet, fruit scones sat on plates next to meat-paste sandwiches. Behind the counter, the proprietor froze as he watched Luca and his men filing through the door.

The only customers were an elderly couple sharing a pot of tea and buttered toast in the corner, and a young woman with a beehive sitting alone at a window table.

Luca gestured with his head for them to leave and the door was held open by one of his men. The moment they'd gone, Luca flipped the sign from *open* to *closed*.

'Stan, it's good to see you again.' He smiled at the owner, who was now visibly shaking. 'I was wondering if you'd come to a decision after our little chat last week?'

Hearing what was going on, Stan's wife, Mildred, came in from the storeroom at the back. She was a solidly built woman, taller than Stan, with thick arms and ankles. She wore slippers, and her paisley nylon dress clung to her droopy breasts. Her thinning grey hair was scraped back, her only make-up a shocking smudge of violet lipstick.

'We paid Rory yesterday.' Mildred's voice was less defiant than her face was.

'But I'm not Rory, am I?' Luca smiled. 'Do I look like fucking Rory?'

'We can't pay both of you,' Stan protested weakly. 'We ain't got that sort of money.'

Luca walked around, partly to distract himself from the burning itch at his crotch. 'I'm not asking you to pay us both. I'm asking you to pay *me*.'

'But we can't.' Stan looked like a cornered animal. 'Even if we could afford it, we daren't. Rory . . .' He trailed, off too terrified to say more.

Luca nodded. The steamy heat of the cafe was stifling. 'Which is why you need to start paying us, Stan. That's what we're here for: to protect you.'

Stan wiped the dripping sweat from his forehead with the bottom of his apron. 'You don't know what he's like, Mr Romano. The Devil himself couldn't protect us from Rory Sheehan.'

'Maybe he couldn't, but I can.' Luca spoke slowly.

Stan's fight-or-flight instinct kicked in and he tried to make a run for it, but before he could make it to the storeroom Gianni and Aldo caught up with him. They dragged him back, slamming him face down onto the chipped counter.

Luca pulled out his stiletto blade and cut through Stan's apron strings. 'One thing we pride ourselves on in Italy is being a gentleman.' He glanced at Mildred, who stood stony-faced. 'Doing a runner, leaving your wife to face the music, isn't what I'd expect of a gentleman.' He put the knife away, helped Stan up, and patted him on the back as if they were old friends.

'Sit down. I want to explain how things are going to work.' He pulled out a chair for Stan.

When the old man just stood quaking in his shoes, Gianni gave him a shove that launched him into the wooden chair, his weight causing it to creak.

Luca's smile never wavered. He straightened his cuffs. 'This is how it's going to be. From today, you no longer pay Rory.' Luca leaned forward. 'And you're going to tell him that you don't need him any more.'

The colour drained from Stan's face. 'Please, I . . . Mr Romano, I can't.'

'You can, and you will.' He nodded to his men who pulled batons from their sleeves. They swung at the glass cabinet, sending a shower of shards across the cafe. They knocked over the tea urn, sending scalding water spraying everywhere. Mildred let out a cry. Cups and plates were smashed against the wall, a teapot, narrowly missing Mildred's head, broke against the mirror, which cracked and shattered. Then they turned their attention on the tables and chairs, kicking them until the wood splintered.

'Next time,' Luca warned, 'it won't just be the fixtures and fittings.' He nodded towards Mildred, who crouched in the corner. 'Think about your wife, your business. Make the right choice . . . Ciao.'

They left the cafe as quickly as they had entered, leaving Stan and Mildred sitting in silence amid the wreckage.

'We need to speak to Rory.' Stan eventually broke the silence.

'You ain't going to tell him that we don't need his protection any more, are you? Don't be a fool, Stan.'

'No. We tell him we need it more than ever.' He touched his face where a shard of glass had nicked his cheek.

'Either that or we leave.' She sounded desperate.

'And go where? This is our home. This is all we've got.' Stan's voice cracked and he wiped his face with his apron, not wanting his wife to see him cry. Twenty years they'd been here, they'd even survived the Blitz, but Stan had a sick feeling that told him they wouldn't survive this.

Chapter Nine

It was late by the time one of Rory's men dropped Maggie off in Camden. She'd wanted to stay in Hampstead at the Murphys' boarding house. They seemed like good people; Mrs Murphy had given her some clothes to change into, since her own were covered in blood. And once the doctor had finished treating her mother and departed with Rory, who had to attend to some urgent business in Soho, the Murphys had insisted she stay for dinner. The roast beef and potatoes they'd served up had been the best meal she'd ever had. She'd felt safe there, and it had been a huge relief to see her mum tucked up in bed, sound asleep.

Before he left, Rory had promised to tell her dad that Mammy had suffered a nasty fall and some friends of his had offered to let her stay with them for a day or two, until she was back on her feet again.

Turning the corner into Chalton Street, Maggie stopped dead when she spotted Pam walking towards her. At first it was as if she'd been struck dumb, but then she saw the smirk on Pam's face and before she knew it she was launching herself at her.

'*You stay away from my da!*' she yelled, grabbing a fistful of Pam's hair.

Pam lost her footing on the wet pavement and they both went

down, rolling on the ground, scratching and kicking. Maggie scraped her knee in the fall and could tell it was bleeding; she hoped she wasn't going to ruin the clothes the Murphys had given her, but she was in too much of a blind rage to stop now. Clenching her fist, she struck out at Pam's jaw.

Breaking free, Pam staggered to her feet and wiped the blood from her split lip. 'What's got into you? You're not right in the head, Maggie Riley.'

In the distance, someone was shouting at them to stop, but Maggie wasn't finished yet. Grabbing the lid from a nearby dustbin, she swung it with all her strength. The edge caught Pam's nose and blood exploded from it as she staggered backwards.

Still holding the bin lid, Maggie stood panting. 'You stay away from him, you hear?'

Pam's eyes were full of hatred. Despite the blood pouring from her nose, she sneered, 'I'll do no such thing. Your da is a real man, and generous with it.'

Maggie stared at her through her tears. 'You don't know what you're talking about! You've no idea what he's like.'

'I reckon I do,' Pam smirked. 'Best man I've ever had.'

'But I thought we were friends,' pleaded Maggie, anger giving way to confusion and hurt.

Pam strolled up to her and pushed her face into Maggie's. 'I was never your friend. You're nothing more than dirt under my feet.'

'I'll tell your mum what you're doing.'

'My mum won't believe a word you say.' Pam laughed cruelly. 'But I bet your dad will believe me when I tell him you're soft on a black boy.'

'Pam, you wouldn't. No, please. You know what da would do to me . . . what he'd do to Thomas.'

'You should've thought about that before you got so friendly with him.' Gloating, Pam turned and began to walk away.

'Pam, please!' Maggie ran after her, clinging to her arm. 'Da will kill me.'

'Best start digging your grave, then.'

Chapter Ten

Maggie was beside herself with worry. The one consolation was that Rory had said her dad would be needed in Soho to do a bit of work for him tonight, so at least Pam wouldn't be seeing him until tomorrow. But the thought of what would happen when he learned about her and Thomas had her stomach in knots.

On reaching the canal path she came upon a group of men passing a bottle between them. Picking up her pace to get past them, she ignored the whistles and catcalls, hoping they wouldn't follow her home. It was a relief when the Cow and Bull came into view and she saw a familiar figure huddled against the wall.

'Thomas?'

Even in the dim light, Maggie could see the terror on his face when he looked up at her. 'Thomas, what's wrong?' She crouched beside him and reached for his hand, but he pulled away, turning his face from her.

'Has my da done something to you?' she whispered. 'Has he hurt you?'

'Your dad? No. It's got nothing to do with him.'

Sighing with relief, she asked, 'What is it, then?'

'I've done something bad. I've done something really bad.'

'What?'

He shook his head, refusing to meet her gaze. 'Thomas, you know you can tell me anything.'

'I'm working for Rory now,' he said flatly.

'That's good, isn't it?' She squeezed his hand.

Raucous voices drifted out from the pub doorway.

'Come on,' Maggie urged, helping him to his feet. 'We can't stay here.'

He shoved his hands in his pockets. 'I'll walk you home. We can go through the back streets, and if we see anyone I'll scarper.'

'And you'll tell me what's upset you?'

Beside her, Thomas stared at the pavement ahead of him. 'If I tell you, you have to promise you won't tell anyone. It must stay our secret. Can you promise me that, Maggie?'

She thought of Rory and his words to her earlier. 'Your secrets are safe with me.'

She had no way of knowing how important those words would be.

Chapter Eleven

'Do you hate me, Maggie?' Thomas asked. 'Now that you know what I've done?'

'No . . . no, I could never hate you.' She was still trying to digest what Thomas had told her.

'Will you look at me differently though?' Tears glinted in his eyes.

She shook her head. Thomas was always full of stories, and she'd desperately wanted this to be just another of his tales. But then he'd shown her where they'd buried the bodies, and after that there was no point in pretending it wasn't true.

Now it was one more thing to lock away in her head, never to be talked about. Like the things her dad did when he was drunk, the way he hurt her mum, the way he hurt her . . . The memory of her mum lying in a pool of blood, screaming, in Doris's kitchen.

'Maggie,' Thomas whispered her name. As she turned to face him, his fingers traced her cheeks and stroked her lips. He'd never touched her like this before, and though she knew she should pull away, she leaned into him. Her lips met his and she felt how soft they were.

Thomas drew back. 'Are you sure this is okay? Is it what you want, Maggie?'

She had never been so sure of anything in her life. Gently she stroked his face and drew him towards her. They kissed deeply and Maggie could feel him hardening against her.

'Come on,' she said. 'My dad's out tonight.' Her words terrified yet thrilled her.

'What about your mum?' Uncertainty leapt into Thomas's eyes.

'She's . . . away. Come on, we may not get a chance like this again.' Taking him by the hand, she led him into the small, terraced house.

Huddled together under the threadbare sheets of Maggie's bed, they lay naked in each other's arms.

'I love you, Maggie.'

She opened her eyes as he kissed her, his hand gently stroking her hair.

'I love you too.' She could feel every part of him: his smooth skin, his soft chest, his erect penis. And when he entered her, it wasn't rushed but slow and tender. Before long they had both drifted into a deep sleep.

The sound of the front door slamming startled them both awake.

'Maggie? Maggie? Where the feck are you?'

Her dad wasn't due home until morning, yet here he was – drunk, by the sounds of it. She could tell by his slurred speech and the way he was stumbling around downstairs.

'MAGGIE!'

Terror gripped her as she heard the first creak of the staircase under his feet.

'Thomas, you need to go.' Her eyes darted to the window, then to the door. But it was too late for that.

'MAGGIE! Where are you?' he roared, his body banging against the sides of the narrow staircase.

'You need to hide. Get under the bed.'

Panicked, Thomas grabbed his clothes as Maggie scrambled to her feet.

'Whatever happens, he mustn't find you . . . No matter what you hear, stay right where you are, you understand me? Whatever you hear, don't move or he'll kill us both.'

The door burst open as Thomas rolled under the bed. Shamus Riley stood swaying in the doorway, his gaze roaming over her naked body as she struggled to put on her nightie.

'I hear you've been causing trouble, Maggie.' He stepped forward and grabbed her by the hair. She screamed and he slapped her hard across the face, splitting her lip. To her horror, she saw Thomas begin to get out from under the bed.

'No!' she yelled.

Thinking she was talking to him, her father grabbed her by the throat. 'Who the fuck do you think you are, telling me "no", and running to Mr Sheehan to complain about me?'

'I haven't, I swear, Da.'

'Then why's he telling me how I should treat you? Like I'm not the man in my own house. Is that what you think, Maggie, that I'm not in charge of my own home?'

'No, Da.'

He grabbed her breasts.

'I'm minded to teach you a lesson you'll never forget.' His fist connected with her eyebrow. The jolt of pain sent her staggering back, blood trickling into her eye, but Shamus wasn't done yet. The next blow knocked her off her feet and she slid to the floor.

Whimpering, she tried to crawl away but his boot caught her in the ribs. When she tried to roll away, her dad straddled her, unbuckling his belt. As he pushed her face to one side, Maggie locked eyes with Thomas under the bed. Overcome by shame, she squeezed her eyes shut, unable to bear Thomas seeing her like this.

Chapter Twelve

'Are you sure that's what the little fucker said?' Rory surveyed the broken furniture and crockery in Stan and Mildred's cafe before furiously stubbing out his cigarette in a heap of spilled sugar.

'Yes, Mr Sheehan. That's exactly what he said.'

Rory rubbed his face. 'Then tell me again . . . go on, tell me a-FUCKING-gain.'

Sweating profusely, Stan gripped his wife's hand. 'He said not to pay you. From now on we're to pay him, and I'm meant to tell you that myself.' He looked at Rory. 'But, Mr Sheehan, that's not why I called,' he pleaded, gripping his wife even harder.

'Point is,' Mildred spoke up, glancing between Rory and Malcolm, who stood over by the door, 'what the hell are you going to do about it? We pay you week in, week out for protection, but look at this place. There ain't one plate that isn't broken.'

Rory slammed his fist on the counter, making the sugar cubes leap. Walking into his manor and smashing up the place – did that slimy bastard have a death wish? Well, if that's what he wanted, then that's what he'd get.

'Like my Stan said, we can't afford to pay you both,' Mildred whined.

Rory spun round and poked her hard in her flabby breasts. 'You think you're going to pay money to those Italian bastards? Have you lost the run of yourself?' Rory's Irish accent always got stronger when he was angry. 'Have you forgotten who owns these streets?'

Mildred shook her head. He shoved her again. 'If I ever find out you've paid them, you'll be sorry. Remember what happened to Arnold's place in Greek Street?'

She nodded. Everyone did. The place had been burned down with Arnold and his family inside, and everyone knew it had been Rory and his men who'd lit the match. Arnie's only crime had been helping out his sister after her old man fell off some scaffolding and couldn't pay the rent. Rather than see them homeless, he'd paid their landlord – leaving him unable to pay Rory his protection money.

Glass and crockery crunching under his feet, Rory paced the floor. First that fucking Shamus Riley had the nerve to show up for work so drunk he could barely stand, and now this. He'd sent Riley home with a flea in his ear; he needed men he could rely on if he was going to deal with the likes of the Romanos. Not to mention all the other pricks trying to move in on his turf: the Mods, the Teddy boys, the Turks, the Maltese. After tonight, he'd need to recruit more muscle, and that was going to cost.

'Payment will have to go up.'

'But we can't—'

The glare from Rory stopped Stan mid-flow. 'We'll find the money somehow,' he gulped.

Rory walked to the door. Not bothering to turn round, he snapped, 'If they come calling again, you tell them that this is *my* turf, and I don't share.'

Chapter Thirteen

Rory was almost home when his car headlights picked out a young woman staggering along the road in obvious distress. He skidded to a halt when he saw who it was.

'*Maggie!*' He jumped out of the car and ran to her. 'Holy Mother of God, who did this to you? Was it your da? If it was, I'm going to kill him.'

Through her swollen eye, she looked up at him. 'No . . . no, I fell. I slipped on the stairs.'

'Maggie, are you lying to me?'

Shaking her head, she burst into tears.

He led her to the car and helped her in, noticing the way she winced when his hand came in contact with her ribs.

'I can see you're hurt, love, but we're not going anywhere until you tell me who did this.'

She obviously didn't want to answer, but the look on his face told her she had no choice. 'I had a fight with Pam Whelan.'

Rory laughed. 'Is that it?'

Maggie looked away.

'I'm sorry, love, I shouldn't laugh . . . Go on, tell me what happened.'

'She threatened to tell my da that Thomas and I are friends.

56

She knows what my da'll do . . . she knows . . .' She dissolved into tears, unable to go on.

'Shhhh.' He kissed her on the side of her head. 'It'll be all right.' He noticed her looking at a small packet wrapped in shiny red paper sitting on the dashboard. He picked it up and handed it to her. 'This is for you, Maggie.'

'For me?'

'I was going to bring it around earlier, but what with one thing and another . . .' He shrugged and smiled. 'Did you think I'd forget what today is?'

Maggie stared at him. She hadn't told anybody what today was, not even Thomas. Her parents had never bothered giving her presents or making a fuss of her, so rather than get her hopes up by thinking of it as a special occasion, she'd learned to think of it as a day like any other.

'How did you know?'

Rory winked. 'A little bird told me . . . Happy sixteenth birthday, Maggie.'

Chapter Fourteen

Maggie woke up next morning to banging on the front door. She hurt all over but it could've been worse. Thankfully, her dad had left the house as soon as he'd finished with her. Thomas waited until he heard the door slam, then crawled out from under the bed and tried to comfort her, but she'd felt so ashamed she couldn't face being in his presence and had begged him to leave, for his own safety as much as her own. Having ushered Thomas out of the house, she'd walked the streets for a while to clear her head, before going home to lie awake for hours, afraid to be alone in the house in case her dad returned.

When the hammering on the door persisted, she swung her legs out of bed and put on her dressing gown. She had to get up anyway to go to the laundrette. With her mum away, there'd be more washing than she could possibly get through alone, but there'd be hell to pay if she didn't go in.

She opened the door to find her mother's best friend, Ivy, gaping at her, open-mouthed.

'I see your da has been handy with his fists again,' Ivy said, taking in her swollen face.

'No, it wasn't my da,' she lied. She hated that everyone whispered about the bruises that regularly appeared on her and her ma's faces. Apart from Thomas's father, and Sean O'Brien the butcher, she didn't know of a single man who didn't raise his hand to his wife and children.

'Mum's not here right now.' Maggie wrapped her dressing gown round herself, hoping Ivy wouldn't ask after her mum. They may be friends, but Ivy was a gossip and her mum wouldn't appreciate her business being spread about.

'It's not your mammy I've come to see, it's you. It's bad news, Maggie. A terrible thing.'

'What's is?'

'Pam – they found her this morning near Chalk Farm station. It looks like she had a fall and broke her neck.'

'Where is she now, in hospital?'

Mouth agape, Ivy stared at her for a moment, then whispered, 'She's dead, love . . . Pam's dead.'

'No.' Maggie took a step back.

'Not only that,' Ivy continued, relishing the chance to gossip. 'They say her dress was torn, and her face was all bruised . . .'

Suddenly aware of the snot and tears streaming down her face, Maggie licked her cut lips and winced from the pain. 'You must've got it wrong. I saw her only—'

Panic rose inside her. Could this have had something to do with her fight with Pam? One of her dad's old drinking buddies got into a fight one night with a bloke down the boozer. The bloke had picked himself up and staggered off home afterwards, but the next day he'd dropped down dead. Dad's mate – Gary, his name was – had been carted off to the nick, sentenced for murder, then hung in Pentonville prison.

'Her mammy is in terrible shock, as you can well imagine. I was only saying to—'

'I . . . I have to go . . . sorry.' She tried to meet Ivy's gaze but then dropped her eyes to look at her hands.

'That's a fine bracelet you've got there,' said Ivy, reaching for Maggie's hand and lifting it up. 'And where would you get something like that, Maggie Riley?'

Maggie snatched her hand away, covering the birthday present that Rory had given her with the other hand. 'I'm sorry. I have to go.' She slammed the door, resting her forehead on it. She felt sick. Pam was dead. She slid down the door, wrapped her arms round her belly and sat rocking and sobbing.

She'd hit Pam with the dustbin lid. She'd walked away, but she must've been dizzy and fallen, snapping her neck in two. Maggie gulped down air, struggling to breathe through the panic. Pam's blood was on her hands.

Ignoring her aches and pains, she got to her feet, dragged herself upstairs and got dressed, then headed out the door. Thankfully the streets were empty apart from a few traders setting out their wares as she made her way to Camden lock, tears streaming down her face as images of Pam flashed through her mind. As she neared the alleyway she broke into a run, stopping only when she reached the door. She wasn't sure why she'd come here, but couldn't think where else to go.

When her first knock on the door went unanswered, she began pounding on the wood, banging on it with both hands. To her relief, the door was opened.

'Maggie!' Rory smiled. 'Now this is a surprise. A good one, but a surprise all the same.' He reached out and brushed the hair from her face, wincing at her bruises and the fresh, dried streak of blood down her forehead. 'Oh, Maggie.' As so often happened when he saw Maggie, Rory felt the start of an erection. 'You don't deserve this.' His breathing was ragged as he continued: 'If I had a girl like you, I'd treat her like a queen.' Then, snapping himself out of it, he took a step back, crossed his arms and leaned on the freshly painted door jamb. 'What can I do for you?'

'I . . . I . . . I killed Pam.' She spoke so quietly, Rory wasn't sure he'd heard right.

'What did you say?'

'Pam's dead.'

Rory wrapped his arms around her as she sobbed into his chest.

When her tears finally subsided, he asked, 'Isn't that a good thing?'

Shocked, she pulled away. 'Good? How is it good?'

He stroked her face and smiled. 'It gets rid of your problem.'

'What do you mean?' She looked at him in disbelief.

Rory tilted his head. 'Wasn't she threatening to cause problems for you? I'm surprised you're shedding any tears for her after the way she carried on. Did she shed any tears for you when she fucked your da, or when she threatened to tell him you were hanging round with that black boyfriend of yours?' He paused, then called over his shoulder. 'Thomas! *Thomas!*'

A moment later Thomas appeared in a navy tailored suit, white shirt and blue tie.

He glanced at Maggie but kept his focus on Rory. 'Yes, Mr Sheehan?'

Rory squeezed Thomas's shoulder. 'Don't you think he looks smart, Maggie? He's going to go far, this one, aren't you, Thomas.'

Looking uncomfortable, Thomas nodded. It was all Maggie could do to look at him after what he'd seen her father do to her.

Then Malcolm appeared, his face grim. 'Mr Sheehan, we've got a bit of bother over in Soho. It can't wait.'

Rory nodded and turned to follow, but paused to whisper to Maggie: 'Yesterday you wished Pam wouldn't say anything about Thomas to your da – remember?'

Maggie nodded.

'So dry those tears. You got what you wanted, didn't you?' He leaned forward until his face was inches away from hers. 'And if you didn't want it, you shouldn't have wished for it.'

And with those words Rory turned and walked away.

Chapter Fifteen

Alone in the pub hallway, Maggie and Thomas stood in awkward silence. Eventually, Thomas spoke.

'About last night . . .'

'I don't want to talk about it.' She turned away.

'But, Maggie, we need to talk.'

'I don't want to!' she snapped, then immediately regretted it. 'I'm sorry . . .' She swallowed. No one had ever made her feel the way Thomas did last night, but then her da had robbed her of that feeling, like he'd robbed her of so many other things. Now, when she thought of lying next to Thomas, her da's face, the stench of his breath, the feel of his fist, the pain of his penis obliterated her memories of Thomas.

'Maggie, what happened with—'

'I said no. Please don't!' Maggie cut him off, raising her voice as a fresh wave of humiliation washed over her. She stood shaking. Ashamed. Thomas had seen her da violating her, and she felt sick at the thought of it. She'd scrubbed herself raw last night but it felt like Da's hands were still on her body.

Over the years, she'd learned to live with the fear of him getting drunk and coming into her bedroom. She'd been too afraid to tell anyone. Too scared of what he might do to her if she did. Most of the time after it had happened, she dealt with it by pushing it to that dark place in her mind, the place she never visited. This time, however, she couldn't, no matter how she tried.

She couldn't bear to imagine what Thomas must think of her now, and she couldn't bear to see the look of disgust in his eyes.

'Maggie, *please*, let me—'

She shoved him away. 'I've told you! I don't want to talk about it. Not now. Not ever.'

'But—'

She backed away. 'Leave me alone – I don't want anything more to do with you.'

Thomas looked ill then. 'You don't mean that, Maggie. Please don't say that.' He lowered his voice and glanced over his shoulder. 'I'll work for Mr Sheehan and save up enough money to take you away from here. We can go anywhere we want.'

Through her tears, Maggie yelled at him. 'Look at you and look at me – we can never be together.'

'We could if we wanted.'

Maggie let out a bitter laugh. Her heart breaking, she turned and walked away without another word.

Chapter Sixteen

By the time Maggie arrived at the Murphys' boarding house with its large green front door, she was shivering and wet through.

Using the lion's head knocker, she rapped on the door, and almost immediately the door was flung open.

'Maggie!' Mrs Murphy took in the sight of the battered and bedraggled young woman. 'This is a grand surprise. Come in, out of the rain. Does Rory know you're here?'

Maggie shook her head.

'Don't worry, come in anyway.' Her hazel eyes were warm. 'Rory's told us a lot about you. He's a good man, Maggie. A family man. A girl would be lucky to have him.'

Uncertain how to reply, Maggie wiped her feet on the thick bristles of the doormat, conscious how shabby she looked compared to Mrs Murphy in her tweed skirt and blouse.

'Can I get you anything?'

'I've come to see my ma, if that's all right.'

'Of course it is. You must be worried. Let me show you up.'

Maggie followed the boarding house proprietor up the carpeted stairs, past the framed paintings and a gaudy porcelain vase on a small table. At the top landing, Mrs Murphy spoke quietly. 'She's weak, so she is, but you can go in and see her.

Don't be tiring her out, though,' she cautioned, opening the bedroom door.

Maggie tiptoed into the room, which smelled strongly of beeswax polish. Her mother was lying on the bed, her skin pale and grey. Her eyes suddenly flickered open. 'What in God's name are you doing here, Maggie? Don't you think I've got enough worries without you coming here to mither me.' She stopped and gawped at Maggie's bruised face. 'I see that you've been giving cheek to your da again.' She shook her head and tutted. 'Will you never learn?'

Maggie fiddled with her fingers. 'I needed to see you.'

'Well now you've seen me you can get off. The clothes at the laundrette won't wash themselves and your da's dinner won't cook itself either. Can I not rely on you to do anything you're supposed to?'

'I . . . I . . . I just had to talk to you.'

'Talk?' Her mum pushed herself up into a sitting position. She straightened the white nightie she was wearing. 'Have you ever heard the like when there's chores to be done and a house to clean! Have you gone soft? *Talk* – I ask you, whoever heard of such foolish nonsense!' Her mother's face was full of scorn.

Maggie dropped to her knees and tried to rest her head in her mum's lap but she was pushed away.

'Get up, girl, you're not a dog.'

'Mammy.' Her voice little more than a whisper, she began to sob. 'I need to tell you what Da did to me, what he does to me—'

'Hush!' Her mother's hand shot out, gripping Maggie's wrist, squeezing it hard, fingernails digging into her skin angrily. 'Not another word, you hear me!'

'But . . .'

No Regret

The slap fell hard across her face.

'Have you no shame?' Her mum's eyes burned into her. 'You came all this way just to cause more trouble?'

Tears rolled down Maggie's face. 'I need your help.'

'Help?' Her mother laughed bitterly. 'We're women, Maggie, and there are a lot of things in this world that we have to bear, whether we like them or not. And we bear them in silence. Do you hear me.' She held Maggie's gaze for a moment before speaking again. 'Now go on with ye. You haven't got time to be sitting around here all day . . . and make sure you iron your da's trousers the way he likes them.'

Her mother sniffed and Maggie rose to her feet as the silence of so many unspoken words stretched between them.

Chapter Seventeen

'I'm sure the boys are fine, Luca. They're young – they're probably out chasing girls.'

A week had gone by since anyone had seen or heard from Luca's three cousins. Only this morning he'd been interrogated once again by his anxious parents, their Italian flowing fast over the breakfast table while his mother crossed herself repeatedly and his father fired questions about when Luca had last seen the boys. And yet here was Marco, trying to tell him there was nothing to worry about!

It didn't help that he was feeling exhausted. Last night he was up late going over the books for the coffee shops, then when he'd finally crawled to his bed and fallen asleep, his fiancée had come into the room and woken him up. Somehow Luca doubted whether she really was the sweet virgin his parents believed her to be.

He hadn't touched Sofia yet, partly out of respect for a good Catholic girl from a family back home, but also because the dose of clap he'd picked up was a brutal one and still hadn't healed. His penis was on fire, and when he took a piss, or the material of his boxers rubbed against his penis, it was agony. The very thought of having sex made Luca shudder.

'Look, I know something's happened to them, and I'm

getting a whole lot of pressure from the family.' Luca glared at Marco as the smell from the coffee shop wafted into his nose. From his basement office he could hear the customers milling around overhead and the sound of the traffic outside. A calendar advertising Bovril hung on the wall over his desk, which was filled with business ledgers – only the legitimate ones, though. The real figures were stored in the attic at home.

Rubbing his forehead, Luca shifted his weight from foot to foot to ease the burn. The morphine he'd taken at breakfast was beginning to wear off, making him even more irritable. He reached into his suit pocket and pulled out a square tin of tablets. He opened it, popped a pill into his mouth and rolled it under his tongue for a moment before swallowing it dry.

Within minutes, the morphine began to kick in, dulling his thoughts, easing the burn until it was only a smoulder. He grabbed a cigarette from the packet on the table, lighting it with a shaky hand, then fixed Marco with a hard stare.

'Someone fucking knows where they are, and we need to find out *subito.*'

'We've asked around, but no one's seen anything.'

Luca slammed his fist on the table. 'So ask again. Have you spoken to those idiots they hang around with? Those Mods, or whatever they're called.'

'They said they haven't seen them. And I believe them.'

Luca nodded. 'What about the Turks?'

'Again, nothing.' Marco paused, choosing his words carefully. 'We don't want to turn it into something it's not. There's enough shit going down already with the Irish and the Maltese, so I thought—'

'You thought what?' Luca cut in. His eyelids felt heavy. He could practically hear his heartbeat slowing from the effects of the morphine. 'My cousins have gone missing and you don't want to turn it into something it's not?' Through gritted teeth he went on, 'I want you to go to Soho and turn every fucking stone upside down. I don't care how you do it, or how long it takes. If you find anyone who knows anything, you bring them back here. *Capisce?*'

Marco, who was tall, olive-skinned and had a liking for teenage boys, nodded.

'Three men don't just disappear into thin air.' Luca walked over to the tray and picked up his cup of coffee, but instead of taking a sip from it, he threw it across the room, smashing it against the wall. Then he grabbed his jacket. 'Get the car.'

'The car?'

'That's what I fucking said, didn't I?' Luca muttered through his morphine haze. 'It's time to pay Rory Sheehan a visit.'

The pub was full of cigarette smoke and its windows were yellowed with nicotine stains. The smell of beer and wet clothes filled the air. Men stood two deep at the bar, huddled over their beer and Guinness, studying the racing papers. Unlike Rory's Soho premises, it had yet to catch the wave of the swinging sixties. It hadn't moved on, time had stood still.

Luca – with his men behind him – paused in the doorway, scanning the room until he spotted Rory sitting in the corner, a bottle of Jameson on the table next to his glass. He clocked Malcolm standing next to a young black guy; on seeing the Romanos, he said something to the black kid, who immediately departed via a side door. No doubt he'd been sent to summon reinforcements.

As Luca strolled towards Rory, the pub fell silent. Rory waited until Luca was standing right over him before slowly looking up from his glass.

'Well, well, well, if it isn't the mafia man himself.' Rory looked round at the punters in the bar. 'Will you look at this fella!'

He nodded to the barmaid, a small ginger-haired woman with a flattened nose that had been broken many times over the years by her bare-knuckle-fighter husband.

She brought over a glass, placing it on the table beside the Jameson's. The Cow and Bull was so quiet it was as if everyone was holding their breath, waiting to see what Rory would do next.

He took his time unscrewing the lid on the bottle and pouring a large glass. He held it out to Luca, who took it and, without hesitation, downed it in one.

Rory gave a nod, then said, 'Now, I'd appreciate it if you'd leave my pub.' He glanced at the brass clock on the wall above the double doors. 'Business hours are over ... gentlemen.' He winked.

The morphine made Luca's mouth dry, but he resisted the urge to lick his lips in case it be taken as a sign of nerves. He pulled a clean, white napkin out of his pocket and slammed it on the table. 'Call this my white flag ... I'm not here looking for trouble ... *this time.*' It was Luca's turn to wink.

Rory shrugged, picked up the napkin and waved it slowly in the air in a parody of signalling a truce. 'What is it you're looking for then?'

'My cousins.'

Rory raised his eyebrows. 'And what business would I be having with them? I've got enough troubles of my own, without having to worry about your family too.' He swigged down the last of his whisky, eyes on Luca the whole time.

The pub remained silent, every ear straining to catch the conversation. The tension hung thick in the air, everyone well aware that the Italians would be carrying under their perfectly tailored three-piece suits.

Luca's hand moved quickly, grabbing Rory's glass and crushing it in his bare hand, the morphine lessening the pain as blood and drops of whisky dripped onto the table.

Rory's face remained calm and his voice steady.

'If you wanted a word with me, all you had to do was say so.' He nodded towards a door marked *private*, and stood up. 'After you,' he added with a smirk.

Marco and Malcolm followed them into the private lounge and took up positions either side of the door.

Rory leisurely helped himself to a Park Drive and lit it. He didn't offer Luca a cigarette.

'You've got some front, boy, coming in here, especially after what's been going down in Soho.' He took a deep drag of the cigarette. 'Give me one good reason why I shouldn't tell my men to take you out right now?'

Luca's face was stony. The morphine dulled not only the pain but also his temper. 'That would be a big mistake. You'll have the whole of the Italian community down on you, and you know it.'

Standing in such close proximity to Rory, with a gun under his jacket, made it very tempting to blow the bastard away. But even under the influence of morphine Luca wasn't that stupid. Undoubtedly the time would come, but this wasn't it.

'Where are my cousins?'

Rory took a seat in one of his wingback leather armchairs and stared back at him, unblinking. 'Like I said, your family troubles aren't any concern of mine.'

Luca turned and nodded to Marco, who reached into his inside jacket pocket and produced a photograph of the three young men. He walked over and gave it to Rory.

'They were last seen a week ago, in Goodge Street.'

Rory studied the photograph of three young Italian men dressed like Teddy boys. He shook his head. 'I've never set eyes on those lads in me life. I wouldn't know them if they walked through that door this very minute.' He held out the photo for Marco to take back.

'Keep it,' Luca said. 'In case you hear anything . . . And if I find out that you *have* seen them, if you've so much as caught a glimpse of their shadow' – he paused to fix Rory and then Malcolm with a stare before turning back to Rory – 'I'll burn down everyone and everything around you.'

Rory remained sitting in his chair as Luca left. He waited until the door closed behind him and then lit another cigarette. Blowing out a cloud of smoke, he tossed the photograph to Malcolm. 'Recognise them?'

Malcolm picked it up from the floor, looked at it and shrugged. 'No. Should I?'

Rory sat forward in the chair, rolling his tongue around his mouth in irritation. 'Well, I recognise them. They're the Teddy boys who attacked Thomas, the ones we butchered and buried – does that jog your memory?' He smashed his fist down on the table. 'How come nobody knew they were Romanos? Talk about a fuck-up. If anyone connects this to us, we've got a real problem.'

Chapter Eighteen

Luca sat in the rear of the black Jaguar, staring unseeingly at the bright lights of the theatre district. His thoughts were elsewhere.

He'd learned long ago to trust his gut, and his gut told him that Rory was lying. When he'd shown him the photo of Donny, Gino and Matteo, there'd been a flicker of recognition in his eyes that didn't go unmissed.

Luca glanced down at the blood-soaked handkerchief wrapped round his palm. It crossed his mind that his cousins' disappearance was a warning to him. But if the intention had been to deter him from expanding into Soho, the result would be the opposite.

He just needed his father onboard.

Vincent Romano used to be hungry. He had built a little empire centred around Clerkenwell but which now extended into Covent Garden. They made a decent profit from the coffee shops and the protection racket, and Vincent seemed to be satisfied with that. But it wasn't enough for Luca. He wanted to be one of the major players in London, for the Romanos to be spoken of with the same respect as the Krays, who ruled the East End, and their South London rivals, the Richardsons.

Everyone was wary of Ronnie and Reggie Kray, Charlie and

Eddie Richardson – their names instilled fear. The same had once been true of Vincent Romano, but these days he was acting like a weak, scared man, a man it was hard to respect. It meant the weight of the Romano name rested entirely on Luca's shoulders.

If he was going to restore the Romano family reputation, he would need to see off all the rival gangs vying for control of the West End – not just Rory Sheehan but the Turks and the Maltese. They would all need to be wiped out before he'd be in a position to take on firms like the Krays and the Richardsons.

Luca glanced at his watch: 9.45 p.m.

The streets of Soho were quiet, the coffee shops closed. Only the basement clubs and walk-ups showed signs of life. The car stopped in Dean Street, and Marco turned off the engine.

'Ready, boss?'

Luca didn't bother replying. He simply opened the door and got out, stretching his legs as he looked up at the three-storey Georgian building.

The bell above the door rang as he opened it.

'*We're closed*,' a voice shouted through from the back. Then a face appeared.

'Ciao, Stan.' Luca winked at the old man.

'Mr Romano. We didn't expect to see you tonight.' The old man stood frozen behind the counter as Luca sauntered through the cafe, running a finger over the mustard Formica tables.

'Where's Mildred?'

'She's . . . sh-she's in the back,' Stan stammered, his face flushed and his eyes darting to the door behind him.

Luca frowned. 'What's going on, Stan?'

'Nothing, Mr Romano.'

'Why do you look like you're trying to hide something? Are you hiding something, Stan?'

'No . . . no.'

Gesturing for Marco, Nestor and Paolo to follow him, Luca stepped behind the counter. Immediately, Stan tried to block his way.

'Mr Romano, *please*.' He stood with his arms stretched wide, his shirt coming out of his baggy grey trousers, which were held up by a belt and braces.

Luca, using only one hand, pushed him aside and walked through to the private residence where he could hear Mildred talking.

'Stan, where did you put that cap? You know, the one you got from Southend last year—'

'Hello, Mildred.' Luca came up behind her.

She jumped and spun round to face him. 'I . . . I didn't hear you.'

Luca leaned forward and moved her hair aside to reinsert the large beige hearing aid that was hanging out of Mildred's ear. 'Can you hear me now?' He smiled widely at her, then his gaze shifted to the four battered leather suitcases standing in the corner.

'Going somewhere?'

'*No*.' Stan's voice came from behind them. 'No, we were just having a clear-out.'

'A clear-out?' Luca repeated. 'Is that right, Mildred?'

'Yes, Mr Romano. You'd never believe how much junk Stan has.' Mildred's voice shook, and she clasped her hands together as if pleading with him to believe her.

Luca sniffed and walked across to the mahogany door that took him through to the tiled hallway and a steep flight of stairs leading to their living quarters. Slowly, Luca climbed the stairs, the wood creaking under his feet.

'Mr Romano, there's nothing up there,' Stan shouted from the hallway.

On reaching the first landing, Luca began opening doors. A storeroom, a bathroom with newspaper over the window, a bedroom where the double bed had been stripped of its sheets.

Luca flung open the wardrobe doors to reveal a rail of empty hangers. He turned to a chest of drawers, opening each one. All were empty.

'Like I say, we're having a clear-out.' Mildred appeared in the doorway, Stan peeking over her shoulder.

Luca noted the two suitcases half-hidden by the thick brown curtains. He turned to look at the old couple, adjusting the bloodstained handkerchief wrapped around his palm. 'Do you know what I think? I think you're doing a runner.'

'No,' Stan protested. 'No, it ain't like that, we just have too much stuff everywhere, and when—'

'Shut up!' Luca roared. Then, his voice quiet again, he asked, 'How old are you?'

'Seventy-four.'

Luca nodded thoughtfully. 'And Mildred?'

'Seventy-two,' she answered.

'And you still haven't learned that people don't like being taken for fools.' He walked over to them and smiled. 'Now, tell me where you were planning on going.'

Stan and Mildred exchanged terrified glances.

'You're running, Stanley. Why? When you owe me money?' Luca's voice was quiet. 'I told you that you had to pay me.'

'Please, Mr Romano.' Mildred clutched her hands together tighter. 'We don't want any trouble. It's just that we can't pay you *and* Mr Sheehan.' Tears flooded her eyes.

'We didn't know what else to do.' Stan wrung his hands nervously.

Luca's hand shot out, grabbing him by the collar. 'And so you thought you'd lie to me?' He released his grip on Stan and pointed to the stairs. 'Let's go.'

They trudged back down, through the hallway and into the cafe, Mildred crying silently and Stan shaking his head.

'Are you a betting man, Stan?' asked Luca, taking a seat at one of the tables.

'I like a bit of a flutter on the greyhounds now and then.'

'Well, you clearly put your money on the wrong runner. If you'd paid me and not Rory Sheehan, none of this would be happening.'

'We had no choice.' Stan was breathless. 'He's doubled his money.'

Luca whistled. 'And where is he now?' He opened his arms dramatically. 'Where's Sheehan when you need him? I'll tell you where. He's in his pub in Camden, having a drink.' He pulled a flick knife from his pocket, opened it and began to clean under his manicured nails. 'How long have you been here?'

'Over twenty years,' Mildred croaked. 'We've put our hearts and souls into this place.'

'Well, that is a shame.' Luca turned to Marco. 'Tie them up.'

Once the couple had been tied to chairs, Luca walked over to Mildred and began pulling out the hairpins that secured her bun. Locks of thin grey hair tumbled down onto her shoulders. Luca grabbed a handful of hair and sliced it off with his knife.

Grey strands fell to the floor as Mildred sobbed. He grabbed another handful, dropping more hair on the linoleum floor. Then he reached into his pocket for his lighter and flicked it open, watching the flame dancing in the dim cafe.

He bent down and touched the flame to the pile of hair. It caught alight quickly, burning with an acrid smell. 'You chose your side, did what you had to do. And now I'm doing what I have to do.'

'*Please*,' Stan begged. 'Please. We're sorry.'

Luca smiled at the sight of the old man pleading, tears running down his face.

'This is business, Stan. Nothing personal.' And then he touched the flame to a stack of newspapers alongside the net curtains. They caught fire immediately, and Luca watched the flames for a moment before signalling to Nestor, who stood waiting by the cafe entrance.

Nestor reached down for the petrol can by his side, undid the lid and began pouring the contents over the chairs and tables. He was joined by Paolo, who doused the counter with petrol before tipping the rest of the can over Mildred and Stan.

'Nothing personal,' Luca said again, reaching down to light the pool of petrol before making his exit. The flames moved rapidly, engulfing the wooden furniture. Smoke filled the cafe as Stan and Mildred struggled against the ropes that bound them.

Luca watched, emotionless, from the opposite side of Dean Street as smoke billowed from the cafe. It was no longer possible to see the old couple through the wall of flames but Mildred's high-pitched wail and Stan's desperate cries rang out in the empty street.

A police constable rounded the corner, his eyes darting from the flames to the well-dressed man strolling towards a waiting black Jaguar.

'Just a spot of bother, officer. Nothing to see here.' Luca reached into his pocket and pulled out a wad of notes, tucking it into the constable's hand.

'I didn't see anything, Mr Romano.'

Luca stared at him. 'And when Rory Sheehan asks?'

The constable sniffed. 'Like I say, I saw nothing.' He turned away, disappearing into the Soho night.

'Where to now, boss?' Marco stuck his head out of the driver's window. 'Home?'

Luca got into the back seat. 'No, we're only just getting started.'

Chapter Nineteen

Rory's Soho club was located in the long narrow passageway known as Bridle Lane. The basement had been used as a bomb shelter during the war and then it had lain empty through the fifties until Rory had bought it and gutted the place, turning it into a successful club, which heaved with punters, drawn by – in Rory's opinion – the best strippers in Soho.

Wood panelling and red velvet curtains covered the walls, chandeliers with red light bulbs hung from the ceiling and the air was thick with cigarette smoke, cheap perfume and music.

Thomas was standing behind the bar, counting the night's takings. He'd been working for Rory for just over a week and he wasn't sure that he'd ever get used to handling so much money. There was more money taken in a night than he'd ever dreamed of. But he'd been warned on his first day not to make the mistake of thinking that Rory had so much he wouldn't miss a quid or two. Before they were allowed to go leave the premises at the end of the night, every member of staff had to submit to being searched, either by Big Arthur, or Malcolm, if he was around.

'Fancy a drink with me, babe?' Christine leaned over the counter, giving him her come-on smile. Her naturally blonde hair was done up in a beehive and the thick make-up she wore on stage accentuated her beauty.

Trying not to stare at her naked, pert breasts glistening with baby oil, Thomas smiled back. Even though his mind hadn't been off Maggie since he'd last seen her a week ago, he enjoyed working here and wished he could spend all his time in Soho instead of having to run occasional errands to Camden. It was always a relief when he was told to get back to the club, especially when it looked as though things might kick off at the Cow and Bull, like earlier tonight when those guys in suits came in.

In Soho, no one gave him a second glance or commented on the colour of his skin. If anything, he was given respect. He knew that was down to Rory, and it could change in a heartbeat if he put a foot wrong. It would definitely change if Rory ever found out he'd slept with Maggie.

The events of last week still haunted him. Most nights he was woken by nightmares, either about Maggie's father or the man he'd killed, the three corpses he'd helped bury. He could still smell their blood. His parents had wanted to know what was going on, but he couldn't tell them. Maggie was the only person he could talk to about things like that.

'Go on, Thomas,' Christine purred. She fluttered the long false eyelashes that framed her piercing blue eyes, and pouted her bright pink lips seductively.

'I'm working,' he reminded her. But when the takings had been counted and locked away, he poured her a glass of vodka and pushed it across the bar.

'Aren't you going to join me?' She took the glass, her fingers brushing his. 'Still hung up on that girl, aren't you?'

Thomas bristled. Stupidly, when he'd been upset, he'd told her about Maggie – not that he'd mentioned her name or said where she was from, but now Chrissy wouldn't let go of the subject.

Turning away from her, he let his eyes drift to the small stage where Josie, a young girl with peroxide-blonde hair and obvious black roots, swayed half-heartedly to a Ray Charles record. A few men near the stage were getting rowdy, throwing money at her. Although that was fine, touching wasn't. Rory didn't allow touching. Not downstairs, anyway. For that, punters needed to go upstairs or to one of the walk-ups Rory had recently purchased.

'Come on, Thomas.' Chrissy stood up, her erect nipples pointing the way as she moved round the side of the bar to join him. Then she wrapped her arms round his neck, her breasts pressed against his chest.

Immediately, Thomas could feel an erection. Embarrassed, he tried to push Chrissy off. At twenty-seven she was more than ten years older than him and much more experienced. Enjoying his reaction, she giggled and let her hand wander down to his crotch. 'It's a shame for this to go to waste.'

'I'm said I'm working, Christine. If Mr Sheehan comes in—'

'I'm sure he won't object to us having a bit of fun,' she cut in. 'Anyway, it's nearly closing time. He wouldn't bother showing up here now.' Her perfume was sickly sweet, and she pressed her hand harder against his penis. 'I could look after you, Thomas, show you a good time – better than that girl you keep mooning over.' She stood up on tiptoes and her mouth found his.

He closed his eyes for a moment, tasting the booze and cigarettes on her tongue and struggling to hold in a groan.

'*Thomas.*'

Thomas jumped and pushed Chrissy away as Davey, the head barman, emerged from the storeroom with a crate of Scotch. He shook his head and grinned. 'Chrissy, do you never give up?' He winked at Thomas. 'Chrissy thinks she needs to fuck everyone who starts here to welcome them to the business.'

Thankful for the distraction, Thomas took the crate from Davey and began stacking bottles on the shelves. He raised his voice over the Bing Crosby record to ask, 'Where's Eddie and Guy?'

'Out the back, sorting the barrels. There was a fuck-up with one of the orders. To say Mr Sheehan wasn't very happy about it is an understate—'

The music stopped abruptly, cutting off Davey before he could finish.

Thomas glanced up to see eight men in suits standing at the entrance of the club. They looked like the same men he'd seen earlier at the Cow and Bull.

Josie stopped gyrating on the stage and the rowdy punters around her fell silent.

Luca Romano paused midway down the stairs to survey the room. He addressed the punters, his tone courteous but ice-cold: '*Buona sera*, gentlemen. I think it's time for you to call it a night.'

They didn't need to be asked twice. Everyone gathered up their things and scurried up the stairs. Luca, meanwhile, made his way to the bar, followed by three of his men. Thomas saw Davey glance towards where the gun was kept, but the sight of Luca's men, all of them obviously armed, made him think twice about reaching for it.

'Whisky. The good stuff,' Luca commanded.

Thomas grabbed the bottle and poured it with steady hands, aware that Chrissy was trying to make herself invisible beside him as Luca looked her up and down.

'You work for Rory.' This was directed at Thomas. Realising it wasn't a question, he remained silent as Luca sipped his drink, glancing around the club. 'Nice place. Doing well, by the looks of it.'

Again, Thomas said nothing.

Behind him, the door opened and Eddie and Guy stopped in their tracks when they saw Luca and his men.

'Ciao, Eddie. Ciao, Guy.' Luca set down his glass. 'Good to see you both.'

Eddie bolted, heading back towards the door he'd come through, but two of Luca's men cut him off, grabbing him by the arms. They dragged him over to Luca.

'That was a very stupid thing to do . . . Let's have a chat, shall we?' Luca nodded towards Chrissy, who looked terrified. '*You* – get a pen and paper, I want Rory to get my message word for word. I take it you can read and write?'

Chrissy nodded, grabbed the pad and pen from beside the till and hurried over to Luca. She stood trembling as he smiled at her.

'I don't suppose you fancy coming to be my secretary, do you?' He flicked her nipple hard and she jumped back, but he pulled her towards him again as his men continued to restrain Eddie.

Thomas stayed by the bar, not sure what he should do, wishing he was anywhere else but here.

Luca picked up his half-empty whisky glass and poured it over Eddie's face, making him gasp and splutter. Then he slammed the glass on the bar edge, smashing it and holding up the jagged edge.

At a nod from Luca, the man holding Eddie reached to prise his mouth open.

Luca gave an evil grin, then slammed the glass into Eddie's mouth and began sawing at his tongue.

Eddie's screams, although muted by the blood bubbling in his mouth, made Thomas feel sick. It was as if he was back at the Cow and Bull, hearing the dying screams of the three men.

The man holding Eddie struggled to keep his jaws open as he

writhed in agony, blood and saliva spraying out of his mouth. Luca just carried on sawing, beads of sweating forming on his brow from the effort. Finally he set down the knife, gripped Eddie's tongue with his fingers and pulled hard, severing it completely.

Luca held the bloody mess up like a trophy. 'Just business, Eddie. Nothing personal,' he said, sounding completely unruffled.

Eddie fell to the floor unconscious, blood puddling around him.

Taking the bloodstained handkerchief that had been wrapped round his hand, Luca placed Eddie's tongue in it. Then he handed it to Christine. 'On second thoughts, no need to write anything down. I'm sure he'll get the message.' He turned to look at Thomas. 'And *you* – you can deliver it. Tell him . . .' He paused. 'Tell him that times are changing, we need to talk about new arrangements for Soho.' Luca straightened his shirt cuffs, which were soaked in blood. Then he took a small tin from his pocket, removed a pill and popped it into his mouth, swallowing it quickly. 'Tell him to enjoy his last weeks as king of Soho.'

Followed by his men, Luca exited the club while Rory's employees looked on in stunned silence.

Chrissy walked unsteadily to the bar and placed the napkin containing Eddie's tongue in front of Thomas. Avoiding her eyes, he slipped it into his pocket.

The war for Soho had just begun and, like it or not, Thomas was caught up in the thick of it.

Chapter Twenty

The inside of the Whelans' terraced house had been trans-formed. The furniture was pushed back against the walls in the small parlour and extra chairs had been borrowed from neighbours.

Pam's coffin, which had been changed at the last minute from a plain model to a mahogany one with gold handles, paid for by Rory, dominated the space. It rested on two kitchen tables with rickety legs, pushed together and draped with a lace tablecloth borrowed from neighbours.

Maggie couldn't bear to look at it. In truth, she didn't want to be here at all. She'd woken up in a real state and she wasn't sure how she'd get through the day.

She bit the inside of her cheek to stop herself from crying as she watched new mourners being greeted at the door by Father Patrick and Mrs Whelan before making their way through the cramped house to file past the coffin. Some of them Maggie recognised, but she didn't speak to anyone. She couldn't. She was afraid she might say something that would give her away.

At the far end of the room, her mother stood pale and sour-faced. She had never seen her mum cry, so it came as no surprise that Kathleen showed no emotion, especially when she hadn't liked Pam in the first place. The only reason she was here was because it wouldn't do not to show her face. Appearances mattered, especially when Father Patrick was in attendance.

'You'll have a wee drop, love?' Mrs Clary pressed a glass of whisky into Maggie's hand. 'I think we'll all be needing some of this before the end of the day. Poor Pam. May the Lord have mercy on her soul.' She crossed herself, an automatic gesture after a lifetime of practice. 'You must be all over the place with sadness, Maggie. I know how close she was to you. It's a terrible shock.' She stopped to tut and shake her head. 'Her mammy told me what great friends the two of you were. That must be of some comfort to you.'

Maggie began to raise the glass to her mouth, thinking a drop of whisky might help matters, but a cold stare from her mother stopped her.

Disappointed at the lack of response, Mrs Clary moved away to offer her condolences elsewhere.

Rory Sheehan had donated a crate of whisky and someone had made sandwiches – plates of neat triangles filled with meat paste and corned beef sat untouched on the sideboard. Beside them stood rows of cups and saucers that didn't quite match.

'For the love of God, the child was young entirely.' Mrs Ryan dabbed her eyes with a clean handkerchief that Maggie had laundered only yesterday. 'A terrible thing. Just terrible.' She stared at the coffin, standing next to other women from the congregation of the local church.

'Joined the angels, so she has. The Lord giveth and he taketh away,' said Mrs Clary.

More people arrived, girls who'd gone to the same school as Pam, and some of Mr Whelan's workmates. They paused beside Mrs Whelan, touching her shoulder, muttering sympathetic words: *Let the saints watch over her; she's with the Blessed Mother now; a grand girl, so she was, always had a smile for everyone; God love her, a terrible shame altogether.*

Making sure her mother wasn't looking, Maggie knocked back the whisky. The burning sensation in her throat made her wince, but she immediately swapped her empty glass for a full one from the sideboard. She needed it.

The clock on the mantelpiece seemed to match her thumping heartbeat.

'Sure, it's an awful way to go, isn't it?' Mrs Clary tried again to draw her in. 'Falling down those stairs, God save us. These things could happen to any one of us. Only the other day, I tripped down a flight meself. Fair caught my foot on an upturned piece of carpet. I swear I thought I'd be joining poor Pam.'

The other women gave Mrs Clary sympathetic nods and continued to chatter about everything from the demise of Pam to the curse of bunions to a neighbour's husband who'd run off with a young girl from Kilburn.

The front door opened again, and Rory entered. As the hallway filled with his bulk, conversation quietened for a moment before quickly resuming. Everyone knew Rory Sheehan, by reputation at least; even those who'd never spoken to him looked anxious as he scanned the room.

Spotting Maggie, he gave her a nod. Surprised how comforted she felt to see him, she found herself blushing. He nodded to Maggie's mum, who reddened for a different reason before hurrying away to get herself a sandwich. Clearly she didn't want to be reminded of what she'd done.

More bottles of whisky appeared and as the alcohol flowed, so did more stories of Pam. Hearing them made Maggie want to run out the door, but she felt a presence by her side and then Rory's voice whispering in her ear.

'I'm glad to see you here.'

Aware of the less than discreet glances being directed their way, Maggie stood looking straight in front of her, offering no reply.

'Is everything, all right? I was disappointed that you ran off last week. I hope Thomas didn't say anything to upset you. I can always have a word with him, if you like.'

She spun round to look at him, not realising he was standing so near that their lips were almost touching. Stepping back, she replied, 'No, of course not. I just needed to go and check on my mum.'

'Good.' He gave her a smile. She looked into his eyes, but she couldn't read what he was thinking. 'Because you know, Maggie, if anyone gives you any bother, all you have to do is come to me, and I'll sort it.' He glanced over at the coffin. 'No matter who it is.' He winked at her and Maggie caught her breath, then she took another step back, banging straight into Father Patrick.

'Maggie, it's time now . . . Time now, everyone!' Father Patrick announced. He rubbed his neck where his white collar stood stark against his skin. Glancing at Rory and then at Pam's father, he said, 'Ready, gentlemen?'

They nodded and moved towards the coffin, and carefully they lifted the lid.

There was a collective intake of breath.

'Would you look at her, so peaceful!'

Pam's mother began to wail again, collapsing on a chair.

Maggie made herself look then.

Pam lay on bright white satin, dressed in an expensive-looking frilly yellow dress that Maggie had never seen before. They'd done something to her face, which made her look like a waxwork model, her expression stiff and severe. The real Pam had been full of laughter and jokes, nothing like the occupant of the coffin.

'I thought it was best to make her look as virginal as possible,' Rory whispered in her ear. 'The dress seemed appropriate.'

Maggie turned to look at him. 'You chose it?' she whispered back.

'Of course. And paid for everything.' His eyes darted over her face. 'We wouldn't want people thinking she looked like a little tart who'd fucked your da, would we?'

Suddenly aware of her mother watching them, Maggie felt as if all the air had been sucked out of the room. Battling her tears, she pushed through the crowd until she reached the kitchen, closing the door behind her.

She leaned forward, resting her hands on her knees as she struggled to breathe.

The door opened behind her.

'Maggie.' Rory's voice was soft. 'I didn't mean to upset you. I'm just a gruff Irishman. I forget meself sometimes.'

She didn't try to move away as he rubbed her back. After all, what he'd said about Pam was true. But when she turned to face him and saw the ever-present smirk on his lips, she glared at him and demanded, 'Why are you here?'

He set down his whisky glass on the draining board. 'I'm paying my respects. The whole street has turned out, as well as Father Patrick's congregation. It would be something if I didn't show up.'

Through the door came the sound of singing, voices slurred with drink and high emotion.

'All these people are talking like they knew her. They didn't, not really. You didn't either.'

He held her gently by the shoulders. 'No, I didn't. Who would think little Pam was fucking men for a few shillings.'

She brushed away Rory's hand. 'Stop saying that.'

'You've got a fire in your belly, Maggie Riley,' he said, the smirk turning to a grin. 'I like that in a woman.' He sounded breathless and his eyes were glazed. She could see his chest rising up and down as he stared at her.

Embarrassed, she looked away. 'I need to go back in.'

'Not yet.' Rory blocked her way. 'You do know I'm serious when I say I'll always protect you. I proved that to you with Pam.'

Maggie didn't want to hear this. She put her hands over her ears, but Rory pulled them down. 'I did it for you, Maggie.'

She shook as the tears ran down her cheeks. 'I didn't ask you to . . . I didn't want you to do that. *I didn't.*'

Rory placed his fingers over her mouth. 'Shhhh, they'll hear you.'

They both looked towards the door, and Maggie took a deep gulp of air to help her calm down.

'Are you telling me you'd rather it was you lying in that coffin instead of Pam? Because we both know that's what would've happened if she'd talked to your da before I got hold of her. Don't you see, Maggie? She had to be stopped. I've told you before – she wasn't your friend. She got what she deserved.' He used his thumb to wipe away her tears. 'If it wasn't for you, Pam wouldn't be lying in that coffin.'

Maggie pulled away, but he caught her arm and drew her to him. 'She's brought us together, made us close. We share a special bond now.' Once again, he began to breathe heavily.

Then the back door opened and Thomas appeared.

Chapter Twenty-One

'Thomas?' Rory whipped round to look at him. 'You'd better have a fecking good reason for showing up here.'

Thomas looked shocked, he was panting as if he'd been running.

Before he could speak, the kitchen door opened and Mrs Clary walked in. Seeing Thomas, she dropped the tray of cups she was carrying. 'Who are you?' she demanded. 'What in God's name are you doing here? Hoping to rob us, no doubt! Well, you can—'

'Mrs Clary,' Rory spoke quietly, 'Thomas here works for me.'

The woman's face paled. 'Y-you have a—'

'He's my employee' – Rory cut her off, waving for Thomas to step inside the kitchen – 'and you will show him respect.'

'I'll do no such thing!' Her words sounded as horrified as she looked.

'Not only that,' Rory continued, wrapping his muscular arm round her shoulders, 'you will address him as Mr Johnson.'

This was all too much for Mrs Clary. She tried to struggle out of Rory's forced embrace, but he was too strong.

'Never.' She shook her head vehemently. 'As God is my witness, there's only one word for the likes of him.'

Rory looked down at Mrs Clary. His voice was ominously quiet. 'Does your husband still enjoy his football, Mrs Clary?'

'His football?' She sounded baffled by the change of subject.

'Yes, he plays for the local team, does he not?'

She looked flustered. 'Of course.'

'Then his legs will be worth saving, won't they?'

'Saving?'

'If I ever hear that you've said anything disrespectful to Thomas, or haven't addressed him properly, I will break both your husband's legs with my bare hands, and I'll make you watch.' He let her go then, giving a curt nod in the direction of the door. She hurried out without a backwards glance.

Immediately, Rory turned to Thomas. 'What do you want?'

'Sorry, Mr Sheehan. I went to the Cow and Bull last night, but the place was all locked up and no one answered. I waited outside until Malcolm came by this morning to open up, and then he sent me here to let you know . . .' He paused and glanced uneasily at Maggie.

'It's fine, Thomas. You can talk freely in front of Maggie.' He winked at her and, knowing that Thomas was watching, she blushed. 'There's nothing that you can't say in front of her.'

Rory and Malcolm had gone over to Dean Street after the call came through about the fire at Stan and Mildred's cafe. A fireman had told them that it looked as though someone had poured petrol everywhere then set the place alight. The old couple had been in the building when it burned down.

Burning down buildings wasn't Luca's style – that was Rory's trademark – but he'd known immediately that this was Luca's way of sending a message. He'd called in a few of the boys and headed up to Clerkenwell to let the bastard know his message wasn't appreciated. Unfortunately, Luca had gone to ground and no one in the tight-knit Italian community could be persuaded to tell them where he was hiding.

'Come on, Thomas, out with it. What's going on?'

Still looking unsure, Thomas blurted, 'It's Luca Romano.'

Rage was building inside him, but Rory knew he had to keep his head. Saying nothing, he nodded for Thomas to continue.

Casting another uncertain glance in Maggie's direction, Thomas reached into his suit pocket and took out a bloodstained handkerchief. When he placed it on the kitchen table, the cloth came unwrapped, exposing the contents.

Maggie let out a cry and turned her head away.

Rory stared. 'Whose is it?'

'Eddie's. Luca came into the club and cut it out in front of everyone.'

Not trusting himself to speak, Rory carefully picked up the handkerchief and its contents and slipped it into his jacket pocket. He was halfway to the kitchen door when he stopped in his tracks and turned to Maggie. 'We never finished our conversation . . . but we can take it up later.' His gaze turned to Thomas. 'You and I are going to the club.'

'Yes, Mr Sheehan.'

'First, I need to say my goodbyes.' He pointed to the back door. 'Head out that way and wait for me by the car.'

Rory slammed out of the kitchen door, leaving Thomas and Maggie alone together.

'What were you talking to Mr Sheehan about?' Thomas asked, keeping his gaze fixed on the floor.

'Nothing,' Maggie lied. 'He . . . he just wanted to know if there was anything he could do to help.' She wasn't sure if Thomas believed her or not.

'You know he likes you.' Thomas looked at her then.

Embarrassed and uncomfortable, she snapped, 'What nonsense are you talking now, Thomas Johnson? You're supposed to be waiting for Rory in the car.'

'So it's Rory, now, is it?'

He reached out and touched her arm. 'Are you and he . . .'

'No!'

'He's too old for you. Too' – Thomas tried to find the right word – 'mature.'

Maggie's eyes flashed. 'What's that supposed to mean?'

'I didn't mean it in a bad way, but you don't belong with someone like him. All he wants is to own you, like you're a possession.'

For some reason this angered Maggie. 'We've got more in common than you think. In fact, he said we share a special bond.'

'Then what about us?' Thomas muttered.

'Us?' She fought back her tears. 'I've said before, there's nothing between us.'

He gave the smallest of nods in reply, and she caught the glisten of tears in his eyes as he turned and strode out of the back door.

What had she done? Why had she said that. 'Thomas, *wait!* I'm sorr—'

'Maggie, what's going on?'

Her mother had entered the kitchen. Maggie looked at her, then turned to look for Thomas. But he'd gone, taking her harsh words with him.

Chapter Twenty-Two

Luca sat in the Romano family home in Holborn. Four storeys of fancy brickwork in a quiet residential road. The decor was Italian: paintings hung in heavy gilt frames, crystal chandeliers lit the gold wallpapered rooms and fine-cut decanters filled with various liqueurs lined the sideboard, catching the light.

Luca sat at the mahogany table, which as always was filled with family and friends. Some habits from back home never changed. Listlessly, he pushed his spaghetti around the plate. His mother and aunt had made their special sauce, the recipe passed down through the generations and brought over from Italy years ago. Too bad his fiancée wasn't interested in learning how to cook.

Usually, Luca would've finished at least two servings by now, but today he had no appetite. For the last hour or so his father had been droning on, repeating the same thing over and over. He was still at it. Sitting there at the head of the table, his liver-spotted hands so gnarled with arthritis that he could barely hold his solid gold fork. But although his strength had left his hands it still remained in his voice. And that voice carried weight in the Romano *famiglia*.

'You burned down one of his businesses?' His father stabbed the meatball that had been evading him for several minutes. 'The cafe that Sheehan protected . . . And half of London saw you do this?' His face was red and he stood, dragging the napkin from under his chin, before throwing the bowl of spaghetti against the wall. 'What were you thinking?'

Luca fought the temptation to challenge his father. Respect was something that was given to Vincent Romano without question. 'Not half of London.' Luca's voice came out quietly. 'Only the people who needed to see.'

'People who needed to see!' He mimicked his son, then sat down and grasped his wineglass with clawed fingers. He took a gulp of wine. 'Who decides this, hmm? *You*? Since when do *you* decide such things?' His tone was cutting.

Luca's mother silently topped up her husband's glass.

'I needed to send a message.'

Shaking his head like he couldn't believe what he was hearing, Vincent glared at him. 'Have you heard yourself, Luca?'

Frustrated with his father but unable to show it, Luca leaned forward on his elbows. 'There's something he's not telling me about my cousins.'

The moment he said this, his aunt wailed, slumping down in her chair. Luca's mother hurried to comfort her. Vincent spoke to his sister in Italian, reassuring her as best he could. Then he turned back to Luca. 'Learn to keep your mouth shut at the dinner table.'

'What am I supposed to do? Just sit here eating pasta and not worry about them?'

His father picked up his knife and pointed the tip at Luca. 'You were supposed to wait. You don't know Sheehan has *any-thing* to tell you about them. It's not like he's your only enemy. You've made plenty of other enemies.'

'Don't you care about Donny, Gino and Matteo?' Luca asked, seething with frustration at his father's weakness.

Vincent slammed his palm on the table, sending the gold cutlery jumping. 'How dare you disrespect me in my own home. Those boys are my family!' he yelled, then broke into a coughing fit and had to take a gulp of red wine to clear his throat. 'We had a plan when it came to Soho. Negotiations. Conversations. Look around you, Luca. You think I got where I am by burning down buildings every time someone crossed me? Or whenever I had a *feeling* I knew something. I was smarter than that, and that's why I'm here and the men who crossed me are long gone.'

Luca watched his father, the resentment building up inside him. He thought of the cafe, the flames creeping up the walls, the old couple's screams. He had felt nothing as he watched the place burn. Nothing at all.

Luca met his father's eyes. 'We couldn't wait.'

His father shook his head, and it was some time before he spoke. 'You mean you couldn't think straight with those pills in your system. What, you think I don't know what you're doing?' He touched his eyes and then pulled at his ear. 'I see and hear everything.'

Luca bristled as his father continued: 'You have a beautiful fiancée, yet you get the clap from one of those Soho tarts. And now you're making decisions with that shit running through your veins.' He threw a bread roll at his son; Luca ducked and it dropped to the floor, where it was eaten by Sofia's white Chihuahua.

'The tablets are medicinal. They have nothing to do with it.' Luca sounded defensive.

'They have everything to do with it! You're not thinking clearly. Never have I seen such stupidity from my own flesh and blood.'

From the doorway came the soft click of heels on the polished floor. Sofia smiled at Luca but saved the warmest smile for her soon-to-be father-in law.

'Ahh, Sofia, come, come.' The old man gestured for her to come closer.

Luca watched Sofia totter in. She was plain but the heavy make-up she wore and the double eyelashes she glued on her lids each morning, gave her a striking appearance.

'Should I come back later, Papa?' She spoke in a hushed tone, practising her English, which still left a lot to be desired.

'No, no.' His mother hurried over. 'Come – sit. Eat something. You're too thin.'

That certainly wasn't the case, but Luca said nothing as he watched Sofia take her place at the table. Nothing about her attracted him, not even the massive tits straining at her bra. He doubted his cock would ever get hard for her. Unfortunately, since the wedding arrangements were already in motion, there was nothing he could do but sit back and accept it.

'We were discussing business.' His father's voice softened for Sofia.

'I heard a little.' She kept her eyes on her plate.

'Then you heard how stupid my son was.'

Luca ground his teeth, not appreciating his father badmouthing him to his future wife.

'Burning down properties makes us look stupid. We don't want to start a war, but now we might have one on our hands, and we're not ready.'

The spaghetti on Luca's plate had gone cold. He pushed it away.

'If we knew for certain Sheehan had something to do with my nephews' disappearance, then the whole Italian community would stand with us. But right now we know no such thing, so we're on our own.' He burped. 'We're businessmen, we use our heads, we don't seek revenge before we even know who's to blame.'

Luca wondered what Sofia made of all this. What she really thought about marrying him, moving to London, sharing this house with his family, memories of Italy everywhere but so far from her own family.

'I'm sorry,' he said finally.

His father looked up, surprised. He nodded but didn't acknowledge the apology. 'This family won't pay the price for your stupidity.' His mother brought a bowl of spaghetti to the table, placing it in front of Sofia. 'We need to stop this situation from escalating.' His father straightened in his chair. 'We need to go and see Sheehan.'

'No.' Luca shook his head.

His father's fist came down on the table. 'If I say we do, we do. I've made my decision. We stop this now, and we offer Sheehan a property from our patch, to show no hard feelings.'

'That makes us look weak.'

'No, what makes us look weak is starting a war we cannot win.'

It was true that the other Italian gangs wouldn't help them bring Sheehan down unless they could prove that he'd disposed of three innocent young men, but that didn't mean Luca agreed with the way his father was running things. How could anyone respect the Romano name if they started giving away their properties to Sheehan? You wouldn't catch the Kray twins doing something like that.

No, if Luca wanted to make a name for himself, he didn't just need to get rid of Rory Sheehan.

He needed to get rid of his father as well.

Chapter Twenty-Three

'You've caused me a lot of trouble.' Rory fixed his piercing blue eyes on Thomas, who shifted nervously in the leather armchair across from him. 'If I didn't like you so much, I'd be thinking about getting rid of you.' There was a threat in his voice, but also a hint of amusement.

There would be no point in reminding Rory that he hadn't been the one who wanted to kill the three Italians, so Thomas sat in silence, waiting to learn his fate.

He winced as Rory picked up the poker, relaxing a little when he began stirring the fire with it. As the logs began to crackle, he turned to pick up the bloody handkerchief from the side table next to Thomas. Then he threw it into the flames, watching with fascination as Eddie's tongue blistered and burned.

'What am I going to do with you, lad?' He rubbed his head. 'I don't want the others thinking I have me favourites, and that's exactly what they'll think if I don't punish you.'

Instinctively, Thomas glanced at the door, but he knew it was futile. Especially when Malcolm was on the other side of it.

'I'll tell you what I'm going to do . . . I'm going to pretend all this never happened. Would you like that?'

Thomas tried to speak, but his lips felt as if they'd been glued together, so he simply nodded.

'In return, there's something I need you to do for me.' Rory walked over to the drinks table to pour himself a large whisky. Then he picked up his packet of cigarettes, offering one to Thomas, who hurried to accept.

Lighting it, Rory took a deep drag, drawing the smoke right down into his lungs. 'That's only fair, wouldn't you say?' He waved his cigarette at Thomas, who was trying to look like he was enjoying his fag. 'You do a simple favour for me, and I'll forget the trouble you've brought to me door.'

Thomas nodded again.

'You're a good lad, Thomas. I knew you wouldn't let me down.' He took another pull on his cigarette. 'Now, this may come as a surprise to you, but I'm planning on asking Maggie to marry me.'

Thomas suppressed his shock and disappointment. He'd been warned off Maggie, so showing any kind of emotion would only raise suspicions that he still had feelings for her.

Rory cracked his fingers and twisted the gold ring on his pinkie finger. 'Well, when I ask her, I want to make sure she says yes. That's the favour you can do for me. You can persuade Maggie to say yes. Then we can forget about this bit of trouble.'

'But what if she doesn't want to?'

The glass Rory had been holding flew across the room, smashing against the marble fireplace. 'You'll do as you're fecking well told! Tell her I won't take no for an answer. She's mine, you understand. And I don't want any other fucker putting his dirty hands on her before I get to her . . .'

Rory smiled at Thomas with such darkness that a cold chill of fear crept down his spine. If Rory ever found out that he and Maggie had been together, he'd be dead. And God knows what would happen if he discovered what her dad had been doing to her.

Panic gripped him. If Maggie said no, his life would be over. But if she said yes she'd be lost to him forever.

'I'm sensing there's something bothering you?' Rory tilted his head to one side to stare at him.

'No, there's nothing wrong, Mr Sheehan.' He swallowed down the bile, trying to find the right words. 'But . . . but what if she needs time to think about it?'

'I'm not expecting her to say yes straight away. Maggie doesn't always know what's best for her, but she's your friend and I'm sure she'll listen to you. And if she doesn't then I've no doubt you'll come up with a way to make sure she does.' He roared with laughter, but it faded to a chilling silence.

At that moment, Malcolm burst in. 'Boss, you're needed in the bar – we've got visitors.'

Rory stood and, as he walked past Thomas, he squeezed his shoulder firmly. 'Remember, I'm relying on you, Thomas. If I can't have her, nobody can.'

The threat hung in the air.

'And I don't want Maggie knowing that we've had this conversation, you understand?'

Thomas nodded.

'Good. So now we understand each other.'

He followed Malcolm into the bar, leaving Thomas staring into the fire, watching the remains of Eddie's tongue turn to ashes.

Chapter Twenty-Four

The last person Rory Sheehan had expected to see in his pub was Vincent Romano. But here he was, along with his son Luca and a dozen heavies in sharp suits.

He glanced at Malcolm, then plastered on a big grin. 'Mr Romano, what an honour! But if you're here to question me about your missing nephews, I'm afraid you've had a wasted journey. As I said to your son, I don't have any information as to their whereabouts.'

It was one thing for Luca to come here, but for his father, a notable gangster who still held considerable sway within the Italian community, to pay a visit was something else.

Back in the day, Vincent Romano had left a trail of corpses across London. He'd been notorious for torturing whole families, including children, and then disposing of them. Luca was weak by comparison. Even so, Rory would rather deal with Vince than Luca. It wasn't that he trusted him – he didn't. But at least you knew where you stood with the old man. Whereas his pill-popping son was becoming increasingly unstable.

Rory wasn't exactly a teetotaller. And he tolerated the girls who danced at his club dabbling in a bit of champagne and 'whites', but if any of his employees were stupid enough to get themselves hooked on it they would be out. One thing Rory hated was a lush.

Grabbing glasses from behind the bar, Rory set about pouring sixteen shots of whisky. 'As an Irishman,' he said, 'I'd take it as insult if you don't drink with me.' He picked up a shot glass in each hand and walked over to Vince and Luca, offering them each a glass.

Neither of the men moved. Vince held Rory's gaze for a long moment before took the glass, knocked back the whisky, then handed the empty glass back, all without blinking.

Aware that Luca hadn't touched his drink, Rory gave Malcolm a nod and he began handing out the rest of the shots to Romano's men.

'But what I find even more of an insult,' Rory said, stepping back to look at them, 'is what you did to my business . . . and to Eddie – one of my men.' Knowing he had to play this very carefully, he turned to face Luca. 'You . . . *you* came here last night. And afterwards you went to Soho and burned down one of the fucking businesses that I protect, then marched into my club and cut my bouncer's fucking tongue out.' He stepped forward, and two of Romano's men moved to block him, but they backed off immediately when Vince shook his head.

'That's why we're here, Mr Sheehan.'

The look in Luca's eyes when his father spoke didn't go unnoticed by Rory. Resentment? Anger? He wasn't sure which, but there was no question Luca didn't want to be standing here, playing second fiddle to his old man.

Rory smirked at Luca, enjoying his discomfort, then turned his attention back to Vince.

'What happened was . . . unfortunate.' Vince's Italian accent was much stronger than Luca's. 'My son here, is . . . how do you say . . . hot-headed. Because of that, mistakes were made.'

Rory's face betrayed no emotion, but the look of humiliation on Luca's face was priceless. He nodded for Vince to continue, hoping he'd come up with a few more put-downs for his son.

'None of us want a war. There's money to be made for all of us, without . . .' Vince searched for the word. 'Conflict. Conflicts are expensive and, in my experience, they distract you.' Vince's gaze moved from Rory to Malcolm. Then, looking squarely at his son, he added: 'Only a foolish man creates conflict for no reason.'

At this, Luca finally knocked back the whisky.

'So, to compensate you and to show that I take this as seriously as you do, I propose to offer you our coffee shop on Rupert Street.'

'And why would I want to accept that?' Rory's voice was gruff.

'Because, Mr Sheehan, it's more than a fair trade for the cafe which was burned down.'

Rory shook his head. 'No offence to you,' he growled at Vince. 'But I want Luca to answer this one.' He turned his focus on Luca. 'Why should I accept Rupert Street?'

Luca said nothing, but anger and resentment seethed from his every pore.

'Mr Sheehan.' The authority in Vincent Romano's voice ensured that all heads turned to him. 'You say in your culture it is an insult not to drink with you. Well, in my culture, I take it as an insult for you to address my son when I'm standing here as head of the family. Do I look like someone to play around with, Mr Sheehan? Respect is something we take seriously.' The cold glare with which this rebuke was delivered left Rory in no doubt that the old Romano darkness still lay very close to the surface.

As if he had all the time in the world, Vince proceeded to adjust the solid gold chain bracelets on his wrist before speaking again. 'So, do we have a deal, Mr Sheehan?'

'The cafe on the south end of Rupert Street?'

'Yes,' Vince said. 'It's yours.'

'And what about Stan and Mildred? The couple who died in the fire. And Eddie, the bouncer at my club. What about him?'

Vince shrugged. 'What about them? It's not as if you or I, or anyone in this room, will lose a moment's sleep over them.' He smiled. 'You want my men to lay a wreath outside the cafe? Would that make you feel better?' His voice was full of sarcasm.

Rory turned to Malcolm, nodded, and turned back to Vince, who held out his hand.

'Well, Mr Sheehan? Shall we shake on it?'

'You'll excuse me, but I'm picky who I shake hands with. Listen, I'm no fool, and I'm not looking for problems either, so I'll take your offer: the cafe at the south end of Rupert Street. As for the wreath – don't bother.'

Vince and Luca exchanged a few words in Italian, before the son, his face flushed red, slammed out of the pub without acknowledging Rory.

'As I say, my son's hot headed, Mr Sheehan,' said Vince, turning to make his way out, followed by his men.

'Do you trust him?' Malcolm asked Rory.

'The question isn't do I trust *him*, it's whether I trust *them*.'

'And do you?'

Rory stared at the pub door through which they'd just departed. 'Not a fucking chance.'

Malcolm poured a whisky and handed it to his boss. 'Good thing they can't connect us to the three missing Romano lads.'

Rory swirled the whisky around in his mouth. He swallowed, enjoying the burning sensation, then lit a cigarette. 'I wouldn't be so sure.'

'No one's going to talk . . . unless Thomas—'

Rory blew out the smoke. 'No, our little Tommy boy hasn't said a word.'

'So what do we do?'

Rory pulled out a chair and sat down. 'For the time being . . . nothing. We sit tight and wait.'

'For what?' Malcolm frowned.

'Luca. Did you see the look on his face? If you ask me, he's tired of playing second fiddle to his old man. Mark my words, it won't be long till he makes a move.'

'What sort of move?'

'Not sure yet – and I don't suppose he is, either. The kid's an addict, and that makes him a loose cannon. And when he explodes we'll be standing by to take the whole shebang.'

Malcom raised his eyebrows. 'Clerkenwell?'

'No, London . . . The whole fucking town.'

Chapter Twenty-Five

Maggie pulled her bedroom curtain aside to see Thomas standing by the outside toilet throwing stones up at the window. The light coming from the kitchen window put him in clear view of anyone looking out. What on earth was he doing here? He knew what would happen if her dad saw him.

'Go away, Thomas . . . *Go*,' she mouthed, and waved him away, but he continued to stand there, not bothering to hide. Maggie dropped the curtain. Her heart raced and she chewed on her thumb, listening to Da yelling at her mum downstairs. Usually she'd be wishing that he'd storm off to the pub before it turned physical and he started lashing out with his fists, but now she prayed that they'd keep on screaming at each other. Because if one of them happened to look out of the window . . .

She pulled back the curtain again, hoping Thomas would have gone, but he was still there. Deciding there was nothing else for it, Maggie crept out of her bedroom and began to tiptoe down the stairs.

'*You fucking cunt!*' Da yelled. The noise drowned out the creak of the hinge as she opened the door, and she was congratulating herself on having made her escape when a deep, low scream from her mother sent her running through to the kitchen.

She took in the scene.

Her mother lay on the floor, her dress pulled up, her peach knickers ripped off, exposing the ugly purple bruises from where Da had kicked her yesterday.

As for her dad, his baggy brown trousers were round his feet and his pasty white buttocks were pumping away aggressively as he lay on top of her mother.

'Get off her, Da!' Maggie ran over and began pulling at his shirt, trying to drag him off. He flicked his arm back and caught her in the face, the power of it sending her crashing into the kitchen door.

Still thrusting away, her dad glanced over his shoulder. 'I'll fucking kill you if you don't get out of here, girl.'

Maggie scrambled up, tears pouring down her face. 'Da, *please*, get off her.' And with all her strength she launched herself at him. This time, it was her dad that went flying. Her shove sent him tumbling off her mother and onto the tiled floor, where he lay, reeking of booze, too winded to move. She wrinkled her nose in disgust at the sight of his penis throbbing red and glistening with a film of wet. 'Why can't you leave her alone?'

'Keep out of it, you,' her mother hissed, snatching her torn knickers from where her husband thrown them and pulling down her dress. 'What happens between a man and wife is nothing to do with you. Do you want to be the death of me?'

'I was trying to help,' Maggie sobbed. 'How can you let him do that to you?'

Her dad was now picking himself up, swaying unsteadily. Once up, he threw one of the chairs across the room, knocking the kettle off the stove. 'You fucking bitch!' he roared, picking up the breadknife and pointing it at his daughter. 'I'll fecking kill you.' He lunged at her but Maggie, much quicker on her feet, dodged out of the way, escaping with only a small slash on her forearm.

Still not finished, he heaved the table aside to get to her. 'I'll swing for you, Maggie! She's my wife and I'll do what I want to her. And as long as you're living under my roof I won't have you telling me what to do. I'll do exactly as I please.'

'Does that include going with Pam, Da? *Does it?*'

Her dad glared at her through a drunken haze. Jabbing the breadknife at her, he demanded, 'What did you say?'

Maggie registered the shock on her mother's face, which was bloody from a fresh cut over her eye.

'I saw you,' Maggie screamed. 'I saw you with Pam.'

'Shut your fucking mouth.'

'It's true!' She whirled round to face her mother. 'I saw him, up against the pub wall with Pam.'

Her mother was vibrating with rage. 'Shame on you! I should wash your mouth out, the lies you tell.'

No matter what her father did, it seemed that so far as her mother was concerned Maggie was the one to blame. But she was done trying to keep all their dirty secrets in her head, just so her mother could hold her head high in the presence of Father Patrick.

'It's true, I swear. And if you don't believe me, ask Rory. He saw it too.'

'Mr Sheehan to you,' her mother snapped. 'There's no truth in your lies. Pam was nothing but a tart, everyone knew it around here. Flaunting herself in front of all the men. Good riddance to bad rubbish, that's what I say.'

'How can you?' Maggie cried, noticing the cross of St Christopher round her mum's neck – the one Rory had retrieved from Doris. 'Only this morning you were at her funeral, making a show of paying your respects, and now you're talking like that about her. If anyone's to blame for what happened, it's Da.'

Thankfully, her father was slumped in a chair, swigging whisky straight from the bottle, oblivious to the fact that his trousers were round his knees and his limp penis was lying on his thigh.

'You're a disgrace, Maggie Riley.'

'Me?' Maggie took a long, hard look at her mother. There'd been a part of her that had hoped recent events might bring them closer together. Sharing a secret, sharing the pain of being a woman and sharing the fear of living under her father's roof. But her mother felt more distant than ever. 'Why is it that I never hear you calling Da a disgrace?' she asked, her voice heavy with hurt and loneliness.

'He's my husband. And I'll thank you to keep your shameful words to yourself.'

Maggie went to say something else, but changed her mind on seeing the hatred in her mother's eyes. It hurt that her mum had no feelings for her. It hurt that she stood by and made excuses for Da.

Determined not to let the two of them see her cry, Maggie grabbed her coat off the hook and rushed out of the back door.

Chapter Twenty-Six

'*Thomas?*'

Hearing Maggie's voice, Thomas stepped out of the shadows.

'Come on, let's get away from here. If my da sees us together, he'll kill us.' Maggie pulled on her coat against the October wind and set off up the road, with Thomas walking a few feet behind her.

At the top of Royal College Street where it met Camden Road, Maggie slowed to a stroll. Just getting away from that house made her feel better. She looked up at the cloudy night sky and let out a sigh of relief.

Being with Thomas calmed her down too. He made the tight anxiety in her chest go away. She felt safe in his company, something that she rarely experienced.

'I came to see you tonight because I wanted to talk about Rory,' Thomas blurted out. He looked uncomfortable, but he knew he had to go on. Like it or not, he needed to get Maggie to agree to marry Rory.

'Is this because of what I said about him earlier? Ignore that. I was just—'

'No. What you said is true. You and Rory have a special bond. You'd be better off with him than you would with me. You're wasting your time thinking otherwise.'

Maggie stared at him in disbelief. 'What? Are you saying you want me to be with Rory?' The tight anxiety in her chest was back.

'Yes . . . I mean . . .' Thomas closed his eyes. He couldn't look her in the face and lie to her. 'Yes, Maggie, I do.'

The hurt on her face when he opened his eyes made Thomas turn away completely, but she ran round, forcing him to look at her. 'Why would you say that?'

'I thought . . .'

'What did you think, Thomas? Go on, what did you think?' she demanded. Then her face crumpled. 'Don't you want us to be together?' she sobbed.

'Well, you said you didn't want anything more to do with me.'

'That was because I felt too ashamed to be with you, after what you saw Da do to me. And now you want to palm me off on the likes of Rory Sheehan?'

'It's not like that. I just think you'd be better off with him. Safer. He'd be able to protect you from your da . . .' Thomas was struggling to get the words out. He loved Maggie, but what choice did he have? 'You did say you have a special bond with him.'

Maggie wiped away her tears. 'I only said that because I was upset.' Suddenly she clasped a hand over her mouth as if she was going to be sick. 'I knew this would happen, I knew it.' She stared into his face. 'After what you saw happen between me and my da, you don't want anything more to do with me.'

Thomas fought back his own tears. He wanted to tell Maggie that nothing could be further from the truth, but how could he? 'I'm not sure what you want me to say to that, Maggie.'

'Tell me it isn't true!' She was getting hysterical.

'Look, you'll be better off with Sheehan. He can look after

115

you.' His voice broke. 'It will be better for all of us – you must see that.'

It was all too much for Maggie.

'You can go to hell, Thomas Johnson!' she screamed, then she took off running.

But she couldn't help noticing that Thomas didn't call after her.

Chapter Twenty-Seven

'*Ciao, bella* . . . Is everything all right, darling? It's late to be out.' The handsome olive-skinned man stuck his hand out of the rear window of the Jaguar as it pulled up beside her, waving a white silk handkerchief. 'Here, you look like you might need this.'

Maggie came to a halt, but made no move to take the handkerchief. Though his accent was mainly cockney, he'd called out to her in Italian.

'I saw you talking to that black boy . . . He wasn't giving you any trouble, was he?'

'No, and it's none of your business anyway.'

'Only, I know he works for Rory Sheehan – I've seen him in the club – so if you want me to tell him to leave you alone, I'll have a little word in his ear.'

'I said he wasn't giving me trouble, didn't I?' Maggie had no idea who this man was, but he had a cheek. 'And Rory wouldn't be too pleased if you start bothering his staff.'

'*Rory*, eh?' He raised his eyebrows, amused at this girl calling Sheehan by his first name. 'Well, so long as he wasn't troubling you.' He waved the handkerchief again. 'Want me to dry those tears of yours?'

'I'm not a child.'

'I didn't say you were.' He waved the handkerchief. 'It's clean.'

Though it went against her better judgement, Maggie walked up to the car and took the handkerchief. 'Thank you.'

'I see you're a fighter . . .' He looked at her questioningly, waiting for her to finish his sentence.

'Maggie.'

'Maggie.' He nodded. 'You're a little fighter.' He pointed to the cuts and bruises on her face.

'Only when I need to be.' She wiped the tears from her cheeks.

'Can I give you a lift anywhere? It's late for you to be out.'

'I'm fine, thank you.' She turned to go. 'Oh, here.' She held out the expensive handkerchief.

'No, you keep it . . . Maggie,' he said with a smile. 'I hope to see you again, *bella*.'

'Not if I see you first,' she muttered under her breath.

Book Two

Four Weeks Later

All women become like their mothers. That is their tragedy.

Oscar Wilde

Chapter Twenty-Eight

As usual, the Riley house stank of cabbage and damp. The November air was cold and dank; it was certainly not drying weather, so the washing hung from the nylon lines crisscrossing the kitchen ceiling.

Maggie bent over the kitchen sink, retching as she'd been doing most of the morning, though she'd long since vomited up her meagre breakfast. Taking a deep breath, she tried to stop herself retching again as saliva filled her mouth once more.

'Jesus, not again.' Her mother suddenly appeared in the doorway, her voice cutting through the quiet. 'It's been five mornings now. You think I don't know what that means?' Her face twisted in disgust.

Maggie said nothing.

Only the dripping tap interrupted the silence.

'Don't you dare ignore me.' Her mother stepped closer. 'Tell me, how far gone are ye?'

Still Maggie said nothing.

'I said, how far gone?' Although her mother wasn't shouting, she was quivering with anger. 'How. Far. Gone?' She prodded Maggie hard in the chest with each word.

Swallowing down the bile, Maggie whispered, 'About six weeks.'

The hard, open-palm slap caught her across the face, sending her staggering back against the sink.

'Six weeks! Sweet Jesus, Mary and Joseph! Six weeks and you're only telling me now?'

Maggie's cheek burned. Her eyes filled with tears. 'I didn't realise. Not really.'

Her mother gave her another slap, which left Maggie's cheek feeling like it was on fire.

'And the father?' Her mother's voice dropped even lower. 'Or don't you even know? Is that what you and Pam got up to? Going around like a pair of tarts, tempting men into evil ways?'

'You know that's not true.'

Above them the bedsprings sounded as her dad heaved himself up. Maggie glanced up at the ceiling. 'We both know whose it is.' There was pain in her voice, and all she wanted was for her mum, just this once, to comfort her. But her mother's face flushed red with fury.

'I don't know what you mean. You're nothing but a cheap tart!'

Maggie shook her head. 'I'm not, and you know it.'

'I don't know anything of the sort,' her mother hissed.

'I've told you before,' she said wearily, voice was almost a whisper.

'I've no idea what you're talking about.'

Maggie stared at her mother, so hurt that she couldn't answer at first. The truth sat between them, as it always had. 'Yes, you do. *YES, YOU DO!*' Finding her voice at last, Maggie shrieked at her. 'You've always known. You've heard it happening. Again and again.'

'I've heard nothing. You're full of lies.'

'You're the one who's lying. You're always saying *lying lips are an abomination to the Lord.*'

'How dare you quote the Bible at me!' Her mother crossed herself furiously. 'You're not fit to quote it. Nothing but the devil's lies come from your mouth. You've always been a liar, Maggie Riley, and to think you're my child. Well, let me tell you, you're no child of mine.'

'*Every* Friday night.' Maggie pressed on, ignoring what her mother was saying. '*Every* payday. *Every* time he took a drink. *Every* time he felt like it.'

'Shut your filthy mouth!' Her mother's hand twitched, ready to slap Maggie again. 'I'll not have such talk in this house.'

Footsteps creaked on the floorboards above as Da got out of bed. She stared at the ceiling. 'He can't know I'm pregnant.' Her words were hardly audible. '*Please.*' All the fight seemed to leave her. 'Please, don't tell him.'

Her mother's face hardened. 'And why would I keep your secret?'

The stairs creaked. Maggie was shaking so hard that she had to wrap her arms around herself to stop the trembling. Her father appeared in the doorway, unshaven, his vest stained with drink and food and the stench of last night's whisky coming off him in waves.

'What's all this fucking racket?' He swayed on his feet, his voice gruff from smoking. 'Can't a man get any sleep in his own home without being woken by screeching women.' He glared at Maggie, who looked away. 'Well?'

'Your daughter,' Kathleen said. 'She has something to tell you.'

'No, *please.*' Maggie's heart hammered. 'Please, Mum, *don't.*'

'Don't what?' Her father's voice was hard as he looked from

his daughter to his wife. He slammed his fist against the wall. *'DON'T WHAT?'*

'Nothing but trouble, this one,' her mother answered. 'She's in the family way.'

Maggie's knees buckled.

She dropped to the floor and wailed.

Her father's features darkened. 'Is that right? Maggie? Been whoring about, have you?'

Maggie stared at the cracked lino, willing it would swallow her whole.

'Answer your da,' her mother prodded, voice tight.

Looking into her father's bloodshot eyes, Maggie told him, 'No. You know I haven't.' Her voice almost a whisper, she repeated what she'd said to her mother. 'You know exactly whose it is . . .'

The accusatory words hung in the air between them.

'What did you say?' He stepped closer and clutched a handful of her hair. She squealed, grabbing his hands to try to prise them off.

One hand let go of her hair, and he balled his fist, driving it into Maggie's face. 'Lying little whore.' He grabbed her by the throat, pulling her up by it. His grip tightened until she struggled for air. 'The filth coming out of her mouth!'

Beside him, her mother made no attempt to intervene.

As black spots floated in her vision, Maggie clawed at his fingers. Just as she was about to pass out, he let her go and she dropped to the floor, coughing and choking. Before she could recover, he brought his fist back and struck her in the stomach. Pain exploded through her.

'That's for lying to your own da,' he snarled.

Maggie doubled over, arms wrapped round her middle.

'Get out,' he said, turning to her mother.

She nodded and backed out of the kitchen door. Raging, he glared down at Maggie.

'You're a tease. I see it now.'

As she looked up at him, she saw the bulge of his erection. She tried to get to her feet and run, but he caught her arm easily, pulling her through to the tiny lounge at the front of the house with its faded curtains and worn sofa, and the large cross hanging on the wall above the hearth.

'Please, Da,' she pleaded. 'Don't hurt me.'

'You're telling me what to do again, are you? I must say, Maggie, you're big for your boots these days.' He stood straddling her.

'Da, get off, *get off*!' She squirmed, desperately trying to break free, to grab hold of the large vase that stood on top of the sideboard – the nearest thing to a weapon within reach – but he was too strong for her.

As he got down, pinning her beneath him, she stretched out her leg and kicked at the sideboard. The vase wobbled, then fell to the floor next to her. Both his hands were occupied undoing his belt, so she was able to grab the vase and bring it down on his head with full force.

The crack to his skull seemed to echo around the tiny house, and as her dad rolled off her blood flowed from a gash on the back of his head.

'You fucking bitch.' He got up and lunged at her, his fist connecting with her jaw. She fell against the hearth, squealing at the pain as her spine hit the sharp corner.

'I'll kill you, and that bastard child inside you.'

She screamed as he drew back his fist to strike her again, but this time it was Maggie who lunged forward, biting down on his arm. He bellowed, clasping the wound with his other hand, giving Maggie the opportunity to grab the poker standing next to the fireplace.

She pointed it at him. 'Stay away from me, you hear me?' she panted, licking the blood and snot from her lips. 'Stay away.'

'Get out of my house,' he growled. 'Get out, and don't come back.'

Her mother came through then.

'Mum!' She was desperate for her mother to help her, but Kathleen grabbed her by the arm, dragging her into the hallway.

'You can't throw me out . . . I've got nowhere to go. What am I supposed to do?'

'You should've thought of that before you brought shame to this house.' Her mother continued hauling her towards the front door. 'Your da has worked hard to keep a roof over your head all these years, he's put food on the table, and this is how you repay him?'

'I didn't do anything . . . I didn't. You know I'm telling the truth,' Maggie sobbed.

Just for an instant, Maggie thought she saw guilt in her mother's eyes, but then it was gone, replaced by the familiar hardness.

'Get your coat and get out.'

'What about my things?'

'You'll get nothing from this house,' her mother snapped, yanking Maggie's coat from the hook.

Her father appeared behind them, whisky bottle in hand. 'You're not gone yet?'

Grabbing her, he shoved her out of the open door into the cold November air then slammed the door behind her. Maggie banged on it. '*Please*. I've got nowhere to go!'

Then she heard the lock turn with a final click.

No Regret

With no idea where she was going, Maggie stumbled along Royal College Street. Swiping away her tears, she told herself that wherever she ended up it couldn't be worse than the place she was leaving behind.

She turned the corner, vowing never to return.

Chapter Twenty-Nine

As she trudged along the street, Maggie looked at the familiar houses, picturing the neighbours who lived behind each front door, trying to think of someone who would take her in. Her first thought was Thomas, but she hadn't seen him since that night he'd told her she'd be better off with Rory. She hadn't seen Rory either, partly because she hadn't wanted to, but mainly because she hadn't been feeling well. Doing her morning chores, working a long shift at the laundrette, then going home to help her mum cook supper and clean up afterwards left her too exhausted to do anything but fall into bed.

And now she understood why she'd felt so out of sorts. The thought that she was carrying her father's child made her want to vomit, but at the same time she felt guilty – after all, it wasn't the baby's fault.

Ahead of her, an imposing building loomed against the greyness of the London skies. As if by instinct, she'd made her way to the church.

She hesitated, gazing up the huge, double oak doors, then pushed them open.

Inside it was calm and quiet. The smell of incense and beeswax candles mingled with the musty scent of old hymn books. She moved into the aisle and dipped, crossing herself as she faced the altar.

She walked up the long aisle, her feet echoing on the stone slabs. Out of habit, she headed for the confessional, which stood in a shadowy corner. Once inside, the smell of polished wood was even stronger. Maggie closed the purple velvet curtain behind her. Normally she would kneel for confession, but her knees still hurt from where her father had dragged her across the floor, so she sat. It was then she noticed the faint scent of tobacco and whisky that always followed Father Patrick around.

The partition of the confessional opened, making her jump.

'Bless me, Father, for I have . . .' She swallowed, the words catching in her throat. She tried again and, as ever, she pushed the images of her father to that place in her head where she didn't have to think about them. 'For I have sinned.'

'Maggie Riley, is that you?' Father Patrick's sharp tone filled the box. She glanced towards the lattice screen; his shock of grey hair and his pointed nose were unmistakable.

Her heart sank.

'Yes, Father.' Her voice was quiet.

'Speak up, Maggie.'

She touched her dry lips nervously. 'I've done something, Father . . . well, I mean, something has happened to me, or . . .' She trailed off. She wasn't sure quite how she was supposed to explain it, because she hadn't wanted any of this to happen.

She tried again. 'Things have happened to me – you know, bad things, things that I didn't want to happen, Father.'

There was silence.

The bells of the church clock rang out, but there was still

silence between Maggie and Father Patrick. She sat nervously fiddling with the frayed hem of her coat sleeve.

'Maggie.' Father Patrick finally spoke, his voice hard. 'I hope you haven't been letting boys touch you in intimate places?'

She tensed.

'Well, have you, Maggie? Have you been letting them touch you where they shouldn't? Tempting them with carnal sins?'

Maggie ran out of the confessional, down the aisle, heaved open the heavy wooden doors, out into the daylight with the watery sun trying to break through the clouds. She ran as fast as she could, pausing only when her shoes, which were too big for her and full of holes, flopped about on her feet.

She ran and ran, her lungs burning, passing shops and cars, passing onlookers who gawped at her.

Then she burst through the door of the Cow and Bull.

'Maggie, for the love of Christ!' Rory Sheehan stared at her bloody and battered face. He glanced at Malcolm. 'Sort out the men and I'll speak to you later.' He reached out his hand and ushered her through to the back.

He looked at her face again, touching her bruises and cuts gently. His voice broke. 'You want me to kill him, Maggie?' he whispered, moving her hair from her neck. 'Because I will. Just say the word and I'll kill your father for you. It would be my pleasure.'

Maggie didn't say anything.

His gaze wandered over her. 'You need to get cleaned up. Come on.'

He held her hand again, leading Maggie up the stairs, along the corridor and to the last door at the end. He opened the door, pushing it wide open.

The bathroom was unlike anything she had ever seen. White

and peach wall and floor tiles gleamed under the lights. It was a far cry from the cracked lino and mould-spotted wallpaper of her own home.

A large porcelain bath with gold taps stood on gold claw feet in the centre of the room. Maggie was sure it was at least twice the size of the tin tub they had in their bathroom.

'You'll feel better after a good soak, Maggie, and then we can talk about what happens next.' Rory spoke quietly, holding her gaze for a moment, then he turned on the taps. Water thundered into the bath, steam rising. He reached over to the shelf and poured a clear liquid under the running water. The smell of lavender filled the room and bubbles began to form, piling high in the bath.

Maggie stood awkwardly by the door, transfixed by the array of jars and bottles on a glass shelf. Pond's cold cream, Brylcreem, rose water, aftershave, and other things that Maggie couldn't even name. A stack of white towels sat neatly on another shelf. Everything was spotless.

'Come in, love.' Rory gestured with his head as he sat on the side of the bath.

She looked down at herself. Rory's spotless bathroom only highlighted how filthy and torn her clothes were.

He stood up and walked over to her. 'Maggie.' He pulled her gently into the bathroom, tapping the door closed with his foot, then he helped her take her coat off.

'Please,' she said. 'I can do this.'

'Nonsense. You need someone to look after you.' Once he'd removed her coat, he started to undo the buttons on her dress.

Her hands went up onto his. 'Really, I can do it.'

Rory smiled. 'Maggie, has anyone ever told you how stubborn you can be? Look at you, you've fair been through the

131

wars.' He continued to undo her buttons. 'And you're my guest, so it's only right for me to take care of you. Come on, let's get you out of those clothes.'

'I can undress myself.'

He roared with laughter as the bathroom filled with steam, and before she could object again, his hands carefully and slowly unfastened each button.

Maggie stood frozen, her arms limp, all the fight gone from her.

Her torn dress fell to the floor, and Rory looked at her and smiled. Gently he unclipped her bra while she chewed on the inside of her cheek trying not to flinch, then he unhooked her stockings, pulling them down and helping her step out of them. Finally he pulled down her tatty grey knickers.

Maggie closed her eyes and balled her hands into fists.

When she opened her eyes, Rory was smiling at her as she stood completely naked, his gaze moving over her body, lingering on the purple and black bruises. He reached out and touched them, and Maggie could see the heat in his eyes and hear the shallowness of his breathing.

'Come on.' He finally spoke, guiding her towards the bath. 'Let's get you cleaned up.'

Obediently, she stepped in, wincing slightly at the heat of the water. It felt good though, and she lowered herself into the bath of bubbles as Rory knelt beside the tub, rolling up his shirtsleeves.

'Lean back, and I'll wash your hair.'

Rory's hands were gentle as he worked the sweet-smelling shampoo into a lather, and she closed her eyes again, trying to ignore the sound of his breathing growing heavier.

'You have beautiful hair, Maggie. Has anyone told you that?'

'No,' she answered truthfully.

'Well, they should've done.'

His hand moved to her shoulder. She tensed.

'We need to wash you properly. You'll feel much better once we've got you cleaned up.'

He reached for the sponge on the side, dipping it into the water before pressing it against her spine, moving it in circles, slow and deliberate. She pulled her knees to her chest and stared straight ahead.

'I'll go and see him tonight. I'll be the last thing he ever sees.'

'No.' Maggie spun round to look at Rory, the bath water splashing onto the tiles. 'No, don't. Please.'

'He can't get away with hurting you like this, Maggie. I told you before: I won't let anyone hurt you.'

But she didn't want Rory to find out why her dad had thrown her out of the house. She didn't want anyone to know.

'I'm sorry, I shouldn't have come here.' She rose out of the water, but, realising her breasts were on display, she dipped under again.

'I'm pleased you're here, Maggie.' He stood then. 'And I want you to stay. I'll leave you to finish off, the towels are over there.' He walked over to the door, but paused before leaving. 'Maggie, if you stay here with me, I promise you that you'll want for nothing. I'll treat you like a princess.'

She didn't answer him.

'Come on, Maggie.' He frowned. 'Didn't Thomas tell you how well I could look after you?'

She wasn't sure why, but it felt important that she should confirm this. '*Yes*, yes, he did . . . but I haven't seen him for a while – I haven't been very well.'

He stared, and as usual she had no idea what he was thinking.

'Well, in that case you know how much you mean to me. So, what will it be, Maggie? Will you stay?'

She smiled at him. 'Why don't I finish my bath, and then I can come and talk to you.'

Rory smiled again. 'I'd like that.' He glanced at her filthy dress lying on the floor. 'I've got some clothes that might fit you.'

She gave him a quizzical look.

He nodded. 'I couldn't help it; I bought some gifts for you. I hope you'll like them . . . Right, I'll be back in half an hour. How's that?'

She smiled. 'That would be nice.'

He turned and walked out.

An uneasy feeling came over her, and as quickly as she could, she got out of the bath, grabbing her dirty clothes off the floor. She crept to the bathroom door, listening to see if Rory was still there.

When she couldn't hear anything, she rushed to get dressed, not bothering to towel herself dry. Then she opened the door, tiptoed down the stairs and through the back entrance, running out into the cold November day.

Chapter Thirty

By the time she reached Soho, Maggie's feet were killing her. She paused to huddle in one of the doorways in Old Compton Street, watching the November darkness beginning to fall.

It was too cold to stay still for long, so she decided to keep on walking despite the pain.

'*Looking for business, love?*'

Maggie glanced to the side of her and saw a small woman with dyed blonde hair and a thick layer of make-up calling over to a man in a bowler hat.

She passed shops, and doorways with signs advertising *private members club* and *models upstairs*. Neon lights started to flicker on in the windows of coffee bars and restaurants. Still she carried on weaving her way through the crowds while the cold seeped into her very bones.

Reading the street sign, Maggie turned right and walked along the narrow passageway of Bridle Lane. She came to a stop and looked down at the basement stairs of the tall Georgian building that had been converted into a club.

Taking a deep breath, she descended the steps, the stench of stale alcohol filling the air.

Pulling open the black doors, Maggie stepped into the club.

Martina Cole

It was warm, there was music playing and the lights gave off a red glow. The place was virtually empty.

'Can I help you, darlin?' A tall man, average build, with a splodge of red hair, nodded at Maggie, his eyes trailing up and down her body.

Conscious of the way she must look, she brushed at her hair with her hand, trying to straighten the tangle. 'I'm looking for Thomas Johnson.'

At that moment, Thomas wandered out of the back storage room. 'Maggie, what are you doing here?'

'I didn't know where else to go.' She felt embarrassed. She hadn't thought what she'd say when she got here, but she didn't know what else to do.

'Davey, can you give us a minute?' Thomas turned to the barman.

'Yeah, of course, I'll be out back.' He nodded at Maggie and sauntered out of the same door Thomas had just come through.

With Davey gone, Maggie walked down the rest of the stairs. 'He seems nice.' She tried to sound calm.

'He is. He's a good friend.'

Maggie smiled. 'I'm glad.'

There was tension between them. They hadn't seen each other for a month, and Maggie found it hard to look at Thomas.

'Did your dad do that?'

She touched her face. 'Yes.'

'I'm sorry.'

She gave a small nod.

'It's good to see you,' Thomas said quietly. 'I thought I might've bumped into you before now.'

Maggie glanced up at him. For all that Rory Sheehan was, for

136

all his power and influence, it was Thomas she wanted to be with. 'I've been busy.'

Thomas looked at his watch, obviously feeling as awkward as she did. 'I better go in a minute. I'm meant to be working.'

'Wait, Thomas. I've . . . I've been thinking.' She used her sleeve to wipe her eyes. 'Remember you said that working for Rory meant you'd be able to save up enough money for us to leave all this behind?'

Thomas frowned. 'Maggie, look—'

'No, please, *listen* . . . I want that to happen, Thomas.'

'Maggie—'

'No, let me finish. If you don't have enough money now, we could run away together.' Her eyes met his.

'*Thomas.*'

A woman's voice came from the side of them and Maggie turned to see a young, voluptuous woman with a backcombed beehive, dressed in a gold miniskirt and black lace silk top. She wore bright red lipstick, and her thick false eyelashes framed dazzling blue eyes.

The woman stared at Maggie as she walked up to Thomas, draping her arms round his neck. Like Davey had done, she looked Maggie up and done, then nuzzled her lips into Thomas's neck.

'Tell me this isn't the girl you were mooning over, is it?' The woman roared with laughter.

'Can you stop, Chrissy.'

'I'm only playing with you, but if it is . . .' She burst into laughter again and kissed Thomas. 'She does know we're together now, doesn't she?'

Thomas pushed her off gently as Maggie began to back away. 'It was a mistake to come here, but I can't go home and I wasn't sure where else to go . . . I'm sorry.'

Chrissy giggled and Thomas gave her a hard stare.

He delved into his pocket and pulled out a clean tissue. 'Here.' He wiped her face gently, avoiding putting any pressure on her swollen eye. 'It's me who's sorry.'

Maggie nodded.

He took her hands and she clutched them tightly.

'Maggie.' He sounded breathless as he whispered her name. 'Believe me, the best thing that you can do is go to Rory. He will look after you.'

And with those words, she snatched her hands away and ran out of the club into the darkness of Soho.

Chapter Thirty-One

Maggie was relieved to finally get to the door of the small, terraced house. She was fit to collapse, it was all she could do to reach up and bang the knocker. Her body ached from the beating her father had given her and the blisters on her feet were so painful she couldn't have walked another step.

And she was cold to the very bones. The rain had turned to sleet and her clothes were soaked through. If she couldn't find shelter here, she didn't think she would last the night.

Leaning on the door for support, when it began to open she almost fell inside. But when the woman saw who it was, she began shoving against the door, trying to close it again.

'Oh no you don't! You and your mum have caused me enough trouble already. You're not coming in here.'

But Maggie jammed her foot in the door, pleading, 'Please, Doris, I need your help.'

'You have got to be kidding! After what happened last time I helped—'

'Please, I've got no one else to turn to.' She reached down and tugged at the hem of her coat, pulling at the place where she'd stitched it up to hide the gold bracelet Rory had given her. 'Here' – she held the bracelet up, offering it to Doris – 'I'm sure it's worth something.'

139

Doris sniffed. 'Even if I wanted to help you, I can't.' She held up her hands. 'Your mate, Mr Sheehan, burned them. Without me hands, I'm useless. He made sure I wouldn't be able to help anyone again.' There was real bitterness in her voice, and Maggie felt terrible, but she was desperate.

'Then is there anyone else who can help me? There must be someone. I swear I can pay.'

'Keep your voice down, will you!' Doris hissed, sticking her head out of the door and looking up and down. 'Come on, then, you'd better come in.'

As she had on her previous visit, Maggie followed Doris into the small hallway and through to the kitchen. To her surprise, the rusty old bed with its stained mattress had gone.

'If you want a drink, you can get it yourself.' Doris nodded towards the bottle of gin on the table. 'And pour me one while you're at it.'

Maggie picked up two chipped mugs from the draining board and poured gin into them, passing one over to Doris.

The woman took a slurp of gin and sniffed. 'How's your mum doing?'

'She survived,' Maggie replied through chattering teeth. The gin burned as it went down but she would have given anything to wrap her hands around a hot cup of tea. She stood as near as she could to the fire, but it was almost dead. Doris must have been getting ready for bed when she arrived.

'I take it she doesn't know you're here.'

Maggie shrugged. 'I don't think she'd care.' She glanced over her shoulder at Doris. 'I'm sorry about your hands.'

'Oh, I've had worse.' Doris took another gulp of gin. 'And maybe it was about time I had a bit of a break from staring up people's fannies. If you'd seen as many as I have, it'd give you nightmares.' She gave Maggie a smile. 'You look fucking freezing, love. Get out of them clothes and dry them in front of the fire. There's a dressing gown on the back of the door. And chuck a few more coals on the fire while you're at it.'

'Thank you.' Maggie placed the mug down on the table then began peeling off her wet clothes.

'Jesus Christ, girl! Who's been battering you around?'

Maggie didn't trust herself to speak. She finished undressing, put on the blue nylon dressing gown and draped her wet things over the clothes horse. Then she took some coals from the scuttle and added them to the fire, before sitting down in the chair opposite Doris.

For a few minutes they watched the flames in silence.

'How far gone are you, then?'

'Six weeks.'

'So what are you going to do?'

Maggie shrugged. She didn't want to think about it. She'd been a fool to hope that Thomas would drop everything and run away with her. Why would he? He knew what she was, and she didn't blame him that he wanted nothing more to do with her. Who would, when she was pregnant with her dad's baby?

'I don't know.' Even though she was beginning to warm up now she was in dry clothes and sitting by a fire, Maggie couldn't stop shaking. 'I can't go back home.'

Doris nodded and finished the last of her gin, then gestured for Maggie to bring the bottle over, which she did, filling Doris's cup to the brim.

'That fella, Sheehan, he's a bastard, and he'd bury anyone that crosses him, but he's sweet on you. He didn't drive over here for your mother's sake – it was you he cared about.'

Maggie continued to stare into the fire. She was exhausted

and the gin was making her sleepy, taking the edge off the events of the day. 'He said he'd look after me.'

'Sheehan?' Doris became animated. 'That's a turn-up for the books . . . He must be smitten.' She rubbed her swollen ankles, the varicose veins bulging in them. 'So there's your answer.'

'What do you mean?'

'Marry him, love.'

'But he's too old for me.' She remembered what Thomas had said: 'Too mature. And I don't love him.'

Doris burst out laughing. 'Love! What's that got to do with it? Women don't love their husbands; they put up with them. They wash their clothes, feed their bellies, bear their children, suffer their beatings and they long for the day they'll be able to bury them, but they certainly don't love them.'

'I can't.'

'Well, I'd say he's your best hope.' Doris wiped the spit away from the corner of her mouth. 'I wouldn't throw it away if I were you. You'll have money with Sheehan. You can have whatever you want with him. Better to be rich and miserable than poor and miserable.'

'But what will he do when he finds out I'm pregnant?'

'You say you're six weeks gone? That's not a problem. Go back to Sheehan, fuck him, and then palm the kid off as his.'

Maggie wrapped her arms round herself, staring into the fire.

'You can stay here tonight, but tomorrow you need to go to Sheehan, get him into bed and fuck him – once, twice, however many times you fancy . . .' She gave a chortle that turned into a bout of coughing. 'He'll be none the wiser that the kid you're carrying isn't his, and then you can get on with the rest of your life.'

'I don't know. It doesn't feel right.'

'What's right doesn't come into it, sweetheart. And it's not as if you've got any alternative, is it? Being out on the streets in the middle of November with a baby on the way, is that what you want?' Doris leaned forward and grabbed Maggie's hands. 'Well, is it?'

Maggie shook her head, tears rolling down her cheeks.

'Play them at their own game, girl. You need to fuck them over in more ways than one.'

Chapter Thirty-Two

After spending the night at Doris's house, Maggie felt better than she had in a long time. Her body still ached, and her face hurt, but she'd slept soundly, no longer having to worry that her dad was going to walk in at any moment, or her mother was going to wake her at the crack of dawn to scrub up her father's vomit from the floor after one of his late-night binges. So, despite everything, she felt almost refreshed when she got up that morning.

Doris had even given her money for her tube fare, to spare her blistered feet having to walk all that way.

As she came out of Camden Town station the market traders were standing by their barrows, yelling their wares. Business as usual.

One of them recognised her and called out, 'How's things, Maggie?'

'Fine, thanks.' With her face swollen and bruised, hair matted, and clothes even more ragged and dirty than usual, she doubted that he'd believe her, but he waved cheerfully as she went by.

When the Cow and Bull came into view, Maggie took a deep breath to steady her nerves.

This was it.

She opened the door to the public bar and walked in.

It was quiet. Empty but for one old man and his dog, both

fast asleep. She glanced up at the clock: 2.30 p.m.. It was later than she'd thought, but Doris had let her have a long lie-in and then insisted on giving her something to eat – fried kippers on toast – before she left.

She smiled at the barmaid, a tall, skinny, dark-haired woman, who looked like she could do with a meal.

'Is Ror— I mean, is Mr Sheehan around?'

Finishing off drying the pint glass, the woman looked her up and down. 'Who's asking?'

'Tell him it's Maggie.'

The barmaid gave a sullen nod and toddled off, swaying on her four-inch stilettos.

A moment later, Rory appeared.

'Fecking hell, girl, what's with you disappearing like that? Where did you go?'

She thought of Doris and what she'd said, what she needed to do. 'I went home to see if I could get my things – my clothes. I was embarrassed for you to see me looking like this.' She glanced down at what she was wearing. 'But they wouldn't let me in, so I slept in the park.'

'You must have been freezing!' Under the watchful eye of the barmaid, Sheehan stepped towards her, taking her gently by the shoulders. 'I told you, I've got some clothes for you to change into.' He leaned forward and kissed her on her cheek. 'I'm glad you're back . . . Will you stay this time?'

Maggie's stomach tightened and she clenched her fists into balls, telling herself that this was the only option she had. She knew that his reputation was well deserved – she'd seen what he'd done to Doris, and she remembered the night Thomas had told her about the men they'd killed – but Rory had always been kind to her . . .

'Yeah, if you'll have me.'

Rory grinned. 'Did you hear that?' he yelled, startling the old man and his dog from their slumbers. Then he picked Maggie up and swung her around, roaring with laughter. 'You won't regret this.'

She let out a yelp at the sharp pain in her ribs.

Rory immediately set her down. 'Sorry, did I hurt you?'

Maggie winced. 'It's fine.'

'No, it's not. I'll not have anything or anyone hurt you, not even me.' He stared at her so intently that she had to look away.

'You'll be taking orders from her now, Nelly.' He nodded to the barmaid, who looked like she was having some difficulty smiling at Maggie. 'Any shit, she'll be putting you in your place.'

Maggie wondered if he was joking, but there was no hint of laughter. If anything, there was a darkness to his expression.

'Come with me.' He grabbed her by the hand, leading her through to the back and up the stairs to a different room to the one she'd gone in yesterday.

'As you can't go home, this will be your room.'

He opened the door.

Like the bathroom, it was beautifully decorated. Cream wallpaper and fresh yellow curtains, with matching yellow sheets and white blankets on the polished brass double bed. There was a large mirror and a chest of drawers, as well as four wardrobes.

Rory turned to her. 'What do you think? If you don't like it, I can change it . . .'

She gave a shake her head. 'No . . . no, it's beautiful.'

'Good. I want to make sure you have everything you need.' He walked over to the first wardrobe, opening one door then

146

another until all four wardrobes were open. Inside them were dresses – ten, twenty, thirty, more. All brand new.

She stared at him. 'Why have you got all these?'

'I got them for you.'

Maggie's mouth dropped open. For some reason, a chill rolled down her spine.

'Why don't you try one on?'

She walked over to where Rory was standing, reached out and touched one of the dresses, then the next. Even if they'd been second-hand cast-offs, she could never have afforded anything this good. There were red ones, yellow ones, blue ones – every colour of the rainbow.

'But I don't understand.' She tried to keep the panic out of her voice.

Rory shook his head. 'All these questions, Maggie. You'll have to learn that too many questions is never a good thing.' He placed his fingers on her lips. 'But if you must know, I've been waiting for you.' He dropped his fingers from her mouth.

'Waiting?'

He nodded. 'Since the first day we met – in church, remember? I've been hoping that one day you'd be mine, and now that day's here.'

Maggie had first met Rory when she was nine. She gave him a tight smile.

He grabbed a navy dress with a white lace collar.

'Try it on.'

'This one?'

'Is there a problem?'

Maggie hesitated but had the sense not to say what was on her mind. She knew now that she'd made a huge mistake coming here, but Doris's words kept running through her mind: *Go back to Sheehan, fuck him and then palm the kid off as his . . . then you can get on with the rest of your life.* How bad could it be?

Forcing a smile, she told him, 'No, it's lovely.'

'Take your clothes off, then. There's no room to be shy, not now.' He began opening drawers full of underwear. He took out a pair of stockings, knickers and a bra made of cream silk, then handed them to Maggie. 'Here you go.'

She'd lived in fear of her father ever since she could remember, but this was a different sort of fear. There was something about the way Rory looked at her, the way he'd had this room set up ready for her, that made her feel like running. But it was too late for that.

Rory sat down on the large bed, leaning back on the pillows. 'Go on, then, take your clothes off.'

Again Doris's words ran through her mind: *you need to go to Sheehan, get him into bed and fuck him – once, twice, however many times you fancy.*

She needed to stop worrying about how she felt, and get on with what she needed to do.

As Rory looked on, she took off her clothes. Once she was naked, she walked across to the bed. Trying not to show the shame and embarrassment she was feeling, she leaned forward to kiss him on his lips.

His hands flew up and he grabbed her by the wrist. 'What the fuck are you doing?'

'I . . . I . . .' She looked at him in confusion. It was obvious from the bulge in his trousers that he was hard, so why was he looking at her with such disgust? 'I thought . . . I thought this was what you wanted.'

'We're not married, Maggie . . . Don't tell me this is what you get up to with fellas?'

She saw his jaw clenching and a flash of anger crossed his face. 'No . . . no . . . never,' she lied.

He narrowed his eyes, his gaze wandering all over her body. 'You see, I wouldn't like to think that you weren't a virgin, Maggie. I wouldn't want to think that you were a fucking scrubber like your friend Pam.'

'I'm not! I swear . . . I swear I've never—'

He stood, towering over her. 'You better not have done, Maggie.'

'It's just . . . when you said you wanted me to stay here with you, I thought that meant . . . you wanted us to get married.'

He smiled, but it didn't reach his eyes. 'All in good time . . . Maybe we could have you as a spring bride.'

Panic gripped her. Next year would be too late. Somehow, she had to get Rory to marry her now, or at least find a way to tempt him to sleep with her.

If she couldn't, she was scared what he might do when he found out she was pregnant . . .

Chapter Thirty-Three

Luca popped a tablet into his mouth and rolled it around under his tongue, mulling over the problem that was foremost in his mind these days.

Ever since his father had put him through the humiliation of having to stand in front of Rory Sheehan while the head of the Romano family grovelled and gave away the family business, he'd been trying to come up with a way to get rid of the old man.

Vincent Romano was past it. His poor decisions were making the family look weak. Soon it wouldn't just be Rory Sheehan trying to muscle in on their business. Every other fucker in London would see how vulnerable they were and start coming in for the kill.

He had thought about trying to reason with his father, asking him to step aside. But the old man was stubborn. He could never admit that the great Vince Romano was capable of making the wrong choices. So the only thing Luca could do was get rid of his father once and for all.

Unfortunately, while his men were loyal to him, Luca knew that they were even more loyal to his father. Tradition ran deep in Italian families, so the idea that he might be plotting the demise of his own father would be difficult if not impossible for most of them to accept.

But as the morphine took hold, a new possibility occurred to him. Maybe there was someone else he could trust. Someone who craved the finer things in life. Someone who loved money, who worshipped power. That person could be his ally in getting his father out of the way so he could take over.

It looked as though Sofia might be of some use after all.

'Boss?'

Luca snapped out of his reverie. 'Yeah?'

'We've just come back from Panton Street. Takings are down. And there was a raid on Suffolk Street last night. We didn't get a tip-off, so a couple of the boys got picked up by the flying squad.'

'Get hold of Miller – ask him what the fuck he's playing at.'

Like so many coppers in the area, Constable Miller was on the take. They paid him handsomely to turn a blind eye when necessary, and to warn them when one of their businesses was going to be raided.

Nico, his hair glistening with Brylcreem, sat down across the table from Luca. He waited until the waitress had set down his coffee and returned to the counter before speaking. 'Word has it that Miller's working for Sheehan now.'

Luca grabbed the glass ashtray and threw it against the wall. It shattered, sending glass everywhere. The only other customers – a couple of women who'd been sitting in the corner – gathered up their shopping bags and hurried out of the cafe. The waitress, having seen it all before, remained behind the counter, careful not to look in Luca's direction.

'In that case, we'd better pay Miller a visit, remind him that we expect loyalty.'

'But your father said—'

'I don't care what my father says, you understand me? *I* say what happens. Not him.'

The uncertain look on Nico's face fuelled his rage.

'You need to decide whose side you're on, Nico.' Luca leapt to his feet, sending his chair crashing to the floor. He reached into his pocket and pulled out a small handgun, smiling coldly as he pressed it to Nico's temple. 'If you don't want me to pull this trigger, then you better start showing me some fucking loyalty.'

The morphine was in control now, and Luca felt nothing as he threatened his childhood friend. 'This is what we're going to do. First, we're gonna drive over to Rupert Street and take back what's ours.'

'But we can't—'

The blow to Nico's head was hard and loud. As the butt of the pistol split his skin, blood spurted across the plastic-covered table. 'Didn't I just tell you?'

Nico licked the blood away, eyes lowered. 'Yes, boss.'

Half an hour later, Luca Romano stood watching as Nico and the rest of his men made their way along Rupert Street battering one business owner after another. He watched with casual disregard as Nico entered a wine bar and grabbed a short woman by her wispy brown ponytail, then smashed her face against the corner of the bar. He stood unmoved as the woman screamed.

This was a message everyone would understand. Luca Romano was the boss now. Not his father, not Rory Sheehan, but him. And if they didn't heed that message, they would reap the consequences.

He strode towards his car, signalling for his men to follow. It was time to pay Constable Miller a visit.

Chapter Thirty-Four

Not too far from where Luca was planning his next move, Maggie was standing next to Rory on the stage of his Soho night club, cringing with embarrassment as he made a grand presentation out of introducing her to his staff.

The heat in the club wasn't helping. Her headache had worsened until she felt like her head was gripped in a vice, and she was finding it difficult to breathe in the smoky atmosphere. She wasn't sure whether it was the pregnancy that was making her feel ill or the fact that Thomas was standing with the rest of the employees listening to Rory announce their engagement.

'. . . And that's why you'll see a grin on me face from now on, because Maggie here has done me the honour of agreeing to be my wife.'

There was a small round of applause, but Maggie stood with her head bowed, feeling like she was a prize cow being paraded at the cattle market while the auctioneer delivered his spiel. This was going to be her life now. She needed to toughen up, play the role. Even if she was dying inside, she couldn't afford to show it.

'. . . So you won't just be taking orders from myself,' Rory informed the crowd, 'you'll now be taking orders from my wife, or rather my soon-to-be wife.'

Maggie gave him a sidelong glance and caught the dark glint

in his eye as he added, 'I hope no one has a problem with that?' His gaze darted around the room. 'Good. So, let's raise a glass to Maggie, shall we?' Then he raised the pint of Guinness he was holding and took a long drag from his cigarette while the staff frantically poured drinks and returned to their places to raise them in a toast.

Rory blew out a cloud of smoke and turned to face her with his cigarette hanging from the side of his mouth. 'To Maggie!'

As everyone echoed him with forced enthusiasm, her eyes found Thomas in the crowd. His eyes met hers, then immediately glanced away. Maggie reminded herself that it wouldn't do either of them any good if Rory caught them looking at each other. But the image of his drawn face and the sadness in his brown eyes seared itself into her mind.

'Are you all right? You look a bit pale.' Rory was peering at her through the smoke.

'I'm fine, it just . . . I'm not used to all this attention and it's a bit hot in here.'

'Do you want to go outside, get a bit of fresh air? I've got some business to attend to here that'll take me a few minutes.'

'If that's all right?'

Rory laughed hard then. 'What do you take me for, Maggie? Of course it's all right. You know you can do anything with me.'

Maggie doubted that, but she hurried off, grateful for some time away from him.

On the way out, she caught sight of herself in the mirror. She almost didn't recognise the person staring back at her. Instead of hanging matted and dirty down her back, her thick brown hair tumbled in glossy waves, framing her face. And though the bruises and cuts showed through her make-up, her skin looked healthy and glowing.

But the cream wool coat and blue dress with its white frilly collar did her no favours. The dress was long and frumpy, almost down to her ankles, and the flat lace-up shoes were the sort of thing Rory's mother used to wear to church. While everyone around her was wearing glitzy clothes and the latest hairstyles, she was stuck like this.

When Rory had gone through her wardrobes picking out the outfit, she'd thought about asking if she could wear something else, but didn't want to risk another outburst.

'Maggie.'

She whirled round to find Thomas looking at her. Nervously she glanced towards the bar where Rory was deep in conversation with Davey and one of his other staff. She stepped into the shadows, pulling Thomas with her. 'He won't like you talking to me, Thomas. You need to go back. If he sees us—' She broke off, not sure why she was so worried. After all, Rory knew that she was friends with Thomas, so why was she panicking?

'I hate seeing you with him . . . but you did the right thing,' Thomas whispered.

'I don't need you telling me I did the right thing,' she snapped. 'If that's all you've got to say, you might as well go back to work.'

'Don't be angry, Maggie – you know I love you.'

Completely thrown by this, she didn't know how to respond. But another glance in Rory's direction brought her to her senses. 'Unless you want Rory to bury you, you better leave me alone. I'm with him now, and . . . and I'm happy. So go back to work, Thomas . . . *Now*.'

He looked like he was going to say something else, but turned away and headed down the stairs. Maggie held on to the stair rail as a wave of nausea hit her. She covered her mouth before rushing out of the club and into Bridle Lane, throwing up the minute she reached the safety of the black railings.

'Got something to tell us?'

Maggie used the hem of her skirt to wipe her mouth before turning towards the voice. Chrissy was smoking a cigarette and watching her with a smirk on her face.

'What are you talking about?' Feeling hot and dizzy, Maggie drew herself to her full height.

Chrissy sashayed up to her, and placed her manicured hand on Maggie's belly. 'Maybe you're in the family way? And there's you going around dressed like a nun!' She laughed nastily and Maggie knocked her hand away.

'Don't touch me,' Maggie hissed. 'And I don't know what you're talking about.'

Chrissy regarded her from beneath her false eyelashes. 'Don't you?'

'No, I don't, and you better not go around saying stuff like that.'

'Why not, you'll soon be showing, and then everybody will be saying it.'

'I won't be showing, because I'm *not* pregnant.' Maggie spoke in a whisper, not wanting to risk anyone coming out of the club hearing her. 'Get back to work.' She wasn't used to giving orders, but knew it wouldn't do to let Chrissy think she'd got the better of her. 'And if I hear any more talk from you,' she continued. 'Or if I hear anyone else saying anything like that, I'll know where it's come from. And as Rory – that's Mr Sheehan to you – just told everyone, you're taking orders from me now. So if you want to keep on working here, you'll do as I say. Got it?'

Chrissy's face dropped, and Maggie turned to walk up the lane, anything to get away from her.

'Maybe I should tell him anyway,' Chrissy shouted after her. 'Maybe I'll tell him you're trying to get rid of me because I know you're up the duff.'

Maggie spun on her heel and made a grab for Chrissy, slamming her against the rails. 'You do, and I'll see to it you'll be fucking sorry.' She brought her face close to Chrissy's. 'And it won't just be losing your job you'll need to worry about.'

Releasing her grip on the other woman, she stormed off. She was upset with herself for losing her temper the same way she'd lost it with Pam that night. But Chrissy had been asking for it. Hopefully, it would have the desired effect and make her think twice about opening her stupid mouth.

Turning into Brewer Street, Maggie looked around her, not sure where to go. The way she was feeling, she needed to put some distance between her and Chrissy, not to mention Rory and Thomas.

She wrapped her new wool coat around her, slowing down at the corner to wait for a gap in traffic so she could cross the road. The sound of a horn beeping made her jump. She turned her head and saw a shiny black Jaguar parked a few feet away. Ignoring it, she walked on.

'Maggie, isn't it?'

She glanced back. The man getting out of the car looked familiar. He was tall and good-looking, but it took her a moment to remember where she'd seen him. It was in Camden, by the station. He was the one who'd given her a handkerchief when he saw her crying.

She waited for him to walk up to her. 'Yeah, that's right.' She smiled. 'Do you want your handkerchief back?'

He frowned for a moment, then grinned. 'No, you can keep it.' He winked, then looked her up and down. 'You look *different* from the last time I saw you.'

She felt herself blushing. 'You mean, I'm not crying and I haven't got torn clothes on.'

He shook his head. 'No. I didn't mean that. I meant . . .' He paused, searching for the right word. 'You look . . . well, you look . . .'

She waited patiently for him to finish his sentence.

'You look lovely.' He shrugged and reached out, touching her hair. 'Beautiful.'

The moment he touched her, she took a step back, looking around nervously. She couldn't let anyone see her with him, although there was something about the way he looked at her that made her stomach tighten. 'I . . . I . . . I have to go.'

'Are you sure? We could go for a drink. I know somewhere nice, not far from here.' His voice was deep and smooth.

'I've just told you I can't. I have to go.'

He tilted his head and stepped forward.

Maggie's heart raced and, as much as she knew this was dangerous, she couldn't quite pull herself away.

'Why do you have to go?'

'I'm expected back, and I don't want them to come looking for me.' She spoke in a whisper.

He stepped even closer, his hard muscular body brushing against hers. She looked up into his dark eyes. 'I really have to go.'

'Don't you want to know my name?'

'No. Why would I?'

He roared with laughter. 'That's fair enough, but I'll tell you anyway . . . it's Luca. Luca Romano.'

Chapter Thirty-Five

Later that night Luca stood outside Sofia's bedroom door, his hand resting on the gold handle. Taking a deep breath, he turned the handle and stepped quietly into Sofia's room. It was the first time he'd been in here since they decorated in preparation for her arrival. The last few months had been spent trying to avoid having any sort of physical contact with her. It wouldn't have gone down too well if he'd given his future bride a dose of the clap. Thankfully, all those doses of penicillin had eventually done the trick.

Just as well, because he needed Sofia as an ally if he was going to take over the family business. Giving her what she'd been wanting all this time would be the quickest way to seal the deal.

Moonlight streamed through the window, illuminating his sleeping fiancée. She was snoring loudly, reminding Luca of the pigs his grandma used to breed back in Italy.

Taking a deep breath and feeling like he'd rather be facing Rory and his men than having to fuck Sofia, Luca walked across to the bed.

He sat down on it and gently touched her shoulder. 'Sofia, Sofia, wake up.'

She groaned, rolled over and opened her eyes. Seeing Luca there, she gasped and sat up, her heavy breasts falling forward.

Luca grimaced to himself but tried not to let it show in his voice – after all, he'd fucked enough old brass in Soho to be able to fuck this one, surely?

'What are you doing here?' She pushed her hair away from her face.

Luca ran a hand over her nightdress. 'Take this off.'

'What?' She frowned.

'Take it off.'

Sofia glanced towards the door. 'But what about your parents?'

As Luca had anticipated, she wasn't putting up even a show of resistance.

'They're asleep. Don't worry about it. But we need to be quiet.'

She nodded and eagerly stripped off her white nightie. There was a hungry look in her eyes as she leaned forward to touch him, but he shook his head. 'I want our first time to be special.' He knew the right words to say, and he kissed her gently on her lips. 'Let me do something for you.'

In truth, he didn't want her pulling and tugging at him with her fat hands. If his plan was to succeed, he needed to make sure that by the time he was finished with her, Sofia would be gagging for more. Thanks to his experience of satisfying women, especially eager ones like Sofia, he was confident that after tonight she would be putty in his hand.

He pulled back the sheets, exposing her naked body, then took his time unbuttoning his shirt, undoing the buckle of his belt and taking off his trousers.

He gently pushed her back onto the bed, cringing as he lay on top of her. Then he spoke the words she wanted to hear. 'Let me make love to you, Sofia. You're so beautiful.'

He knew it sounded corny, but Sofia would think he meant

it. His only problem was going to be getting hard when she was so repulsive to him.

He kissed her breasts, circling his tongue around them, and the more she groaned, the more it turned him off. When she grabbed his hair and started pushing him down towards her hairy fat cunt, he found himself thinking about Maggie. He didn't know anything about her, where she lived or what she did or even if she was married. Not that it would make any difference to him.

'Oh, Luca, oh God, oh God . . .'

He lifted his head. 'Shhhh, Sofia, you don't want my parents to come in, do you?'

Thankful to be able to make that excuse to shut her up, he let his thoughts return to Maggie and put his head back between Sofia's flabby legs.

'I love you. Oh, that's it,' she muttered as, trying to stop himself from gagging, he continued to work on her. 'Don't stop . . . Don't stop, Luca.'

Ignoring her wishes, he pulled himself up and clambered on top of her, continuing to think about Maggie as he shoved his penis into his fiancée.

The moment he entered her, Luca decided that the likelihood of Sofia being a virgin was as slim as him being one. Still, that didn't matter now. His mission was to get Sofia to support his plan. Once his father was out of the way, he could ditch her.

Wanting to get this over and done with as soon as he could, Luca thrust away hard and fast, listening to Sofia's grunts. The moment he was about to climax, he withdrew, coming all over the sheets instead.

Sofia, covered in sweat, stared up at him. 'Why did you do that?' She sounded disappointed and he gave her a tight smile.

The last thing he wanted was to get Sofia pregnant. Women changed when they were pregnant, and especially once they had a child. Their attention went elsewhere and he didn't want Sofia focusing on anything other than him.

He kissed her stomach and sat up, wiping himself down with his shirt. 'As much as I'd like to get you pregnant, I'm not sure your family or mine would like that. It won't be too long until we get married and then we can have as many children as you like.'

Sofia lit up with delight and hugged him. 'You mean it? I wasn't sure – you've been so distant with me.'

'I've had a lot on my mind . . . I only hope I can give you the wedding you want though,' Luca said slyly.

'What do you mean?'

It was time to put phase two of his plan into action. He knew that Sofia wanted a big wedding to impress her family back home, and that she was greedy for expensive things. 'I'm not sure if my father's still willing to pay for it – of course, I'll do everything I can, but that's one of the things that's been worrying me.'

Looking puzzled, Sofia said, 'He's always said that he wanted to give his only son the best wedding any Italian has ever seen.'

Luca nodded. 'But things change, and . . .' He gave a dramatic pause. 'It doesn't matter. I shouldn't be saying this.'

'Saying what?'

The other thing about Sofia was that she liked to know what was going on. This was going to be easy; it was like bringing a moth to a flame. And he wasn't the one who was going to get burned.

'I'm sure you don't want to hear business talk . . . and, in any case, I shouldn't be telling you. I don't want to upset you.'

She grabbed his hand. 'Luca, we're going to be man and wife. There shouldn't be secrets between us.'

He nodded as if overcoming his reluctance, while inwardly congratulating himself on the way he was reeling her in. 'All right . . . My father's cutting back on the family business. He doesn't want to run things any more – or not as many things, anyway.' He smiled sadly. 'I suppose that's understandable, given his age, but it means that our plans for the big house we were going to buy, the cars, the jewellery I wanted to buy you, the diamonds I saw in Hatton Garden – none of that will be possible.' He stood up and grabbed his trousers from the floor, heading for the door. 'It's a shame, because I'd always dreamed of passing everything down to my children.' He shrugged. '*Ma così è la vita*. What can you do?'

He reached for the door handle.

'*Wait*, Luca . . . Why can't *you* run the business if he doesn't want to any more?'

'Pride sometimes stands in the way of sense. There's nothing I can do.'

'I'm sure there's a way,' she said softly.

'You think so?' He walked back to her, sat down on the bed and took her hands in his. 'I wish I knew what.' He stroked her face, leaning down to give her a soft kiss on her mouth. 'I'm lucky to have you.'

'I'll help you.'

'There's nothing to help with. My father's stubborn and when he's made his mind up about something, no one can convince him otherwise. And, as their only child, it pains me that I have to sit back and watch the legacy I wanted to pass on to our children disappear because of him . . . But thank you.' He laughed ruefully, playing the part well. 'It's not as if I can force him out, is it?'

163

There was silence between them.

'Why not?' she asked.

'Why not, what?'

She hesitated. 'I don't want to speak out of turn.' She lowered her head, but Luca raised it with his fingers.

'Say it. It's fine, Sofia. I won't be angry.'

'Well, why not force him out?' She looked at him, wide-eyed. 'I'm sorry, I shouldn't have said that. He's your father and—'

Luca hid his smile. 'It's fine. But I couldn't do it on my own.'

Sofia lowered her voice. 'No, of course not. I'd help you.'

'You?'

She nodded. 'Yes. We could do this together, and then . . .'

'Go on.'

'Then we can pass the legacy of the Romano name on to our children.'

And, with those words, Luca knew that in a very short time his father would cease to be a problem.

Chapter Thirty-Six

In her bedroom above the Cow and Bull, Maggie was also planning her next move. It was the most comfortable room she'd ever been in: warm, dry, clean and it smelled of lavender. But it wasn't helping her get to sleep. Her mind was too busy mulling over the Rory problem.

He'd been adamant that he wasn't going to sleep with her until they were married. He'd looked at her as if she was dirt when she'd suggested that, now they were engaged, they were as good as married. She was afraid to push him and risk his temper, but at the same time there was no way she could sit back and do nothing.

If she didn't act now it would be too late. Very soon he'd see her growing belly, he'd hear the bouts of morning sickness. She thought again of Chrissy; she'd known right away that Maggie was pregnant and, if she could tell, others would be able to as well.

The thought galvanised her into action. She took a long cotton nightdress from the drawer, put it on, then nervously made her way down the hallway to Rory's room.

She wasn't sure whether she should knock, go back to her own room or just walk in. She touched her stomach, trying to work up the courage to open the door. Doris's voice in her head reminded her that it was a choice between passing the baby off as Rory's, or trying to survive winter living on the streets.

Determined to see it through, she opened the door.

The room was dark although the curtains were open allowing the moonlight to stream in. She stood looking at Rory, asleep in bed. It was now or never. Chewing on her lip, she crossed the room and, without bothering to wake him, she lifted the sheets and climbed into bed next to him.

A hand gripped her neck, then she felt the sharp tip of a knife against her skin. She tried to scratch his hands away as he tightened his hold, letting out a gasp of relief when he suddenly released her.

'Maggie?' He dropped the knife. 'What the fuck are you doing?'

Terrified, she stared up at him, his nose almost touching hers. 'I was scared. I had nightmares,' she lied. 'I didn't want to be on my own . . . I'm sorry.'

She could feel him getting hard on top of her, but she didn't move, she wasn't sure what he was going to do.

'I didn't know it was you. A man can't be too careful when he's got enemies.'

Since when do enemies climb into bed with you, she wondered. But she kept silent and waited for Rory to say something.

It seemed to take forever before he finally spoke. 'What do you want from me, Maggie?'

'Like I said, I was scared, that's all.'

His erection pushed against her leg. 'Do you think I'm stupid, Maggie?'

'I don't know what you're talking about.' She felt sick with panic. Had Chrissy said something after all?

'I think you do.' Rory's voice was low and Maggie found she was trembling.

'I don't, honestly.'

166

'I'm only flesh and blood, Maggie, and you doing this – well, what am I supposed to do? What's a man supposed to think?'

Terrified as she was, she had to keep playing the game. 'I swear, it's just that I wasn't used to being in that room. Everything's new to me . . . I wanted to be with you. Is that so wrong?'

There was another drawn-out silence before he gave a sigh and said, 'No. But you can't keep on tempting me like this.' The note of anger to his voice didn't go unnoticed by Maggie.

'I'm not trying to tempt you. I just feel better when I'm with you. If I'm going to be your wife anyway, I don't understand why that's so wrong.'

'I'm a good Catholic boy, Maggie, I thought you knew that? I like to think you were a good Catholic girl. Didn't Father Patrick teach you about the sins of the flesh?'

Maggie nodded, shocked at the way Rory was acting. She'd never heard of a man behaving like this. She'd been warned by her mother to keep her distance from men in case they tried it on or forced themselves on her. It was hard to believe that any bloke, especially a bloke like Rory, would behave like a nun.

Part of her was relieved that he wasn't forcing himself on her, but in the current circumstances she couldn't afford to have him push her away. She briefly considered letting her hand wander down to his erect penis, but the moonlight glinting off the knife by his pillow made her change her mind.

'I don't want to wait till next spring,' Maggie said.

Even in the moonlight she could see his steady gaze. 'Is that right?'

She gave him a small nod. 'Why don't we get married sooner? Like in two or three days.'

Rory laughed. 'It takes much longer than that, Maggie. All the arrangements, sending out the invites, that takes time.'

Swallowing hard, she stroked his face. 'I just want to be your wife.'

'You will be, Maggie. Why the rush?'

She knew she had to be careful now. She didn't want to raise his suspicions. 'I saw the way your staff in the club looked at me, and I know everyone else will look at me the same. They think we're living in sin because I'm under your roof. But they won't think that if I'm Mrs Sheehan.'

'Is that what you're worried about?' He chuckled.

'Yes. I want to walk down the road with my head held high.'

'Are you sure that's all?' His tone was even.

'Of course, what else would it be?'

He kissed her on the forehead then. 'I tell you what I'll do, Maggie. I'll speak to the staff and make sure they never make you feel uncomfortable again.' There was a threat in his voice.

'No, don't do that. I don't want them to hate me.' Chrissy already hated her. Being ordered to kowtow to Maggie would only make that worse. She was the type who'd kick off and let everyone in on Maggie's secret.

Rory fell silent. 'Then what can I do?'

'Let's get married as soon as possible, *please*. I don't care about a big wedding. All I care about is being your wife.'

Her words seemed to please Rory. 'All right, all right.' He laughed. 'How could I say no to that? I'll speak to Father Patrick tomorrow. We'll need your da's consent, but I'm sure that won't be a problem' – he gave her a wink – 'a bottle of Jameson's should do it. And by next month we can be married.'

The words next month rushed round Maggie's head. Next month might be too late. She was already six weeks gone. What the hell was she going to do?

Chapter Thirty-Seven

Maggie sat in the club feeling ridiculous in her long green dress, but after the lecture he'd given her about his dear old ma, and what a good Catholic wife and mother she'd been, choosing the ugliest dress in the wardrobes had seemed like the best way to appease him. And now he wasn't even here to appreciate the gesture, because he'd rushed off to Rupert Street on some urgent business.

'I want a word with you.'

Maggie looked up and saw Chrissy standing over her.

'Go away, Chrissy,' Maggie hissed. 'Rory will be back any minute, and you wouldn't want me telling him about the way you speak to me, would you?'

'I think you'll want to hear what I have to say,' Chrissy slurred, swaying on her feet.

Maggie shook her head. 'I don't wanna hear anything you've got to say, so piss off.' Chrissy being drunk was making her edgy. Things were difficult enough without some silly tart making a nuisance of herself.

'I ain't going anywhere.'

The other dancers and the bar staff were glancing their way. The last thing she wanted was to aggravate Chrissy when she was in this state, because then she'd start raising her voice.

'All right, I'll talk to you, but not here.'

A smug smile lit Chrissy's face when Maggie got up and led the way to the exit.

'I'm just going to get some fresh air,' she told the barman. 'I won't be long.'

It was true – she did need some fresh air. Having Rory's watchful eye on her at all times made her feel as if she were suffocating.

Of course it was better living with Rory in a warm dry place where she didn't have to scrub the floors every morning than lying in a damp, cold bedroom, terrified of what her dad might do next. But she missed the freedom of being able to come and go as she pleased. Even when Rory wasn't there, she knew his men were keeping an eye on her. If it was like this now, what would it be like when they were married?

At the top of the stairs, Maggie turned to Chrissy. 'Okay, what is it you want to tell me?'

'I don't think you want to talk here, do you?' Chrissy said. '*Mr Sheehan* might come back and overhear us.' She giggled drunkenly.

Maggie nodded and walked further down Bridle Lane, leaving Chrissy to totter along behind in her stilettos.

Stopping halfway down the lane, Maggie turned again and looked at her, not bothering to conceal the hatred she felt. 'I already told you, I'm not pregnant, so you can get that out of your fucking mouth.' She wasn't usually like this, but there was something about Chrissy that made her feel she needed to protect herself, just like she had done with Pam.

Chrissy laughed. 'If you say so.' Then she took a cigarette from the little purse she was carrying, lit it and blew smoke in Maggie's face. 'But you seemed so upset that I might say anything it got me thinking.'

'What the hell are you talking about?' Maggie snapped. She didn't have time for this; if she was going to keep Rory sweet, she needed to be waiting for him in the club when he got back.

'Come off it, Maggie. Nobody gets that upset if they've got nothing to hide,' Chrissy sneered. 'What would *Rory* say, if I congratulated him on him becoming a father?'

'He wouldn't say anything.' Maggie tried to stay calm. Why had she been so stupid? Why had she shown Chrissy how worried she was? Now the woman was a like a dog with a bone and she wasn't going to let it drop. Deciding the best course of action was to call her bluff, she stepped in closer, clenching her hands into fists. 'So go ahead and speak to him, why don't you. Then you won't have a job.'

'Okay, I will. I'll go tell everyone the good news, then we can raise a toast when he walks in.' She turned to go, but Maggie grabbed her.

'Wait!' Maggie was filled with fear, no matter how much she tried to hide it. Right now, Chrissy had the upper hand.

'So it's true, then?'

Maggie shook her head. 'I'm not saying that. I just don't want you causing trouble.'

Chrissy chuckled. 'I'm not stupid.'

'What are you going to do?'

'I'm not going to do anything. *You're* going to do it.' She paused. 'I want money. I want you to give me money. Fifty pounds.'

Maggie shivered. 'Fifty pounds?'

'Fifty pounds a week.'

'You're mad. I can't get that kind of money.'

Chrissy shrugged. 'That's not my problem. If I don't get it, then I'll tell him. Your choice.'

'I've already told you – there's nothing to tell.'

'Then you don't have to worry, do you? . . . Make sure I have it by next week, Maggie, otherwise you know what will happen.'

She laughed and tottered back to the club, leaving Maggie standing watching her. There was no way she could get that sort of money, but at the same time she knew there was no way Chrissy would keep quiet if she didn't find a way to pay for her silence.

Chapter Thirty-Eight

The front room of Doris's terrace smelled of damp washing and carbolic soap. Stockings and threadbare underwear hung from a piece of string that hung across the fireplace. Steam rose as they dried in the heat.

Maggie perched on the edge of the sagging armchair, a chipped teacup balanced on her knee, while Doris sat opposite her.

'So this Chrissy,' Doris said, 'you're telling me she wants fifty fucking quid a week to keep her trap shut?'

Maggie nodded miserably. She hadn't known where else to go, who to talk to, and somehow she'd found herself at the door of Doris's house. 'Yeah, that's right.' Maggie stared into her tea.

Doris took a slurp of her tea. 'Fifty bloody quid! Girl's got a nerve.'

'And I haven't got that sort of money.'

Doris's sharp eyes missed nothing as she stared at Maggie. 'Course you ain't. Not unless you start working the streets.' She let out a cackle and leaned forward, tapping ash into a battered tin lid. 'And I can't see Rory being too happy about you doing that.'

The room fell quiet except for the crackle of the fire and the wireless in the background playing Cliff Richards' 'The Young Ones'. 'And you reckon she's serious,' Doris said eventually. 'You think she'll definitely blab?'

Maggie nodded. 'Yeah, yeah I do.'

'And we both know what Rory will do if he finds out.' She held up her scarred hands.

'What am I going to do?' Maggie's nerves were shot; her life seemed to consist of one disaster after another.

'Well, it's like I told you, Maggie, you've got to fuck men over in more ways than one. Same goes for life.'

'I don't understand.'

'Course you don't.' Doris put her tea on the side and picked up her cigarette. She pointed at Maggie. 'All your life you've been a pretty face with big eyes, but that'll only get you so far.' Doris's tone wasn't unkind, just matter-of-fact. 'Men like Rory – most men, actually – only see what's on the outside. Tits and arse and a nice smile . . . They don't give a monkey's about what's up here.' She tapped her temple with a nicotine-stained finger.

Like Doris, Maggie set her cup down. She leaned forward. 'So what are you saying?'

'I'm saying, start using your bleedin' brain, girl. Take control of your life. Be clever.' She tutted. 'You should've learned by now that no one else is going to look out for you, so you've got to look out for yourself. Getting together with Rory was smart, but that's only the start. When I'm long gone, you'll still be up against bastards like your dad, blokes like Rory and tarts like Chrissy. They're ten a penny. As much as I don't like what she's doing, at least Chrissy's using her brains. She's spotted an opportunity and she's making the most of it.' Doris reached for her teacup again. 'And that's what you need to start doing. Use this' – she tapped her head – 'cos men don't expect us to think, and that's their weakness. You need to start keeping an eye out for opportunities. And right now, darlin', there's one staring you right in the face.'

'You?'

Doris roared with laughter, her feet raised off the floor as she cackled. 'Not me, you daft bleedin' cow – *Rory*. He's got money, hasn't he? Lots of it. And where there's money, there's ways of getting some.'

Maggie frowned. 'You want me to steal from him?' She chewed the inside of her cheek. 'He'd kill me, Doris. You know he would.'

'Not steal. Christ, you're green!' Doris grimaced as she shifted on her arthritic hip. 'I like to call it "paying yourself some house-keeping".' She grinned. 'Men like Rory, they've always got fiddles on the go. Books that don't add up. Money that doesn't get reported.'

'You mean all the accounting books and the ledgers he has?'

'There you go.' Doris nodded approval. 'Now you're thinking.'

'But I don't know anything about keeping books.'

'So learn.' Doris shrugged like it was the simplest thing in the world. 'That's where your face comes in, and those big eyelashes of yours. Tell him you want to help with the business. Tell him, how much you admire him.' She chortled and rolled her eyes. 'Men love that kind of shit. It makes them feel important.'

Maggie considered this. 'He might go for it.'

'There's no *might* about it. You have to make sure you per-suade him. Then learn the books. Learn where the money comes from, where it goes. Find the gaps, who they pay and who they don't pay. You need to look out for the gaps.' Doris reached across and patted Maggie's knee with surprising tenderness. 'Listen to me, girl, the world ain't kind to women, especially women like us. Never has been, and I doubt it ever will be. If you want to survive, you've got to be tougher. You can't go around playing this innocent angel any more.'

Maggie frowned and touched her stomach. 'I'm hardly an inno-cent angel.'

'Then stop playing one,' Doris said bluntly. 'I know you've had it hard with your da, but knock on any door in this bleedin' street, and there'll be a whole lot of girls with a story just like yours. Believe me, in my line of work, I should know. I had girls and women of all ages begging me to help them get rid, just like your mum did, with stories about fellas that would make your fucking toes curl.' She sniffed, then reached out for the bottle of gin and poured a hearty measure in her teacup.

'Thanks, Doris.'

'Don't thank me yet, darlin'. You've still got a fuck of a lot to deal with.' Doris grinned, her harshness falling away. 'But you've got a brain, and it's about time you started using what God gave you – and I don't mean what's between your legs.'

Chapter Thirty-Nine

Luca was sitting at the table opposite his father in the back room of their house in Holborn. He watched the veins on the side of his father's temple throbbing while his face turned red and his bloodshot eyes blazed with fury.

'Who gave you permission?' Vince Romano banged on the table, and it crossed Luca's mind that he'd never seen his father look quite this angry. Not at him anyway. 'I gave Sheehan my word of honour when I handed over the Rupert Street business. By taking it back, you've made it look as though I have no honour. You've humiliated me.'

'You made a laughing stock out of the Romano name. People were saying we're weak, we're giving away our businesses, our money, our legacy.' He waved his hand in the air passionately, every bit as furious as his father. Right now he felt nothing towards his father but hatred. The morphine heightened that feeling. It numbed any guilt, any loyalty he might have once had.

Luca stared at the knife in front of him. He was tempted to use it right now, to slit his father's throat. But he couldn't. Patience was needed.

He glanced at Nestor and Marco, who stood in the corner

listening to their conversation. They were loyal, but if he acted now, or let them know what he was planning to do, that would soon change.

No, he had to be smarter than that. Much fucking smarter.

Vince stood. He rested his arthritic hands on the table as he spoke. 'Even though you're my only son, that doesn't mean you can show me disrespect.' Vince nodded to the other men, giving the go-ahead for what was to come next. 'This gives me no pleasure, Luca.' He walked out with Nestor following him.

Luca knew what was about to happen. He'd seen it many times before, he'd even been the one to give the order, but that didn't make it any easier.

Marco strode across the room and, betraying no emotion, drove his fist into Luca's face.

Luca's lip burst open. His mouth filled with blood. Then came another blow, this time to the side of his skull. Luca fell forward, but he knew it was pointless fighting back; this was a punishment that his father had ordered, and no amount of struggling would change that.

Before he could get up, Marco grabbed a handful of Luca's hair, pulling his head back then slamming it hard against the table. His nose crunched and blood splattered everywhere.

In pain, Luca clambered up from the chair, trying to get on his feet, but Marco brought back his foot, kicking Luca in the side, connecting directly with his ribs. He kicked him again, winding him, then stamped down on his hand, breaking a couple of his fingers.

The punishment stopped as quickly as it had started, and Marco walked out without saying a word, leaving Luca on the ground in a pool of blood and pain.

No Regret

A few minutes later, Luca heard the door open.

'Oh my God, oh my God. Luca! What happened?' Sofia rushed up to him, dropping to her knees to prop his head on her lap. He opened his swollen eye and looked at her.

'Sofia.' He attempted a smile, but found he had to turn his head to the side to spit out the blood and a chipped tooth.

'Was this your father?'

Luca groaned and laughed bitterly. 'I tried to talk to him about running the business. This was his fucking answer.'

'I can't believe he did this,' she whispered.

Luca said nothing. His breathing was shallow as he struggled with the pain in his ribs.

'Go into my pocket.'

Sofia did as she was told, bringing out Luca's tin of pills.

'Give me two.'

Shaking, she opened it and took the tablets out and gently placed them under Luca's tongue.

He attempted another smile. He knew exactly what he was doing. Marco might have delivered the beating, but he was delivering something far more dangerous, and a few bruised ribs and broken fingers was worth it. 'My father thinks pain will teach me a lesson.'

Sofia's hand cupped his face. 'He can't do this to you.'

'He already has.'

Sofia leaned closer, her breath against his ear. 'Then we have to stop him.' She stroked his face again. 'Permanently.'

Luca watched Sofia's eyes burn with anger.

Although he was in pain, he held back his laughter. With her on his side, it would be easy. Within a month, the Romano family legacy would be his. Luca could almost taste it. The business would be under his control. Every fucking part of it.

Everything that he had worked for would finally be in his hands.

He closed his eyes, letting the morphine slip through his veins. Within a few minutes, the pain started to fade. Everything was going exactly the way he'd planned. His father wouldn't see it coming until it was too late . . .

Chapter Forty

A week after Maggie's conversation with Doris, she was still mulling over what they'd said. It felt too risky, so for the past few days Maggie had tried to come up with alternative ways of raising the money to keep Chrissy quiet.

She'd thought about selling some of her expensive clothes, the ones that Rory had given her, but apart from the fact that he'd probably notice they were missing Maggie had no idea where to sell them.

She doubted any of the Camden pawn shops would take them, and if they did she wouldn't get much. It would be a struggle to raise a single payment of fifty quid, and Chrissy had made it clear that she wanted a payment each week.

Calling Chrissy's bluff was too risky. She had too much to lose. Chrissy didn't just know about the baby – she knew that Maggie and Thomas had been close. She had seen the anger bubbling underneath the surface when she even looked in the direction of another man. Most of the time he didn't say anything; he didn't need to – the look alone was enough.

She sighed. Despite it the risk, she'd have to do as Doris had advised. After all, Doris's advice so far had been a life-saver for Maggie. But she needed to be clever about it and make sure no one would be any the wiser. Tits and arse . . . and brains.

Her mind made up, Maggie walked along the corridor behind the main bar of the club. This area wasn't open to the public; it stank of stale smoke and alcohol, with cigarette butts littering the sticky floor and empty bear crates lining the walls.

When she reached the door at the end, she knocked twice.

'What? This better be fucking good.' Rory's voice was sharp and irritated.

Maggie pushed open the door, and saw Rory hunched over his desk, a cigarette hanging out of the side of his mouth. 'I'm busy,' he snapped.

She closed the door behind her, which made him look up.

Something like a smile spread across Rory's face. His eyes narrowed. 'What's this then?' He leaned back in his chair, taking a deep drag of his cigarette. 'I thought you'd be resting at home. I hope there's no trouble. I've got enough on me plate as it is.'

'No trouble, I just needed to talk to you.' Her voice was steadier than she felt. Apart from being nervous, she was struggling with morning sickness, but there was no point feeling sorry for herself. Like Doris said, she had to be smart, and that meant being tough.

She'd had to find a way to make sure Rory couldn't hear her retching of a morning, because it wouldn't take a genius to work out what was wrong. So she'd mastered the art of vomiting silently. Kneeling on the cold tiles, her head hanging over the lav and one hand pressed hard against her mouth, she'd let the sick run slowly through her fingers to stop it splashing into the toilet bowl.

The hardest part was when the nausea came without warning. She recognised the signs – the cold sweat breaking out on her forehead, the saliva flooding her mouth – but often there was nothing she could do to stop it. And now the *morning* sickness wasn't just coming in the morning – it was coming all hours of the day and night.

The one piece of good news was that Rory had gone to see Father Patrick to arrange for them to be married in three weeks' time. But she was scared that three weeks might be too late. It seemed so far away when she was keeping a growing secret.

'You want to talk, do you?' It seemed to amuse him and he reached over to the bottle of whisky that was sitting on his desk. He unscrewed the top and poured himself a large drink, keeping his eye on her the whole time.

She, meanwhile, had to resist the nausea brought on by the sickly smell of the whisky. It made it harder to focus on the little speech she'd been rehearsing.

'I know I'm gonna be your wife,' she said, 'but I'd still like to earn my keep. I've worked since I was a kid, and I want to carry on working, not just sit around doing nothing.'

His silence and that unwavering stare made Maggie speak more quickly as her nerves got the better of her. 'I wanna help. I can read, I can write, I'm good at numbers – I want to be part of all this.' She could hear her own breathing in the quiet room.

Rory's laugh was hard and ugly. 'So you don't want to just sit around looking pretty – is that what you're trying to tell me? Isn't what I've given you enough? We're not even married and you're telling me that you're not happy.'

'No, no. That's not what I mean. I am happy,' Maggie lied. 'I'm looking forward to being your wife.' She smiled at him, desperately hoping her lies sounded convincing. She wouldn't be marrying Rory at all if it wasn't for the baby growing inside her.

He leaned forward on his elbows and blew a stream of cigarette smoke from his nostrils. 'I won't have my fucking wife standing behind the bar, serving men, looking like a little tart. Is that what you want? You want the men to look at you?'

Maggie shook her head vigorously, but kept her mouth shut.

Rory pushed his chair back and got up, slowly walking to where Maggie was standing. He put his fingers under her chin, lifting her head up. 'Do you want them to look at you Maggie?' he hissed, then he moved his hand over her breasts and her hips. Then he pulled up her long dress to reveal her thighs, gripping the grey material in his fist and using it to draw her into him.

Maggie could feel his erection against her as he breathed heavily. She wished that he'd have sex with her and get it over with. Every time she felt him becoming hard, she hoped it'd be the time his willpower would break. But she daren't push it. She needed him to think she was innocent and inexperienced.

'Is this what you want them to do to you? Is it, Maggie?'

'No.' Her voice was small.

'Fuck, Maggie, you do know if any man so much as touches you, I'll kill both of you.' He leaned his head on her shoulder and groaned. 'You haven't let anyone touch you, have you, Maggie?'

'Never.' She squeezed her eyes shut, her heart racing.

Rory suddenly pushed her away. He ran his fingers through his hair, looking like he was trying to calm himself down, then he went to sit on the edge of his desk.

'So go on, then, tell me what it is you want to do.'

She fidgeted with her fingers, trying to think what Doris would say. 'I want to learn the books.'

'The fuck you do!' He laughed again, his lips curled in a sneer.

Undeterred, she stepped closer. 'I want to help with the business. If we're going to be married.'

'If?'

'*When* we're married, I want to be part of this.'

'Since when?'

'Since you told your staff that they should take orders from me. How am I supposed to give them orders when I don't know anything about the business? I've seen how they look at me. They know I don't know anything.'

'And I said *I'd have a word*.' His face darkened.

She shook her head. 'I'm not asking you to do that. I'm asking you to involve me in the business. Show me how it all works.'

This time she was the one who moved closer, coming to stand within inches of Rory. He didn't push her way as he so often had before. 'Isn't that what it's all about? Making money, making a name for yourself? Because *when* we're married, your name will be mine.'

Rory held Maggie's stare, his eyes cold and calculating.

'I'm not stupid, Rory.' She forced herself not to look away. 'I could be useful to you.'

'Could you now?' He stubbed out his cigarette, stood up slowly from the desk and once again stood towering over her. 'And why would my pretty little Maggie suddenly want to get her hands dirty?'

'I've already told you.'

His hand shot up, grabbing her throat. Not hard enough to bruise, but hard enough to make her flinch. 'Is that right – *you've already told me*, have you?' He pushed his head against hers. 'Do I look like a man who's going to be *told* anything by a fucking woman?' Then his thumb stroked her cheek. 'You've got a lot to learn, Maggie, if you think you'll ever be able to tell me what to do.'

'I was—'

'Shut-up.' His grip was tight enough to hurt now. 'I've been good to you, haven't I?'

She gave a tiny nod. 'I just thought . . . it might be a good idea.'

'A good idea? Why would I need you to know about the business when I've got Malcolm running the books?'

Maggie had given some thought to this. 'Because if anything happened to you, or to Malcolm, or to both of you . . . you'd need someone else to make sure this place continues to run smoothly.'

'So you think something's going to happen to us?' He raised his eyebrows.

'Yes— No, I mean . . .' Maggie stammered. 'I've heard you talk, I've heard how there's been raids all around London, I've heard how the Italians want to take over, so I thought, if anything did happen, well, who better to support you than your wife?'

'Don't push your luck, Maggie. I've seen how women have been the downfall of many a man.' He burst into laughter. 'I always did say you were a smart one though.' His grip softened and became a caress. 'But the books, Maggie? That's my business. A business I've worked hard to build up with blood and sweat.'

'I know, but I was good with numbers at school.'

'This isn't school, Maggie.' He tilted his head, thoughts racing behind his eyes. 'But if I show you, and I teach you, the question is, can I trust you?' His voice dropped, a note of menace creeping in. 'My little Maggie would never screw me over, would she?'

'Never.'

His lips brushed the side of her ear then he held her lobe with his teeth for a minute, biting down enough to make her let out a yelp. 'Because you know what happens to people who betray me, don't you? You've seen it.'

Maggie's body was rigid. It was true – she had seen it. Only last week, she'd had to stand and watch while Malcolm sliced open the face of one of the barmen after he'd pocketed a couple of quid. So there was no doubt in her mind, none whatsoever, what Rory did to people who took advantage of him.

'All right, then.' He suddenly stepped back, gesturing to the desk where some of his books were piled up. 'Maybe it is time you learned . . . *Malcolm!*' he bellowed.

The door opened almost immediately and Malcolm stood there in a finely tailored suit.

'Maggie here wants to learn the books,' Rory said, amused.

Malcolm's eyebrows rose a fraction. He nodded, but didn't say anything.

'So I want you to show her a few basic things . . . Only a few things, mind. We don't want her knowing all our secrets, do we?' Rory laughed. 'See how she gets on.'

Maggie glanced at Malcolm and saw distrust in his eyes, then she turned back to Rory.

'You can trust me, Rory.' She spoke firmly. 'You can trust me with your life.'

Chapter Forty-One

Later that night Maggie sat in the bath. She felt as if things were finally moving in the right direction. While it was clear Rory had no intention of teaching her everything about how the business worked, it was a start. And in learning how to keep the books she was hopefully showing Rory that he could trust her. She smiled to herself.

If she'd had time, she would've liked to have gone to tell Doris how it went. Despite what had happened with her mother, Maggie believed that Doris genuinely did care what happened to women like her who found themselves in trouble. She was tough and loud, but that didn't mean she didn't have a heart of gold.

Apart from Pam, she'd never really had any female friends, and she'd certainly never been able to speak to her own mother. Doris was different: she made her feel stronger. Whenever something made her resolve wobble – like seeing Chrissy draped all over Thomas, or the look of disgust on her mum and dad's faces when they passed her in the street – she held her head high and didn't break down.

Her parents were another problem she had to deal with. Chrissy was only guessing, but her mum and dad knew she was pregnant. Part of her couldn't imagine that they would say anything, not now she was with Rory. They'd be too scared. However, she couldn't leave it to chance.

Sighing, she leaned back in the bath, the steam filling the plush bathroom. She sank deeper into the bubbles, watching the water ripple against the porcelain tub. She closed her eyes, letting one hand drift to her stomach, the secret growing heavier with each day.

The bathroom door crashed open, smashing against the wall. Maggie sat up.

Rory stood in the doorway swaying. 'Well, will you look at you. If it isn't my beautiful girl.' His voice was slurred. A bottle of whisky dangled from his hand. His shirt was half unbuttoned, and Maggie could see blood spatters on his shirt. His face wasn't injured, but his knuckles were. Whoever he'd been in a fight with had clearly come off worse.

'Is everything all right?' she asked. Keeping her voice neutral, she gestured towards his hands. 'Are you hurt?'

Rory leaned against the heavy door frame, lifted the bottle and took a long swig. 'Nothing I can't handle.'

He stared at Maggie through the steam, his eyes moving over her naked body. After a moment, he took another long swig from the bottle before turning away and stumbling down the hall towards his bedroom.

Maggie watched him go. Then she stood up, splashing water everywhere. This was the chance she'd been waiting for. She reached for the thick white towel hanging from the rail, wrapped it round herself and ran down the hallway.

The door to Rory's bedroom was open, and he sat slumped on the edge of the bed. The whisky bottle hung precariously from his fingers, the liquid sloshing about inside.

'Rory?'

He grunted, then lifted his head, looking confused, his eyes bloodshot. 'What do you want?'

She could hardly understand what he was saying. He was drunker than she'd ever seen him before, and saliva dribbled down his chin. But she walked over to him anyway, taking the bottle from his hand. She paused before lifting it up to his lips. 'Here, have some more.'

His head swayed and his lips parted as if to speak, but he allowed Maggie to pour the drink into his mouth.

'There's still some more. Go on . . . That's it.' She supported the back of his head with one hand and watched him empty the bottle. Then she placed it on the floor.

She knelt in front of him, putting her hands on his thighs.

'Rory? Rory?' She tapped him, but he only gave a grunt before flopping onto the bed with his eyes closed.

With some difficulty, Maggie rolled him further into the middle of the bed. Taking a deep breath, she began to unbutton the rest of his shirt, struggling to pull his arms out of it, feeling like they were made of stone. Next, she undid the buckle on his belt. She tugged his trousers off, along with his boxer shorts. Then she dropped her towel, climbed into bed next to him, wrapping his arms over her, before kissing him gently on his lips.

Rory stirred, she kissed him again, tasting both whisky and cigarette.

'Rory.'

He opened his eyes and she could see the darkness in them. Her heart raced and she held her breath, wondering what he was going to do. She didn't have to wait long for his hand to reach up and tangle in her damp hair, pulling her closer.

'Rory?'

He murmured something she couldn't understand and pushed

190

his lips onto hers while his hand fumbled her breasts, his fingers digging into her skin, leaving marks.

Maggie's hand went down to his penis, and although he was drunk it was semi-hard. Recoiling inside, Maggie started to massage it, trying to get him more aroused, worried that at any moment he'd shove her away. This was her chance, and she didn't want to mess it up.

After a while, Rory began to groan, then he clambered on top of her, his weight pressing down so hard it was suffocating. When he thrust into her, Maggie bit down on her lip and turned her head to avoid his stinking breath.

When it was over, he collapsed beside her and, within minutes, began to snore loudly.

Maggie lay still.

She closed her eyes, daring to breathe out, grateful but hating what had just happened. Not that it mattered how she felt. She'd done what she needed to do. Tomorrow morning Rory would wake up and see her next to him. There'd be no denying it then.

Doris would be proud of her.

Chapter Forty-Two

Over the next few days, Maggie started to feel better and stronger. Not just because the nausea had lessened, but because the deed was done: she'd had sex with Rory. Now he would think the baby was his. He hadn't touched her since, but that was fine by her.

She still had to be careful, especially with Chrissy sniffing around. She intended to keep hiding her pregnancy for as long as possible after the wedding. It would be a relief when the news was finally out and she could stop worrying about Chrissy. In the meantime, there was nothing for it but to keep paying her hush money.

Which meant sneaking into the office while Rory and Malcolm were otherwise occupied. Right now they were talking with a guy who had information about a shipload of cigarettes coming in; Rory had a nice little sideline selling stolen goods on the black market, and he relied on tip-offs from the men who worked on the docks.

She had the combination of the safe off by heart, so it was a matter of opening it, pulling out one of the ledgers and making a small adjustment. Malcom had shown her the basics, and she was now allowed to enter orders for booze, takings, staff pay. She was careful not to make mistakes; she knew Malcolm didn't trust her and checked everything she did. So when it came to turning a six into a zero, or a seven into a four, she copied Malcolm's handwriting, sticking to small adjustments that wouldn't raise suspicions. And she didn't skim the money she needed all from one place. A few quid from the Greek Street collection on Friday, a couple of quid from the barber shop on Rupert Street on Wednesday, and various amounts from the clip joints on Wardour Street. Everything had to be spread thinly so no one could spot it. Everything had to be balanced so that no one would know.

After replacing the ledger, she used the second combination she'd memorised to get into the safe where the money was kept. She always changed the books before taking the money; that way, if she was interrupted before she could get to the money, they would find themselves with *more* cash than expected and be less likely to question it. But she knew if she was ever caught red-handed there wouldn't be enough excuses in the world to get her out of the shit she'd be in.

With the cash safely in her pocket, she sauntered back into the noisy bar. There were punters sitting about drinking, Brenda was dancing topless to some new Elvis Presley song and Chrissy was standing by the bar smoking a cigarette. She nodded to her then headed for the back door which led to a small concrete yard behind the pub where deliveries came in.

A moment later Chrissy appeared. 'Well?' She stuck out her hand. 'I hope you've got my money.'

Maggie pulled the notes out of her pocket and slapped them down on Chrissy's palm.

She counted the notes and, satisfied it was the full amount, tucked the money into her knickers. 'See, not so hard to get, is it? And don't think next week's going to be any different.'

Chrissy sneered. 'Unless of course you want me opening my mouth about your little secrets.' She took another drag on her cigarette, blowing smoke straight into Maggie's face. 'You know, I think—'

'Is there a problem out here?' Malcolm, having entered through a side door unnoticed, stood watching them.

Maggie gave Chrissy a nervous glance, then shook her head. 'No, no. Chrissy wasn't feeling too clever so I said she could come out here for a breath of fresh air.'

Malcolm looked between them and Maggie's heart thumped.

Finally, he nodded. 'Rory's waiting for you.'

'Thanks.' Maggie's stomach tightened as she wondered how long he'd been there. And how much he'd seen . . .

Chapter Forty-Three

Sofia lay naked under the sheets, her dark hair spilling across the pillow while her eyes tracked Luca's movements.

'How am I supposed to fucking wait?' he fumed. 'Every day feels too long.'

'You must have patience, Luca.' Her voice was smooth but it did nothing to comfort Luca. If anything, it irritated him.

'And we need to figure out what to do about Marco. He follows my father like a fucking shadow.'

'Marco can be handled,' Sofia said simply.

'How?'

She smiled at him, a glint in her eyes. 'Men are simple creatures: money or pussy.'

Luca shook his head. 'Not Marco.'

'All men.' Sofia reached for her cigarettes. 'Some just take longer than others.'

'And if that doesn't work?'

'It will.'

Her smug demeanour infuriated him. He slammed his hand against the wall, glaring at her. 'I said, *if it doesn't fucking work, what then?*'

Sofia, as usual, ignored his tantrums. She laughed. 'Then a bullet will work just as well.'

The casual way she said it made Luca laugh. He doubted he could ever love her, but she was the perfect business partner. Cold and calculating. The woman had ice where her heart should be.

'Nothing can be traced back to us, though.'

'It won't be.' She threw back the sheets and swung her legs onto the floor, crossing the room to stand behind Luca and press her naked body against him. She slid her arms round his bare chest and kissed his neck. 'Your father trusts me, but timing is everything, Luca.'

Luca reached across to his tin of pills, opening it and popping one inside his mouth. Two weeks after the beating, his cuts and bruises were almost healed, but the broken fingers were still taped together, and his ribs hurt like hell whenever the morphine started to wear off.

'I want to be there when it happens. I want to see his face when he realises it's me.'

'Don't be silly, Luca. You need an alibi.' Her tone was matter-of-fact. 'You want revenge, but you also want to get away with it. You'll need to look like you're grieving, like you're broken-hearted. You need your father's men to stand by your side when you take over, not to stand against you.'

What Sofia was saying was true. Hard as it was to wait for his revenge, he nodded in agreement. 'Okay, okay, I'll do as you say.'

'Good,' Sofia purred. 'Because when the prize is worth the risk, Luca, there'll be no regret.'

Chapter Forty-Four

Maggie still couldn't work out whether Malcolm had seen money changing hands, or whether he'd heard the conversation she'd had with Chrissy in the back yard, but ever since that day he'd been different with her. She could see it in the way he looked at her, as if he knew something that she didn't.

It made her feel edgy, as well as worried about what she would do in the long term. She couldn't go on skimming the books for much longer. Once she was married, and able to tell Rory she was pregnant, then she could stop dishing out the money to Chrissy. Right now, though, she had other things to worry about.

With Rory having announced this morning that he and Malcolm would be gone all day, she could finally look forward to escaping the constant scrutiny. Knowing that his men would never dream of knocking on her bedroom door, she'd taken the opportunity to sneak out of the Cow and Bull while no one was looking.

Pulling her woollen coat around her against the winter chill, she stood outside the terraced house. As usual, it was her mother who answered the door. There were no words from her, just a long, cold stare, her eyes tracking over the new coat and leather shoes. Without waiting for an invitation, Maggie stepped in.

The hallway smelled the same: damp and cabbage and stale beer. The wallpaper still peeled and Maggie doubted it would ever be fixed.

Her mother went into the kitchen and she followed her through. It felt like a lifetime ago since she'd last been here. She was a different person now. The girl who'd peeled vegetables, washed floors and huddled terrified in the corner when her father came in had disappeared.

She stared at her father, who sat at the table, a bottle of whisky in front of him, wearing a grubby string vest and baggy brown trousers. 'Oh, look what the cat's dragged in,' he slurred. 'Come to show off, have you, Maggie? Flaunting what you get for being a whore.'

Maggie stood her ground, her head held high. This pathetic excuse for a man no longer frightened her.

'Look at it.' He took a swig of his whisky. 'All high and mighty in her fancy new clothes, all thanks to Mr Sheehan.' He leaned forward, his eyes bloodshot. 'I wonder if he knows what a little slag you are.'

Maggie bristled, but didn't react.

Her father gave a cold, ugly smile, the one that she'd seen so often when he used to come into her room at night. His eyes fixed on her stomach. 'You haven't told him, have you?' He roared with laughter and then began to cough, bringing up phlegm, and spitting it into the corner.

He lurched to his feet, swaying, and threw the bottle at Maggie. It missed her head, but only by inches, smashing against the wall behind her, glass and whisky splattering and shattering everywhere.

Maggie stepped forward. Even though her heart raced, she refused to run. Those days of cowering from her father were over.

She reached into her coat pocket and pulled out an envelope.

She threw it on the table. 'There's money in there.' She knew it was probably more money than the house had seen for a while. Rory had stopped using her father the moment she'd gone to live with him. So, without a doubt, they were having to rely on her mother's meagre wages from the laundrette.

Since most of their money went on booze, her parents would be reduced to eating soup made from scrag ends and vegetable peelings.

'Think you can buy us off, do you?' he sneered.

'Would you rather I tell Rory what you've done to me, and what you were doing to me all through my childhood?' She turned to her mother. 'While you stood by and did nothing.'

The slap came hard.

Maggie should have expected it, but it took her by surprise. Her cheek stung, but she didn't react.

'How dare you speak to me like that in my own home. Who do you think you are? You were always too big for your fecking boots. You always thought you were above us when you're no better than the rest of us . . . You're just like I am, Maggie. You're just like me.'

'I'm nothing like you.' She wouldn't give this woman another one of her tears. 'But that's the last time you ever raise your hand to me . . . otherwise you'll regret it.'

She turned to her father. 'None of us wants the truth to come out.'

He pulled the envelope towards him, opened it, looked inside and whistled.

'That's all you're getting,' Maggie said firmly. 'And you're lucky you're getting that and not a beating from Rory.'

Her dad's face darkened. 'You threatening me in my own home?'

'It's not a threat, Da. We both know what Rory will do to you if you tell anyone the baby isn't his . . . So what is it going to be?'

'You're passing off that thing in your belly as his?'

'I am . . . We all are. Understand?'

Unable to meet her stare, he bowed his head and gave a nod of acknowledgement as he shoved the envelope into his trouser pocket.

Knowing this would be the last time she ever returned, Maggie took a last look around the room, then she walked past her mother without looking at her, made her way down the hallway and out into the fresh air. The icy chill hit her, but Maggie didn't feel the cold any more. Instead, it felt like a huge weight had been lifted.

And she walked down the path and back out into Royal College Street, without looking back, leaving her childhood and all its ghosts behind.

Chapter Forty-Five

Wanting to make the most of her freedom while Rory and Malcom were away, instead of heading straight back to the pub she decided to take the tube to Leicester Square and then cut back through Soho to the club. She felt alive, the nearest she'd been to happy for a long time.

Doris had been right, as always. Better to be rich and miserable than poor and miserable. She would put up with Rory and do what was necessary to get by in the years ahead. Because, whatever lay ahead, it couldn't be worse than life with her parents.

Halfway down Whitcomb Street, the nausea came on without warning. After throwing up in the gutter, she had to lean against the wall, waiting for the dizziness to wear off.

But instead of easing, it got steadily worse.

The next moment, Maggie blacked out . . .

'Maggie . . . Maggie?'

Maggie frowned, not knowing where she was or what had happened.

'Maggie?'

She found herself facing Luca Romano.

'Where am I?' She was flustered. 'What happened?'

'Nowhere very glamorous, darling. You're in the back of my car.' He laughed. 'We need to stop meeting like this.' He smiled as the black Jaguar idled at the kerb.

'Why am I in your car?' Maggie pushed herself up.

'You fainted.'

She winced at her throbbing headache. 'Why did you put me in your car, though?' she snapped.

He shrugged. 'Would you rather I left you on the pavement?'

'No, I suppose not.'

He narrowed his gaze, a neutral expression on his handsome brooding face. 'A thank-you wouldn't go amiss.'

'Sorry . . . yes, thanks. Thank you,' she mumbled.

Luca laughed again. 'Actually, it was Nico who picked you up. I just gave him the orders, but I got the pleasure of sitting here waiting for you to come round.' He winked.

'I better go.' Maggie reached for the door handle, but the dizziness hit her again, and she had to lean back on the seat, taking deep breaths, to stop herself from vomiting again.

'Why don't you rest for a minute? It won't do you any good rushing out into the cold. You'll catch your death, darling.'

She didn't say anything, but she threw him a glance.

'Look, I won't bite, Maggie. Nico will be back shortly, so we can drive you to wherever it is you're going.'

'No, I'll be fine.'

Maggie wished now that she'd gone straight back to the pub after seeing her parents.

'Here, you look very pale.' Luca shrugged out of his jacket and handed it to her. 'Put this over you. Go on.'

Feeling too unwell to argue, she let him drape the jacket across her shoulders, grateful for the warmth. It smelled of cigarettes and cologne.

Luca lit a cigarette, the sharp flare of his match lighting his face, and once again she was aware of how handsome he was. But it was more than that; there was something about him that intrigued her, even though his presence beside her felt dangerous. She knew, of all the places she shouldn't be, here with Luca was top of the list.

He smiled slowly. 'I'm glad I've seen you again – not that I know anything about you.'

Maggie shrugged. 'There's nothing to know.'

'Everybody's got a story to tell.'

'Well, I haven't, all right?'

Luca's eyes moved to her hand. 'You married?'

She frowned. 'No, but I will be soon.' She longed to get out of the car, but right now she didn't trust her legs to carry her.

Luca took in this information. 'But you don't wear an engagement ring?'

Irritated, Maggie balled her hands into fists. 'You ask a lot of questions, but my life is no business of yours.'

Luca shrugged. 'I just want to know a bit more about you . . . So tell me, why were you in Camden that day when we first met?'

'Why were you?' Maggie snapped back.

Luca laughed. 'Fair enough. I was there with my father to see someone I was doing business with. Now your turn.' He winked at her.

'I was there . . .' Maggie stopped and shrugged, choosing to tell him only part of the story. 'I was there to see my fiancé.'

He turned his head to the side to look at her. 'And does your fiancé often batter you about?'

'No, no, that wasn't Rory. He wouldn't raise a hand to me.'

Luca raised his eyebrows. 'Rory . . . That wouldn't be Rory Sheehan, by any chance, would it?'

203

She turned a shade paler as panic hit her. It didn't bear thinking about what would happen if it got back to Rory that she'd been seen sitting in a Jaguar with Luca Romano. 'Look, I shouldn't be speaking to you.' She reached for the door. 'I need to go.'

'Maggie, calm down.' Luca's voice was firm but gentle. 'I won't say anything, if that's what you're worried about. Rory and I aren't exactly what you would call friends . . . Look, let me take you home. You don't look well enough to walk.'

'I told you I'm fine . . . Well, I will be in a minute.'

'You want another handkerchief?' He laughed, and Maggie couldn't help but smile, then they fell into silence and Luca wound down his window, blowing out his smoke before turning to her again.

He reached out and touched her forehead and she pulled back slightly. 'You aren't burning up . . . Maybe you'll live.' Studying her face, he grinned.

Their eyes met and Luca leaned across to her again, though this time, Maggie didn't back away. She let him kiss her, his hand cupping her face, his thumb brushing her cheek.

Then reality crashed in.

What the hell was she doing?

She broke away. She glared at him. 'Don't you ever fucking do that again!' Then she pushed his jacket back at him and fumbled for the door handle.

'Wait, Maggie . . . It's okay!' He reached for her, but Maggie was already out of the car. Even though she still felt unwell, she hurried away down the street, hoping no one had seen.

But someone had seen.

Chapter Forty-Six

Maggie stood in her plush bedroom, looking at herself in the mirror. The white satin and lace of the wedding dress felt like a heavy weight on her. It was suffocating and it pooled around her feet. Of course, like everything else, it had been Rory's choice. He'd just brought it home, laid it on her bed, and that was that. No conversation, nothing.

She sighed.

If she was honest, she didn't care. Getting married to Rory was hardly about love, was it? It was about convenience, it was about her baby having a father, and that was it. Nothing about the wedding was what she would've chosen. Not the flowers, not the guests, not the food and not the groom. All she had to do was show up.

In just over an hour she'd be walking into the church to sign away the last of her freedom. She would emerge as Mrs Sheehan, and Maggie Riley would disappear forever.

There was a soft knock on the bedroom door, and Maggie took a breath, trying to calm her nerves before answering.

'Who is it?'

There was a pause.

'It's me.'

Thomas's voice sent a ripple of tightness through her chest.

'I . . . I . . . I don't think you should be here, Thomas.'
Another pause.

'I had to see you . . . Mr Sheehan's gone to the church with Malcolm, so we're safe . . . Let me come in.'

Maggie's heart raced. She knew that she should send him away, because what was the point in speaking? But then she caught a glimpse of herself in the mirror. What difference would it make now? What harm could it do?

She breathed out slowly and called, 'Come in.'

The door opened and Thomas stood in the doorway dressed in a fitted navy suit, red tie and a crisp white shirt setting off his dark skin. Maggie caught her breath. 'You look good, Thomas.' She tried to smile, but there was a lump in her throat.

Thomas glanced down at his suit. 'Mr Sheehan bought everyone's wedding outfits.'

Maggie nodded. That didn't surprise her, but she said nothing.

'You look beautiful, Maggie.'

'Don't say that. I look ridiculous in this dress. It's like I'm wearing a sheet.'

Thomas stepped inside the room, closing the door with a soft click, and for a moment Maggie felt like they were shutting out the world.

He moved towards her, the floorboards creaking beneath his weight. 'Maggie, look at me.'

She looked at him, then the enormity of what she was about to do crashed in on her.

'Oh God, I don't know if I can do this.' She gulped down air. 'Oh fuck.' What was wrong with her? She had her plan, and she was determined to stick to it, so why was she feeling like this? Maybe it was just pre-wedding nerves. She remembered when

Pam's cousin was getting wed. It took half an hour to find her after she'd run off, too scared to walk up the aisle.

'This morning I woke up thinking, *I can do this*, but standing here in this dress, I don't know if I can. It's like I'm giving myself a prison sentence.' She swallowed hard, and gave him a small smile. 'I always hoped this might be you and me one day.' She wiped her face with the sleeve of her wedding dress. There was no place for tears. She'd promised herself she wouldn't cry, not any more. Pulling herself together, she spoke with a steadier tone. 'Ignore me, Thomas. I've just got a bit of bride jitters, that's all.'

'Maggie, I came here to say I'm sorry. I shouldn't have listened to Sheehan. I should've—'

'What do you mean?' Maggie slumped on the bed, crumpling the ugly, long white wedding train underneath her.

'He told me not to tell you. He told me . . .' He shrugged, and Maggie knew exactly what that shrug meant. She knew what Rory was like. 'He told me I had to persuade you to choose him. Because if you didn't he'd make sure that something happened to me . . . and to *you*. He would've hurt both of us.'

She squeezed his hands. 'Thomas, it's fine . . . It wasn't your fault.'

His eyes were deep and wounded. 'You don't have to marry him, not if you don't want to.'

'But I do, for lots of reasons. Besides, where am I supposed to go if I don't? Men like Rory don't let go of things that they think belong to them. Not now. Not ever. He'll come looking for me. He'll always come looking for me. This is my life now and I have to accept it. Bloody hell, it could be worse. I could be still stuck with my da.'

They held each other's stare, then Thomas's hand found her

face and before she could stop herself she pressed her mouth on his. He kissed her back hard then his arms wrapped around her waist, pulling her into him.

'You have to go,' she whispered, pushing him away.

Outside, the church bells began to ring, suddenly sounding less like wedding bells and more like a funeral knell.

Chapter Forty-Seven

Luca stepped through the front door of his father's house. The marble-tiled hallway stretched out empty before him. He was tired and had wanted to go and relieve his stress in one of the massage parlours off Tottenham Court Road. He was in need of some proper relaxation; being around Sofia was hardly what he'd call relaxing. He also needed Nico to collect more of his pills, but his father had insisted on this meeting.

All his fucking life, he'd jumped when his father said jump. He'd done everything the old man had asked him. He'd been a loyal son, a son who followed Italian traditions even though he felt more cockney than Italian. But tradition was important to his father, so Luca had gone along with his wishes.

But the old man's days were numbered. Soon he wouldn't have to put up with anyone who humiliated him, who wouldn't listen to reason. His demise couldn't come quickly enough.

'Luca!'

He heard his father calling from the front room. He plastered a wide smile on his face and opened the door only to be greeted by Sofia, who was sitting in his father's leather chair, legs crossed and a cigarette burning between her fingers.

'Surprise, Luca.'

He frowned.

That was when he saw his father, moving to stand by her side, his face impassive.

'What's this?' Luca kept his voice steady. 'What's going on?'

Sofia blew smoke toward the ceiling, but she didn't answer him.

Vince nodded to his son. 'Sofia has been filling me in on your plans.'

Luca's mind raced. He glanced at his fiancée then back at his father. 'I don't understand.'

'You will.' His father looked over Luca's shoulder as Nestor and Marco walked in. The first blow came from behind, Nestor's fist connecting like a hammer with Luca's kidney. He staggered, nearly falling, but he kept his balance.

Sofia sat passively watching on while Vince spat out his orders.

'Hold him,' the old man commanded.

Nestor and Marco stood on either side of Luca, their arms locked round his, as Vince walked up to him.

He stared at Luca, then raised his hand and slapped his face. 'When will you learn? Haven't I taught you anything? Haven't I for years taught you the meaning of being a son?'

Sofia stood up, glaring at Luca, then she walked over to him and crushed her cigarette out on his neck. 'Fuck you, Luca.'

Even through the morphine it was agony. Luca winced and gritted his teeth, trying to work out what the hell was going on. This wasn't part of their plan, or at least they certainly hadn't discussed it.

'I thought he needed to know.' Sofia stepped in closer. 'I thought your father needed to know that you were taking me for a fool.'

It was then that cold panic took hold of him. 'What are you talking about, Sofia?'

But she nodded at his father, leaving it to him to explain.

'Sofia has told me everything . . .' He poked Luca hard in the chest and brought down his voice in the familiar threatening tone that Luca had heard used on others over the years. 'She thought it was important that I knew you thought you could take over this family.'

'How fucking thoughtful of her,' he snarled, struggling against Nestor and Marco's grip. He laughed bitterly, shaking his head. 'To think I trusted you.' He spat at her.

The spit slid slowly down her cheek and she wiped it away, a look of disgust on her face. 'No, Luca, to think I trusted *you*.'

With the sting of the burn still on his neck, Luca frowned.

It was Sofia who laughed now. 'I saw you, Luca, kissing that whore.'

He had no idea what she was talking about.

'In the car. I saw you kiss her.'

Luca heard the burn of jealousy in Sofia's voice, and suddenly he remembered Maggie. He glared at Sofia, growling angrily at her, once again pulling against the hold of Marco and Nestor. 'For a kiss, for a fucking kiss, Sofia? You fucking betrayed me for nothing more than a meaningless kiss?'

The anger flashed in Sofia's eyes. 'No, Luca. You betrayed me.'

'What man doesn't have a whore as well as a wife? Ask my father!' Luca glared at his dad, then back at Sofia.

'I know how it works, Luca. I know what I have to accept in a marriage. But no one looks like that at a whore. I saw you. I was watching.'

As she stepped back, Vince stepped forward. He leaned into Luca. '*Ti amo.*' Then he nodded to Nestor and Marco, took Sofia's arm and walked out of the room without a backward glance.

The moment he'd gone, Nestor brought out a knife and

plunged it into Luca's side. White-hot pain shot through Luca and his knees gave way, but not before he threw his head back, connecting with Nestor's nose, and taking him by surprise. The crunch of cartilage was loud, and he felt Nestor loosen his grip, and despite his pain Luca managed to catch Marco's wrist, while grabbing and twisting his crotch.

Marco doubled up and Luca, knowing that they intended to kill him, ignored the gaping wound in his side, and slammed Marco against the wall, elbowing him hard in the face, causing him to crash into the table.

The blood was pouring from Luca's wound, but he snatched Nestor's knife off the floor and slashed wildly at him, slicing his ear off. Nestor yelled and Luca, feeling weaker with each passing moment, staggered over to the door, locking it and tossing the key into the fire.

Seeing Marco begin to get up, Luca charged forward and drove the knife into Nestor's neck. Blood spurted like a fountain, splattering across the room, then Luca's gaze landed on the window. It was his only chance.

Holding his side, he staggered towards it, driving his shoulder through the glass. The shards tore at his skin as he crashed through, smashing onto the ground outside.

The impact drove the air from his lungs, and twisted his ankle beneath him. Pain engulfed him, but he knew he had to get up, and fast.

Limping across the garden, he heard the front door open.

Gritting his teeth, he ran for the road, using the wall to keep his balance. He ran blindly, each step agony. Behind him he thought he heard a gunshot.

At that moment he saw a taxi coming down the road. Desperate and weak from loss of blood, he waved it down.

The taxi slowed and Luca opened the door, forcing his battered body inside. 'Get me to a hospital.'

As the taxi drove through the streets, Luca Romano could only hope this wasn't the end.

And, with that thought, he blacked out . . .

Chapter Forty-Eight

Maggie leaned on the church wall, having just thrown up. The cold from the stones cut through her dress and she shivered, trying to take deep breaths through the dizziness.

'Mary Mother of God, pull yourself together. Look at the state of you. No one would think this was your wedding day.'

Maggie jumped at the sound of her mother's voice.

'What the hell are you doing here?'

Kathleen looked her up and down with her usual sneer. 'Do you think we wouldn't have been invited to our own daughter's wedding?'

Maggie began to shake. She hissed through her teeth. 'Well, you should never have come.'

Her mother stepped closer, lowering her voice. 'Don't get lippy with me, Maggie. We both know what you are, what you've always been. You're lucky I'm here. How would it seem to everyone if the mother of the bride didn't turn up? What would people say?'

'I don't fucking care what anyone says.'

Her mother went to slap Maggie, but Maggie caught her wrist. 'I told you already, you will never put your hands on me again.'

'Maggie.' Behind her, another familiar voice.

This time it was Chrissy.

Maggie stared at her, noticing with growing horror what she was dressed in.

Chrissy laughed. 'Mr Sheehan thought it would be a nice surprise for you to have a bridesmaid, so here I am.' She spun round in her long peach satin bridesmaid gown.

'I want you gone, both of you. I don't want you here at my wedding.' She glared at them both, the corset biting into her ribs.

'It's not down to you, Maggie.' Chrissy smirked. 'I don't take my orders from you.'

Her mother tutted. 'And neither do I, Maggie.'

Maggie shook her head, backing away, wondering why Rory had done this to her. Was this some sort of game to him? 'I said, I want you gone.' It was barely a whisper, but the anger Maggie felt was clear to hear.

But her mother just turned and walked into the church, leaving Maggie standing with Chrissy.

'Rory bought me this dress,' Chrissy purred. 'What do you think, Maggie? He's very good to me.' She licked her lips suggestively. 'He was especially good to me last night.'

The church doors opened before Maggie could react, and the organ music washed over her as she felt Chrissy's hand pushing her forward.

And with no other option Maggie put one foot in front of the other and slowly made her way up the aisle. The church was packed. Faces turned to stare and Maggie's eyes moved over the congregation. Most of them she didn't know, and at first she didn't recognise her own father, who was booted and suited for the occasion.

Then she saw Thomas.

There in the third row. Her beautiful Thomas, but Maggie daren't meet his eye.

She looked up, her dress weighing heavily, scratching at her skin. She saw Rory waiting at the altar, wearing a black tuxedo with Malcolm standing next to him, dressed the same.

Father Patrick nodded at Maggie, but his eyes were cold as she reached the altar.

'You look beautiful, Maggie,' Rory whispered, his breath heavy with the scent of cigars and whisky.

Unable to trust herself not to scream, she faced forward. She could feel the sweat running down her back and it was hard to stop her legs shaking.

'Dearly beloved,' Father Patrick began, his voice echoing through the stone church. 'We are gathered here today . . .'

His voice faded into the background and Maggie swayed slightly as the service continued around her in a blur.

'Margaret Mary Riley,' Father Patrick droned, 'do you take Rory James Sheehan to be your lawfully wedded husband, for better or for worse, in sickness and in health.'

Rory leaned forward, whispering in Maggie's ear. 'Till death do us part . . .'

Book Three

Seven Months Later

If you want to keep a secret, you must also hide it from yourself.

George Orwell

Chapter Forty-Nine

'Make way for the pregnant lady.' Rory grinned at Maggie as he helped her down the stairs of the club. It was heaving with punters and smoke hung thick in the air. Maggie moved uncomfortably, her swollen belly huge.

She slumped in one of the velvet couches, grateful to get off her feet. Not that she wanted to be here: she didn't. Maggie couldn't remember the last time she'd had a decent sleep. The baby in her stomach liked to kick at night, keeping her awake, and forcing her to lie staring at the ceiling night after night next to Rory, who felt like a stranger in her bed.

The summer heat was making everything worse. It wasn't just her belly that felt swollen, every part of Maggie did. She felt huge and she longed to have a cool bath and go to bed, but Rory always insisted that she stayed with him until the club closed, which was often not until the early hours of the morning.

Trying to get comfy, Maggie moved back in her seat as her belly pressed against the edge of the table. She grabbed the cocktail menu, fanning herself with it, desperate to cool herself down. She tried not to think how many hours she had left until she could go home. Yesterday, she hadn't got into her bed until well past three in the morning, then had got up only a few hours later to sit with Rory as he tucked into a breakfast she didn't eat.

As the girls danced topless to the Ronettes, and the punters sat smoking and watching them, Maggie glanced across to where Rory was holding court at his usual table. He caught Maggie's eye, and raised his glass to her, winking.

She smiled, but looked away quickly. Since she'd told Rory she was pregnant shortly after their wedding, he'd treated her like she was going to break. At first, he'd looked surprised, then he'd grinned, and within seconds of him digesting the news he'd cracked open the best champagne and the bottle of single malt whisky he'd been saving for a special occasion.

The cigars had come out and the celebrations had begun. Surrounded by people drinking her health, it struck Maggie that she had never felt so alone. As on the day of their wedding, Rory had taken control. He'd already decided on the names: if it was a girl, Rose Mabel Sheehan, after his mother. Maggie had been a kid when the poisonous old cow died, but she remembered her giving clips round the ear to the kids and acting like she was better than everyone else, bossing the adults about and passing judgement on them. Then if it were a boy, Rory James Sheehan, named of course after him. It didn't matter whether Maggie liked the names or not; she was never consulted.

It turned her stomach to see Chrissy serving drinks at the bar. When Rory had announced that his new bride was pregnant, Chrissy's face had been covered in a knowing smirk. Maggie had thought the weekly payments would stop at that point. But when the time came to tell Chrissy that she wasn't getting any more money out of her she'd been too exhausted to put up any sort of fight, especially as she now knew that Chrissy was fucking Rory.

So far as Maggie was concerned, they deserved each other. But she could have done without constant worries about the fallout if she were to stop the bitch's money, and the fear of Malcolm finding out she was fiddling Rory's books to pay her off. The only good thing about it was that she was using her brain, as Doris had told her, gathering information about Rory's business deals and associates.

The baby kicked hard against Maggie's ribs, making her wince. He or she had been restless all day, turning and stretching out their limbs. Maggie rubbed her side, hoping that somehow it might comfort her baby.

'How are you, Maggie?'

Thomas was standing by her side, a glass of orange juice in hand. He placed it down, glancing nervously at Rory before speaking to Maggie. 'Can I get you anything else?'

Maggie shook her head. She hadn't seen much of Thomas for the past couple of weeks. The truth was, since she'd got married, she had tried to avoid him, and she'd certainly avoided having any sort of conversation with him. It was easier to focus on her pregnancy and not think about what might have been.

'I'm fine, thank you.' Instinctively she glanced in Rory's direction and saw him staring at her.

'Maybe you should get one of the girls to ask me if I want a drink next time. I don't think Rory likes you talking to me.'

Thomas glanced over his shoulder again, and saw that Rory was busy talking to Malcolm. 'You should be at home, resting. It's not good for you to be sitting here until the small hours.'

'Are you gonna tell that to Rory, or shall I?' Maggie laughed humourlessly.

'I'll check on you in a bit, all right?' He walked away without giving Maggie a chance to answer.

As he went, Maggie sipped her juice, but then out of nowhere a wave of pain wrapped itself around her middle like a steel clamp. She dropped her glass, and sucked in a breath as another agonising wave rushed round from her back to her belly. She closed her eyes, willing it to pass, her whole body gripped in pain.

When she able to open them, Rory was standing over her, a cigarette dangling from his mouth. 'What's wrong?'

She forced a smile as the pain began to ebb away. 'Nothing's wrong. I'm tired, that's all.' She tried to keep her voice light.

Rory's eyes narrowed. 'And that's why you dropped a fucking glass, is it? Because you're tired?'

'Yeah, I must have been nodding off, and it slipped out of my hand . . . I'm sorry.'

Rory bent down and kissed the top of her head. 'What are we going to do with you, hey? I'll get Davey to sweep up the mess.' He studied her again. 'Malcolm's out the back. I can get him to drive you home if you want.'

'I'd rather wait here for you, Rory.'

He smiled at her. She'd given the correct answer. No other response would have been acceptable in his eyes.

'I've got some business to finish, so I'll see you later.'

Maggie nodded and slid out of her chair to go to the toilet, but she froze as she felt a flood between her legs. At first she thought she'd peed herself, then she realised.

'*Rory*.' She had to shout above the music until he turned around, looking annoyed at her for delaying him. 'Rory, my waters have broken.'

'What?'

'My waters. They've broken.'

He scowled at her and walked back. 'It's too early.'

Maggie had been prepared for this moment. Doris had told her exactly what to say.

'Tell that to the baby . . . The midwife said babies arrive whenever it suits them.'

Another contraction gripped her, much stronger than before, and she grabbed Rory's arm, breathing out and bending forward as her fingers dug into him. The music around her seemed to fade as faces turned towards them. She was vaguely aware of Thomas pushing through the crowd.

'Get Malcolm!' Rory barked at him. '*Now*. Tell him to meet me out front with the car.'

Thomas did as he was told, while Rory scooped Maggie up as if she weighed nothing. As the crowd parted to make way for them, Maggie clung to his neck until finally they made it out into the street, where Malcolm was already waiting by the car, his face expressionless.

'Let's get her to hospital,' Rory said, placing her on the back seat.

The contractions began to come faster as the car pulled away, speeding through the streets of Soho, then up Tottenham Court Road to University College Hospital.

Malcolm pulled up outside the entrance and swivelled round to face Rory. 'You want me to come in?'

'No, wait here,' Rory snapped, getting out of the car. He helped Maggie out and picked her up, carrying her through to reception.

'*Oi*, she needs help, now!' he bellowed at the elderly nurse manning the desk.

He placed Maggie in one of the wheelchairs lined up by the wall.

'We'll take her from here, sir.' Clearly shocked by Rory's manner, she looked at him disapprovingly. 'If you'd like to wait here—'

'I'm fucking coming with her!'

Taken aback, the nurse frowned. 'That's not hospital policy, sir. Fathers wait in recep—'

'Do I look like I give a fuck about your policies, darlin'?' Rory stepped closer to the nurse. 'That's my wife, and I'll not be told by anyone where I can and can't go. I want to make sure she gets to the right place, and gets seen.'

The nurse paled and another contraction seized Maggie. She let out a cry.

'Follow me.' With the nurse reluctantly leading the way, Rory pushed the wheelchair through the double doors and into the lift.

When they reached the third-floor maternity unit, he finally stepped back and let the nurse take over.

'Maggie.' He fixed that intense gaze on her. 'Don't you worry. I'll be right here . . .'

But, far from providing comfort, Rory's words heightened the rising fear inside her.

Chapter Fifty

'That's it, Maggie. That's it, sweetheart. Just a few more pushes. You're doing so well.' The midwife's voice faded in and out as pain flooded through Maggie. She gripped the metal bed rails, her face and hair plastered with sweat as it to stuck to her forehead as another contraction tore through her.

It was as if all her energy had been drained away. 'I can't,' Maggie gasped. 'I can't.'

'You can, and you have to, unless you want it to stay there forever.' The nurse, a middle-aged woman with deep frown lines and warm brown eyes, smiled. 'Come on, Maggie. The baby's head is crowning. One good push now, and then you can meet him or her.'

She pushed again, and a loud, deep scream ripped from her. The pressure and sting between her legs felt unbearable, then it gave way in a rush.

'That's it! That's it. Well done, Maggie.'

She collapsed back against the thin pillow, her chest heaving.

'You've got a daughter.' The nurse took her baby to the other side of the room. 'Let me just clean her up.'

Overwhelmed by happiness, Maggie tried to get a look at her baby.

She felt as if she'd been caught up in a nightmare, and now it was finally over. She could stop worrying and concentrate on herself and the baby, and making the most of life with Rory.

'Have you got a name for her yet?' the nurse asked.

Maggie thought of Rory's chosen names and nodded. 'Yes. Rose. She's going to be called Rose.'

She strained her neck to see what was going on across the room, where the two nurses were standing with their backs to her.

'Why isn't she crying? What's wrong with her?' Panic set in. 'Let me see her.' Maggie tried to sit up. 'Please.'

One of the nurses glanced over her shoulder. 'Give us a minute, love. Sometimes it takes a bit for them to get going.'

The silence stretched out, then finally a thin wail cut through the room.

Maggie closed her eyes and relief washed over her.

'We need to get her warm, and I think she needs a bit of oxygen to help her. Nothing to worry about, though.'

Maggie heard the concern in the nurse's voice as they rushed Baby Rose out of the room. 'No wait! I want to see her . . .' she shouted after them. 'I said, wait! Just bleedin' wait!'

The younger nurse, a tall, slender woman with sharp features and thin brown hair, came and laid a hand on her arm. 'Let's get you cleaned up while they take care of Rose, shall we?'

Maggie nodded and the next twenty minutes passed in a blur as they helped her get washed and into a fresh nightgown.

'When can I see her?' Her voice trembled as they wheeled her into a single room which reeked of disinfectant.

'Soon.' The nurse fluffed her pillows behind her back. 'I'll come back and check on you in a short while.'

She walked out, leaving Maggie alone.

The door opened.

Rory stood there and Maggie noticed the dark circles under his eyes and wondered if he'd waited all night.

'Well?' He walked into the room. 'Boy or girl?'

'Girl.' Maggie's voice cracked. 'You've got a daughter.' Desperately she tried to smile. 'Rose . . . They said she needed some oxygen.'

Rory sat on the edge of the bed and took her hand. 'Are you all right?'

'I'm tired, that's all.'

He lit a cigarette and smiled, the smoke weaving past his eyes. 'I better go. Now I know you're still alive, I can get back to the club.' He winked.

'Don't you want to meet your daughter?' Maggie asked. 'They said they wouldn't be long with her.'

He laughed and let go of her hand. 'That's the thing, Maggie.' He reached out and stroked her hair with surprising tenderness.

'What?'

He leaned forward, pressing his lips onto her mouth. Then his hand closed in her hair, tight enough to make her gasp.

'I can't have children, Maggie.' His voice dropped to a whisper, and he moved his lips against her ear. 'The doctor told me years ago.'

At that moment, the world stopped.

'What?' Her mouth went dry.

Rory's fingers pulled her head back and he pressed his face into hers. 'You heard me.' His voice was calm and controlled.

All these months, all this time, he'd known the child wasn't his. She began to shake as he let go of her hair, throwing his cigarette down onto the floor and grinding it out with his foot. Then his hands grabbed her milk-filled breasts and squeezed them hard.

227

She squealed.

'So here's what's going to happen now, Maggie.' His grip on her breasts tightened, and she could see he was getting aroused. 'You're going to tell me who the father is and I'm going to kill him . . . And if you don't tell me I'll find him anyway, then I'll kill the both of you.' He grinned. 'You see, I love you, Maggie. But I won't share you with anyone.' He kissed her hard, pushing her back on the pillow. Then he suddenly stood up and straightened his tie.

'And the baby?' Maggie thought about her father, she thought about all the trouble she'd gone through to hide his dirty secret. 'What about, Rose?'

'What do you take me for, Maggie?' He smiled coldly. 'I wouldn't hurt my daughter. We're a family now. That's never going to change. Ever.' He walked to the door and paused. 'You're mine, Maggie, and I want the world to know that I've got two girls who are mine now.'

Chapter Fifty-One

'I hear you're going to call her Rose.' Her mother sniffed, looking in disdain at Maggie as she carried the baby into the hospital room.

Seeing her mother holding her daughter before she'd even held Rose herself, enraged Maggie. 'Give her to me!' Trembling, she raised her voice, stretching out her arms.

Her mother laughed and shook her head. 'Oh, Maggie, by the time Rory's finished with you, you'll wish your da had fathered this child.'

'What are you talking about?' Maggie edged towards her mother.

The laugh that left her mother was even louder and nastier than before. 'You don't get it, do you? You stupid little whore.' She pushed Rose into Maggie's arms.

Maggie stared at her daughter.

She was beautiful.

Soft black curls, light brown skin and green eyes.

Rose was the image of Thomas.

It felt like the room was spinning. Why hadn't she ever considered the possibility that Thomas could be Rose's father? But, given the number of times her da had forced himself on her, it hadn't even occurred to her that it could be Thomas.

And then her blood turned to ice as she realised that Rory, too, would clock instantly who the father was.

She held Rose against her, rocking her, but it was just as much for her own comfort as Rose's.

Her mother stood by the door. 'I heard the rumours of you hanging round with that black boy . . . and now I know it was true.'

'Mum, what am I going to do?' Maggie cried.

'Pray, Maggie, because with a bairn who looks like that, you're going to need a miracle to survive.'

Chapter Fifty-Two

The bus to the East End bumped over the potholes on Whitechapel Road, each jolt sending pain through her body. Rose slept against her chest, wrapped in thin blankets, her tiny face pressed into Maggie's coat.

Maggie sighed, watching her daughter sleep, oblivious to the danger she'd been born into. The tin of formula milk and a couple of bottles she'd stolen from the hospital rattled in her pocket. She wanted to make sure she had something to feed Rose if her own milk didn't come through properly. She also wanted to make sure that Rose would accept a bottle, especially now she knew there was no way she could go back to Camden or Soho. She'd have to survive on her own, providing for them both, which meant getting a job, and finding someone to mind Rose even though she was still so tiny.

'Last stop, miss.' The conductor's voice startled Maggie and she looked around and realised they were the last passengers on the bus.

'Thank you.' She got up from her seat and caught the conductor eyeing Rose. 'Have you got a problem, mate?' she snarled.

He didn't say anything, but he didn't have to. It was obvious in the way he looked at Rose, and this was just the start of it. She'd seen the way people looked at Thomas, heard the stories of how people had treated his family. Well, that wasn't going to happen to Rose. It was down to her to protect her daughter as best as she could.

She kissed the top of Rose's head. 'I promise, Rose, I won't let anyone hurt you. I swear.'

With renewed determination, Maggie stepped off the bus.

The warm air hit her and Rose stirred slightly, whimpering. She had such a tiny cry, and Maggie wondered if she'd done the right thing taking her baby and running out of the hospital. But what other choice did she have? Rory had said he was coming back to see her, which meant he'd see Rose. And the moment he did, he'd know that Rose was Thomas's daughter. Within hours, Thomas Johnson would be dead.

Rose gave out another small cry. 'It's all right, sweetheart, we're gonna be all right.' But how could they be? Maggie had hardly any money to her name, only what little she'd had in her pocket when she'd been in Rory's club. A thin blanket for Rose, a tin of milk and a couple of bottles, and that was it. They were all the possessions she owned in the world.

Knowing that this was the time she needed to be stronger than ever, Maggie looked around her. The street stretched out before her, terrace houses packed tight, washing lines strung across the narrow alleyways with dogs roaming and a few kids riding on their bikes.

Maggie walked along, her arms wrapped protectively around her daughter. After a few moments, she walked up to the now familiar house, knocking on the peeling paint door.

It opened and Doris stood there.

'Jesus Christ, look at the state of you.' A cigarette dangled from her lips. Her thin grey hair was set in rollers. 'Come on in, love. Come in.' She hurried Maggie into her house and through to the tiny front room where Maggie slumped on the chair.

'I see you've had the baby, then.' Doris nodded at the bundle in Maggie's arms. 'When?'

'Early hours of this morning. Her name's Rose.'

Doris raised her pencilled in eyebrows. 'And you're running around already?'

'Rory knows she's not his.' Maggie's voice broke. 'He told me he can't have children. He knew all along that the baby wasn't his. It must have been some sort of game for him.'

This information had Doris leaning back into her chair. She shook her head and took a deep drag of a cigarette. 'Fucking shady bastard.'

'He wants me to tell him who the father is so that he can kill him. That's why I had to leave the hospital. Once he sees Rose, he won't need me to tell him who her father is.'

'So does that mean it's not your dad's?' Doris must have seen the look on Maggie's face. 'We all know what your old man was like. But if it's not his, whose is it?'

Maggie pulled back the blanket to reveal Rose's perfect face. Doris's eyes narrowed.

'Well, fuck me.' She glanced at Maggie. 'You kept that one quiet!' Doris cackled. 'I would have liked to have seen your mum's face when she saw Rose. God knows how many Hail Marys she'll have to say to get over that shock.' She burst into laughter again, and even though Maggie was feeling terrible she couldn't help but join in.

'So, Rory doesn't know?'

'No, and he can't find out.' Maggie took a deep breath. 'The minute he sees her, he'll know who the father is – Thomas works for Rory. And I can't let anything happen to him . . . I love him, Doris. I always have.'

Doris nodded, understanding. 'And Rory would skin him alive . . . What you gonna do, then?'

'I was wondering if I could stay here with you for a while? I'll earn my keep. I can do the housework and cook, I'll get myself a job, and when I do I'll pay you rent . . . *Please*, Doris, I need your help.'

Doris shook her head. 'I would love you to stay, I really would. I could do with some company, especially now I'm getting on a bit. But I wouldn't be doing you any favours if I let you stay.'

Maggie tried to speak, but Doris held up her hand.

'No, hear me out, love,' Doris continued. 'If you stayed here, it would only be a matter of time before Rory finds you. He'll turn up every fucking stone in London looking for you, and we both know that, don't we?' Doris lowered her voice. 'That doesn't mean I won't help you, though. I'll be here for you when you need me, but, if you want to keep that little one of yours safe, then you can't stay here.'

Though she realised what Doris was saying was true, that didn't make it any easier.

'Come on, why don't I make you a nice cup of tea and we can talk about what we're going to do with you.' A loud creak sounded as Doris pushed herself up from her chair. 'Bleedin' hell, I don't know which one will break first, this chair or my frigging bones.'

Doris disappeared into the kitchen, returning minutes later with two steaming mugs of tea. 'I put an extra spoon of sugar in for you. I thought you'd need it after what you've been through today.' She smiled and placed one cup next to Maggie then settled back down in her chair, kicking off her stained green slippers.

'You'll need to be careful. With a baby like that, you'll have people talking,' Doris said, slurping her tea. 'Girl as white as you with a baby who looks like that, questions will be asked, darlin'. Mark my words.'

'They can ask all they like,' Maggie said firmly.

'Easy for you to say, love, but people like to judge, even though they've got enough skeletons in their own wardrobes to fill a graveyard.'

'We'll be fine.' Maggie leaned to the side and took a sip of her tea, careful not to spill any on Rose. She pulled a face at how sweet it was, but it was probably just what she needed.

Doris smiled at her almost proudly. 'I'm sure you will, Maggie . . . Look, it's not gonna be easy, but you're not the first woman to fall for a black fella and have their kid, and you certainly won't be the last.'

Maggie yawned, her eyes getting heavy.

'I tell you what, why don't you finish your tea and get a couple of hours' kip? I'm sure you could do with it. You can use my spare room, and I'll see what clothes I have around here for you. I'm sure I've got a few baby bits and pieces as well, from when I used to sell stuff down Brick Lane.'

'Thank you, Doris.' Maggie's stomach tightened. 'I just wish things were different.'

Doris lit a fresh cigarette. 'Well, no use crying about it. You're a mother now, and believe you me you'll shed more tears for Rose over the years, so best save them.'

Maggie winced at the burn between her legs.

'You'll soon heal up,' Doris said matter-of-factly. 'It's all part of being a woman. Men don't know the half of it.'

When Rose stirred in her arms, Maggie kissed her on the head. In that moment, she knew she'd give her life for her daughter. She only hoped that she wouldn't have to give it any time soon . . .

Chapter Fifty-Three

The boarding house in Stepney Green was worse than Maggie could have imagined. It had certainly seen better days. The paint peeled off the window frames and the steps leading to the cracked front door were broken and uneven. Maggie shifted Rose to one arm and placed her suitcase, full of the things that Doris had kindly given her, on the step.

It was a long minute before the door cracked open. A woman with a hard stare, a sharp nose and a scar across her cheek opened it. 'It's a bit late for callers. What do you want?' the woman snapped.

'I need a room,' Maggie said simply.

The woman's eyes settled on Rose. 'No babies – they cry, and the last thing I need is a screaming baby.' She started to close the door, but Maggie jammed her foot in it.

'She doesn't cry – she's good as gold – and, anyway, Doris sent me.'

At the mention of Doris's name, the woman opened the door wider. 'How do you know Doris?' She licked her lips, which were stained with pink lipstick bleeding into the wrinkles around her mouth.

'We're friends,' Maggie said truthfully. Doris had been more help than her mother had ever been, and she'd always be grateful to her.

'Did she tell you how much it was?'

Maggie nodded. 'She did, and I know that I've got to pay two weeks up front.' It was Doris who had lent her the money, and Maggie had every intention of paying it back with an extra bit on top to show her thanks.

The woman held out her hand, and Maggie reached into her pocket and pulled out the envelope with the rent money in it, placing it in the woman's palm. 'It's all there.'

The woman raised her eyebrows. 'It better be. I won't have anyone trying to turn me over, Doris's friend or not.' She shoved it into her apron and gestured with her head. 'You'd best come in, then.'

Maggie stepped inside.

She looked around. The place was filthy: damp wallpaper slid down the walls and black mould festered in the corners, but she supposed it was no worse than the house in which she'd grown up.

'Your room's on the second floor, end of hall. Bathroom is shared and there's no men and no noise after ten at night, you understand? Otherwise, you're out on your ear, and that includes the baby. Breakfast is at seven, any later than that you go hungry. Any other time the kitchens are off limits. And don't touch nothing that ain't yours, you hear me?' Like everything about this woman, her tone was harsh.

'But I'll have to make her bottles,' Maggie said.

The woman shrugged. 'That's not my problem, love. If you don't like it, you can piss off.'

Clearly there was no point arguing with the woman, so she

followed her up the narrow wooden staircase then along the corridor, stepping over a broken floorboard.

'This is yours.' The woman opened the door.

The room, if you could call it that, was tiny. Just enough space for a single bed with a sagging mattress. It had a chipped wash basin in the corner with rusting taps and a broken chair that lay on its side. But it was a roof over their heads, and that was all that mattered right now.

'I'm Mrs Mills, by the way, and I'd appreciate it if you call me as such.' Her expression was cold and she stared at Rose, getting a proper look at her for the first time. 'I didn't see it wasn't white.'

Maggie stared at her. 'Her name's Rose.'

'I don't bleedin' care what it is. Just keep it quiet and out of sight. Some of the girls in here won't take kindly to seeing it, and I don't want anyone being upset by it.'

Maggie fought the urge to slap the woman's face, but she knew that, if she did, they'd be thrown out, and where would that leave her and Rose. She swallowed her anger. 'She's a baby, not an *it*, and I told you already her name's Rose.'

Mrs Mills looked like she was going to say something, but instead she walked around the room as if she'd never been in there before. 'So has . . . *Rose* . . .' She emphasised the name. '. . . got a father?'

'I should think so, wouldn't you? Bit of a miracle if she hasn't.'

'You're a cheeky cow, I'll give you that.' She shook her head. 'No wonder Doris likes you.' She sniffed again and for a moment Maggie thought she was going to smile, but the smile didn't come. 'Anyway, she better not disturb my girls – they work nights and sleep days, most of them. They don't need a screaming baby, especially not one like that.'

Maggie clenched her hand, but she held her tongue . . . and her fist.

'So have you a job?' Mrs Mills asked.

'Not yet, but I'll get one.'

'Well, you better, because this isn't a charity I'm running. I expect the rent every week on the dot. But, mind, if you get stuck for work, there's plenty of work around here for a young girl like you.' She looked at Rose again. 'And, from where I'm standing, you can't be that proud . . . Well, I bid you goodnight, and, like I say, breakfast is in the morning. Seven sharp.'

Mrs Mills departed, leaving behind her a strong smell of cheap perfume.

Maggie opened the suitcase and took out one of the blankets that Doris had given her, and she put it on the bed before she laid Rose on top of it. The mattress was filthy and Maggie could see traces of mould on it.

Rose's eyes fluttered open and Maggie smiled at her, staring into her beautiful green eyes. 'Hello, darling.'

Rose gurgled and Maggie once again felt a surge of love and protectiveness, something she'd never felt before.

There was a tap at the door, which made Maggie jump. The door opened without her inviting whoever it was in, and a young woman with bleached hair and a bad case of acne appeared. Maggie noticed her black eye straight away.

'I thought I heard someone new arrive.' Her eyes glanced round the room. 'Shithole, innit? This room is worse than mine, and I thought mine was bad. I'm Bernie, by the way.'

Maggie smiled, pleased to see such a friendly face. Bernie tottered up to look at Rose, who was lying with her eyes open on the bed. 'She yours?'

'Yeah. Problem?' Maggie said defensively.

Bernie grinned, shaking her head. 'No, she's beautiful. You're lucky. I was pregnant last year, but my old man, he kicked it out of me. Lost me womb because of it.' She shrugged as if it was an everyday occurrence. 'I got fed up with him battering me around, so I'm here. Most of the girls are here because of fellas. I'm sure you're the same, ain't you?'

Maggie didn't want to talk about anything, and thankfully Bernie seemed to pick up on that.

'Look, you don't have to tell me if you don't want to. If you need anything, I'm just down the hall, I've got a kettle and some extra tea if you want it. Mrs Mills doesn't let us into the kitchen apart from at breakfast, but all of us sneak in there. I'll show you the ropes tomorrow when you're settled in . . . You'll be fine, Maggie.'

'I hope so.'

'Oh, and Mrs Mills, her bark is worse than her bite. She ain't really a miserable cow.' She headed for the door then. 'I'll bring you some tea later . . . And, Maggie, it's nice you're here, and your daughter. We look after one another here, you know, so you'll be fine.'

Bernie left Maggie who stood by the small grimy window that looked out onto an alley. In the distance were the London lights, and Maggie thought of Soho and of Rory, who would be looking for her already, and of course she thought of Thomas who she needed to keep safe, like she wanted to keep Rose safe.

Doris's words rushed into her head: *We don't need men, Maggie. Remember that. All we really need is ourselves and a bit of money in our pocket.*

Maggie had no money, no mum or dad, and no Rory. She just had herself and no matter how difficult things might be from now on, or how dirty the room was, it still felt good. She had herself and she had Rose, and for now that was all Maggie needed.

Chapter Fifty-Four

The sun shone through the window and Maggie woke instantly. She jumped up, not knowing for a moment where she was, and then she remembered . . .

She could hear Rose's soft breathing, and she watched her daughter curled up next to her fast asleep. Rose hadn't woken once in the night; it had been Maggie who'd woken up several times, just to touch her, just to make sure she was still breathing.

Clambering out of the bed, Maggie moved carefully to avoid waking Rose until she needed to. She moved too quickly though and winced, a reminder that she'd only given birth yesterday. She shook her head. Yesterday seemed so long ago.

Feeling an itch, Maggie looked down at her leg and saw several large red bites. It was probably bed bugs. She was used to them from living at home, but she quickly checked Rose over, hoping they hadn't nipped her. The idea of her daughter, who wasn't even two days old yet, being bitten, upset her. When she had enough money, she hoped she could find another place, one that didn't have insects crawling everywhere.

Over the next half hour Maggie got herself ready, then Rose, changing her the best she could given the water in the bathroom wasn't working right now. She dressed her in one of the outfits that Doris had given her.

'Maggie, are you up?' Bernie's voice called from the other side of the door. 'Ready for breakfast?' Bernie's face appeared round the door. 'It's not too bad – some of the girls cooked it. You only have to worry when Mrs Mills does it.' Bernie laughed and looked around, puzzled. 'Haven't you got her a pram?'

'No, but I'll get one when I've got some money.'

'You don't need to, there's one in the shed downstairs. I don't know whose it is, but it's been there since I've been here, and nobody uses it. I can't imagine anybody will mind. It's hardly a chariot, but it's got four wheels . . . just about.' Bernie laughed again and Maggie couldn't help but like her. 'I reckon with a bit of soap and water it'll come up all right, and it'll save you having to carry Rose everywhere you go.'

Maggie smiled. 'That would be really good, thank you.'

Bernie grinned. 'You ain't seen it yet. Fucking hell, you might not be thanking me once you do.'

Maggie laughed as she carried Rose and followed Bernie out of the room, down the stairs to the kitchen.

It was chaos. The room was filled with cigarette smoke and smoke from cooking. There were at least a dozen women sitting around the large table, smoking fags and looking exhausted from their night's work.

'Move your bleedin' self.' A stockily built woman with eyes slightly too close together pushed Maggie as she hesitated in the doorway. 'Some of us have been working all night.'

'Don't speak to Maggie like that.' Bernie frowned.

'What's it got to do with you?' The woman turned on Bernie, who shrank back.

'It hasn't got anything to do with her, but *everything* to do with me,' Maggie snapped, holding the woman's stare.

The woman whistled then looked over her shoulder at another

woman who was cooking some eggs on the stove. 'We've got a right one here.' She turned back to Maggie. 'If it wasn't for the fact that you're holding your baby, I'd knock you through that fucking wall.'

Maggie glared at her. 'If it wasn't for the fact I was holding my baby, I wouldn't be going through that fucking wall – it would be you – so count yourself lucky.'

The woman burst out laughing. 'I like you . . . I'm Sarah, by the way. Welcome to the shithole . . . Make room for another one,' Sarah shouted over to the women, who shuffled up on the long bench they were sitting on. 'How old is she?'

'Just the day.'

Sarah nodded, mulling over this information. 'Running away from your fella?'

Maggie gave a nod. 'Something like that.'

'Well, you've come to the right place.'

Her eyes dropped to Rose's face, which was now visible above the knitted shawl she was wearing. 'Christ, I see now why you're hiding.'

'What's that supposed to mean?'

'Nothing, love. You won't get any judgement from me.'

Maggie moved over to the table and sat down. She glanced back at Sarah. 'Good, because she's my daughter, and if any-body's got a problem they need to say it now.' She looked defiantly around her.

The room fell silent.

No one said anything.

Then a tall redheaded woman placed a plate of egg, tomato and a small slice of bacon in front of Maggie. 'Here you go, love, you have that.'

The unexpected kindness caught Maggie off guard. 'Thank you.'

Sarah sat down opposite her. 'I couldn't care less what she looks like. Me mum had enough boyfriends coming in and out the house from every bloody nation. I thought at one point she was servicing the whole of the Foreign Office.' She laughed, breaking the tension, and all the other women laughed along, continuing with their own conversations and smoking their cigarettes.

Sarah took a sip of her milky tea. 'So what sort of work are you looking for?'

'Any kind of work I can get. I'm not fussed,' Maggie said honestly.

'Well, you could try a couple of the shops across from here, but I don't hold out much luck for you, especially not the bakery – the minute Mrs Jones sees your baby, she'll be shouting blue murder and barricading up the door . . . Oh don't look like that, Maggie. It's just the way it is, and you'll have to get used to it. You can't fight everyone.' Sarah reached across and touched Maggie's hand. 'Though I bet you're gonna try, ain't you?' She winked at her.

Maggie smiled and tucked into her breakfast as Sarah continued to talk. 'There's also the Annabelle's laundrette, just round the corner from Bethnal Green Road. I know they were looking for someone. I think the last girl who was working for her got nicked for shoplifting, so it's worth a try. Annabelle is a right moody cow, but she pays all right and she pays on time.'

'I'll give it a go.'

Sarah took a packet of cigarettes out of from her cleavage. 'But you gotta be careful out there. Not everyone will take kindly to you or your daughter, and if you're trying to lie low it won't do you any good to get into fights. You don't want to be nicked and carted off. So be clever, right.'

This time Maggie didn't say anything, but she heeded the warning.

Chapter Fifty-Five

Maggie pushed the pram along Bethnal Green Road. Bernie had been right – it certainly wasn't a chariot by any means, but they'd taken a good couple of hours to scrub away the dirt and some of the stains, and although it was far from perfect, as Bernie had said, it *just* about had four wheels, and it did the trick.

She smiled at Rose, who was fast asleep again. Her love was growing for her daughter with every passing moment. Even though it was warm, she had wrapped her up in the rest of the blankets that Doris had given her, worried that she'd get cold.

She tried the few shops opposite the boarding house, and, like Sarah had said, Mrs Jones had nearly fainted when she'd seen Rose, but this time Maggie hadn't bothered fighting. She just left the shop and tried the next one.

But now she was on her way to the laundrette.

Bethnal Green teemed with women doing their shopping at the market, and Maggie glanced nervously over her shoulder. In all the time that she'd known Rory, he'd never mentioned this area, mainly because it was ruled by another gang, one more ruthless than Rory and his crew. So, as much as she could, Maggie tried to convince herself that she'd be safe.

Turning the corner, she navigated one of the wheels of the

pram over the kerb. It bent slightly and for a moment she was afraid it was going to fall off. She kicked it straight and continued towards the laundrette, which was sandwiched between a pawnbroker's and a butcher's.

Pushing open the door with her back to pull the pram inside, Maggie was met by the familiar smell of soap and bleach, reminding her of the endless days that she'd spent at the laundrette when she was working with her mum.

A woman, probably in her thirties, looked up from behind the counter, hair scraped back into a bun. She had a thick layer of make-up on that looked like it was running down her face from the heat, and her hands were red and cracked from life in the laundrette.

'If you want a service wash, you'll have to wait until this afternoon. I'm run off me bleedin' feet and there ain't any more machines available right now.'

'No, I'm not looking for a wash. I heard that you might be looking for someone to help you? I know what I'm doing – I worked in a laundrette for the past couple of years.' Maggie looked at her evenly.

'So you've done laundry work before, only it's not an easy job. It ain't about swanning in here and sitting about all day having a fag and going home.'

'I know, and I'm not shy of hard work.'

'It's six days a week, eight until seven.' The woman folded her arms. 'You'll be on your feet all day.'

'I can handle that,' Maggie said confidently, though she wasn't looking forward to working all those hours, especially when her body was still aching. But she had to earn money and that was all there was to it.

'Is the baby yours?' The woman nodded towards the pram.

'Yes.'

'How old?'

'Two days.'

The woman pulled face. 'Fucking hell, you should be in bed.'

'I can't afford to be.'

It was a moment before the woman spoke, and Maggie could already feel the sweat running down her back. 'Right then, you seem like you know what you're doing. I got a back room where the little one can sleep during your shift, as long as they don't make too much of a noise and cry all day . . . You can start on Monday.'

Relief washed through Maggie. 'Thank you. I won't let you down.' And she meant it. There was no way she was going to let this opportunity slip through her fingers, especially as it meant she wouldn't have to find anyone to mind Rose. It couldn't have been better.

'I'm Annie, by the way. I own this gaff.' She nodded with a smile.

'Maggie.'

'Well, Maggie, you've just got yourself a job.' She laughed warmly then she froze. 'It's black.'

For a moment Maggie didn't know what Annie was talking about. She gazed around, puzzled. Then she realised Annie was staring straight at Rose.

Annie's face curled up into a sneer, a look of disgust. 'I can't have that thing in here. This is a respectable establishment.'

'What?' Maggie couldn't believe what she was hearing. 'She's a baby.'

'I don't care what the hell she is. I said take that dirty thing out of here.' Annie went to grab the pram, and Maggie moved without thinking, reaching out and grabbing Annie by her top.

247

'What did you call her?' Maggie was raging.

Annie staggered back, but she wasn't about to silenced. 'You heard me.' Full of hatred, she screamed, 'I don't want it in here and I don't want the likes of you in here neither.' She tried to break free, but Maggie clung on hard.

'Get your fucking hands off me!'

'Not until you take it back,' Maggie growled.

'Hell will freeze over before I do.' Annie raised her voice as loud as she could. 'You're nothing but a filthy whore! Coming in here with your black bastard where decent folk are, you should be bleedin' ashamed of yourself.'

Maggie's fist connected with Annie's jaw before she thought about what she was doing. In return, Annie grabbed a clump of Maggie's hair, twisting it round her fingers and pulling it as hard as she could.

Maggie bit down on Annie's arm.

Annie screamed, 'I said you were an animal, just like your daughter.'

The more Annie spoke, the more enraged Maggie became. 'How dare you talk about her like that!' Tears of anger and frustration rolled down her face. Then she slapped Annie hard, this time across her cheek, causing the woman to stumble backwards and crash into one of the tumble dryers.

She immediately righted herself and ran for the door. The moment it was open, she screamed out, 'Help, *help*, the crazy cow's attacking me!'

Maggie was only half aware of a crowd forming as she shoved Annie out into the street. And this time it was Maggie who grabbed a clump of hair, dragging Annie onto the pavement and jumping on top of her. She carried on pummelling her around the head as Annie scratched at her face.

'*Officer!*' someone shouted, but Maggie was too busy yelling at Annie to notice.

'She has a name,' she yelled. 'And she's worth twenty of you!'

From the corner of her eye, she saw a policeman coming towards them. Panic replaced anger, and she clambered off Annie and raced back into the laundrette.

With Rose crying, Maggie turned and ran, pushing the pram up the street as she heard shouting from behind her.

She didn't dare to look back.

Her lungs burned as she weaved through the alleyways with Rose screaming as the pram bounced and juddered over the potholes.

Finally, when Maggie was sure no one had followed her, she slowed. She breathed hard, leaning against the brick wall, before scooping Rose up. 'Shhhh, I'm sorry, I'm so sorry, Rose.'

Still cradling her daughter, Maggie slid down the wall. 'I'll do better. I promise I'll do better,' she whispered to her daughter as Rose began to settle down. 'I'll make it all right for you, I promise.'

But the problem was Maggie had no idea how she was going to deliver on that promise.

Chapter Fifty-Six

Rory's fist connected with a sickening crack. Blood sprayed across the peeling wallpaper of the tiny front room. Shamus Riley, covered in blood, his lip already torn, fell to the floor. Rory brought back his foot, booting Maggie's father in the ribs. Not finished yet, he grabbed the man by his head, bringing it back before smashing it on the corner of the hearth. Shamus yelled out in agony.

'I'm going to ask you one more time.' Rory's voice was quiet and threatening. He flexed his fingers, playing with the sovereign rings on them. 'Where is Maggie?'

Her father could hardly talk as blood bubbled out of his mouth. 'I don't know. I haven't seen her.'

Rory's foot shot out again, coming down on the man's face. He ground his heel into his ear. 'You better not be lying to me.'

Behind them, Maggie's mother pressed herself against the wall, her face drawn with terror. 'He's telling the truth. We haven't seen her. We'd tell you where she was, Mr Sheehan, if we knew.'

Rory glanced across at Malcolm. He nodded to him and Malcolm walked over, bringing his lit cigarette. He passed it to Rory who took it, then he pressed it into Maggie's father's split lip. His shriek of agony was heard down the street and he writhed on the floor, wetting himself through the sheer pain.

Rory let out a sigh and brushed the dirt of his suit. It seemed he was about to leave. Then his foot came back a final time, landing in Shamus's ribs with full force.

Rory turned then and grabbed Kathleen Riley by the throat. His grip tightened, forcing her to struggle for air, then he tipped his head back and headbutted her. 'I won't have my wife running out on me. She's my wife and she always will be, until I take me last breath.'

Rory let go then, and Kathleen covered her face.

Ignoring her muffled sobs, he told her, 'If Maggie contacts you, if you find out where she is, you tell me straight away. Because if I find out you're hiding anything I'll be back, and I promise you'll wish you were dead by the time I've finished with you.'

It was another half hour before they pulled up outside the club in Soho. Rory didn't wait for Malcolm to open the door – he was walking before the engine was turned off, rage driving him forward.

The doorman straightened up at the sight of Rory. 'Evening, Mr . . .'

But Rory had swept past by the time he'd finished his sentence.

Standing at the top of the stairs, he bellowed, 'Everyone out – now!' His voice carried to every corner and the club fell silent as punters and staff turned towards him.

'I said, *now*.'

Terrified, the customers got up and scurried out, leaving Rory with Malcolm standing behind him, staring down at the staff. They stood frozen, their expressions full of unease.

Rory walked down the stairs slowly. The music was turned off. No one spoke and no one met his eye.

'I want to know where Maggie is.' He fixed his gaze on each one of them in turn. 'Someone must fucking know . . . Well?'

Again, no one spoke.

Rory reached into his pocket and pulled out a flick knife, which he twisted in his fingers. 'If you don't tell me where she is, and you know something, I'm going to slice you up, piece by fucking piece – and that goes for you all. If one of you knows and you don't tell me, every last one of you will find yourself at the wrong end of this.'

He flicked open the blade, then stared at Thomas.

'You . . . You must know something.'

It wasn't a question, it was a statement. Thomas didn't know how to react, whether to answer or not.

Rory strode round the bar and grabbed Thomas by his shirt. He brought the knife up so it was touching the tip of his nose. 'You want me to slice it off, Tommy boy?'

'No, Mr Sheehan.'

Rory leaned close to him, whispering in Thomas's ear. 'Then you'll tell me where she is, if you know what's good for you.'

Terrified, Thomas tried to speak. 'I . . . I . . . I don't, I swear. I wouldn't lie to you.'

Rory nicked Thomas's ear with the blade and it started to bleed. 'But I think you would lie, Thomas. I think if you knew where Maggie was, you'd keep it to yourself.'

'My loyalties lie with you, Mr Sheehan. I wouldn't lie to you after how good you've been to me.' Thomas's voice shook.

Tossing him aside, Rory turned to Davey. 'What about you? I've seen the way you look at her.'

The barman shook his head, his pale face drawing even paler.

'So you're not denying it, then?' Rory asked.

'No, I mean, yes . . .' Davey swallowed. 'I don't know

anything about where she's gone. And, as beautiful as Maggie is, I would never look at her, not like that, Mr Sheehan.'

Rory turned away and strode up to Malcolm. He lowered his voice. 'What do you think?'

Malcolm mulled it over. 'I reckon they don't know where she is.'

Rory licked his lips and pulled out a packet of cigarettes from his inside jacket.

'So what do we do now?' Malcolm spoke evenly as he clicked his fingers to Thomas, indicating that he wanted two large glasses of whisky.

Rory pulled deeply on his cigarette, enjoying the smoke going down to his lungs. 'We keep looking, Malcolm. We turn London upside fucking down until we find her.' He glanced towards the door, pointing with his cigarette. 'Because she's out there. Maggie is out there somewhere, and I'm not going to rest until we bring her back.'

Chapter Fifty-Seven

The single bed sagged in the middle as Maggie and Bernie sat on it. Sarah was leaning against the wall, her legs stretched out on the bare wooden floor. The evening light was fading through the single grimy window in Maggie's room. The bottle of gin by Sarah's side was already half empty.

Rose nestled fast asleep in Bernie's arms as Maggie repeated the story of what had happened to her.

'So you floored her with one punch, then?' Bernie rocked Rose as she grinned at Maggie. 'Right there outside the laundrette? Fucking hell, I would have loved to have seen that. Stupid cow, she deserved all she got.'

'She shouldn't get into fights,' Sarah said firmly reaching for the gin. 'I already told her that.'

'Oh, stop being so fucking up your arse. She was sticking up for her daughter.' Bernie rolled her eyes. 'Sometimes you can be a right moody mare.'

Sarah took exception to this. 'I'm not being moody.' She poured the gin in three chipped mugs and handed them out to Maggie and Bernie. 'I'm only looking out for her.' She smiled at Maggie. 'Go on, drink this. It looks like you need it.'

Maggie took it gratefully, enjoying the burn of the gin as it went down her throat. She was in pain, and she was also shaken up from what had happened. She knew she shouldn't have got into a fight with Annie, but there was no way, no matter what Sarah said, that she could stand back and listen to what that woman was saying about Rose.

Maggie felt exhausted, and she closed her eyes for a moment. The smell of damp competed with the smell of smoke and Sarah's cheap perfume. Outside, she could hear raised voices from the pub round the corner. Her mind flickered once again to Rory. Immediately her heart begin to race. She pushed all thoughts of him away, into that dark place in her mind, and took another large gulp of the gin.

'So what are you going to do now, if you can't get a job,' Sarah asked, refilling Maggie's mug.

'I don't know.' Maggie stared at her drink, feeling the mattress springs digging into her thighs. 'I don't think my money will last even a week.'

Bernie and Sarah exchanged a glance.

'Well . . .' Sarah put down her mug and stared at Maggie. 'You could always join us.'

'Join you?' Maggie looked puzzled.

Bernie laughed. 'We ain't talking about coming for a night away at the seaside with us, you dozy cow.'

'It's quick money,' Sarah went on. 'You can earn when you want without worry . . . Don't get me wrong, I ain't saying that selling your arse is everyone's idea of fun, but it's a job and it pays, and in my book that's all that fucking matters.'

Bernie nodded. 'You need money, and it's a way of getting some.'

'All the girls here in the boarding house are on the game, so one more won't make any difference. We all look out for each other, so you'll be safe, and most of us work for a pimp. He's all right as pimps go, and it saves you being knocked around by any fella that fancies it out on the street. He takes a cut, but it ain't nothing compared to some of the pimps around here.' She fell silent, drinking her gin as she gazed out of the window. 'He ain't bad, could be worse.'

Maggie shook her head. 'I can't.'

'Can't or won't?' Bernie's voice didn't hold judgement, but she frowned. 'We've all said that at one time or another, Maggie. You can't let your pride get in the way.' She looked down at Rose stirring in her arms. 'You've got this little one to think about.'

'That's what I'm doing – I'm thinking about her.'

'Not if you're getting into fights, you're not, and not if you're turning your nose up at a good job.'

'I can't anyway.' Maggie gestured vaguely at her body. 'I'm not healed yet.'

Bernie giggled and smiled warmly. 'There's other ways to earn, ain't there? Hand jobs. Blow jobs. Plenty of men are happy to pay for that.'

Maggie suddenly felt shy. 'I . . . I . . . I don't know how to . . .'

Sarah raised her eyebrows. 'I think you'd pick it up pretty quickly. There's nothing to it.' She laughed, but not unkindly. 'And how come you don't know how to do it, when you've got a kid and you're running from your old man?'

Maggie shrugged. Sex with Rory had been rough but never anything more than him climbing on top of her. The sex with Thomas had been gentle, special, but again there had been nothing more than him being on top. As for her dad, it had been awful, and even thinking about it made her feel sick. But it had only been him attacking her, raping her, never anything other than him forcibly climbing on top.

Maggie turned away from that thought; she couldn't think about it, so she shut it away in that box in her head.

'Here, take her.' Bernie gently placed Rose in Maggie's arms. She stood up and reached for the empty formula bottle on the cracked windowsill. 'Pretend this is your old man's cock.' She waved it around suggestively.

Maggie laughed despite herself. 'I'd rather not.'

'Watch me. I'm going to make you rich.' Bernie gripped the bottle in one hand. 'So all you have to do is open your mouth, use your tongue, make noises like you're enjoying it.' She giggled. 'That sometimes gets you a few extra bob. And that's all there is to it.' Bernie put the bottle in her mouth with exaggerated enthusiasm, slurping noises and groaning as Sarah doubled over with laughter.

'Christ, Bern, you'll give her fucking nightmares! If that's how you do it, I'm surprised you earn any money.' Sarah grinned, showing off her rotten teeth.

Bernie threw the bottle on the bed and collapsed into fits of laughter as Rose opened her eyes at all the noise.

'See what you've done now! Poor little mite, she's probably wondering what sort of bleedin' madhouse she's landed up in.' Sarah shook her head and divided the last of the gin equally between their mugs.

The laughter died down, leaving the three women sitting in silence in the dingy, stuffy room.

'None of us like it, babe.' Bernie's voice was quiet as she came and sat cross-legged on the bed. 'But it pays the rent, it keeps a roof over our heads.'

Sarah nodded, looking serious. 'And the main thing is' – she knelt by Maggie's side, stroking Rose's cheek with her bitten fingernail – 'it keeps you, it keeps us all, from having to go back to our old man.'

Sarah's words hung in the air and eventually Maggie spoke.

'And I earn enough to pay the rent, to buy food and to buy milk?'

'Yeah.'

Maggie looked at them both. 'I'll think about it.'

'That's good,' Bernie said encouragingly.

'And thank you.' Maggie swallowed hard against the tightness in her throat. 'For everything.'

Sarah looked at Maggie then and her eyes shone with warmth. 'There's no shame in trying to survive, darlin'. That's all any of us are trying to do.'

Chapter Fifty-Eight

A fortnight passed before Maggie built up the courage. Although, it was only when she got to the point of desperation that she decided to give it a go. Because, for all Maggie had seen and done and been put through in her life, she was naïve to a lot of the ways of the world.

However, she had to admit it was less about courage and more down to the fact she had no money. The tin of formula milk for Rose stood almost empty on the windowsill, and the makeshift nappies needed replacing, plus the rent was due tomorrow. Which meant Maggie no longer had the luxury of time to think about it, and certainly couldn't afford to worry about her pride or dignity. The only thing she needed to focus on was Rose – nothing else mattered.

Trying not to look as nervous as she felt, Maggie stood next to Sarah on the corner of Bradwell Street near the Mile End Hospital. The warm summer evening swished the hem of the red dress Bernie had lent her and the black patent shoes she'd borrowed from Sarah rubbed the backs of her heels.

'Don't look so worried, Maggie. Bernie's good with kids,' Sarah said as she lit her cigarette. 'Try not to worry about Rose.'

Maggie nodded, but it was hard not to. Rose had been grizzling when she'd left her, and she would have given anything to stay with her daughter, but she knew Mrs Mills wouldn't wait for her rent, and Rose wouldn't wait for her milk, so here she was. There was no turning back now.

'It's not just that.' Maggie's stomach tightened. The weight of what she was about to do filled her with panic.

'First one's always the worst.' Sarah squeezed her hand. 'Once you've done the first one, you'll see it as just a job, no different from working in a laundrette, no different from working in the bakery.' She winked at her, but so slowly it looked as if her thick false eyelashes were weighing down her eyelids. 'If it helps, keep your eyes closed.' She laughed and Maggie attempted to smile. 'And remember what we told you.' Sarah blew out rings of smoke. 'Just stick to the hand jobs and blow jobs, don't let them pressure you into anything else – that's what blokes always try to do.'

Maggie nodded, feeling more miserable by the minute.

'And if they get rough . . .'

'I use the knife.'

'Jesus Christ, girl – not straight away! You wanna get banged up? That's only if you're desperate, babe. If they get rough, just call for help. I'll be here; Susie's over there. We never leave this area, so someone will always be able to hear you.'

It was small comfort to Maggie, but she nodded anyway.

As they continued to talk, a man approached them on foot. He was short and heavyset. Maggie could see he was dressed well, and she could also see the wedding ring on his fat fingers.

He came to a stop, eyeing Maggie up and down as if she was a piece of meat.

'All right, Sid?' Sarah nodded her greeting.

'She new?' He spoke to Sarah while continuing to stare at Maggie with beady, lustful eyes.

'Fresh as they come, mate.' Sarah pushed Maggie forward. 'This is Maggie, and she's pleased to meet you.'

Sid leered, revealing his tobacco-stained teeth, and Maggie tried really hard not to run back to the boarding house to grab Rose, but she knew there was no option but to go through with this.

'She'll do,' Sid sniffed.

'But it's only blow jobs or hand jobs,' Sarah said firmly. 'That's all you get, mate.'

He shrugged, not bothered. 'I'll have a blow then.'

'Usual price, mind – no trying to rip her off, you hear me? She may be new, but she ain't anyone's fool.' Sarah stared at him. 'You know where the alley is.'

It was Sid's turn to nod. Sarah gave Maggie a little shove. 'Go on, then. You'll be okay. I'm right here. I ain't going nowhere.'

Maggie followed the man, reminding herself she was doing this for Rose, reminding herself that, no matter what, she couldn't go back to Rory. If selling herself was the only way to keep herself and her baby alive, then that's what she would have to do.

Besides, she'd had worse, hadn't she? Much worse than some fat old bloke she didn't know. Nothing could be as bad as what her da had put her through. And she'd managed to survive that, so she could survive this . . . couldn't she?

The alleyway stank of piss and there were piles of torn-open rubbish bags with stinking bits of meat carcasses thrown out by the butcher's round the corner.

Sid stopped by the wooden crates stacked up against the wall. He began to unbuckle his belt. 'Make it quick,' he sniffed. 'Me missus is expecting me home.' He dropped his grey baggy trousers to his ankles, revealing pale flabby thighs, which were thick with varicose veins.

His belly hung over the waistband of his paisley underpants and as he began to pull those down too, revealing a mass of unkempt sticky pubic hair, Maggie closed her eyes and tried not to gag.

'Go on, then, get on your knees,' he ordered her impatiently.

Without saying a word, Maggie knelt down.

Her face was inches away from Sid's unwashed penis, and the urge to retch grew stronger as she caught the sweet-sour smell of it.

Looking at Sid's penis as it stood half-erect, withered and spotty, she told herself that it was just a job.

A job that would keep Rose fed and safe.

As Sid climaxed, Maggie pulled back and turned her head. There was no way she was going to swallow. Sid tucked himself away, adjusting his clothing.

'Money.' Maggie just about managed to say.

Sid went into his pocket and dropped the money on the ground next to Maggie, then hobbled away on his swollen ankles. Maggie stayed on her knees to say a prayer. After a few moments, she got to her feet and put away the money, telling herself once again it was for Rose. As she walked back to Sarah, she saw her talking to a man. Hearing her footsteps, the two of them turned to look at her.

'Well, well, well. Look who it isn't.'

Maggie stopped in her tracks as she came face to face with Luca Romano.

Chapter Fifty-Nine

By the time Maggie had run back to the boarding house, she was a mess. What the hell was Luca doing here? More importantly, how long would it be before he told Rory that he'd seen her? Fuck.

Charging into the dingy hallway, she slammed the door behind her. Sarah's shoes had rubbed the skin off her heel, but she took the stairs two at a time.

'Bernie! It's me, open up! Bernie.'

Getting no answer, Maggie tried the handle, and swung open the door.

Bernie was sprawled unconscious across the bed, an empty bottle of gin in her hand. Rose's face was red from crying as she lay on blankets in the large open dresser drawer, which had been turned into a makeshift crib.

Maggie hurried over and picked Rose up, stroking her head and kissing her. 'I'm so sorry, Rose. I'm so sorry.' She cradled her at the same time as kicking Bernie's leg. 'Bernie . . . Oi, wake the fuck up!'

Bernie stirred and slowly opened her eyes. 'What? Maggie? You're back early,' she slurred. 'How did it go, darlin'?' She gave a crooked smile.

'I don't want to talk about it. I want to know why you're drunk.

You're supposed to be looking after Rose, not pissed out of your head.' She raised her voice. 'How could you? I trusted you.'

With some difficulty, Bernie pushed herself up on her elbows. 'Oh, she's fine. Stop getting your fucking knickers in a twist – that's if you're wearing any.' She cackled loudly and searched on the bed for her packet of cigarettes, which she found under her pillow. 'I gave her some sugar water and a bit of gin to settle her.'

'Gin! She's a baby – what the fuck do you think you're doing, giving her that?'

Maggie couldn't believe what she was hearing. It was then that she felt how wet Rose's bum was. She was soaked through. 'Bernie, she's wet. How long has she been like this? Bernie!' Maggie kicked the bed. 'I said, how long has she been like this?'

'I don't know, do I? I've been asleep,' Bernie mumbled, grabbing the other quarter bottle of gin which was on the floor next to her. 'Have a drink with me, Maggie. Come on, don't be angry.'

'Angry? I'm not angry, Bernie – I'm fucking livid, you stupid cow. I trusted you with the only thing in the world that matters to me.'

Bernie's face hardened as she became defensive. 'Well, excuse me! Next time I won't bother doing you any favours.'

Maggie turned away, not trusting herself to hold her temper. Since she'd had Rose, her emotions were all over the place; she was either raging or crying, and right now she felt like doing both.

She slammed out of Bernie's room and marched down the stairs to her room, grateful for her own tiny space. She kicked off Sarah's shoes. As bad as it was with Bernie, her main problem now was Luca. She was terrified he was going to ruin everything.

Rose started to cry louder, distracting Maggie from her own problems. She walked around the room rocking her, not wanting the screams to become any louder. Only yesterday Mrs Mills had given her a warning about Rose's crying, and Maggie couldn't afford to be booted out.

'I know, love, I know. I'll sort you out. Shhhh, Rose. It's all right, darlin'.' Maggie laid her on the bed and changed her.

There was a quiet knock on the door, which made Maggie freeze.

'It's Sarah. You all right?'

Maggie cracked the door open, making sure Sarah was alone before opening it fully.

'I came to make sure you were all right after you ran off like that. But then I heard you shouting at Bernie. It's all kicking off this evening, ain't it? Can I come in, babe?'

Maggie nodded. She had no beef with Sarah.

'What was it all about?' Sarah asked, getting straight to the point.

'She was passed out, drunk.' Maggie shook her head. 'Rose hadn't even been changed, and then she tells me that she'd given her some gin.'

Sarah sighed. 'She's been hitting the bottle hard lately.'

This irritated Maggie. 'Well, someone could've told me that before I let her look after Rose.'

'She was trying to help, Maggie. Don't be too hard on her. She's really struggling. She puts on a brave face, but she's not doing as well as she makes out.'

Maggie frowned. 'That's no excuse, though. Rose is only a few weeks old.'

Sarah sat on the bed. The mattress sagged like it was going to give way this time. 'No, it's not, but we've all got a way of coping, ain't we? And the bottle is hers.' She raised her eyebrows. 'It's the same for a lot of us.'

Maggie turned away, picking Rose up from the bed and placing her in the pram, which doubled as a cot. She was angry, but she didn't want to take it out on Sarah. Of course she got where Bernie was coming from. Just lately, she'd been finding that the odd glass of booze made things seem not quite so bad. But, no matter how much she understood, that didn't make it right for Bernie to get pissed when she was looking after Rose. It was wrong, and that wasn't just because Maggie could remember how terrified she'd been when she was little and left alone with her drunken dad. Anything could've happened to Rose while Bernie was out of it.

'And what was all that about earlier?' Sarah said quietly. 'You looked like you'd seen a ghost. Then you ran off.'

It felt like she had seen a ghost, but Maggie didn't say as much. She simply asked, 'How do you know Luca?'

'Everyone round here knows Luca. He runs a bunch of us girls.'

This was news to Maggie. Rory had never mentioned that Luca was a pimp. She knew that he and his family ran protection rackets, coffee shops and sold a lot of goods on the black market, but she had no idea that he had expanded down that route.

'He's all right, as they go,' Sarah continued. 'He's only been in the area for a few months, but he seems to know what he's doing. Last thing I heard he was trying to take on some girls up near Aldgate.' She shrugged. 'Though it probably helped him that this part where we are was a bit of a no-man's land when it came to poncing, so there wasn't any agg from any of the other pimps when he wanted to start looking after us. Don't know much about him or where he comes from. All I know is that he's got a nasty habit, but he looks after me.'

Maggie frowned. 'You work for him?'

'I wouldn't choose to have a pimp – I've never liked the idea

266

of having to give a cut of my money when it's only me that's putting the hard graft in. But around here you have to watch your back. It's not safe otherwise. Before he came along, I was working for myself, but I was getting knocked around a fair bit.'

Taking a moment to digest this, Maggie asked, 'What habit?'

'Pills – a bit too many, if you ask me, but who am I to fucking judge? Anyway, my mate Shelley said that her fella, who did a bit of work for him, saw him banging up the gear. He likes to pop it in his veins.'

Maggie wasn't really listening any more. Seeing Luca made it feel like Soho was closing in on her, and she was doing her best not to show Sarah how panicked she felt.

'Anyway, what about you? How do you know him?'

'I used to see him around the West End.' She tried to be as vague as possible. She could see that Sarah wasn't buying it, but she didn't say anything, and for that Maggie was grateful. 'I met him a few times, that's all. It was weird seeing him here . . . Anyway,' Maggie said, changing the subject, 'I'm not sure what I'm gonna do about Bernie. I can't have her looking after Rose.'

'Look, how about I have a word with her? Give her another chance, cos who else are you going to get to look after her? I can do my bit, but I need to work to pay for my own kids.'

'You've got kids?'

Sarah nodded. 'They're with my mum, only she's getting on a bit now. She's a miserable old cow, but she looks after them fine. It was better than me leaving them with my old man. He didn't give a shit, and he was forever knocking them into next week.' She began to look upset. 'So . . .' It was Sarah's turn to change the subject. 'Shall I speak to Bernie for you?'

Maggie wasn't sure. It wasn't like she was giving her another chance at doing a cleaning job, or working in the laundrette – this was another chance at looking after Rose. The thought of her baby being hurt was painful to even think about. But what would she do otherwise? She didn't want to leave Rose ever again, but right now she had no choice.

'Try not to worry, Maggie. I promise I'll speak to Bernie, and make sure she knows that when she's looking after Rose drinking is off limits. Otherwise she'll have me to deal with.'

Maggie wasn't sure if Bernie would listen to Sarah, but right now she was too tired to argue about it.

'Come on, Maggie. Don't let it get you down. How did it go with Sid?' Sarah grinned and started to laugh. 'Once you go with Sid, babe, you can go with anyone. The rest is easy, but I'm telling you, the smell of his dick will stay in your nose for a long time to come.'

They both laughed, then Maggie rolled her eyes. 'I don't know if I want to do it again.'

'None of us want to do it again, but here we are. Listen, I've got a bottle in my room. Why don't I bring it down, and we can have a drink together? It's quiet out there anyway, and Luca won't mind if I'm not working tonight. He knows you were a bit upset, and I was going to come and see how you were.'

Maggie's blood ran cold. 'He . . . he . . . he knows where I live?'

'Is that a problem?'

'Yeah, because he knows my husband.' Maggie's words tumbled out as the panic rose in her. 'What if he tells Rory where I am? What then?'

Sarah sat up from the bed and took hold of Maggie's hands. 'It sounds to me like you know him better than just seeing him around the West End.'

Maggie nodded, taking comfort in Sarah holding her hands.

'Why don't you tell me about it?' Sarah's voice was warm and full of concern. 'You can trust me. I swear you can.'

'I'm scared that Luca will say something because his family and Rory are rivals. More than rivals . . . sworn enemies.'

'So, if they're enemies, what's the problem? If they hate each other, Luca's not gonna say anything, is he?'

'I don't know.' Maggie tried to think straight. 'What's to stop him telling Rory just to wind him up?'

Sarah looked puzzled.

'Luca can use the fact he knows where I am to taunt Rory. Then he'll end up telling him.' Maggie suddenly jumped up. 'I have to go.'

'Go where?'

'I don't know, but I can't stay here waiting for Rory to find me, can I?'

'Maggie, you gotta calm down, girl. You can't just up and run.'

'Why not?'

'Because you've got Rose, and out there you've got no one to look out for you. At least here you've got us. We're all running from one thing or another, Maggie. I'm running from my old man and I don't think there'll ever be a time when he'll stop looking for me, but I'll be damned if I spend the rest of my life running from him. I can't. I won't. I won't live my life as if it's not my own.' She patted the bed. 'Maggie, come and sit down.'

Maggie did just that.

'Why don't we have a drink, like I said, and see what tomorrow brings. Maybe things won't look so bad in the morning.'

Maggie smiled, but she had a feeling that things would look even worse . . .

Chapter Sixty

It was a couple of days later and Maggie hesitated outside Doris's door. For the past two days she'd been lying low. She'd felt ill and too scared to go out, apart from letting Rose have a bit of fresh air, and even then she'd just sat outside on the concrete stairs. Not that she'd ever called Stepney's air fresh, but she wanted Rose not to be cooped up in the stuffy room.

Her mind had been on Luca and of course that made her think more and more about Rory. Even though Sarah had told her repeatedly not to worry, it was really hard not to. As for Bernie, she had apologised, and Maggie could see that she meant it. So much so that Bernie had shoplifted a tin of formula milk for Rose, along with a few other bits that Maggie was grateful for. But Bernie meaning she was sorry and trusting her with Rose were two different things.

At the moment, Maggie didn't want to go anywhere, even if it meant her not having enough money to eat. As long as she had milk for Rose and the rent money, it was all that mattered. But then last night Mrs Mills had given her a message: Doris wanted to see her.

Even though Maggie had waited until it was almost dark, she kept glancing over her shoulder, feeling jumpy. Only when she was sure the street was empty did she run along the terrace and knock on the door.

The curtain twitched and through the crack Maggie saw Doris. She waved and a moment later the door opened. 'Maggie.' She grinned, showing off her broken teeth, and Maggie was hit with the smell of bad breath, fish and booze. 'I'm glad you came round.' She frowned. 'Where's Rose?'

'Do you mind if we talk inside?' Maggie said nervously.

'No, of course not. Come in.'

Maggie walked in and Doris shut the door behind her then shuffled through to the lounge. A half-eaten plate of kippers and a glass of gin sat next to Doris's chair.

As Doris creaked into her seat, Maggie told her, 'Rose is with Sarah at the boarding house. I thought it would be safer coming alone.'

She watched the concern growing on Doris's face. 'Safer?'

Maggie nodded. 'I saw Luca Romano, and I'm worried he might have told Rory where I am. He knows where I live now. He's running some of the girls.' Maggie proceeded to tell Doris all that had happened, although she left out the part about Sid.

Doris took a sip of her gin and leaned back in her chair with a sigh.

'Why did you want to see me?' Maggie asked.

'I don't know if it's connected, but I heard through the grapevine that a couple of blokes had been asking if anyone had seen a young girl with a baby. Now, before you panic, it might not be you, it might not have anything to do with you at all. Up and down the East End there are loads of young girls with kids, but I thought I'd mention it so you can keep your eyes open.'

'What else was said?' Maggie wasn't sure she wanted to know, but she had to ask.

'Word is they were offering money.'

'Then it must be Rory. Who else would be offering money to find out about someone?'

'Well, I don't think you should worry too much. Like I say, it was the East End grapevine. For all I know, it's two blokes looking for their pet dog and, by the time everyone's finished adding their two penn'orth, they're looking for a young girl with a baby. It might be something and nothing.'

'How can I not worry?' Maggie snapped. She knew it was only a matter of time before they found her. 'What will you do if they come here? What would you say?'

'What do you think I'll say?' Doris took a swig of her gin. 'I'll say I haven't seen you. I haven't seen you since your mum came here. Don't worry, Maggie. I know how to keep my mouth shut.'

Doris began to cough, a deep hacking cough. She grabbed for the grubby towel next to her, spitting into it as her face turned red.

'Are you all right, Doris? That sounds nasty. Have you seen the doctor?'

This caused Doris to laugh between bouts of coughing. 'What for? To tell me that my lungs are on their last legs? I don't need to spend good money to hear that. Anyway, you don't look too clever yourself. You need to look after yourself as well as that little baby of yours, you hear me? You'll do her no good if you come down ill.'

'I'm fine, or I will be, when I get enough money to get out of that place. The girls are nice enough, but not being able to wash Rose or boil bottles properly makes life difficult.'

Doris nodded. 'It ain't easy being on your own, but it ain't easy getting your teeth knocked in by a fella, either.'

Maggie tried to smile. 'It's not that that I'm worried about. It's Rose.'

All she cared about was not letting Rory see the baby. She couldn't be responsible for what he'd do to Thomas, or Thomas's family for that matter. She remembered what he'd done to Pam. She wasn't going to have more blood on her hands.

'Now listen. I'm not saying it is Rory who's looking for you, but maybe it's a good idea to lay low for a while,' Doris said eventually. 'Round here, people don't grass each other up, but when money is involved it's a different matter. Half of this street would sell their own mother for a couple of bob, the rest would sell her for less.' She laughed and coughed again, and fresh fear twisted in Maggie's stomach.

'Maybe I should leave the area, get out of London completely.' Maggie's words rushed out. 'I dunno, go to the coast or something, or maybe to the countryside.'

Doris shook her head. 'You are joking? First off, what with? These things take money. And secondly . . .' She paused to scoop up a piece of kipper with her fingers, shoving it into her mouth. 'It sounds like some of those girls at the boarding house are looking out for you. If you piss off, it will be harder than ever.' Doris smiled. 'You just need to be careful right now, Maggie.' She wheezed out her words. 'Don't talk to too many people, and keep your business to yourself. But don't run off cos you're panicking. Keep your head.'

Maggie nodded

'How are you getting on with money, by the way?' Doris asked. 'You got a job yet?'

Unable to look Doris in the eye, she stared at the empty coal scuttle. 'Sort of. I tried getting a job at the laundrette off Bethnal Green Road and a few other shops, but the minute they saw Rose they didn't want to know.'

'That doesn't surprise me.' Doris frowned. 'So what you doing for money, then?'

Maggie didn't say anything.

'You on your back, now?' Doris said, but there was no judgement in her voice, only concern.

'No, well, not yet. It was just a quick fumble in an alleyway. Only the once, cos it was right after that I saw Luca. I've been scared to go out ever since, but I know I'll have to go back to it.'

'There's no shame in it. We've all done it at one time or another. I did it myself when I was younger, before I got into the abortion game.' Doris pointed over to the corner. 'Pass my bag.'

The tatty brown handbag in the corner had clearly seen better days, but Maggie got up and handed it to Doris.

Opening it, Doris fumbled with her purse and took out some money. 'Here you go – take this.'

Maggie shook her head. 'No, you've already loaned me some money, and I still need to pay that back.'

'This is a gift. Go on – take it. I like you. I liked you the first time I set eyes on you. There's something about you that reminds me of myself when I was your age. So if I can help, I want to . . . Now take it.'

'Thank you, Doris.' Maggie's eyes welled up with tears as she took the money, knowing that it would cover her for a couple of weeks at least with the rent and a bit of food.

'But what have I told you about those bleedin' tears?' Doris said, not unkindly. 'You need to toughen up, Maggie. This life ain't easy for women, but we make damn sure we give it as good a shot as we can, which means there's no time to feel sorry for ourselves. We just keep dusting ourselves off every time we get a knock.'

Maggie leaned forward and kissed Doris on her cheek, making the old woman smile.

'I better go. I don't want to leave Rose too long with Sarah.'

At the door, Doris caught Maggie's arm, and there was a surprising strength in Doris's bony fingers. 'Be careful, love. I've known Rory for a long time, and if it is him looking for you, well, we both know he ain't right in the head. He's probably tearing up Soho as we speak and battering anyone he can, making examples of people that he thinks might know something.'

Maggie didn't say anything. Her gut told her it was Rory. Who else would it be? So the only thing now she needed to work out was how long she had left . . .

Chapter Sixty-One

Rory sat in the back of the car as Malcolm drove him through the West End. Beside him was Thomas, who he'd been sending out to look for Maggie. Though a couple of times he'd wondered if he was really bothering to look, and he'd had to slap him around a bit to make sure he got the message. Maggie needed to be brought back, no matter what.

He cracked his neck, the pressure building up. He was finding it hard to concentrate on anything apart from that little bitch Maggie. The thought of what she might be doing ran through his veins, distracting him from everything. He'd had a couple of meetings that he hadn't bothered showing up for. He'd also told Malcolm to ignore the message which had been sent through from the Romano family for talks.

Right now he had nothing to say to them, mainly because he couldn't think properly. For the time being there was an unsteady truce between them while he decided what he wanted to do about Vince Romano's cunt of a son burning down some of his business. He'd heard that Luca had pissed off somewhere after falling out with his father. He didn't know if that was true – he had other things to think about. Though it wouldn't surprise him if it was, because Luca's addiction had made him a liability.

Business and drugs didn't go. Just like Maggie and business didn't go.

And speak of the devil—

'Stop! Stop the fucking car!'

Malcolm slammed on the brakes and Rory jumped out.

He rushed towards the store he'd seen the woman walk into.

It was Maggie, marching around bold as fucking brass.

Shoving an old couple out of the way, he was just in time to see Maggie disappear behind a display at the back of the department store. He rushed past the perfume counter, closing in on her, then made a grab for her.

'Got you, you fucking slag!' Rory grabbed the back of her coat and yanked her round so hard her bag went flying, spilling lipstick and loose change across the polished floor. 'Who the fuck do you think you are, fucking off like that?'

But it wasn't Maggie.

The woman staring back at him had Maggie's colouring, but she was older, heavier. Nothing like his Maggie.

'Get your hands off me!' she screeched 'Who the bloody hell do you think you are?'

Rory didn't let go. His face flushed as shoppers paused to stare. 'Shut up, you silly cow,' he hissed, not appreciating a woman screaming in his face. 'Just shut your mouth.'

'Boss?' Thomas ran up, confused by the scene in front of him, not quite knowing what was happening.

'I'll have the law on you!' the woman continued to yell, trying to twist away from Rory's grip. 'Someone get the police!'

'Everything all right here?' A man appeared beside them, sleeves rolled up over his thick forearms. His flat nose and cauliflower ears marked him out as a boxer.

'This isn't anything to do with you, mate.' Rory's eyes flashed. 'So if I were you I'd piss off.'

The man scowled. 'Is that right? Well, I make it my business when I see a fella roughing up a woman.'

'She needed some manners, a bit like you.' Rory released his grip on the woman's coat and took out his frustration on the man. 'You should've kept walking.'

While Thomas looked on, helpless, Rory took a swing at the man, his fist cracking against the boxer's jaw and sending him stumbling into one of the counters. The man recovered quickly, lowering his head and charging at Rory driving him backwards into a glass display case, but Rory began hammering short, vicious punches into the man's sides. He gasped and fell back, but Rory didn't give him time to recover. He grabbed his collar, dragging him backwards like he was an army of men, pulling him towards the entrance with Thomas following on.

Outside, Rory threw him into the gutter. Then he ran at him, kicking him hard in the ribs, dragged him up again and hauled him to where his Jaguar waited at the kerb with Malcolm.

With a grunt of effort, Rory slammed the man's face against the bonnet of his car, slamming his head on the metal. 'Next time you might want to think twice before sticking your fucking nose in other people's business,' Rory snarled as he let the man's unconscious body slide to the pavement.

He dusted himself down, nodded to Thomas and they both got into the car.

Malcolm drove away as Rory lit a cigarette with hands that didn't shake.

This was Maggie's fault. All Maggie's fault. And if it took him forever, he was going to make sure he found her and brought her back to where she belonged.

Chapter Sixty-Two

Maggie had missed the bus. Annoyed, she began to walk back to the boarding house. It crossed her mind how much she hated living in fear, the feeling that any minute now she could be found. She just wanted it to stop. If it wasn't for the fact that Rose looked so much like Thomas, she might have been tempted to go back to him. Better the devil she knew.

As controlling and claustrophobic as it had been living with Rory, it was better than the life she was now living. She was tired of having to battle. Plus, she could do with a long, hot bath. Maybe the next time she went to see Doris, she'd take Rose and she'd ask her if she could use her tub. Then they could both get clean.

With that small thought making her feel slightly better, Maggie cut through the alleyway, wanting to keep off the main road. But, hearing a noise behind her, she paused to peer into the darkness. Her eyes darted around and she realised that she'd left it late to get home. She touched her pocket, comforting herself that she was carrying the knife Sarah had given her.

She picked up her pace, but at the end of the alleyway she saw that she'd reached a dead end. She must've taken a wrong turn.

Sighing, she turned round, and gasped as she came face to face with a tall, stocky man, his eyes bloodshot. He swayed on his feet. 'How much?' he slurred, leaning closer to Maggie, his breath sour with beer and cigarettes.

'Not tonight, mate.' Her voice was firm. She was still debating whether she could make a run for it when he grabbed her arm.

'Get off me. Get the fuck off me.'

The man laughed, his face darkening, as Maggie tried to pull away.

'I said, *let go of me.*'

'Shut up, you silly tart.' His grip tightened, and he shoved her into the wall, the darkness surrounding them both.

The impact had winded her, and it took a second to catch her breath. By that time, he was pinning her to the wall.

'Little fucking tease, aren't we?' He slapped her face so hard it made her ears ring.

She could taste the blood in her mouth where he'd split her lip. Her hand slid into her pocket and she pulled out the blade. She swung it blindly, feeling it connect with his flesh.

The man yelled, stumbling backwards. 'You cut me, you fucking whore! I'm going to kill you for that.'

Maggie didn't wait to see where she'd cut him; she knew it couldn't have been a very deep wound, not enough to keep him from coming after her. So she took off, sprinting along the alleyway, back the way she'd come.

'Come here, you fucking slag!'

She could hear him raging behind her, his footsteps pounding the ground as she skidded round the corner into another alleyway. But, like the last one, it was a dead end, and the wall was too high for her to climb.

She spun round just as the man appeared at the entrance of the alleyway. He was bleeding from the shoulder, his hand pressed against the wound. Despite his obvious pain, he grinned nastily. 'Got you now, you bitch, and I'm gonna make you sorry for what you just did.'

Trembling, Maggie clutched the knife, pointing it towards him. 'You stay away from me, you hear . . . *Stay away.*'

He laughed coldly. 'Or what? You going to try to stab me again? Because I'll snap your fucking neck when I'm done with you.'

He continued to close in on Maggie, but as she tried to back away, he raised his foot and kicked the knife from her hands. Maggie tried to grab it, but the man lurched towards her, ripping his belt off as he did.

He wrapped it round his hand and swung it at her, catching the side of her body. She yelped and jumped away, but he thrashed her again: once, twice, three times. Pain rushed through her, but she was used to that. Her biggest worry was that she had no idea what this man was going to do. She yelped again as the metal buckle cut at her leg.

That's when she saw the punch coming.

She managed to dodge out of the way, avoiding the full impact of the man's fist, but he caught her jaw and she stumbled backwards, tumbling to the ground. He grabbed a clump of her hair, and slapped her face.

'Get off me . . . Get off!' Maggie tried to fight, but he was too strong.

He hauled Maggie back up to standing position, bringing his fist back and thumping her in her stomach. The pain this time was something else and she screamed in agony. There was nothing she could do to save herself when he put his foot behind her heel, causing her to smash to the ground.

Immediately, he jumped on top of her, spreading her legs

apart as she continued to struggle against him. He leaned forward, pulling up her skirt and tearing her knickers.

'You better get off her, unless you want me to blow your fucking brains out.'

With that Maggie passed out.

Chapter Sixty-Three

Taking a minute to come round, Maggie tried to work out where she was.

'Nice to see you're back in the land of the living.'

Hearing the voice, Maggie scrambled up from her bed in the boarding house. She winced in pain as she stared at Luca.

He lit a cigarette and grinned at her through the smoke. 'Twice I've come to your rescue now, and twice you don't seem very grateful.'

'I don't need your help,' Maggie said indignantly.

Luca nodded and came to sit down on the end of the bed.

'Next time I'll remember to leave you to it.' He gave her a brooding smile. His dark eyes looked into hers. 'If you only knew how much trouble you've caused.'

Maggie frowned, looking around the room. She'd scrubbed every inch of it from top to bottom, not that it had made much difference. 'What do you mean?'

'Nothing that should concern you.'

They fell silent, and Maggie nervously fiddled with her sleeve.

'I need to get my daughter,' she said eventually. She started to stand up, but she immediately felt dizzy and had to sit down again.

'Rose is fine. Sarah's got her.'

Maggie bristled at the way Luca talked about her daughter as though he knew her.

'I didn't know you had a kid.' He blew out smoke from the side of his mouth.

'Why would you? You barely know me,' Maggie snapped, but then she paused to look him straight in the eye. 'Are you going to tell Rory you've seen me?'

'Are you?'

Seeing the confusion on her face, Luca rephrased his question: 'Are you going to tell Rory you've seen *me*?'

'Why would I do that?'

'Exactly. Why would *I* do that?'

He touched her hand gently, sending a shiver through her, and she silently caught her breath.

'We're both running, Maggie, and neither of us wants to be found.'

Maggie began to relax a bit. 'What are you running from?' From what she'd heard about the Romanos, it was hard to believe that Luca would need to run.

'It's a long story. But we have more in common than you might think.' He ran his finger along her palm. 'So, do we have a deal? You keep your mouth shut and I'll do the same?'

Maggie nodded. 'Deal.'

He smiled at her and changed the subject. 'Nice place you've got here.' He winked. 'You know, it would be safer for you if you worked for me. You might even be able to afford to rent a better place than this.'

Maggie laughed. 'You want me to work for you?' She wasn't sure if he was joking or not, but she shook her head, feeling a weight lift off her shoulders. Whatever was going on with Luca, she believed that he was telling the truth about wanting to lie low. And she wasn't sure why, but knowing he had secrets he needed to protect made her feel better. 'I could never work for you.'

He laughed as well. 'That's a shame.'

She tilted her head to look at him. 'Is it?'

Luca got up then. 'Maybe it isn't. Maybe I'm glad that you don't want to earn money lying on your back.'

'I didn't say that.' Maggie stared at him evenly. 'I said, I don't want to work for *you*. How I earn money to support myself and my daughter is my business, and I certainly won't give a ponce a part of what I earn.'

His face dropped and Maggie wasn't sure if he was angry or not. Then it broke into a smile.

'It's good to know that's how you see me, Maggie.' He winked again and headed for the door. 'What about a bit of protection? It's not safe around here. You saw that for yourself. Surely that's worth paying for?'

'I've looked after myself up until now, and I'll keep on looking after myself.' She gave him a smile. 'But thank you . . . Luca.'

'Goodnight, Maggie. Hope to see you around.'

Outside in the street, Luca smiled to himself. God, she was as stubborn as she was beautiful.

'Did it work, boss?'

Luca shook his head. 'No. She doesn't want to give a ponce a cut.' He laughed.

'You want me to try again?'

Luca thought about it, and shook his head. Most girls who worked for him had been subjected to the same treatment as Maggie. He'd pay Clive to jump on them, slap them around a bit, frighten them – just like he'd done earlier with Maggie – making them feel that they needed protection. And it worked especially well when he showed up at the end, making it look as if he'd stopped Clive giving them a serious beating.

Then Luca would pick up the pieces, sweet-talk them, take them out for something to eat, convince them that he'd treat them well when they worked for him. As a result, he was now running an ever-increasing number of girls who were indebted to him. Enough to keep him ticking over, to help him rebuild his life, his money . . . his power.

Up until this point, getting Clive to jump them had worked like a charm. Maggie was clearly different. But then why didn't that surprise him?

Chapter Sixty-Four

'There's not much business tonight,' Bernie grumbled as she lit her cigarette. Her blonde hair hung in wispy strands around her face, and her make-up was already smudged, her mascara running down her cheeks in the cold October rain.

'Well, any business is better than nothing,' Maggie said, scanning the street. She'd moved on from blow jobs and hand jobs to full-on sex a couple of months ago. It certainly wasn't her first choice and, unlike a lot of the others, Maggie didn't think she'd ever get used to it. So she tried to stick to anything other than having some sweaty bloke riding on top of her, but if it was that or turn a punter away, she just pulled her knickers down, thought of something else, and let them get on with it.

She hadn't set foot in the East End since her visit to Doris back in July. Though she still kept a low profile and only took Rose out to places where there weren't many people around, or when it was dark, she was getting on with life as best she could. With each day, her confidence grew, and with it her reputation.

'I've heard there's another group of women trying to move in on our patch.' Bernie took a pull on her cigarette. 'Luca will go mad when he finds out.'

'I think the other girls work for Luca too,' Maggie said, eyeing one of the regulars, who nodded her over. 'So long as he gets money in his pocket, he doesn't care who's on whose patch.' She shrugged. 'Look, I'll be back in a minute.' She winked at Bernie. 'And I do mean only a minute.'

Trying to ignore the tightness in her stomach that came on every time she went with some fella, Maggie approached the punter.

'All right, Ernie, how you doing?'

Ernie was a small bald bloke whose eyes seemed too wide apart, and his features were blotted with red, angry spots. 'I'm glad to see you, Maggie.' Ernie leered at her. 'I've missed you.'

Maggie rolled her eyes and walked with Ernie to the alleyway round the corner where all the girls took their punters. It was full of used condoms and litter as well as the occasional rat.

Maggie struggled to smile, but she knew what to say and, as clients went, Ernie seemed harmless enough. 'I've missed you too, Ernie.'

He groaned as they stood in the filthy alley.

'Show us your tits, Maggie.'

Trying not to sigh, she did as she was told. She hoped that, as was often the case with Ernie, he'd get so excited that he'd come without her having to have sex with him.

Ernie reached out to grab one of her breasts, and fondled it like he was making dough while he put his other hand down his trousers, rubbing himself and groaning loudly as spit formed at the corners of his cracked mouth.

'Maggie . . . ooooh, Maggie, this feels good, does it feel good to you?' His voice became high-pitched.

'Yeah,' Maggie said flatly, stifling a yawn before – as she had expected – Ernie came within the minute.

'Same time next week?' He dropped the money into Maggie's hand.

'I can't wait, Ernie.'

Clearly delighted at this, Ernie pottered off, leaving her to saunter back round the corner to where Bernie was.

'I told you I would only be a minute,' Maggie laughed as she walked up to her.

Bernie wasn't listening, though. 'What the fuck is she doing here?'

Maggie glanced towards where Bernie was looking. She watched a large woman approach from the direction of the butcher's. Reenie Jacobs. She was a nasty old cow who mainly worked the docks. Working the docks was harder than working the streets, and it took a certain woman to be able to do it.

Though she had never spoken to Reenie, Maggie had taken an immediate dislike to the woman. She knew trouble when she saw it, and Reenie Jacobs was certainly trouble.

'Oh, fucking hell,' Bernie muttered.

'Well, look who it is,' Reenie called over to Bernie, her voice carrying in the quiet street. 'You still owe me a packet of fags.'

'Keep walking, Reenie,' Maggie shouted back.

'Why should I? It's a public street. I can go where I like.'

'No one wants you round here, so move it, or I'll move you.'

Reenie squealed with laughter, unfazed by Maggie's threat. 'Fuck me, that's big talk from a kid. What are you, eighteen? Nineteen?'

'Sixteen, actually – not that it's any of your business.'

'You think you're something special, don't you. Well, let me tell you, you're nothing but a little scrubber.' She smirked. 'A little scrubber who likes fucking the blacks.'

Maggie moved like lightning, her fist connecting with Reenie's flabby jaw. The bigger woman staggered back against the wall, but she didn't fall.

'You little cunt!' Reenie swung a fist, but she didn't have speed on her side and as a result, Maggie was able to duck easily, delivering a punch to Reenie's stomach.

Reenie farted and wheezed at the same time. Undaunted, she charged like a bull, wrapping her arms round Maggie's waist and slamming her against the lamppost.

Despite the pain exploding in her spine, Maggie brought her knee up, at the same time grabbing Reenie's brittle hair. The distraction allowed her to twist free and escape Reenie's grip.

Knowing that her opponent wouldn't back down until one of them couldn't get up, Maggie swung her fist again at Reenie, connecting with her mouth, but all that happened was Reenie spat a mouthful of blood onto the pavement, and brought her own hand back, slapping Maggie hard across the face.

Ignoring the pain and the ringing in her ears, and realising she had to finish this pronto, Maggie head-butted Reenie, splitting open the skin on her forehead with a deafening crack.

Reenie dropped to the floor, grunting in agony, her dress riding up to expose her naked, pasty-white bum. She screeched at Maggie. 'You're a nasty bitch, no better than that black bastard of yours.'

That was it for Maggie, she leapt on Reenie, raining blows on her head. 'Don't you ever speak about my daughter like that, you understand?'

'Maggie . . . Maggie, leave her now.'

She allowed Bernie to pull her away. Then she glared down at Reenie, who was covered in blood. 'Next time, when I say keep walking, you should take my advice.'

'Christ, Reenie!' Shelley walked up to her, lighting a cigarette. 'You shouldn't have taken on Maggie.' She laughed as she helped Reenie up. 'She has the Irish in her, all right.'

Maggie turned away, linked arms with Bernie and they walked back towards the boarding house. She was looking forward to seeing Rose, who was being looked after by Mrs Mills after Doris had had a word with her. She had to pay her, of course, but it was an extra babysitter for Rose when both Bernie and Sarah were working.

As they turned into the street where the boarding house was, Maggie spotted Denise, a woman who had recently rented a room next to hers. She was running towards them, her face pale.

'What's happened? Is it Rose?' Maggie started to panic.

'No . . . it's Sarah. Her old man found her. He caught up with her. The police are on their way.'

'Her old man?' Bernie frowned.

Denise nodded.

'Where is she?' Maggie asked.

'This way.'

Maggie and Bernie followed Denise round the corner. A crowd had gathered, and Maggie had to force her way through. And then she froze.

Sarah's body was slumped against the wall in a pool of blood. She'd been stabbed several times in her chest and her throat was partly slit. Her eyes were open and fixed on the sky. Her face was almost unrecognisable, it had been beaten so badly. Blood dripped from her torn mouth.

It was a cold reminder that none of them were safe.

Chapter Sixty-Five

The next couple of weeks went by in a blur. A deep sadness settled in Maggie's heart, and she became even more nervous of going out.

A car pulled up next to her as she was walking, and the window rolled down.

'Get in.'

It was Luca.

Maggie sighed. 'When are you going to accept that I'm not interested in being one of your girls.'

'I'm not saying you are interested. Just thought you might want a lift.'

She came to a stop. 'What do you want from me?' She'd had several brief conversations with him since the day she'd been attacked, but right now she wasn't in the mood.

Luca smiled, his handsome face lighting up. 'Nothing. Just let me buy you dinner.' He leaned across to open the passenger door. 'Don't look like that, Maggie. Can't a man ask a woman out to dinner?'

Maggie smiled, and despite herself she felt flattered. 'I've got food back at the boarding house, so I don't need dinner from you.'

He wiped his hand over his chin. 'Has anyone ever told you how stubborn you are?'

She pushed the thought of Rory out of her head. He'd often said that. 'Why do you want to take me out for dinner?'

Luca laughed again and lit a cigarette. He blew out the smoke and it wafted towards Maggie. 'Because you don't look like you've eaten a proper meal in weeks.' His dark eyes lingered on her. He shrugged. 'And you're a very beautiful woman . . .'

Maggie had heard enough sweet talk to last her a lifetime, and look where it had got her. 'I'm not working tonight, so you can save the chat.'

'What do you take me for, Maggie? I like you, that's all . . . Look, how about if I pay you, will you come out to dinner with me then?'

'I already told you I'm not working.'

'Oh, come on. It's just dinner. Don't you want to be treated once in a while?'

She stared at him. 'Just dinner?' She stepped towards the car. 'Nothing more?'

'Nothing more.' He pushed the passenger door open and Maggie got in, trying to tell herself she wasn't about to make yet another mistake . . .

The restaurant was tucked away on a side street near the Isle of Dogs. It was a small place, run by an old Italian family. The place was empty, but the minute Antonio, the proprietor, saw Luca, he smiled and broke out in Italian, laughing and patting him on his back while Maggie stood patiently.

'Come on, let's go to this table over here.' Luca pointed.

Maggie had never been in a restaurant. In a pub, in a cafe, but never a restaurant. Not that it was fancy, but it was clean and the tables were laid out with crisp white tablecloths, slim red candles in the middle, and knives and forks already set out.

'How do you know this place?' Maggie asked, suddenly feeling nervous.

He pulled back her chair for her to sit down. 'I live upstairs. I rent a flat from Antonio. It's perfect for me, gives me time to set up my business.'

He sat opposite her and Maggie wanted to ask him about what had happened with his family. He'd said a few things, though nothing she could really piece together. But she decided against probing for answers, conscious that she wouldn't want anyone to ask her about her own family.

Antonio came over with a bottle of red wine and two glasses. He placed them on the table and left without speaking, and within minutes he'd come back bringing them plates of pasta in a rich meaty tomato sauce, bread which was still warm and a salad.

It was another first for Maggie. She'd never eaten pasta, and she didn't know if she'd ever eaten a salad before, either. Of course she'd seen a lettuce in the grocer's in Camden High Street, but tomatoes and cucumbers, they'd never been able to afford. Instead, they had lived off soups and stews.

She tried to eat slowly, but her hunger won out, and she forked the spaghetti into her mouth, hardly giving herself time to breathe between each mouthful.

Luca refilled her wine glass and sat back in his chair.

'I know you don't want to work for me, and I understand. In fact, I'm not sure if I could take your money knowing where it's come from.'

It was Maggie's turn to laugh now. 'You run girls, Luca. You do it all the time.'

He shrugged. 'I know . . . but I don't care about the other girls. I care about you . . . I want to help you, not as a pimp but as a friend.'

Maggie was surprised by what Luca was saying. 'I don't need friends.'

He reached out and touched her hand, his fingers against hers, and Maggie caught her breath. 'What do you need, then? How can I help you, Maggie? I want to help.'

'I'm fine.' She couldn't tear her eyes away from his.

'Then come upstairs for a nightcap with me.'

She didn't say anything, but she did continue to hold his gaze, and, as it had been since the first time she'd seen Luca Romano, Maggie couldn't help but feel drawn to him, no matter how dangerous that might be.

She followed him out of the restaurant, and up the stairs to his flat.

'Maggie.' He stepped closer to her, his hand sliding down the back of her neck. 'What is it about you?'

He shook his head and, even though Maggie knew she should leave, when he kissed her slowly and gently, she didn't pull away. Instead, she let herself sink into his embrace, allowing herself, for this one moment, to think of nothing else.

Afterwards, Luca traced patterns with his fingers on her skin. 'Stay,' he murmured against her face, and it was then that Maggie noticed the track marks on his arms.

She got up, naked, from the bed. 'I have to go.' She reached for her clothes scattered all over the room. 'This was nice for what it was. But that's all.'

'Come on, Maggie, don't be like that.'

She grinned at him. 'I'm not being like anything.'

'Maggie, please, stay.'

She shook her head. Deep down, she knew Luca was nothing but trouble. She dressed in silence, aware that he was watching her. She smiled and walked up to him, giving him a gentle kiss on his lips. 'Goodbye, Luca.'

'What I said about helping you, I meant. If there's anything I can do for you, Maggie . . .'

She nodded and walked towards the door.

'Maggie,' he called after her. 'No regret?'

'Never.'

Chapter Sixty-Six

Maggie knocked at Doris's door, remembering the first time she'd ever been here. It seemed so long ago now, that day when she'd come here with her mum. She'd grown up so much since then. Looking back, Maggie could hardly remember the girl she used to be.

Sighing, she knocked again, only this time harder, but there was still no answer. She looked to see if the curtains had been open. They weren't. They were still closed, which was strange because Doris never usually kept her curtains shut at all. She would laugh and say she was too nosy, always wanting to know what was going on in the street.

When she tried the handle, it was unlocked. She pushed the door open slowly. 'Doris? It's only me – Maggie. Are you there, Doris?'

There was still no answer. She tried the front room, which was empty. There was a half-drunk cup of tea on the table with mouldy skin forming across its surface. The fire, which was usually full of coal, was empty and cold.

'Doris?' Maggie called out again as she headed towards the back of the house. But like the front room it was empty. Growing increasingly anxious, she made her way up the stairs. 'Doris?'

She heard a feeble cough coming from Doris's room, and

relief flooded through her. The door was slightly ajar, and she walked in.

Doris lay propped up against her pillows, her face grey and pale as she lay in the iron bed. 'Maggie,' Doris said, triggering a bout of coughing. Fresh blood dotted on her lips along with the spit.

'Doris! Why didn't you tell me you were ill? Why didn't you send a message? I would have come earlier.'

Doris gave her a grin, and Maggie had to force herself not to recoil from the stench of her breath. 'I'm not up to taking a piss, darlin', let alone sending a message. Listen to me.' Doris struggled to speak. 'I saw one of Rory's men. I don't know his name, but I've seen him hanging around with Rory.'

Maggie went cold. 'Where was this?'

'He came round here.'

'Oh my God, when . . . when?' Maggie's words tumbled out.

'A few days ago, but I didn't answer. You won't be able to come round here again, though.'

'But I can't leave you like this. Have you seen a doctor?'

'Oh, you know what I think about them.'

Maggie held her hand. 'But you should—'

'Stop bleedin' fussing, Maggie. We all have to go at some time or another.'

'Doris, we need to get a doctor to see you.'

'They're a waste of time that lot. You think I'm going to waste the little time I've got left hanging around the surgery so they can tell me I'm dying?' She shook her head.

'What about going to hospital?' As worried as she was about Doris, Maggie was now feeling edgy about being here.

Again Doris shook her head. 'I used to say to my old man, if anyone wants me out of this house, they'll have to carry me out in a coffin.'

Maggie looked around helplessly. There was a chamber pot in the corner, unemptied, and a pile of cloth covered in blood from where Doris had been coughing.

'You better get off now,' Doris said weakly, giving her hand a squeeze. 'But, listen to me, in that wardrobe there's some money in a brown envelope that I want you to have. It's not a lot, but maybe it'll help you get yourself a little flat to rent. I always wanted to get a place on the south-east coast meself, but I never actually got there . . . Me sister's kids have already got their eye on this house, otherwise I'd give you this as well.'

'Doris, stop. You're gonna be fine.'

She smiled at Maggie. 'And you're gonna be fine as well.' She gulped to find her breath. 'Remember everything that I've told you, and remember how strong you are. You're a fighter, Maggie, and that's what I love about you. Rose is lucky to have you as a mother. Now go on – piss off. But pass me the gin first.'

Doris cackled again and coughed, using the dirty rag to wipe away the spit and blood. 'There's a bottle on the side over there.' She nodded to the table tucked away in the corner.

Maggie grabbed it. 'I'll get you a glass.'

'I wouldn't bother with that – life's too short. Well, mine is anyway.' She grinned but Maggie was finding none of this funny.

The old woman reached for the bottle, but her hand was shaking so badly that Maggie had to help guide it to her cracked lips.

Doris took a small sip, closing her eyes. 'That's better. Helps with the pain. I reckon gin's the tonic to life . . . How's the baby anyway?'

'Rose is doing well.' Maggie smiled. 'I can't imagine life without her.'

'And to think you came to me wanting to get rid. Well, it's a good job you didn't. I reckon that little girl will be the making of you, Maggie Riley.'

Silence fell between them, which was only broken by Doris's laboured breathing. A trickle of blood ran down the side of Doris's mouth and Maggie wiped it away with a cloth. Then she held her hand until a few moments later when Doris stopped breathing altogether.

She stood up and kissed Doris on her head, before going into the wardrobe and taking out the envelope of money which Doris had said she could have. Then she walked out of the door, her heart heavy.

In deep thought, Maggie walked home. Doris had been more of a mum to her than her mother ever was. At least now, with the money that Doris had given her, she could move out of the boarding house and get her and Rose a place somewhere.

She wasn't sure where she'd go. Anywhere outside London might be harder because of people being unwilling to accept Rose, but maybe it would be safer. Or perhaps she'd move to South London; she'd never been there herself, but she'd heard all about it from one of the girls.

Nearing the boarding house, Maggie slowed.

A car idled at the kerb, its engine running with its headlights on. As it began to move away, instinctively Maggie pressed into a doorway, watching as it drove past.

Fear gripped her as she recognised the driver.

It was Malcolm.

Chapter Sixty-Seven

Maggie sprinted for the front door of the boarding house and raced up the stairs. 'Bernie!' She pounded on the door. 'Bernie, open up!' The door was unlocked and Maggie flung it open. It was dark and Maggie fumbled for the light switch. The bare bulb flooded the room with light.

'Oh my God . . . Bernie! . . . *Bernie!*'

Bernie lay across the bed, her neck bent at a strange angle, her open eyes staring at nothing.

'No, no, no.' Maggie rushed over to her. 'No, no, no.' As she began backing away, her gaze moved to the drawer which doubled as a crib.

'Rose?' The word escaped Maggie's throat. 'Rose?'

Maggie turned and ran out of the room back to her own, throwing open the door. It was empty. The room began to spin and she had to grip the end of the bed to keep herself from falling.

Then she ran out, banging on everybody's doors. 'Have you seen Rose? Mary, have you seen Rose? Denise, have you seen Rose?'

No one had seen her.

Rose was gone.

Chapter Sixty-Eight

Maggie pushed through the doors of the Hen and Cock pub which stood on the corner of Whitechapel Road. It was the place where all the girls hung out and everyone knew each other. Smoke hung thick in the air with voices raising over the clatter of glasses and chat.

Maggie shoved her way through the crowd to the bar. 'Jo, have you seen Luca?'

The barman nodded. 'He's through there as usual. Everything all right?'

She didn't bother answering. Instead, she hurried into the back room, where she spotted Luca sitting alone, his shirtsleeves rolled up and a bottle of whisky on the table in front of him.

She glanced at his arm, and she could see a fresh track mark. No doubt he'd shot up in the bathroom.

'Maggie, I didn't expect to see you again so soon.' His eyes were glazed as he tried to focus on her.

'Did you tell him? Did you tell Rory where to find me?' She rushed at Luca.

He grabbed her. 'What the fuck's the matter with you? What are you talking about?'

'He's got her.' Maggie could barely say the words. 'Malcolm took Rose. I saw him.' The terror of it started to sink in and it was all that Maggie could do to stop herself collapsing and screaming.

Luca let her arms go. 'When?'

'Just now.'

'I've got nothing to do with it.' His eyes were half closed as he spoke to her and he unsteadily poured himself a drink.

'When he sees Rose, Rory is going to kill Thomas.' Her words came out in a whisper.

'Who?'

'Thomas, he's gonna kill him . . . I need to get back to Soho.' She moved round the table and began to pull Luca up. 'Luca, can you take me in your car?'

Luca shook his head. 'I can't, Maggie. I can't go back there, not yet anyway.'

Maggie was desperate. 'Luca, I need your help, please.'

Luca's eyes hardened. 'I told you I *can't*. I can't help you with this.' His head fell forward in a drugged stupor and Maggie shook him.

'You said you'd help me.' Maggie raised her voice. 'Luca, you said you'd help!'

She'd wasted valuable time coming here. Why had she thought Luca might be different?

She headed back out into the darkness.

Back to Soho.

Chapter Sixty-Nine

The bus hadn't even come to a stop on Charing Cross Road, and Maggie was already jumping off. She raced along Shaftesbury Avenue, pushing past an elderly woman who was carrying shopping bags and ran across the road, ignoring the oncoming bus.

She ran as fast as she could down Old Compton Street, turning right into Greek Street. Coming to the walk-up's open blue door, Maggie took the stairs two at a time.

'Sally, it's Maggie . . . *Sally!*'

An ex-girlfriend of Davey's, Sally used to work at the club until she left because she couldn't stand working for Rory and hated Chrissy. She'd got on well with Maggie, though, and was one of the few people in Soho she reckoned she could trust.

Without waiting for a reply, she barged into the walk-up room.

Sally was on her knees, giving a blow job to a well-built bloke with thick glasses and a large paunch.

Sally's eyes widened as she stared at Maggie. She pulled back from the man, his throbbing penis dripping as she stood up.

'Oi, what about—'

'Oh, fuck off.' Sally shut him down before he had time to finish his sentence. She shoved Maggie gently out of the door.

'I can't believe you're back,' she whispered. 'Does Rory know?

Oh my God – he's put a price on your head.' Her words came out in a rush.

Brushing the warning aside, Maggie gripped her arm. 'I need you to go to the club. You have to find Thomas, tell him—'

'Thomas?' Sally was puzzled. 'What's this got to do—'

'Just find him and tell him to come here.' Maggie panted. 'He needs to get himself here, fast as he can. Sally, please, hurry.'

Picking up on Maggie's distress, Sally nodded. 'All right, all right, but you're crazy coming back here. Rory's been going berserk since you left.'

Maggie began pushing her towards the stairs. 'If you see Rory, whatever you do, don't tell him I'm here. But you've got to get word to Thomas *now* – this is urgent.'

'Okay, I'm going – if my punter gives you any grief, tell him I'll be back in a minute.'

Sally ran down the stairs and out the door, leaving Maggie to wait.

She locked herself into the lavatory on the landing, listening for Sally's return. Each second felt like a lifetime.

Sally had been gone for what seemed like forever when she heard footsteps on the stairs. Relief washing over her, she opened the door a crack.

'Thomas?'

But it wasn't Thomas.

It was Davey. She stepped out on to the landing.

'Maggie, I've just seen Sally.' He sounded worried.

'Where's Thomas?' she demanded.

'He's gone.'

'What do you mean he's gone?' There was a rush of white noise in Maggie's ears.

Davey ran his hand through his mop of red hair. 'Malcolm told him Rory needed him at the warehouse.'

Maggie clutched her stomach. 'No, no . . . when did he leave?'

'A minute or two before Sally showed up.' Davey grabbed Maggie's arm as she moved towards the stairs.

'He's my friend, Maggie. If he's in trouble, you need to spit it out.' His grip was firm.

'Thomas is Rose's father.'

'What?'

'He doesn't know it yet, but he's the father. And now that Rory has found out, he's going to kill him.'

Davey let go of her in surprise and she tore down the stairs and out of the walk-up. She kept running, turning right into Moor Street. Ahead of her, she could see the bright lights of Cambridge Circus. A black Jaguar was pulling away as the lights changed to green. Sitting in the back seat was Rory, with Thomas beside him.

'No!'

The scream ripped through her as the car disappeared into the distance.

Chapter Seventy

'Why are we here, Mr Sheehan?' Thomas licked his lips nervously as he stood in the derelict front room of a boarded-up terraced house.

Rory didn't answer. He just circled him slowly, looking him up and down. Malcolm stood by the door, arms folded across his chest, his massive frame blocking the only exit.

'Mr Sheehan, is there a problem? I thought you wanted me to check—'

'Change of plan, Thomas,' Rory said, his voice soft in the empty silence.

Thomas knew what it meant when he used that tone of voice. He eyed the door nervously.

'I should probably be getting back to the club—'

'You can try.'

Rory pounced, grabbing him by his throat. His fingers pressed into Thomas's windpipe as he slammed him face-first against the wall.

Thomas yelled as blood sprayed, his nose smashing on the impact. He dropped to the floor, gasping, while blood poured into his mouth. 'Mr Sheehan . . . please.' His words came out in a whisper. 'What have I done wrong?'

Rory's boot stamped down on his ankle with a loud crunch,

bending it to the side. Thomas screamed, trying to pull his broken ankle away, but Rory ground down on it harder.

'*What have you done wrong?*' Rory bellowed, bringing his foot down again. 'That's what you're asking me, Thomas?'

Thomas's screams echoed through the empty house. He clawed at the floor, trying to drag himself away. 'I've done everything you asked, Mr Sheehan,' he pleaded.

Rory lit a cigarette and looked down at Thomas writhing in agony on the floor. 'Yes, Thomas, you've been a good worker. That's true.' He lifted his foot, releasing Thomas's broken ankle. Then he pulled a length of chain from his overcoat pocket, wrapping it round his fist. 'But that's not what this is about.'

Malcolm stepped forward and grabbed Thomas by his hair, yanking him up to his knees.

'I don't know what I've done . . . *I swear.*' Blood bubbled from Thomas's mouth.

'Really?' Rory took some smoke down into his lungs. 'Hear that, Malcolm? Thomas doesn't know what he's done.' He laughed, but then it faded. He glared at Thomas and lowered his voice to a whisper. 'Then I'll tell you, shall I?' He paused to finish his cigarette and flicked it at Thomas.

Ice-cold fear rushed through Thomas as he looked at Rory's chain-wrapped fist.

'I warned you, Thomas. I told you never to go near my wife. But you did, didn't you?'

Rory's fist connected with his mouth, smashing the metal into Thomas's face. His teeth shattered from his gums, and the pain caused Thomas to collapse as Malcolm dropped him.

Gagging on his own blood, Thomas was unable to speak as Rory drove his knee into his stomach and then into his balls.

As he spewed vomit and blood, Rory leaned down over him.

No Regret

'What did you do, Thomas? Did you force her?'

'It wasn't like that.' Thomas's words were barely audible.

'Then what was it like?' Rory signalled to Malcolm, who hauled Thomas back up on his feet and held him while Rory pummelled his ribs, breaking them.

'You touched what was mine, Thomas.' Rory unwrapped the chain to its full length. 'No one touches what's mine . . . I warned you.' Rory reached into his pocket, pulling out a gold lighter, and the flame jumped to life with a click. 'And do you know how I found out, Thomas?'

Thomas could only manage the slightest shake of his head.

'Was that a *no*, Thomas?' Rory put the lighter near his face. He laughed. 'Well, tough. You're never going to find out—'

The last thing Thomas saw before he blacked out was Malcolm, standing over him with a can of petrol, ready to pour.

And the last thing he heard was Rory's voice saying, 'Burn in hell.'

Book Four

Ten Days Later

I am no bird, and no net ensnares me. I am a free
human being with an independent will.

Charlotte Brontë

Chapter Seventy-One

Rory leaned back in his armchair, watching Maggie pace the floor like a caged tiger.

'Just tell me where she is.'

'Maggie, we've been over this already. Rose is perfectly safe – safe from you, at least.' He stood up and walked over to her.

'From *me*? What's that supposed to mean? It's you she needs to be kept safe from.'

He grabbed her and Maggie tried to push him away, but she was no match for him.

'Listening to you, anyone would think that I'm going to harm my own daughter.'

'She's not your daughter. She's mine. Mine! Why couldn't you have just left us alone?'

It was now ten days since she'd been forced to return to Rory's flat above the Cow and Bull in the hope of being reunited with her daughter. But Rory was still refusing to tell her where Rose was being kept. And since she was being kept prisoner in the flat, where the only person she saw aside from Rory was Malcolm, she had no way of finding her daughter.

'Come on, Maggie. You're my wife. Did you really think I'd let you and Rose get away from me?'

The moment he loosened his grip, she pounded her fists against his chest.

'She *needs* to be with me,' Maggie screamed. 'Give me back my daughter – that's all I ask.'

'She's my daughter as well. We're married, remember. Everything that's yours is mine – and that includes Rose.'

Maggie grabbed the fruit bowl from the sideboard and threw it against the wall. It shattered into tiny pieces. 'She's not yours!' she shrieked. 'She's mine and Thomas's, and I'm glad she is.'

Rory grabbed her by the hair and flipped her neck back. Then he placed his hand on her throat, squeezing it, before kissing her hard on the lips. He pulled away as he began to breathe heavily. 'Well, that's a shame, isn't it? Because Thomas went up in a ball of flames.' His face twisted with anger. 'If you want to see Rose again, you better start behaving yourself. She doesn't want a fucking whore for a mother, do you understand me?'

Maggie gave a tiny nod, trying to breathe as the tears blocked her nose.

'Good. It's time you learned.'

He let her go.

She tried again, keeping her voice low this time. 'When can I see her?'

The response was a cold stare. 'I think you're forgetting your fucking manners.' He slapped her.

Her head flicked to the side, and she swallowed hard. She daren't try to fight back. She caught a glimpse of herself in the mirror. Her hair was brushed back into a long ponytail and the grey woollen dress she wore was buttoned up to her neck. 'When can I see her, *please*?'

He winked at her and planted a kiss on her cheek. 'See, that wasn't difficult, was it?'

'It's been over a week . . . You said yesterday that I could see her.'

He went over to the sideboard and poured himself a large glass of whisky. He swirled it round before taking a swig. 'Did I?'

'You promised. *Please.*' She hated having to beg him.

He waved the glass in the air. 'Here's the thing, Maggie, promises are strange. They have a habit of being broken. You of all people should know that.'

Despite her better judgement, she launched herself at him, her fingernails drawing lines of blood down his cheeks. 'You bastard!'

Rory caught her wrists, laughing as she struggled and kicked at his shins.

'I hate you! I'll always hate you,' she hissed through her teeth.

He backed her up against the sideboard. 'Hate me all you want, Maggie, so long as you do what you're told.'

His mouth pressed against hers in a kiss that tasted of whisky and cigarettes, while his hand yanked up her dress, his hand moving between her thighs.

She stood rigid, not responding and not fighting, even when he entered her roughly.

Eventually, he broke away. His face tense, his jaw moving as he ground his teeth, he stomped over to the door, opened it and called out. 'Malcolm, you can come up now. And bring Chrissy with you.'

He sneered at Maggie. 'You wanted to see her.'

Malcolm entered the room, followed by Chrissy, who carried a bundle wrapped in her arms.

Maggie rushed forward and gently pulled back the blanket from around Rose's face. There she was with her tiny fists clenched and her green eyes blinking up at her. Maggie carefully took her from Chrissy, holding her close and kissing her head of brown curls.

'My beautiful little girl,' Maggie whispered.

Rose gurgled, looking like she had grown in the ten days since she'd last seen her. She was clean and well dressed in expensive baby clothes and she smelled of lavender.

'She doesn't stop bleedin' crying.' Chrissy tutted. 'Gives me a right fucking headache, she does.'

'What are you talking about?' Maggie snapped, wanting to smash the smug smile off her face.

'Chrissy's looking after her.' Rory smirked. 'She's doing a fine job of it.'

'No . . . No.' Maggie couldn't believe what she was hearing. She clutched Rose to her, the baby nestling against her neck. 'No. Chrissy's not going anywhere near my daughter. I won't let that bitch have anything to do with her. Rose belongs to me.'

'And you belong to me.' Rory took a swig of whisky. 'So I'll decide who looks after Rose.'

Glaring defiantly at Chrissy, Maggie snarled, 'You keep your fucking hands off her.'

'It's not your decision to make – it's Rory's. As I told you on your wedding day, I take my orders, amongst other things, from him, not you.' Chrissy smiled at Rory and batted her false eyelashes at him.

Maggie spun to look at Rory. 'You can fuck her all you like' – she jerked her head at Chrissy – 'but she's not looking after my daughter.'

Rory's face darkened. 'That's it. Time to say goodbye, Maggie.'

'What?' she stared at him in disbelief. 'No, you can't.' She began to back away, holding Rose to her chest. 'You're not going to take her, none of you are. She's mine and she needs to be with me. You can all go to hell.' Maggie was becoming hysterical.

'Malcolm.' Rory jerked his head at Maggie.

Malcolm stepped forward. Maggie tried to back away, but she found herself cornered. His strong arms closed around hers and he began to pull Rose from her.

'Get off her, get off her!' Maggie screamed as the baby began to cry. '*Please*, Malcolm, let go.' She struggled against his grip. 'Please just a little longer, *Rory*, please. I'll do anything you say—'

With one last tug, Malcolm ripped Rose from Maggie's arms. She tried to reach out, but was blocked by Rory. Helpless, she watched as Malcom handed her baby to Chrissy. Rose's cries grew louder as Chrissy walked out of the room with Malcolm.

'No! *No!*' Maggie fought wildly. 'Rose! *Rose!*'

Rory threw her to the floor, where she crouched, sobbing.

He leaned down and gripped her chin in his hand, forcing her to look at him. 'If you behave yourself, I'll let you see her again – next week.'

'Next week! No, Rory, you can't do this to me. I can't live like this. Why can't we have her here with us?'

Rory stroked her face. 'And risk you running off again? The minute I turn my back, you'll be gone. I can't have that, can I? At least this way I know you won't be going anywhere in a hurry.' He leaned forward and kissed Maggie.

'Some day, I swear to God, Rory, I'll kill you.'

He kissed her again and smiled. 'Maybe.' He laughed. 'But not today . . .'

Chapter Seventy-Two

Rory's club on Bridle Lane hummed with Saturday-night business. The cigarette smoke hung thick in the air as the band Rory had hired for the evening played the Shadows' 'Wonderful Land'.

Maggie sat alone at a corner table, nursing a glass of gin. She'd lost count how many she'd had, but she didn't care as long as it dulled the world around her and the pain she felt inside.

A week had gone by, but Rory hadn't allowed her to see Rose. He'd dangle the promise of a visit, then snatch it away to punish her.

The only escape left to her was the gin, and she was happy to drown in it. Every day since she'd been back with Rory, she'd woken up with a hangover. Then she'd start drinking again the moment she got out of bed.

Her focus beginning to blur, she watched Rory, holding court as usual, with Malcolm and a couple of his cronies hanging on his every word. Then she glanced towards the bar. No friendly faces there, either. No one had seen Davey since the day Thomas had been taken away.

Her breath caught in her throat. She couldn't let her thoughts wander to Thomas. Not on top of everything else. If she did, Maggie was scared what she might do. And then what would happen to Rose?

There was a loud bang and suddenly uniformed policemen began thundering down the stairs into the club.

A tall, slim detective in plain clothes stepped on to the stage. The band stopped playing as he stepped up to the mic.

'Nobody move.'

Rory rose slowly to his feet. 'Evening, officers, is there something I can help you with?'

The detective, who looked to be in his mid-thirties, stepped down from the stage and crossed to Rory's table. He took an official-looking document from his pocket and held it out in front of Rory. 'I'm Detective Inspector Simons of the Metropolitan Police. We have a warrant to search these premises, Mr Sheehan.'

Rory glanced at the warrant and passed it to Malcolm without reading it, then he painted on a smile and shrugged. 'Search away. I've got nothing to hide. Though I'd appreciate it if you were quick about it and your boys didn't make too much mess.' He sneered at Simons. 'I've got a business to run here, you know.'

'Your business is exactly why we're searching the property, Mr Sheehan.' Simons nodded to his men, who began moving through the club, checking behind the bar, opening cupboards, while some of their colleagues headed through to the back. 'We've had information about illegal goods moving through this establishment,' Simons added.

'Illegal goods?' Rory smirked. 'This is a club, Inspector. What sort of goods are you hoping to find? Things move through here all the time, but nothing illegal, I might add.'

'I'm talking cigarettes, Mr Sheehan. American cigarettes and tobacco. Large quantities being brought in and sold on the black market.'

Rory shrugged and, taking the mickey, he pulled out a packet of cigarettes and lit one. 'I have no idea what you're talking about.'

Maggie took another swallow of a gin, embracing the burn. 'You should listen to Rory, Inspector.' Unsteadily, she got to her feet and tottered across to where DI Simons was standing. 'He's such a good man. Everything he tells you is the truth.'

'And who's this?' Simons asked, turning to Rory.

'This is *my wife* . . .' Rory took hold of her hand, squeezing it a little too firmly.

'Hello, Inspector.' Swaying, she leaned on Rory to keep her balance.

Simons studied her for a moment, then reached out and gently turned her face so the light caught it. 'Those are some nasty-looking bruises you've got there, Mrs Sheehan.'

Maggie jerked her head away. 'What's it to you?'

'You'll have to excuse my wife, Inspector.' Rory dug his nails into her wrist. 'She's had a bit too much to drink.'

'I can see that. Are you all right, Mrs Sheehan?'

Maggie gave a slow deliberate smile and leaned towards Simons, giving him a clear view down the front of her frumpy dress, which she'd partly unbuttoned. 'Never better, but I might need someone to look after me tonight.' She licked her lips as her hair tumbled over her face.

She winced as Rory's grip tightened.

'Maybe you shouldn't have any more to drink, Maggie. Come on, you wouldn't want to miss seeing Rose tomorrow, would you?'

Even in her state, Maggie knew a threat when she heard one. She lowered her voice to a whisper. 'I'm sorry . . . I'm sorry.'

Rory gave her an indulgent smile and turned back to the

inspector. 'If there's anything I can do for you, just let me know . . . *Anything*.' He emphasised the word.

'Mr Sheehan, a word of advice,' Simons said coldly. 'I won't be bought.'

'Sir.' One of the uniformed officers approached them. 'We found nothing suspicious in the back room or storage areas or in the yard.'

Simons nodded. 'And in the office?' He sounded frustrated.

'We've checked there too, sir. Nothing. It's clean.'

Rory grinned widely. 'Perhaps I can get you a drink, then, before you go?'

Simons glared at him. 'We're not finished with you yet.' He turned to the officer. 'Check again. Check everywhere.'

The search continued for another thirty minutes. Maggie watched, knowing they'd find nothing. The tobacco shipment had arrived yesterday and had already been broken down into smaller packages and distributed to the network of shops, pubs, casinos and clubs that Rory sold to.

'Satisfied?' Rory asked smugly when Simons finally called off the search.

'For now. But we'll be watching you very closely, Mr Sheehan.' He turned to Maggie. 'If you need anything, Mrs Sheehan . . .' He left the offer hanging in the air.

Maggie raised her empty glass. 'I need another drink.'

After the police had gone, the atmosphere in the club slowly returned to normal, the band struck up again and conversations resumed.

Rory slid into the seat next to her. 'Did you enjoy that little performance?'

She smirked drunkenly as her head lolled to one side.

'You think it's funny, Maggie? What you did there, embarrassing me in front of everyone, embarrassing yourself. You think that's how I want my wife to behave?' He leaned forward. 'Just for that, you won't get to see Rose this week.'

The words cut through her drunken stupor. 'You can't—'

'Oh yes I can. I can and I bloody well will.' His hand covered hers and he pressed down with his thumb so hard it made her gasp. 'Next time you want to flirt with a copper in my club, remember it's going to cost you.'

He stood up, straightened his jacket and returned to his table where Malcolm was waiting.

Maggie signalled for another drink. If she couldn't see Rose, she might as well stay drunk. But there was a small part, a clear part, in her mind that knew one day she would pay Rory back for everything he'd done . . .

Chapter Seventy-Three

The Speckled Hen on Greek Street was a shithole. Like a lot of the pubs in the area, it stank of cheap beer and perfume, and it was packed wall to wall with punters. Most of the tables were full, and the bar area was crowded. Maggie sat in the corner, hunched over a glass of gin.

Rory would be going out of his mind that she'd snuck out of the club, but let him fucking rage. She didn't care any more. As the days without Rose ticked by, she found it hard to even care about herself.

The room felt like it was swaying each time she moved her head. She'd lost count of how many gins she'd had. Five doubles? Six? Maybe more. Who was counting? The more the merrier.

The empty glasses lined up in front of her blurred before her eyes as a barmaid with a large droopy bust collected them with a tut. 'I reckon you've had enough, love, don't you?'

'Not even close.' Maggie didn't bother looking up. 'Until I can't think straight or see straight, I haven't had enough.'

Her eyes drifted across the crowded bar, settling on a man who was sitting on his own. From where Maggie was she could just make out he was in his late forties, perhaps a little older. He was well dressed, at least as the punters in this pub went, and he'd been watching her for the past ten minutes or so.

She raised her glass in his direction, booze spilling over the rim. 'Want to join me, sweetheart? I could do with a little company.'

The man hesitated and then got up, bringing his pint with him. He walked unsteadily to Maggie, patches of sweat under his arms. 'Mind if I sit down?'

She nodded to the chair next to her. He sat close enough that his knee pressed against her. 'I'm Reg.'

As he leered at her, Maggie noticed the bits of food in his wiry beard.

She gave a shrug. 'I couldn't care less who the fuck you are.' She drained her glass. 'As long as you buy me another drink.'

Reg looked slightly surprised and then laughed and signalled to the barmaid. 'Bring her whatever she's drinking, put it on my tab.' He turned back to Maggie. 'Haven't seen you in here before.'

'I don't wanna talk,' she snapped.

The fresh drink arrived and she knocked it back in one, wiping the drips off her chin.

'So if you don't want to talk, what do you want?' Reg stared at her, a hungry look in his eyes.

'It's not what I want, it's what you want, Reg.' She slurred her words.

His face brightened then. 'What I want . . .'

Maggie felt his hand moving up her thigh.

A large grin was spreading across his face.

'*Reg!*'

A woman's voice screeched across the bar and he jolted his hand away from Maggie's thigh as if he'd been burned. A peroxide blonde in a tight-fitting blue dress tottered over, her face flushed red. 'What do you think you're doing?'

'Lil!' Reg half rose from his chair. 'I was only . . .'

'Only what?' Lil cut in. 'Getting cosy with another little tramp, are you? I can't turn my fucking back for one bleedin' minute, and you've already got your hands up her cunt!'

Maggie snorted. 'Who are you calling a tramp?'

Lil's eyes narrowed. 'If I were you, love, I'd keep your trap shut. I'll deal with you in a minute.'

This was an invitation Maggie was keen to take up. 'Why wait a minute? I'm ready now.'

Lil snorted, a look of disgust on her face.

Reg raised his hands, trying to placate her. 'Lil, just—'

'Shut it, Reg.'

As Maggie got to her feet, Lil knocked the glass from her hand. It smashed to the floor. 'You want my husband? Is that it, you little slag? You can't find your own, so you want to nick someone else's?' Her face twisted in anger. 'Well, he's my husband and you're not gonna get your hands on him.'

Maggie roared with laughter at this.

In return, Lil spat in her face.

Grabbing Lil by the hair, Maggie gave her a hard slap that split her lip. Lil shrieked and clawed at her, and the two of them staggered sidewards, banging into a table, sending more glasses and ashtrays crashing to the floor.

Ignoring the shouts from outraged customers, Maggie brought her fist back and drove it into Lil's face, but the momentum overbalanced her and she toppled over.

'Bitch! You ain't going to steal my husband!' Lil jumped on top of Maggie, and they rolled across the floor, which was sticky with spilled drinks and littered with broken glass. Lil grabbed Maggie by the hair and tugged her head to the side, while Maggie kicked out with her legs, forcing Lil off her.

'Whore!' Beside herself with anger, Lil reached for a piece of broken glass and tried to slash Maggie's face, but she moved her head and it just nicked her chin.

Furious, Maggie slammed her knee into Lil's stomach.

The woman groaned and rolled on her side as Maggie began to pummel her face with punches. Until suddenly she felt herself being hauled backwards.

'That's enough.' A uniformed police constable restrained her. 'I said, *that's enough*.'

A second officer grabbed Maggie's arm, yanking her roughly to her feet. 'You're nicked.' He looked at Lil. 'Both of you.'

Maggie continued to struggle. 'Get your hands off me.' She tried to twist out of their grip. 'Don't touch me! Do you fucking hear me?'

'Calm down, miss.' The constable tightened his hold. 'You're only making it worse for yourself.'

'No, you're making it worse . . . You'll regret this,' she hissed. 'My husband's Rory Sheehan, and he won't take kindly to you lot carting me off.'

The constable looked at his colleague. Everyone knew Rory Sheehan, the things he did, the things he got away with, the people he had in his pocket.

The second constable shrugged, nonplussed. 'We still need to take her.' There was uncertainty in his voice, though. 'Let's get her down the station. She can sober up there.'

Still yelling, Maggie was escorted into the street.

Chapter Seventy-Four

Unaware of what was happening only a few streets away, Rory was in a rage. He was trying to focus on the business meeting he was having, but as usual Maggie was at the forefront of his mind. She'd been gone for almost three hours now – what the fuck did she think she was playing at?

'Rory?' Malcolm was speaking. 'What do you think?'

'What do I think about what?' Rory snapped.

'About Simons. It doesn't look like he's going to be bought.'

Rory knocked back his whisky. 'Rubbish. Everyone has their price.'

Barry, a burly Scot who'd done a ten-year stretch for battering his wife to death, and who'd been offered a job by Rory on his release from prison, shook his head. 'Not Simons. Word has it he's been brought in to stamp down on things around here.'

'That doesn't mean he can't be bought,' Rory snarled.

'But if he can't that's gonna make it hard to bring in the goods,' said Frank, a Port of London employee who'd been on Rory's payroll since he'd started work at the docks.

Rory rubbed his head. He didn't need this shit. 'We've managed so far, so I don't see there being a problem.'

The men all looked at Rory, unconvinced, as he shouted

across to Guy, who was busy cleaning the bar. 'Has Maggie come back yet?'

Guy shook his head. 'Not yet.'

Rory's face was a picture of fury and it didn't go unnoticed by the men.

'And the warehouse fees have gone up again,' Malcolm said, glancing at Frank. 'The greedy fuckers want another oner on top of their usual.'

Rory took in this information and nodded at Frank. 'Then pay them. We don't want any delays. We want to get the shipments into Limehouse, then get them taken straight to the warehouse without any grief, especially if we've got the filth sniffing around.' He clicked his fingers for Guy to bring him another whisky.

The higher tax rates that the government had slapped on tobacco made it more expensive in the UK than in other countries. Every fella smoked, demand was high, but money was short what with the cost of living, so for most families life was a squeeze. But they still wanted their fags and tobacco, so selling it at discount rates while racking up a profit was a lucrative side gig for Rory. Apart from a bit of grief now and then, it was easy money compared to the protection rackets. And the profit he made on tobacco put everything else in the shade. It was getting to the point where his club, pub and other business ventures combined didn't match what he was earning on tobacco.

'It looks like the Turks are getting bolder,' Andy chipped in. He was the oldest man present, and loyal to the core. Like Malcolm, he was ready to give his life for Rory. 'Apparently, they're going round some of our shops trying to flog the cigarettes they've brought in for a cheaper price. We need to watch them, especially if they've got eyes on our shipments.'

Rory didn't need this headache. He could deal with the Turks but, like a lot of things, the timing had to be right. He had a big shipment coming in on Friday – very big, worth thousands – and an even bigger one the week after, so right now he didn't want to start a war with anyone. He needed things to run smoothly. He'd forked out a lot of money for these shipments, so nothing could go wrong. If it was true that Simons couldn't be bought, that could cause him a lot of grief.

'Boss? Do you want me to go and look for Maggie? Put your mind at rest?' asked Malcolm.

Rory gave a tiny shake of his head.

'Are you sure? It might help you to focus.'

'You saying I can't concentrate on my own fucking business?' Rory wasn't having any of it.

Malcolm knew not to argue with Rory, especially when he was in this mood.

'Mr Sheehan,' Guy called over. 'Sergeant Jones is out the back. He's hoping to have a word with you.'

Rory nodded. 'Show him through.'

Jones was in Rory's pocket. He'd been the one who'd warned them that Simons was going to raid the club looking for contraband tobacco. It wasn't cheap paying everyone on his books, but Sergent Jones was worth his weight in gold.

'What can I do for you, Jonesy? You want a drink?'

Jones, a lanky man with bland features, shook his head. 'I'm on duty, guv. But there's been a bit of a development I thought you might want to know about. The raid last Saturday – turns out it wasn't our division that gave it the go-ahead. There's a new special unit been set up, which I didn't know about until today. Scotland Yard have teamed up with Customs and Excise, and Simons is handling the Soho side of things.'

'And he can't be bought?' Rory grunted.

'No, and it's not worth trying – he'll be down on you like a ton of bricks. He's already got his beady eye on you. I'll do my best to tip you off, of course, but it would be wise to keep everything in the warehouses for the time being, rather than bringing stuff in here. Simons likes to do double raids. He wants you to get cosy after the first one, and then he'll come in again a day or so later.'

Rory sighed and ran his hand through his hair. 'I appreciate the warning.'

'Word has it, Simons is like a fucking terrier once he gets his teeth into something. He's got a lot of men watching your place in Camden as well.'

Rory shrugged. 'Let them watch. There's nothing to see, not around there anyway.' He nodded to Jones, dismissing him. He needed time to mull this over. It was too late to cancel the shipments, not to mention too costly.

'There's something else . . .' Jones looked uncomfortable.

'Come on, then, spit it out.' Rory took a deep drag of his cigarette.

'Your wife – Mrs Sheehan.'

'I know who she fucking is,' Rory snapped. 'What about her?'

Sergent Jones looked towards Malcolm, and then back to Rory. 'She's been arrested.'

Rory went very still. 'What?'

'Drunk and disorderly. A fight broke out in the Speckled Hen about an hour ago.' Jones didn't meet Rory's eyes. 'She's in the cells down Charing Cross nick.'

'Fucking hell!' Rory's calm composure cracked. 'Who the fuck thought it was a good idea to take her in?' He slammed his fist on the table. 'I want names.' He turned on Jones and poked him in the chest.

Jones swallowed. 'Simons brought in some new fellas from his old station . . . it was probably one of them.'

Rory chewed on his lip.

'Want me to go, boss?' Malcolm said quietly.

'No.' Rory drained the last of his whisky and ground his cigarette into the ashtray. 'I'll handle this. I need to see what my fucking wife has to say for herself.'

And, with that, he marched out.

Chapter Seventy-Five

Cell 5 at Charing Cross nick measured little more than eight feet by ten. It was cold and damp, and the walls were grey from decades of grime. There was a small, barred window, and in the corner a bucket for sick or piss.

Maggie slumped on the bench, her head hanging between her knees, trying desperately not to vomit. She was still drunk, but the numbing effects of the gin were wearing off, leaving a hollow emptiness in its place.

Hearing a key rattle in the lock, she looked up.

'Mrs Sheehan.'

DI Simons entered the room and stood in front of her.

'I thought I told you the other day, fuck off,' Maggie muttered.

Simons stepped into the cell, closing the door behind him. 'I hear you put up quite a fight out there. Is that how you got the other bruises to your face, Mrs Sheehan, or have you been in more than one fight recently?'

Fighting off another wave of nausea, Maggie slurred, 'I just want to know where she is . . .'

Simons frowned. 'Know where who is?'

'She should be with me.'

'Mrs Sheehan, you're not making any sense.'

'He's got her, did you know that?' The words tumbled out. 'He won't let me see her. He's given her to his tart of a girl-friend.' Maggie wiped away the tears with her sleeve. 'I don't know what to do. What am I supposed to do?'

'Mrs Sheehan, I need you to slow down. Who has her? And who is she?'

'Don't you fucking know anything? I'm talking about my daughter. She's only five months old and I want her back.'

'Mrs Sheehan, maybe it would be a good idea for us to speak about this when you're a bit more . . . a bit more yourself.'

Maggie laughed scornfully. 'I am my fucking self.' She glared at him. 'What do you want to know?'

'Well, I had hoped to talk to you, but, as I say, maybe we should leave that for another time.'

'The only thing I want to talk about is getting Rose back. If you can't do that . . . get out, get fucking out . . . Go on.'

Simons crouched before her. He brought his face level with hers. 'Mrs Sheehan, I'd like to help you.' He paused. 'Maybe we can help each other.'

Her eyes came into focus. 'What do you mean?'

Simons stood up. 'I think we'd better speak when you've sobered up. I'll be in touch, Mrs Sheehan.'

She watched him walk towards the cell door, then shouted after him. 'My husband won't like me speaking to you.'

Simons gave her a look of sympathy. 'From what I gather, he doesn't like you speaking to anyone . . . so that's why we're not going to tell him.'

Chapter Seventy-Six

Not a word had passed between them since Rory had signed Maggie's release papers. Not even when he'd gripped her arm hard enough to bruise her, steering her past the desk sergeant's knowing look. And not during the drive back to Camden.

By the time they reached the flat, Maggie had sobered up completely. And now she was terrified of the punishment that lay ahead.

The flat door slammed behind them, making her flinch.

Rory shoved her into the front room.

He circled her, then rapped her hard on the head with his knuckles. 'What have you got to say for yourself?' His voice was deceptively gentle.

She bowed her head, not daring to speak.

'Nothing?' Rory's jaw tightened. 'Have you got nothing to say to me, Maggie? No fucking excuses?'

'What's the point?' she muttered.

The slap snapped her head to the side, flooding her mouth with blood where she'd bitten her tongue.

'The point' – Rory's eyes flashed – 'is for my wife to show me some fucking respect.'

She straightened up then. 'Respect?' She couldn't keep the scorn from her voice.

The second blow caught her across the temple, sending her staggering back against the sideboard. The glass whisky decanters rattled with the impact.

'You're making a fool of me, Maggie. Is that your game?'

'No, I—'

'Shut it,' he growled. 'Blind drunk and scrapping in public like a cheap tart. And I have to pay the Old Bill to get you off a drunk and disorderly charge.'

Another blow, this time hard enough to make Maggie's ears ring. She had to grab the sideboard to stop herself from falling.

'Rory—'

'I said *shut it*!' He was breathing hard now, and he grabbed her jaw, forcing her to look at him. 'I've tried to be patient with you, Maggie, and look how you repay me.'

He drove his fist into her stomach. She doubled over in pain, gasping, but before she could recover, he punched her again, cracking his sovereign ring across her cheekbone, sending her sprawling onto the carpet.

The coffee table overturned as she fell, the ashtray crashing to the floor. She tried to crawl away, but he grabbed her by the hair, yanking her head back.

'Rory, please, I just want her back, that's all . . .'

Ignoring her pleas, he hauled her to her feet and threw her against the wall. The force of it left a spray of blood on the wallpaper. She whimpered as she slid down to the floor again.

'You seriously think you can get away with making a fool of me?' He stormed over to her, and began raining down slaps and punches. 'Is that why you let Thomas have his way with you?'

'No . . . no.' Maggie covered her ears. She couldn't bear to hear about Thomas.

'You're lying!' He caught her wrists as she tried to shield

herself. Holding them above her head with one hand, he wrapped the other around her neck.

Maggie clawed at his hand as she struggled for breath.

'I've given you everything, and this is how you repay me.'

He let go of her throat, then dragged her by her feet into the middle of the room. He clambered on top of her, his weight pinning her to the floor. 'You belong to me – every fucking part of you belongs to me.'

He tore at her dress then, the buttons popping open. As he ripped off her knickers and undid his zip, she lay motionless, her mind disconnecting from her body as it had so many times before in her young life.

When it was over, Rory stood over her, fastening his belt. 'Get cleaned up now. We've got people for dinner. I expect you to join us.'

Blood trickled from her split lip and from the cut above her swollen eye as she looked up at him.

He paused in the doorway. 'Oh, and, Maggie, I'll kill you if you ever try to leave me again.'

She turned her head away.

Without Rose, she was already dead.

Chapter Seventy-Seven

The dining room at the back of Rory's pub was quiet aside for the scrape of cutlery against plates. The heavy velvet curtains were closed, and the overhead light cast shadows across the large table. The smell of gravy and smoke mingled in the air while the clock on the mantelpiece ticked away.

Maggie sat rigid at the far end of the table. Her face was a mass of purple and red bruising, her left eye swollen shut.

Rory sat at the other end of the table, cutting into his pork chop while Malcolm and Barry sat on either side of him, their plates half empty having tucked into the chops, boiled potato, carrots and cabbage that the cook had made.

'Eat up, Maggie.' Rory spoke without looking at her as he continued to saw into his chop. His voice was calm. 'Cook's gone to a lot of trouble.'

Maggie didn't move, the untouched plate of food growing cold in front of her. Malcolm busied himself with his meal as Barry shovelled food into his mouth.

'I said, *eat up.*' This time Rory's voice was harder, and when Maggie didn't answer, he pushed back his chair with a loud scrape, and marched over to her. He stood behind her, reached down and took her fork, stabbing a piece of potato with it. 'Open wide.'

When she didn't, he grabbed her jaw with his free hand, his fingers digging into her bruised flesh, and when Maggie's mouth opened in pain, he shoved the potato in. 'Now chew the fucking thing.'

He leaned down to watch as she began to eat, then he patted her on the head. 'That's my girl.' Casually, he returned to his seat and pouring himself a glass of whisky.

He took a swig, then turned his attention to Malcolm and Barry. 'So, everything's in place for Friday's shipment?'

Malcolm nodded. 'The tobacco's coming into Limehouse, and the crates will be marked *Smith's Furniture* as usual.'

'And the unloading?' Rory asked.

'We'll have men down there, ready and waiting,' Malcolm continued. 'They'll take the shipment straight to the warehouse. We'll be able to move everything before midnight.'

'What about the Turks?' Barry asked as he wiped up gravy with a piece of crusty bread.

'Fuck the Turks,' Malcolm said flatly. 'They know better than to cross our patch in Limehouse.'

Rory leaned back and lit a cigarette. 'I want to be sure they won't fuck this up.' He took a drag and rubbed his chin. 'We can't have anything going wrong. Not at this stage, not with the second shipment only a week away. I've put too much money in for the Turks or the Old Bill to mess this up for me.' He looked at Barry. 'The shipment on the twenty-seventh is going to be the big one. It'll change everything.'

'Rather than leave this smaller shipment in the warehouse overnight, maybe what we should do is break it down, load it on a lorry and move it somewhere else.'

'Like where?' Malcolm asked. 'Simons has men watching all our properties.'

Rory took another gulp of whisky. 'I say we take it to the church. Father Patrick has no problem with us using the place. And who's going to look in a fucking church vault?'

Malcolm laughed. 'Hiding behind the big man himself, Rory?'

Rory joined in the laughter, but stopped when he caught sight of Maggie slumped in her chair. 'How about you crack a fucking smile when we've got guests, *Mrs Sheehan*?'

She raised her head, blinking her eyes as if he'd woken her.

Rory shrugged. 'Well, I'll tell you what *will* put a smile on your face, Maggie darlin'. If you behave yourself, I'll get Chrissy to bring Rose to see you on Sunday. You'd like that, wouldn't you?'

'Really?' Her eyes pleaded with him.

Rory nodded. 'Yes, really, Maggie . . . as long as you behave yourself. You be a good girl for me, and I'll let you see our daughter . . .'

Chapter Seventy-Eight

As Sunday morning dawned, Maggie sat by the window, waiting for Rose to arrive.

She was due to arrive at eight o'clock.

At nine thirty, Maggie reluctantly tore herself away from the window. Once again, Rory had gone back on his word. Rose wasn't coming.

She went to the sideboard and picked up the bottle of gin.

The burn of it in her throat promised at least some relief from the pain.

Twenty minutes later, still clutching the bottle of gin, she went downstairs, grabbed her coat and headed out the side door. If that was the way they wanted it, then she'd fucking show them.

By the time she stumbled off the bus, the world seemed to be tilting from side to side as she navigated the street in her drunken state. The gin bottle, now empty, slipped from her hand and smashed to the pavement.

She kicked at it, lost her balance and fell into the gutter, muddying her cream coat. Using the wall to get up, she wiped her hands on her coat, and crossed the road.

When she pushed open the heavy wooden doors, the congregation were on their feet singing 'Guide Me, Oh Thou Great

Redeemer'. Maggie scanned the rows, her vision blurring with the booze.

She staggered into the aisle, banging into a stack of bibles on the table by the door. They tumbled down with a crash and one by one heads began to turn.

Maggie didn't care who was looking. She continued to scan the pews until she saw them.

On the second row from the front, Rory sat in his Sunday best with Chrissy beside him, dressed up like mutton. There was no sign of Rose. He wasn't about to parade 'his' daughter in front of the congregation – not when she was the spitting image of Thomas Johnson.

A row behind them, Maggie saw her mother.

She stumbled down the aisle, knocking into the ends of the pews, vaguely aware that the organ had stopped playing and the church had fallen silent.

'I want my baby back!' Her shrill voice echoed around the church.

Father Patrick glared at her from the altar. 'How dare you enter the house of God in such a state, Maggie. Have you no shame?'

'I WANT MY DAUGHTER!'

Father Patrick recoiled and looked to Rory, who got to his feet.

'Maggie, you're making a show of yourself.' Rory looked her up and down in disgust. 'You're drunk.'

'And, if I am, whose fucking fault is that?'

'Don't try to blame me for your drinking!' He spat out the words for the whole congregation to hear.

Maggie wrapped her arms around herself. 'Who else should I blame. It is your fault I'm like this. Yours!'

Her mother stood up then, thin-lipped and rigid. 'Margaret

341

Riley Sheehan, you get yourself outside this minute. Haven't you shamed us all enough?'

Maggie laughed, a harsh, broken sound. 'Shame? You want to talk about shame, Ma?' Her eyes were full of angry tears. 'Well, you are the expert. After all, you stood by while my da raped me – that's shame.'

There was an audible gasp from the congregation.

Kathleen's face was ashen. 'Lies, all lies!'

'But it's not, is it.' She turned to Rory. 'You know I'm telling the truth.' Her voice broke in pain.

Father Patrick stormed down the aisle and grabbed her by the arm. 'How dare you speak of such things! Get out now and don't come back. I shall pray for your sins, and God have mercy on your child with a mother like you.'

Maggie pulled free, stumbling backwards. 'I'll get her back. I'll get my baby back if I have to burn this whole fucking place down.'

She turned and fled, stumbling over the bibles that she'd knocked to the floor.

As the cold air hit her, Maggie started to run.

Chapter Seventy-Nine

By the time Maggie returned to the Cow and Bull, she had sobered up. She'd expected Rory to be waiting there, ready to give her another beating, but the flat was empty. She walked through the door and sank to her knees as the shame of how she'd behaved in church pressed down on her.

She didn't regret what she'd said to her mother, though, and she wasn't sorry that she'd told everyone she wanted her daughter back. Speaking those truths was something she would never regret.

Letting the shame and humiliation wash over her, she put her head in her hands. The only thing she'd achieved in speaking out that way was to prove to everyone that she was unfit to be a mother.

Feeling sick, she got up and walked upstairs to the bathroom. She turned on the taps and splashed her face, the cold water a shock against her sore and bruised skin. When she looked up, her reflection stared back from the ornate mirror.

She froze, truly looking at herself for the first time since she'd returned to Camden.

Her face was bloated from crying, her left eye surrounded by a blue-and-purple shiner. Her other eye was bloodshot and her long hair hung messily. Her clothes were stained with mud where she'd fallen in the gutter.

She barely recognised herself. Where was Maggie Riley? Where was the Maggie who'd survived the things her da did to her? The Maggie who'd worked all hours, but still managed to have a smile on her face. The Maggie who'd been prepared to take on anyone who insulted her daughter? The daughter she loved with all her heart, the daughter she'd give her life for.

Where was that Maggie?

Gone.

She'd drowned herself in gin and self-pity.

Seized by fury, Maggie grabbed the heavy bottle of bath salts and hurled it at the mirror. Both bottle and mirror shattered in an explosion of glass fragments. She sank to the floor, breathing heavily, her head bowed low.

And the face that came into her mind then was Doris's.

Old Doris, the woman who'd help girls in trouble. She'd survived a lifetime of troubles, and despite her suffering she'd been a friend to Maggie.

Be smarter than them, Maggie, Doris had told her.

Drying her tears, she got to her feet, stepping carefully over the broken glass. She was going to get Rose back. But not by screaming, not by begging Rory, not by drowning in gin or wallowing in self-pity. No, she would follow the advice Doris had given her. She'd use her brain, she'd take control, she'd be clever. She'd start keeping an eye out for opportunities.

With a new sense of determination surging through her, Maggie walked out of the bathroom, her mind now focused on what she needed to do . . .

Chapter Eighty

'Open up . . . *open up*!' She banged so hard on the dark blue door that her palm stung. Her voice was hoarse from where she'd screamed in the church that morning. But she was stone-cold sober now. 'Luca . . . Luca, if you're in there, open up. I need to talk to you!'

She heard footsteps on the other side of the door. A moment later, Luca opened it, frowning as if he didn't recognise her.

Maggie was having trouble recognising the handsome young Italian in the gaunt figure standing in the doorway. In the few months since she'd last seen him, his eyes had dark circles under them, his cheekbones had grown more prominent and he had lost weight. The track marks on his bare arms gave the reason for the transformation.

'Maggie? What are you doing here? I didn't think I'd see you again.'

'Can I come in? I need to talk to you.'

The urgency in her voice penetrated his drug-induced lethargy. With a long sigh, he nodded and beckoned her to enter.

She followed him up the stairs, remembering the night she'd been here with him. It felt as if it had been five years ago, not five months.

His once-tidy room was now littered with dirty plates, empty

345

glasses, syringes and needles. The ashtrays overflowed and the curtains were partly drawn.

He slumped down on the couch and opened his arms as if to ask what she wanted.

Maggie paced the room as she talked. 'I know you couldn't help me last time I saw you, but we need to work together now, to help each other.'

He frowned. 'With what? What sort of help are we talking about?'

'I need to get Rose back, and to do that I need to bring Rory down.'

Luca shook his head. 'What's this got to do with me?'

She sat down next to him, and he reached up to touch her face, his fingers tracing the bruises.

'Because Rory's always been your enemy too. And the only way we can bring him down is if we work together.'

'Maggie, I've got my own problems right now, and Rory isn't one of them. All that's in the past for me.' He shrugged. 'I'm building myself up again. I'm not looking back.' There was a hint of the old Luca as he added, 'But I am going to get back what's owed to me. I'm going to get my life back. That's got nothing to do with Rory, though.'

And then he sat nodding to himself, muttering something about the Romano name and respect, as if he'd forgotten that Maggie was there.

Maggie laid her hand on his arm. 'Luca, please, you have to help me.'

He pulled his arm away to reach for a bottle of pills on the floor. Shaking several into his palm, he asked, 'What do you expect me to do? Walk into his pub and kill him?' He swallowed the pills dry, then laughed bitterly.

'You've got contacts,' Maggie insisted. She got up and opened the curtains on the weak December sunset, then sat back down again.

'No. I *had* contacts. Things change, and the people who you once thought were your friends become your enemies. But my time will come.' He gave her a smile as his eyes began to shut.

'But how long are you going to wait, Luca? How long?'

'There's an old Italian saying: *La pazienza è la virtù dei forti.* It means, patience is the virtue of the strong.'

Maggie knew she didn't have time for patience. Somehow she needed to persuade Luca that he didn't have it either, because what she had planned wasn't something she could do alone.

Since pleading wasn't getting her anywhere, she'd have to find another way.

Use your bleedin' brain, girl! She could picture Doris, teacup of gin in hand, cheering her on.

'Don't you want revenge?' Maggie asked.

'Of course I do – but the revenge I'm looking for doesn't involve Rory. Like you, it's all about family for me. But Rory isn't my family. Your revenge has nothing to do with mine.'

'You need revenge on Rory for what he did to your family.'

Luca rolled his eyes. 'How many times do I have to tell you? As far as I'm concerned, Rory's the past. He's way down the list of my concerns.'

'Really? What if I told you . . .' She leaned forward, her eyes locked on his, making sure she had Luca's full attention. 'What if I told you it was Rory who killed your cousins, and I can prove it?'

347

Chapter Eighty-One

Maggie was aware how late it was. She was also aware of what would happen to her when she got back, but whatever the punishment Rory doled out, it was going to be worth it.

Besides, after her outburst at the church, Rory would punish her whether she was home early or late.

She wiped the condensation from the windscreen. The moon filtered through gaps in the trees, casting long shadows across the clearing as she watched Luca in the car headlights, digging.

On the way here, Luca had barely spoken as she gave him directions to the place Thomas had taken her, just over a year ago, to show her where the bodies were buried.

Of course, she hadn't told Luca that it was Thomas who had stabbed his three cousins. She'd placed all the blame on Rory – after all, he was the one who'd forced Thomas to do it. He was the one who'd given the orders.

Luca said he'd known in his gut that Rory was responsible, but he'd never been able to prove it. So now he wanted to see the evidence, even if it meant taking a shovel and digging an hour in frozen ground to find the remains of his cousins.

The December chill had seeped into the car and Maggie's fingers were numb in her pockets. She tried rubbing her hands together and blowing into them as she continued to watch Luca, his breath clouding in the cold, his shirt stuck to him with sweat despite the freezing night air.

Suddenly, Luca threw down the spade and dropped to his knees, scrabbling frantically at the earth with his bare hands.

Then he went still for a moment before lurching backwards and crawling away from the hole he'd dug. He began to vomit, the deep heaving sounds carrying through the night. When he looked up, his face was a mask of grief. In that moment, Maggie knew he'd found them. His three cousins. The boys he'd grown up with who'd turned into men, working beside him to help build the Romano business.

Maggie had hated them for what they'd done to Thomas. They'd dragged him out of a cafe, beaten him and then thrown him in the canal, leaving him to drown. Not because he was an enemy – he didn't work for Rory back then – but because he was black.

Even so, she felt for Luca. She could see how much it hurt him, finding their decomposing bodies.

Luca staggered to his feet, wiped the vomit from his mouth with the back of his hand and walked across to the car. Exhausted, he leaned on the roof and gazed at Maggie through the open window.

'Will you help me now?' she said quietly.

He nodded. 'I'll help you . . . I'll bring Rory down.'

She closed her eyes and put her head in her hands. Relief washed over her. She knew now there would be no going back. For either of them.

Rory's days were numbered . . .

Chapter Eighty-Two

Maggie was a bundle of nerves. If Luca screwed this up, her one and only chance would be lost, and then what would happen to Rose? It didn't bear thinking about. As she'd done so often in her life, she pushed the thought into that dark place in her mind and tried to forget about it.

She glanced at the watch Rory had given her, making sure she had time to get back to the club before Rory returned from Lime-house docks. Not that he would suspect she was planning his downfall; he was more likely to assume she'd run away again. If he decided to have her followed whenever he wasn't around to watch her himself, that would put a major spanner in the works. Fortunately, he was confident that Maggie would never run away so long as he had Rose stashed away; he'd seen how he could control her simply by denying or granting access to her daughter.

The car windows were fogged with condensation. Maggie spoke with a quiet urgency as she sat in the back seat, watching the entrance to the church.

'Mrs Donovan and Mrs O'Malley will be arranging the flowers. They usually leave around six and then one of them comes back to lock up for Father Patrick at seven o'clock.' She glanced at Luca to make sure he was paying attention. 'Mrs Donovan's routine runs like clockwork, so you'll need to be out before seven, otherwise you won't be able to get in or out once she's gone, and there won't be any other chances – Rory is planning to move it out again tomorrow.'

Luca nodded, his gaunt face illuminated by the glow of his cigarette. 'And this priest? Father Patrick, what about him? There can't be any fuck-ups, Maggie.'

'You think I don't know that?' she snapped. 'I'm putting my life on the line here. I'm putting all my trust in *you*.' The thought was enough to make her jittery. Luca had been hell-bent on retribution since seeing the corpses of his three cousins, but could she trust him to get the job done? He was, after all, an addict.

'Father Patrick's out in the community today,' she said, trying to stay calm. 'He always visits his parishioners on a Friday, and he never gets back till late in the evening. The curate's in hospital, so Mrs Donovan is in charge of locking up.'

Maggie would have preferred to wait a week for the main shipment, which would give them more time to prepare. But it turned out Luca didn't have enough money to hire all the men they'd need for the job; she could only assume that was down to his addiction – back in the summer, he'd been rolling in cash.

'You know what you have to do?' she asked.

He gave a nod, but she decided to run through it one more time just to be on the safe side.

'So, once you're in, you need to go straight down the aisle.' Maggie pictured it in her mind's eye. 'Then when you get to the front row, where the tall gold candlesticks are, turn into the right wing. The stairs to the vault are behind the confessional.'

It crossed her mind that giving Luca all this information could be dangerous; he might not use it in the way she'd intended. But it was too late to worry about that now.

'The keys are kept above the wooden door. You can't miss them. They hang on a nail behind the crucifix.'

A black car rolled past and Maggie fell silent as she watched it drive by. She knew Rory was in the East End right now, but that didn't stop her feeling nervous. She turned to look at Luca again.

'Fifty per cent,' she reminded him. 'That was the agreement – half the profits, not a penny less.'

Luca's mouth tightened. 'I've been thinking about that. Since I'm the one taking the bigger risk, how about we say sixty/forty.'

She shook her head. 'That's not what we agreed.' It angered Maggie that he'd left it till now to try to renegotiate their deal, and it didn't reassure her that she'd been right to trust him. 'I need that money and, besides, I've got to live with Rory – if anything, I'm the one who should be demanding a bigger cut.'

Luca didn't answer immediately. He took a deep drag on his cigarette and blew out the smoke before finally agreeing. 'Fine – fifty/fifty. I'll make sure my men turn the job round tonight. Then tomorrow I'll meet my contact. He's prepared to buy the shipment outright. We'd get more if we broke it down and started to sell it, but that would take time and we need a quick turnaround on the money, so this way is as good as any.'

Maggie agreed. Selling it to clubs and pubs and other venues, the way Rory did, would bring in more money, but it would take time they didn't have – and put them at risk if either Rory or the police got wind of someone with a shipment to sell.

'And then we can focus on next week's shipment. The money from that one will set you up for life, and I'll be back in business, only this time, bigger and better. It'll show my father he can't get rid of me. It'll change everything.'

'You're right – it will,' Maggie agreed. 'Because, once you're back in business, that's when you're going to kill Rory.'

Chapter Eighty-Three

As the bus back to Soho trundled along the Euston Road, a thousand thoughts flashed through Maggie's head.

If all went to plan, by New Year's Eve she would have enough money to start a new life with Rose. Somewhere far from London, where nobody would know them.

Provided nothing went wrong.

She got off the bus two stops early, even though it was pouring with rain. She was hoping the walk would calm her nerves. The moment Rory found out the shipment was gone, all hell would break loose. She didn't want anyone recalling that she'd been acting strange on the day the tobacco went missing.

Fortunately, the rain made it perfectly natural to walk along holding your brolly at an angle that covered your face, so there was little chance of anyone noticing her. It also meant that she didn't see the man stepping out of the newsagent's on the corner of Old Compton Street until it was too late.

She banged into him and almost lost her balance.

'Sorry,' she said, raising her umbrella. 'I didn't see . . .' But the words died in her throat when she saw who she'd collided with. It was DI Simons.

She tried to dodge past him, but he caught her arm. 'Mrs Sheehan, it's good to see you.'

Maggie pulled her arm free.

'And you're looking so much better than you did last time we met.' He studied her face. 'Although it looks as though some more bruises have appeared . . .'

His gaze was so intense she had to turn away. 'Leave me alone.' She began to walk off, but Simons blocked her way.

'You may remember, I was hoping to talk to you.'

'I've got nothing to say to you.' There was no way Maggie could risk anyone seeing her with Simons. Desperate to get away, she told him, 'Look, I'm meant to be meeting my husband at his club and I'm late.'

'Well, that's all right, because he's not there right now.'

Maggie knew this, but the fact Simons was aware of it suggested that he had men watching the club. She hoped that wouldn't be a problem. 'He's probably running late too, then, isn't he. So if you'll excuse me.' Her voice was sharp.

'Maggie, you and I can help each other. I'd say you want your husband out of your life as much as I want him off the streets.'

'That's not true . . . I love my husband.' The lie came easily to her. She tried to sidestep him, but again he blocked her way.

'Do you love him when he beats you?'

Instinctively, Maggie's hand went to her eye, the bruising around it now faded to black and yellow.

'What is it you want from me?'

Simons gave her a tight smile. 'I've been hearing some very interesting things lately about your husband's business arrangements.'

She kept her face neutral. 'I don't know anything about his business. It's got nothing to do with me.'

Simons raised an eyebrow. 'So you don't know anything about shipments of tobacco?'

'He doesn't discuss his business with me. I can't help you.'

'Then what about your daughter?'

That got Maggie's attention. She didn't say anything, but Simons continued to talk.

'Last time we met, you said he'd given her to his tart of a girl-friend. I understand you'd like her back.'

Maggie could barely remember what she'd said when she'd been locked up in the cell, but everything about this conversation with Simons now felt like it might ruin her plans. 'Keep out of my business. I can't help you with anything.'

Simons narrowed his stare. 'Can't or won't? There's a big difference.'

'I need to go.' Gripping her umbrella, she pushed her way past a group of men coming out of the pub. But as she hurried down Old Compton Street she could hear him calling:

'You know where I am, Mrs Sheehan . . . You know where I am.'

Chapter Eighty-Four

Luca crouched in the shadows beside the main entrance of the church. The two vans he'd borrowed were parked close by, the men he'd recruited waiting inside them. Everything was in place, but the sensation of ants crawling under his skin was gaining in intensity. He reached for the small tin in his pocket. He'd been trying to cut back, but this was no time to go cold turkey. He dry-swallowed two, and hoped that would be enough to get him through.

He could see Willy keeping lookout across the street. He couldn't count on Willy to lay down his life for him the way his Romano cousins would have done, there was none of that Italian loyalty, but as hired muscle went, he was reliable. Luca had used him in the past and was confident he'd get the job done.

'. . . to say she liked the drink as much as any sailor would be an understatement!' An old lady shuffled out of the church, talking to the younger woman who was walking beside her.

Luca pressed himself deeper into the shadows as they passed, and when their chatter and footsteps had faded, he waved to Willy, who gave a low whistle.

Three figures emerged from the parked vans across the street and walked briskly towards the church.

'Ladies gone?' Mickey, a short, muscle-bound man asked as he drew level.

'The two flower arrangers left,' said Luca. 'I didn't see anyone else go in there.' He flicked a glance at the door and then up at the church clock. 'We haven't got time to hang around. They lock up at seven, so we need to go in sharpish.'

'And if we meet anyone?' Willy asked.

'We do as little harm as possible. We're there to get the crates, that's all. Clean tracks. If we batter some old girl in a church, the Old Bill will be swarming all over the place.' He nodded to the others. 'Ready? Then let's go.'

Each carrying several large canvas bags, they slipped through the wooden doors.

The lights inside were still on and Luca tried to step quietly, but he couldn't avoid his footsteps echoing in the church. Following Maggie's instructions, he led the way down the aisle, passing the rows of wooden pews until he reached the front row.

'Right wing.' Luca gestured with his head, hurrying past the gold candlesticks. 'Behind the confessional.'

His men followed in silence, looking from side to side, checking the pews for anyone kneeling in prayer. When Willy knocked against a rack of hymn books and sent them tumbling to the floor with a crash that sounded like thunder, everyone froze.

'For fuck's sake!' Luca hissed. 'Why don't you ring the fucking church bells while you're at it.'

'Sorry, boss,' Willy mumbled, stooping to replace the books.

'Leave them,' Luca ordered. 'Come on, I want to get in and out of this fucking place. Churches have always made me nervous.'

They reached the confessional, a dark wooden structure with heavy purple curtains, and slipped behind it. Just as Maggie had said, there was a narrow wooden door set into the wall.

Luca reached up, his fingers finding the crucifix hanging above. Behind it, he felt a small iron key hanging on the nail. 'Got it,' he whispered, inserting the key into the lock. 'Fuck . . . fuck.' It wouldn't turn. He tried wiggling it, but it still wouldn't open. Agitated, he banged his fist on the door, and the resulting boom echoed around the church.

'Here, let me try.' Jimmy stepped forward, and Luca moved aside.

A moment later, the door swung open with a shrill creak. Narrow, winding steps led down into darkness. Luca pulled out his torch, its weak beam lighting the way. 'Careful,' he warned. 'The last thing we need is one of you cunts falling down them.'

They set off down the stairs, the air growing damp and cool as they descended into the vault. The beam of Luca's torch swept across stone walls lined with wooden shelves holding dusty books.

At the end of the vault, there was another door with a modern padlock. Luca produced a short iron rod and prised the hasp securing it out of the old wooden door frame. The wood splintered and the door flew open.

He turned to the others. 'We're in.' He grinned and pushed open the door.

Boxes lined one wall and in the centre stood what they'd come for: six crates of tobacco, each one stamped with the false furniture labels.

'There's our payday, boys.' Luca winked at Willy. He moved across to the crates. 'Knife.'

Jimmy pulled a large knife from his pocket and handed it over. Luca worked it under the lid, breaking the top off one of the crates.

He smiled. Inside there were dozens of packets of tobacco wrapped tightly in cellophane.

'Move fast,' Luca ordered as he shone the torch. 'Last thing I want is to get locked in here.'

They worked quickly, transferring the tobacco into their canvas bags. There was more tobacco than Luca had anticipated, and he was wondering whether they'd have to risk a second run to get all of it.

Like the other crates, the sixth was tightly packed. As fast as he could, Luca began transferring the contents to the remaining canvas bags.

His fingers touched something hard beneath the final layer of tobacco, and he pushed the packets aside to expose what lay beneath.

'Hello.' A whistle escaped from his lips. Hidden in the bottom of the crate, lying on top of a hessian sack, were ten handguns. He pulled one out and grinned at Willy, spinning the empty chamber. 'Seems like Rory's been enjoying himself . . . Let's take these as well.' He took the rest out and they began tucking them in their waistbands and pockets,

'Let's go.' They hurried back up the stairs, locking the vault door behind them and replacing the key on the nail.

'I'm sure I left my purse in the vestry, Mary.'

'Bloody hell,' Jimmy mouthed as they heard a woman's voice.

The men crouched in the shadow of the confessional, listening to the women's footsteps approaching along the aisle.

Jimmy brought out his knife.

'You want me to sort them out?' he whispered, turning the blade in his hand.

Luca shook his head and held up a hand.

The footsteps grew fainter as the women turned left at the

altar, and then they heard the sound of a door opening and closing.

'Move!' hissed Luca.

The men hurried down the aisle, each weighed down with several canvas bags. Thankfully the street was empty when they came out of the church with their haul, and they made it to the vans without incident.

Once everything was loaded and they were on their way, Luca leaned back against the passenger seat, a smile on his face. 'Now that was easy.'

It was the first step in the bigger plan. A way back to the top for him. And, for Maggie, it was the beginning of her way out . . .

Chapter Eighty-Five

The day after the robbery Maggie was slumped in her usual corner of the club in Soho with a half-empty glass of gin in front of her. She'd been nursing it for an hour, occasionally spilling drops on her dress. Playing the part she needed to play.

She wasn't drunk, but she needed to look like she was. She needed to reek of the stuff. She needed to convince Rory, and everyone else, that nothing had changed, when the truth was that everything had changed.

And she sat and watched and listened . . .

In the centre of the dance floor, four men knelt with their hands tied behind their backs, blood dripping from their split lips and broken noses, terror on their faces.

These were Rory's delivery men. The ones who'd moved the tobacco from the warehouse to the church. And Rory stood with his fists covered in blood while Malcolm and Barry looked on, their faces impassive, almost bored, as they watched their boss at work.

'One more time,' Rory said, his voice calm. 'I'm going to ask you again . . . where the fuck is my tobacco?'

The driver, Archie, spat blood onto the floor. 'I told you, Mr Sheehan. We delivered it all. Locked the door ourselves.'

'I'm not saying you didn't. What I'm saying is, it's not there any more, and I want to know which one of you cunts is responsible. Or maybe it was all of you?' He narrowed his gaze. 'Is that it? You were all in on it? Did you think I wouldn't notice when I went back to get the crates and every single leaf of that tobacco had vanished? How much of a cunt do you take me for?'

'Mr Sheehan, I have nothing to do with this.'

The chain Rory liked to use to dish out his punishments whistled through the air, connecting with Archie's back. He fell forward and, unable to break his fall with his hands, his face smashed to the floor. He let out a scream.

'Wrong answer.' Rory unwound the chain, letting the links clank together. 'Someone took it, and someone knows who.'

Maggie took another pretend sip of gin, watching through half-closed eyes. When Rory glanced her way, she raised her glass unsteadily in a toast, as she often did when pissed, continuing to play along.

He winked at her, then returned his attention to the men.

'What about you, Freddie?' Rory lifted the man's chin.

'It could've been anyone from the dock or the warehouse. We just did what we were told, Mr Sheehan. Delivered it to the church.'

'See, that's the part I don't understand, Freddie. No one would have known where we were taking it, unless one of you lot opened your fucking mouth. Did you talk, Freddie? Did you open that fat fucking mouth?'

Freddie's eyes were wide. 'No, no, but it wasn't just us who knew.' He glanced at Malcolm and Barry. 'There were other people.'

Rory laughed hard, but it was hollow. 'You think it had something to do with them? Did you hear that, Malcolm? Freddie reckons it was you. Maybe I should have you kneeling down here too.' His face turned into a snarl. 'Or maybe it was the priest. Maybe, while I'm at it, I should bring Father Patrick in here? Or how about the women who arrange the flowers? Maybe it was them.' He leaned down, bringing his face close to Freddie, who was shaking. 'But I don't think any of them did it. So that leaves me asking, who the fuck did it?'

'I don't know,' Freddie sobbed.

Maggie reminded herself who these men were. She'd seen them in the Cow and Bull, where they were regulars. They worked for Rory, not only delivering contraband but delivering beatings as part of his protection racket. For all the time she'd known them, they'd revelled in violence, dishing it out to people who didn't deserve it. So she pushed aside the guilt she was feeling.

'I swear.'

The chain came down again, this time across Freddie's shoulders. His scream filled the club.

Malcolm shrugged. 'Not sure they know, boss.'

Rory straightened up, cracking his neck from side to side. 'Then who? Who else knew about where we stored it?'

'Are you sure Father Patrick wouldn't have slipped up by mistake?' asked Barry.

'No. He never has before.' Rory was adamant.

'Could be the Turks,' Malcolm suggested, lighting a cigarette. 'They've been pushing into our territory.'

'Maybe, but it feels too much like an inside job. They had to go through the church doors and the one to the vault. And, even if it was them, how would they know?'

Malcolm looked down at the tied and battered men. 'Something just doesn't feel right.'

Maggie let out a little groan and let her head loll against the back of the chair, trying to make it look as if she was struggling to stay awake. Rory glanced at her, but immediately returned his attention to Malcolm and Barry.

'The main shipment's coming next Friday,' Rory said thoughtfully. 'How are we supposed to fucking prevent this from happening again if we don't know who is behind it? It makes me jumpy,' Rory admitted. 'It makes me wonder who we can trust.'

'Maybe we should get in touch with the Turks. Warn them off? Send a message to them?' Malcolm lowered his voice. 'If it is them, we can't let them get away with it.'

Rory was silent for a few moments, mulling it over. 'Trouble with that is, if it isn't them, not only will we be letting them know we can't look after our own shit, we'll be creating a war that we don't need right now. Simons is already sniffing around, so we need to keep as low a profile as we can.' He poured himself a glass of whisky and took a large sip. 'If it turns out we need to go after the Turks, we'll do it once next Friday's shipment is in and safely distributed. I don't want to start dragging any more cunts into this – that wouldn't be good for us right now. Agreed?'

Barry nodded. 'Agreed.'

'What about changing the location of the shipment? You want me to try to find another warehouse to store it in?' asked Malcolm.

'No.' Rory's decision was immediate. 'We don't want to go shouting about the fact we're looking for somewhere. That'll only advertise the fact we're expecting a large shipment and make us a target. But we use double the men. Armed.'

He turned back to the kneeling men and, without warning, swung the chain at Freddie's head, smashing it down with a sickening crack. Freddie collapsed to the ground, his body twitching as his eyes rolled backwards. Not finished yet, Rory brought his foot down with full force on Freddie's neck, snapping it.

Shocked, Maggie let her glass slip, gin spilling across the table. The sound drew everyone's attention.

'I'll take her home, shall I?' Malcolm glanced at Maggie, then back at Rory.

'Take her in the office for now. You can drive her home after you've helped Barry get rid of them.' He nodded towards the men.

'All of them?' Barry's face remained expressionless.

'All of them,' Rory said coldly.

A shadow fell across Maggie. Malcolm leaned over her. 'I need to take you to the office. Can I get you another drink?'

Maggie forced herself to stand, swaying slightly. 'I'm fine.' She allowed Malcolm to lead the way, leaning heavily against him, playing her part. As they passed the kitchen, he pushed open the door and shouted, 'Davey, I'm leaving Mrs Sheehan in the office. Listen out for her.'

Davey shouted back. '*Okay, Malcolm.*'

She'd had no idea that Davey was back.

Malcolm opened the door to the office. 'I'll be back for you soon.' The distrust in his eyes when he looked at her made her feel uneasy.

'Are you sure I can't get you anything else?'

'I'm fine,' Maggie muttered, and slumped in Rory's chair. 'Gonna have a nap.'

Once Malcolm had gone, closing the door behind him, she began to worry. Did he suspect? Did he know what she was trying to do? Her heart began racing. How could he? Maybe it was just her imagination working overtime because she was terrified.

The door opened then.

Maggie looked up. 'Davey.'

'Sorry, Mrs Sheehan. Should I get you some water. Malcolm said you might need some.'

Maggie straightened, her eyes suddenly clear and focused. 'Close the door, Davey.'

He looked unsure.

'Davey, *please*, close the door.'

He did as she asked. She got up from the desk and went over to him.

'I need your help,' she whispered.

Davey looked nervously at the door. 'Maggie, I can't—'

'Please.' Maggie cut him off. 'I'm not drunk. I just need to know where Rose is. You're close to Chrissy.'

Davey shook his head. 'Not any more.'

'But do you know where Rose is being kept? I wouldn't ask you if I wasn't desperate.'

Davey looked away.

'You do know, don't you?' She grabbed his arm. 'Davey, look at me. I need to get Rose away from Rory. He doesn't care about her – he knows she's Thomas's daughter. And anyone who sees her will know that, which is why he never shows her off. For now, she's useful to him, but what will happen when she gets older? I need to get her somewhere safe.'

As she pleaded with Davey, a gut-wrenching scream filtered through from the main club.

'Please, Davey, I have to get her away from here. I don't care what Rory does to me, but if I'm dead, who'll protect Rose then?'

Chapter Eighty-Six

Standing under the trees on the north side of Regent's Park Zoo, Maggie leaned against the railings, keeping an eye out for anyone who might be watching her. She needed to be careful. She would have preferred to meet Luca further away from Camden, but she didn't want to be out of the area too long.

Still raging about the stolen shipment, and with so much riding on the shipment due in on Friday, Rory was even more suspicious than usual, and his temper was more unpredictable. He'd even had a blazing row with Malcolm, which was unheard of, so she daren't risk being out of his sight for more than an hour. He'd only agreed to let her out this afternoon because it was two days till Christmas and she'd told him she wanted to buy Rose a present. She'd nip into the zoo shop when they were done and buy her a panda teddy.

She was still keeping up the pretence of drinking, though it was a struggle. Slurring her words and acting drunk was easy, but resisting the urge to down the drink and let the booze take the edge off, that was the hard part. Now she could feel everything and it was so raw and painful that she longed for something to numb that pain.

On the plus side, Rory now dismissed her as a lush and spoke to his men in front of her as if she wasn't even there. She'd learned a few bits and pieces, but not as much as she would like.

'Open your bag.' Luca suddenly appeared beside her. The black hat he was wearing was pulled down low.

Maggie frowned. 'Why?'

'Just fucking open it,' he snapped, his eyes scanning the park.

Maggie did as she was told. He took a black-plastic-wrapped package the size of a brick from his pocket and dropped it into her bag. 'That's your money. Fifty per cent, like we agreed.'

'Where am I supposed to keep it?' Maggie's heart rate shot up. She had assumed he would hand over her share from the first shipment, plus an upfront payment for the main swoop, on the day she was leaving. Together with the money Doris had given her, that would be enough to find somewhere she and Rose would be safe, and she'd meet up with Luca later to get the rest.

'It'll be difficult to store it somewhere that Rory won't see it.' The envelope with Doris's money was taped under the wardrobe, and every time Rory went near it her heart would start pounding.

'That's not my problem.' He shrugged. 'There's more than I thought there'd be, cos it turns out Rory is smuggling more than just tobacco.'

'Like what?'

'Like this . . .' He reached into his coat again and pulled out a small hessian pouch. 'Take it. Be careful, though.'

'What is it?'

'It's a gun.'

'No.' Maggie yanked her hand away. 'I don't want it.'

'Don't be so fucking stupid. You might need it.'

She shook her head. 'I don't even know how to use one.

I'm not taking it, Luca. I can't. It'll be hard enough hiding the money, let alone a gun.'

'Suit yourself.' He slipped it back into his pocket. 'But you might regret not taking it.'

'I won't.' She was adamant. 'Look, I have to go soon, so we need to run through the plan for Friday. They're going to move the crates from Limehouse to the warehouse this time, so that's where you'll need to hit them.'

'And the address?'

'I'll show you where it is on the day.' She knew if she gave him the address, he wouldn't need her any more. This was her guarantee that he would wait for her and things would go the way she'd planned.

'On the day?' His head whipped round to look at her.

'Yes. Rory's so paranoid after the last shipment was stolen that he keeps making changes to his plans. Malcolm reckons they should hire a warehouse, but he wants to use his own. They've been at each other's throats over it.'

'Why not hit them at the docks, then?' Lucas took a drag from his cigarette. 'Why not spring it straight away?'

'He's doubled his men for this one. It's made him nervous, not knowing who stole the tobacco from the church, so there'll be twenty, maybe twenty-five of his men when the crates come in.'

'So we follow them to the warehouse. Once they've finished unloading, he's not going to leave all his men there overnight, just a few guards. So we jump the crates during the night.'

Maggie shook her head. 'No. If he does use his own warehouse, it's isolated and there are no roads nearby, except the track down to it, and inside the layout is mostly open,' she said, remembering how it looked the last time she'd been there with

Rory. 'There's nowhere to hide. They'll see you coming from miles away.'

'All the more reason to wait until most of them are gone, then. We can still get the shipment, and still make our money.'

'No. We have to do this my way. When I get away with Rose, I don't want anyone coming after us.' She turned to look him in the eye. 'So I need them dead . . . I need Rory dead.'

'And I can do that any time, after you've gone. I want him dead as much as you do.'

She shook her head. 'I doubt that. And no, Luca. We don't wait. You put a bullet in his head on Friday.'

Chapter Eighty-Seven

Maggie had spent Christmas Day wishing she'd taken the gun Luca had offered her. If she had, Rory wouldn't have had to wait until Friday to get a bullet in the head.

She'd wanted Rose's first Christmas to be special, and he'd promised that Chrissy would bring her over for the day. He'd even given her money to buy her daughter a present and a Christmas tree to put it under. She should have known it was never going to happen. On Christmas Eve, Chrissy had arrived at the club dressed up to the nines and snogged Rory under the mistletoe. When Maggie had a go at her – not because she cared what that slag got up to with her husband, but because she wanted to know who was looking after her daughter – Malcolm dragged her out of the club, drove her back to Camden and locked her in the flat.

And that was where she stayed – trapped and alone, wondering if he'd found out what she was planning, wondering where Rose was and if she was okay – until yesterday morning when Rory finally came home.

It had taken every ounce of willpower she had not to scratch his eyes out. But she knew she had to be on her best behaviour. She couldn't give him any excuse to lock her up again.

But now it was Friday at last.

Her money, her future, Rose's future, all hung on the next

371

twelve hours going as planned, and that thought made Maggie feel sick no matter how many times she told herself everything would be all right.

She heard a door slam, and knew immediately that something was wrong.

Rory stalked into the flat. He shrugged off his coat, hanging it on the hook by the door. 'Where've you been, Maggie?' he asked, trying to make it sound casual.

'Just here. Cleaning up a bit.'

'All day?'

'No.' Her heart began to race. 'I went to the chemist's earlier.' She placed a glass on the side, trying to ignore the churning in her stomach. She knew what was coming. When he needed to release stress, he'd pick a fight with her, slap her around. He'd done it in the past when there was trouble with a rival gang or a business deal with a lot riding on it. And tonight's shipment had *everything* riding on it for Rory – and, though he didn't know it, for Maggie too.

'Just to the chemist's – nowhere else?'

She nodded.

'Funny that,' Rory said, cracking his neck. 'Because a little bird told me that he saw you.'

Her gaze wandered over his face. 'Saw me where . . . ? Saw me where, Rory? I swear I haven't been anywhere, or done anything except go the shops and for a walk.'

'And what about the other day, Maggie? Where were you then?'

'I don't know which day you mean, Rory.' Her mouth had gone dry. Had someone seen her with Luca on Monday? They'd been so careful. Maybe this was Rory playing games as he so often did.

Rory was in front of her now, close enough that she could smell his cologne. 'Which day? Are you up to no good on other fucking days?'

'Don't forget I was indoors by myself all Christmas Day and most of Boxing Day.'

'Yeah, that's right, you were. And I went to see Rose.' He curled his lip.

Maggie went rigid.

'When she looked at me, Maggie, do you know what I saw?'

She gave a shake of the head.

He put his mouth against her ear, whispering. 'I saw *him* . . . Like he was fucking looking at me, laughing at me, Maggie. I can't have that. No man would put up with that.'

Maggie's blood ran cold. 'You didn't hurt her, did you, Rory?'

The slap came without warning, snapping her head to the side. With no booze inside her to cushion the blow, the pain seared, sharp and hot, into her jaw.

'Don't question me, Maggie.'

She backed away, her mind racing. 'Rory, please . . .' She pleaded with him. 'I just want to know if she's all right . . . That's all.'

'I think you should stop worrying about Rose and start thinking more about me.'

'I do . . . I think about you all the time.'

He shook his head. 'Like I say, I can't have it. I can't have that happening any more.'

'Have what?'

'Have him looking back at me every time I see Rose . . . She needs to go, Maggie.'

'No . . . no, no, no.' Maggie couldn't think straight. 'What have you done to her? Rory, please, tell me you haven't done anything to Rose . . . RORY!'

His fist connected with her stomach and the air rushed from her as she doubled over, retching. The next blow caught her across her face, sending her sprawling to the floor.

As she tried to crawl away, his boot connected with her ribs. She curled into herself, but he dragged her by her feet across the room towards the bedroom, her vision blurred with tears and pain as thoughts of what he might've done to Rose whirled round her.

'You're staying right here,' he growled, shoving her through the doorway. She fell hard against the side of the bed. 'I'll deal with you after I get back tonight.'

Maggie struggled to stand. 'Rory!'

The door slammed, and the key turned in the lock with a loud click.

'Rory, no!' Maggie threw herself against the door, pounding with her fists. 'Rory, let me out! Rory, you have to let me out!'

The sound of his footsteps disappeared down the hall.

She tried the handle again, knowing it was useless. The door was solid oak.

Somehow she had to get to Luca. She needed his help now more than ever, given what Rory had just said about Rose. But what if he had already done something to her? The thought of it made Maggie feel faint.

She hobbled over to the window, pain radiating through her body. It was too high to jump. Two storeys up with no ledge, nothing to climb down either, and the street below was empty. This was even worse than when she'd been locked in over Christmas; at least then she'd had the run of the entire flat.

She glanced at the clock on the chest of drawers. The shipment would arrive at eight this evening, but before that she needed to meet Luca.

'Think,' she muttered to herself.

She'd come too far for the plan to fail now.

There had to be a way out. She couldn't give up.

She got up and began to search the room. She looked in the wardrobe, under the bed, in the chest of drawers, for anything that might help.

Nothing.

No key, no scissors, no loose screws in the hinges – there was absolutely nothing to help her. She slumped against the wall, defeat crushing her.

It was over.

All her careful planning, all the risk, for nothing.

She thought of Rose. Her beautiful Rose.

Then Maggie frowned and let her eyes drift to the window . . .

Chapter Eighty-Eight

The Limehouse docks stretched out before Rory. He scanned the cranes that lined the harbour, breathed in the smell of the Thames and the strong smell of oil. There was a thriving dock-land community here, a lot of people who Rory knew. He loved the place. He always had. His first job had been working as a docker. It was fucking hard work too: early-morning starts and late nights. At the end of the day his hands had been raw and bloody from hauling the coarse, heavy ropes used for mooring ships and securing the cargo. The constant friction, combined with brackish water and harsh weather, had caused infections and open sores, but he hadn't minded.

Rory prided himself on the fact that he never shirked from grafting. It was in his blood; the men in his family had always been hard workers. It was that drive, along with his ruthless-ness, that had got Rory to the top of his game.

He and his men were out on the very edge of the docks. It was the perfect spot to avoid snooping eyes. The lorries they'd need later to transfer the crates were already parked and ready for tonight.

Pulling up his collar against the sharp wind, Rory leaned against the wall. He checked his watch. Everything needed to go like clockwork today. The tides were in their favour, and there'd been no delays. All being well, the ship should arrive in the next few hours.

Barry came and stood beside him. 'How many men shall we leave here?' he asked, his voice competing with the slap of the water against the docks.

Rory blew into his hands. 'We need to have at least ten men, maybe twelve, here in case anything goes off. The rest can wait at the warehouse.' He glanced across to some of his men who were waiting by the lorries. All armed. All paid well enough to keep their mouths shut. Well, he hoped so. He'd hand-picked them.

After what happened with the last shipment, Rory needed to be sure. There was too much riding on this – he knew that.

Malcolm crushed his cigarette under his heel. 'The men all know the drill, so I can go to the warehouse and wait there along with Barry, unless you want him here with you.'

'No, he can go with you,' Rory said. 'It'll be a long wait for everyone, but we need to stick to that cargo like shit on a cow's arse.'

Barry nodded towards the water. 'What about river patrol?'

'Taken care of.' Rory smiled 'The new sergeant down at Wapping, I knew him from before, so he was happy to go on the payroll.'

'And our men know to keep their mouths shut,' Malcolm added. 'They heard what happened to Freddie and the others, so they won't utter a word. Soon as the crates are at the warehouse, we should be home and dry.'

'I fucking hope so,' Rory said, and fell silent, listening to the creak of moorings and distant voices from the main dock. 'Once it's in, we'll load the crates and move straight to the warehouse. No stops. Benny and Matthew are going to drive behind in their cars, make sure no one is following.'

'And then we divvy it up and start distributing it on Saturday?'

'Yeah. First vanload will go to Liverpool. Next one's for Hull. Then Manchester and Glasgow.' Rory drew on his cigarette. 'They're hungry for it. Everyone's looking for a cheap smoke this time of year.'

Barry rubbed his hands together for warmth. 'And the special merchandise? That still going the same route?'

'No.' Rory's voice dropped. 'Change of plan. The guns will go to the Meadow boys in Birmingham.'

Malcolm nodded in approval as Rory checked his watch again and laughed. 'Fags and guns, two products that will always turn a profit in war or fucking peace.'

A ship's horn sounded, low and deep, and Rory flicked his cigarette into a puddle where it went out with a soft hiss. He looked at Malcolm and Barry. 'Right, why don't you two round up the men who are going with you, and get down to the warehouse. Remember, this time there can't be any fuck-ups . . . Oh, and Malcolm – that other business.' Rory glanced at his watch for the second time in as many minutes. 'I'd like you to sort it out today.'

He gave Malcolm a knowing look and smiled . . .

Chapter Eighty-Nine

Maggie picked up the lighter Rory had left sitting in the ashtray. She flicked it once, twice, then the flame sparked to life on the third try.

She held the flame to the bedroom curtains.

And waited.

At first, nothing happened, then a wisp of smoke curled upwards, followed by an orange glow that spread with surprising speed.

'That's it . . . Come on,' she whispered, stepping back as the flames began to climb the curtain.

Soon the fire was consuming the dry fabric and sending plumes of dark smoke towards the ceiling. Forcing to retreat to the far side of the bedroom, Maggie crouched down below the growing cloud of smoke.

The flames must be visible from the street. Someone would see and raise the alarm . . .

The smoke was getting thicker, stinging Maggie's eyes. She grabbed her nightdress from the bed and used it to cover her mouth and nose to stop the smoke getting into her lungs. The fire was taking hold much faster than she'd anticipated. The ceiling above the burning curtains was starting to blacken as the paint blistered in the heat.

Panic set in as she realised she was trapped in a burning room with no escape.

Maggie crawled to the door and pounded on the heavy wood with one hand, still clutching the nightdress to her mouth with the other.

She screamed as the window shattered from the heat. The fresh air fed the flames and she looked on in horror as they soared higher.

Terrified, she began to crawl toward the nearest wardrobe, but stopped in her tracks as she heard shouting in the hallway. There was a thud as someone tried to kick down the door, but the heavy oak resisted.

More thuds followed as they tried again, and again. Then suddenly the door burst open, wood splintering around the lock as Kenny and Pete, the barmen from downstairs, stood in the doorway.

'Jesus Christ!' Kenny lunged forward, grabbing Maggie's arm and pulling her out into the hallway. 'Someone just ran in the pub and said the place was on fire. Good job they did!'

Pete was holding a fire extinguisher. He stepped into the bedroom to try to tackle the blaze.

'Fire brigade's on their way,' Kenny told her. 'But if this takes hold the whole place will be in flames before they get here.' He looked anxiously from Maggie to a second fire extinguisher that stood by the door. 'Do you think you can get yourself downstairs, Mrs Sheehan, or do you need me to help you?'

'You go help Pete,' she croaked, already making her way down the hall. 'I'm all right.'

As he ran back into the bedroom, she reached into the hall cupboard for her coat and the handbag containing the envelope stuffed with money, then took off down the stairs, wheezing from the effects of the smoke.

When she stepped through the side door, the cold air brought on a coughing fit, but she bundled herself into her coat and set off down the alleyway. Outside the pub, everyone was now looking up at the smoke billowing through the shattered bedroom window. No one noticed her as she hurried away from the pub, heading for Camden High Street and a bus that would take her to the East End.

Finally, after a journey that seemed to take forever, Maggie stepped off the bus and headed for Luca's place. Her chest still felt tight and she kept coughing, but she knew she had to force herself to keep going. Afraid she wouldn't make it on time, she clutched the handbag to her and tried to run.

If it hadn't been for Pete and Kenny breaking down the door, she knew she wouldn't have made it at all.

She pushed the thought aside. There'd be time to dwell on what might've been later, when she and Rose were far away. The main thing now was to get to Luca, as arranged. Then they'd join up with the men he'd hired so she could lead them to the warehouse.

The door beside the restaurant that led up to Luca's flat was slightly ajar. She could someone talking in Italian as she climbed the stairs.

'It's only me, Luca,' she called. There was no reply. Her voice sounded so hoarse she wondered if he'd recognise it. 'It's Maggie, mind if I come . . .'

The door to the flat was wide open. Antonio, the old man from the restaurant below who was Luca's landlord, was standing just inside the doorway with his wife. And beyond them, lying on the sofa, was Luca.

Still.

Pale.

Dead.

Dried vomit crusted the corner of his mouth, his eyes were wide open.

'No . . . no,' Maggie whispered, rushing forward. 'Oh my God, Luca, no . . . no, no, no, no, no.'

He couldn't be dead. He couldn't. Not today. Not now. She needed him. Gently, she touched him. 'Luca . . . Luca.' Then, desperate, she grabbed his shoulders to shake him, but he was already cold and stiff. 'Luca! Luca! Oh my God, why?' she sobbed as the reality of what this meant crashed in.

The old lady crossed herself, then smiled kindly at Maggie. 'It's too late. He's gone. So sorry.' Struggling to express herself in English, she continued: 'We find him like this . . . He put too much of the poison in him.'

Maggie could see for herself what had happened. And what it meant.

It was over. She didn't know where Luca had arranged to meet his men and, even if she did, she knew they wouldn't take orders from her. Her chance of escaping Rory was gone. Worse, she'd lost her chance to save Rose.

Or had she?

She stepped past the old couple, went into Luca's bedroom and threw open the wardrobe door. Her eyes fell on two black-plastic-wrapped packets. She stuffed them into her bag and took off, running as fast as she could.

Chapter Ninety

The club in Soho wasn't due to open for a couple of hours. Maggie knew that most of the men would be with Rory, so hopefully she'd be able to slip in and out without being seen.

She snuck in via the side yard, using the key she'd had duplicated to open the back door. Pausing to checking that no one was in sight, she crept down the corridor that led to the office, her ears on red alert.

Though she knew Rory and Malcolm would be in Limehouse, that didn't stop her expecting them to appear at any moment.

She went straight to the safe and entered the combination. Glancing back at the door, she pulled out the red leather-bound ledger, grabbed a notebook. Rory had his own version of shorthand, but she knew every symbol and abbreviation. Translating as she went, she scribbled down the information she needed.

Footsteps sounded in the hallway. Frantically she shoved the notebook into her pocket and placed the ledger in the safe.

The door swung open.

Maggie gasped.

Davey stood there, his eyes widening when he saw her. 'Mrs Sheehan, I . . . I . . .' He looked back down the corridor, then stepped into the room and closed the door behind him. 'You shouldn't be here.' He sounded frightened for her.

'I know. Please don't tell anyone you've seen me.'

He gave her a sad smile. 'I won't. You can trust me.'

'Thank you.' She reached into her bag, pulling out one of the packets of money she'd taken from Luca's wardrobe. She pressed it into Davey's hand. 'Here take this.'

He shook his head. 'You don't need to pay me to stay quiet.'

'That's not what this is for.' She glanced nervously at the door. 'This is so you can leave here. Today. That's what I'm doing . . . There's enough for you to set yourself up somewhere.'

Davey stared at her in confusion.

'Take it . . . please.' She threw her arms around him. 'Look after yourself.'

And then she made for the door.

'Wait, Mrs Sheehan—'

'Maggie.'

Davey nodded and smiled. 'Maggie.' His eyes scanned the bruises on her face. 'I'm glad you're going.'

She nodded. 'So am I.'

She left the club the same way she'd entered. Sticking to the backstreets and alleys, she made her way to Covent Garden. Seeing a telephone box ahead of her, she made a beeline for it.

Closing the door behind her, she lifted the receiver and dialled 0. When the operator put her through, she fed the coins into the slot with shaking fingers.

Chapter Ninety-One

The wait was excruciating. Each passing car made her tense, and each minute felt like forever. She'd found a doorway to wait with a clear view of the building and alternated between watching the entrance and checking her watch, nervously chewing her lip all the while.

Then at last she saw him.

'Maggie.' DI Simons came to a stop in front of her.

'Inspector.'

She reached into her pocket, bringing out the notebook. 'I've written down the names of every bent copper on Rory's payroll. Every fucking judge. Every customs official who looks the other way when his shipments come in. The numbers are bribes paid, and the dates.' She pushed it back into her pocket and glanced around. 'Come on, let's walk.'

Simons's face remained neutral as he walked beside her.

'The shipment I was telling you about on the phone – it came in this morning and it's going out first thing tomorrow. They're turning round the crates in the early hours.'

'Where are they storing it?'

She shook her head. 'I don't trust the Old Bill, so I'm not saying a word until you agree to my terms.'

He looked puzzled, but nodded for her to continue.

'If you don't do it tonight,' Maggie warned, 'you'll lose your chance.'

'Why are you doing this?'

Maggie came to a halt, looked him in the eye. 'I'm afraid for my daughter, Inspector. The law doesn't protect women like me, and it certainly doesn't care about girls like Rose.'

He nodded, looking like he understood.

'But I'm not doing this for free.' She glanced around her, checking if they were being watched. 'It comes at a price.'

Chapter Ninety-Two

The terraced house in Kilburn Park Way looked like all the others on the street. It had a neat front garden, and lace curtains in the windows. The lights were on.

She crossed the street with purpose, her eyes fixed on the front door.

Within moments of her hammering on the knocker, the door swung open.

Chrissy's eyes widened. 'Mag—'

Before she could finish, Maggie's fist connected with her face. Chrissy stumbled backwards, hand clasped over her split lip. 'You fucking cow!'

Maggie followed her in, dropping her bag and kicking the door shut behind her. 'Where is she?' she demanded. 'Where's my daughter?'

Instead of answering, Chrissy launched herself at Maggie. They crashed into the hallway table, sending the vase of flowers smashing to the floor. Maggie grabbed a handful of blonde hair and yanked hard.

'Where is she?'

Chrissy's knee came up, catching her in her already bruised ribs. Pain shot through Maggie's side, but she kept hold of

Chrissy's hair and headbutted her, feeling the crunch of cartil-age as Chrissy's nose broke.

Blood pouring from her nose, Chrissy screamed. 'You fuck-ing cunt, you ain't having her.' She clawed at Maggie's eyes, but Maggie rammed her weight into Chrissy, pushing her back against the wall.

'Tell me where she is.'

Chrissy snarled. 'Over my dead body.'

'Oh, that can be arranged.'

She tried to fight back, but Maggie was like a woman pos-sessed; she threw Chrissy down on the floor, then straddled her, pinning the woman's arms with her knees. 'I want my daughter.'

'Fuck you!' Chrissy spat, blood and saliva speckling Mag-gie's face.

Her response was a sharp right fist that snapped Chrissy's head to the side. The next moment, Chrissy went limp beneath her, knocked out cold by the blow.

Stepping over Chrissy, she ran down the hallway and took the stairs two at a time.

The landing had four doors, which were all closed. Maggie rushed to the first one, throwing it open.

A bathroom. Empty.

The second door was a box room used for storage.

The third room was clearly Chrissy's bedroom.

Maggie rushed to open fourth door.

She yanked it open.

The room had pale yellow walls and a small wardrobe.

And there, in a white wooden cot by the window, was Rose.

Maggie felt her breath catch in her throat. She ran to the cot and laughed when she saw Rose looking up at her with those green eyes, her chubby cheeks dimpling with a smile.

Scooping her up, Maggie cradled her against her chest. Closing her eyes, she kissed her head. 'I'm here,' Maggie whispered, pressing her face against Rose's soft hair. 'I'm here now.'

She turned to leave.

Maggie screamed.

Malcolm filled the doorway.

And Maggie clutched Rose tighter against her.

'Give her to me, Maggie. I'm here to take her away.'

'No.' Maggie backed away until her legs hit the cot.

As Malcolm stepped into the room, Maggie placed Rose back in her cot and turned to face him.

'Rory sent me to get her.' Malcolm laughed. 'He doesn't like to look at her any more. It's time to get rid.'

'No . . . No, please, Malcolm, she's only a baby. Please, I'll do anything.'

He looked Maggie up and down and began to undo his belt. 'Anything?' he smirked. 'Maybe you and me should have a little fun, then.'

Maggie saw the bulge in his trousers. She shook her head. 'Rory will kill you.'

'He's not going to know, is he?'

Suddenly there was a loud bang and Malcolm's body jerked, his eyes widening in surprise. A dark red stain appeared on his jacket, and then he toppled forward, crashing to the floor.

Behind him in the doorway stood Davey, holding a gun.

'Davey!' Maggie's eyes went from him to Malcolm's body and the pool of blood spreading across the pale carpet.

'Go, Maggie. Go now.'

She didn't need to be told twice. She lifted Rose into her arms, wrapping her tightly in the blankets from the cot.

'What about you?' she asked, turning back to face Davey.

Davey smiled at her. 'I'll be fine. I'll sort this . . . Just go.'

She held his gaze for a moment longer, then, holding Rose tightly to her chest, she ran down the stairs, picked up her bag and headed out the front door.

There was just one more thing that she had to do . . .

Chapter Ninety-Three

Maggie sat in the darkness of the police van, clinging to Rose as she peered through the small tinted window at the warehouse across an expanse of wasteland. She'd given Simons the address and layout of the place, and now all she could do was wait.

There was no one else here; all the coppers had gone with Simons. The wind was getting up, howling around the van, making eerie noises that heightened Maggie's anxiety.

She kissed Rose's head, grateful for the comfort of her daughter's presence. The sooner she was gone from here, the better . . .

Inside, the warehouse was a hive of activity. Rory's men were hauling wooden crates to the loading bay and stacking them in neat rows while Rory stood watching.

'Barry, has Malcolm come back yet?'

The burly Scot broke off from supervising the unloading to answer him. 'No, boss.'

'Make sure he comes to see me the moment he's back.' Rory gritted his teeth in irritation. He'd deal with Malcolm later. Thankfully, everything else was going to plan. The ship had been bang on time, and the lorries had been loaded and driven to the warehouse without incident.

'Once you've done—'

A shot rang out, followed by the sound of tyres screeching to a halt on the gravel outside.

'Boss! Trouble!' a lookout yelled as police vehicles surrounded the warehouse.

Rory was already moving, heading for the back.

'Police! Open up!'

The shout echoed through the warehouse, followed by a pounding on the metal doors.

'Get the guns!' Rory bellowed.

His men abandoned the crates and ran for the weapons. Barry kicked open the crate next to him and began distributing revolvers and ammunition.

The hammering grew louder as the police tried to break through the metal doors.

'Take ten men and go cover the front,' Rory ordered Barry. 'I want the rest of you covering the windows and back. And if anyone gets a clean shot at a copper, blow the fucking cunt's head off. There's a drink in it for you.'

As his men sprinted to their positions, there was a loud bang and a window shattered, spraying glass across the warehouse floor. The main doors burst open, flying off their hinges and uniformed officers came charging in.

'Armed police! Nobody move!'

The first shot came from Barry. A copper went down, blood spurting from his neck.

Then it all kicked off.

There was a barrage of gunfire from both sides, bullets ricocheting off the metal pillars. The sound was deafening, and Rory's orders to his men were lost in the chaos. While windows shattered above him, Rory took down two officers with head shots.

He spun round in time to see a copper raising his truncheon

at Tony. Rory charged forward and smashed the butt of the gun in the policeman's back, causing him to drop to his knees. Then he proceeded to ram the gun into the man's face until he went limp.

'Boss! This way!' Barry called from across the warehouse.

As Rory, now covered in the police officer's blood, charged towards him, Barry brought up his gun and fired. Another officer went down, and Barry charged forward, pulling out a knife he kept tucked into his boot, and plunging it into the officer's chest and twisting the blade to finish him off.

'Cover me,' Rory ordered. 'Then follow on. We should be able to get out this way.' He sprinted across to a tower of crates in the far corner. Hidden behind the crates was a metal door. Rory opened it and slipped into the dark corridor.

Unable to stand the confinement of the police van any longer, Maggie opened the door and stepped down. Rose stirred against her chest as she got out. She'd heard the noise as the raid kicked off, but now she could see the warehouse across the clearing, lit up by the headlights of the police vans.

She could see Rory's men being led out in handcuffs. There was no more gunfire. It was over.

Maggie watched as Rory's empire crumbled before her eyes.

Rose let out a whimper and she looked down at her little face nestled in the blankets. Smiling, Maggie rocked her gently in her arms, soothing her.

'Maggie.'

At the sound of that voice her blood turned to ice. She turned to find Rory standing ten feet away. His face and clothes were soaked in blood. His stare was cold and hard.

'So . . . it was you.'

'Stay away from us.' It came out as a whimper not an order, and she began to shake.

'My own wife. My own fucking wife betrays me again.' He glanced at Rose in her arms. 'You can't stop disappointing me, can you, Maggie? I gave you everything, but it wasn't enough for you.' His hand moved to his waistband, pulling out a blade. 'I warned you, didn't I?' He stepped forward. 'I said I'd kill you if you betrayed me again.' His lips twisted in that familiar smirk. 'And now I can kill my two little birds with one stone.'

Panic surged through Maggie. The police were focused on the warehouse and no one was watching this lone police van on the edge of the clearing.

Her heart pounding, Maggie turned and ran. Triggered by the sudden movement, Rose began to cry.

She lost her footing on the uneven ground and stumbled onto one knee.

Behind her, she could hear Rory's footsteps getting closer.

'Maggie, you might as well stop running, because you're not going to get away from me this time.' His voice was raw with rage. 'And, once I catch you, I'm going to make you watch what I do to your fucking daughter!'

She tried to run faster, but a hand grabbed her hair from behind, yanking her backwards with brutal force. Maggie twisted as she fell, landing hard on her side, her arms still wrapped protectively around Rose, using her body as a shield.

Rory stood over her, knife in hand.

But before he could move a shout rang out from behind them and three officers charged forward to tackle Rory to the ground.

They piled on top of him, one kneeling on his back to keep him face down, while the other two forced his arms behind his back.

'Rory Sheehan, you're under arrest.' The tall policeman read

Rory his rights, while his colleague snapped handcuffs around his wrists.

As they hauled him to his feet, Rory's eyes turned on Maggie. She could see the hatred burning in them as he hissed, 'This isn't over. I'll find you – both of you. Then I'll finish off what I started.' He laughed as they pushed him towards a waiting police car.

Rose wailed against her chest as Maggie began to tremble uncontrollably.

A thunderous boom echoed across the wasteland as a lorry trying to escape the warehouse compound collided with a police vehicle. Flames shot up, illuminating the night sky.

'Are you all right, Maggie?' DI Simons appeared at her side, concern on his face.

'I need to get out of here,' she whispered, her voice unsteady. 'Now.'

Simons nodded, then he returned to the van and emerged a few moments later with a leather satchel and Maggie's handbag. He handed her the handbag, and then the satchel. 'Your money,' he said. 'As agreed.' He paused, then asked, 'Can I take you anywhere?'

'No,' Maggie said, already backing away.

'Are you sure? Not to a train station, to a bus station?'

Again Maggie shook her head. She looked down at Rose, then raised her eyes to Simons. 'No, wherever I'm going, I'll get there on my own.'

And, as the warehouse began to burn, Maggie turned and walked away, leaving behind the life that had held her captive for so long. Rose, quiet now against her chest, clutched her hand with her tiny fingers.

Then Maggie Riley vanished into the darkness, vowing never to return . . .

Epilogue

1977

The wheel is come full circle.

William Shakespeare

Chapter Ninety-Four

'Mum! Mum! We're here.' Maggie spun round in her coach seat and smiled at Rose, who'd been chattering away with the other youngsters at the back of the coach. 'It looks amazing!' Rose's piercing green eyes shone with excitement as she stared out of the window. 'Can we go to Leicester Square first?'

'We can go anywhere you want. It's your day.'

'And the Queen's, don't forget!' Shirley cackled as she pulled herself up out of her seat. 'Bloody hell, I'm glad we're here. I thought I was going to piss meself.'

Maggie grinned at her daughter, then the two of them made their way down the aisle and off the coach, setting foot on London pavement for the first time in over fourteen years.

She hadn't wanted to come back, but Rose had been so keen and it wasn't fair to make her daughter miss out on something just because Maggie didn't want to be confronted with her past. But now she found herself standing in the place she'd run away from, it struck her how stupid her fears had been. After all, what was she afraid of? Rory had died in prison five years ago when some lag stabbed him to death. She'd been informed of it at the time, but it was only now that she felt truly free.

As their fellow coach passengers chattered excitedly around

them, taking in the Silver Jubilee decorations, Maggie looked at Rose. 'You know I love you.'

Rose, conscious of her friends watching, blushed and giggled. 'Mu-umm!'

'Come on,' called Mavis, rounding everyone up. 'We need to get to the Mall – the Queen ain't going to wait for us lot!'

Rose tugged on Maggie's sleeve. 'Mum, can we go and see where you used to hang out first?'

Her daughter's question caught her off guard. She'd told Rose she'd been born in Camden and spent time in Soho, but she'd skimmed over the details. 'I er . . . I'm not sure. Don't you want to go with your friends?'

'We can meet up with them later. Come on, Mum, *please.*'

Maggie moved out of the way of a group of young girls with painted Union Jack faces. 'I don't know . . .'

'Mum, please.'

She smiled at her daughter. They were as close as any daughter and mother could be. She'd always loved Rose's happy-go-lucky nature, breezing through life as if she hadn't a worry in the world, something that Maggie couldn't have dreamed of when she was a kid. She'd been determined to give her daughter the childhood she'd missed out on.

Going to live in Margate had been a spur-of-the-moment decision. She'd had no idea where she was heading when she'd left London that night. She'd looked at the station departures board, overwhelmed, and then she saw a poster that said, *Escape to Margate!* It was then she'd remembered Doris saying she'd always wanted to live on the south-east coast. So she'd taken the first train there, and she'd been there ever since.

'If that's what you want,' Maggie agreed. She glanced over to

Shirley. 'Shirl, Rose and I are going to look around for a bit. I'll join you later.'

'Are you sure you should? What if you get lost?'

'I'll be fine.'

'London's not like Margate, girl. You hear all sorts.'

Maggie winked at Shirley. 'You certainly do.' She laughed then and linked arms with her daughter as they walked down Charing Cross Road.

Rose chatted away excitedly as she took in the sights. Around them, everyone was intent on enjoying themselves. Maggie drank it all in. As much as she loved Margate, a part of her heart belonged to London. For all the good and bad, this had once been her home.

Red-white-and-blue bunting fluttered above Leicester Square, crisscrossing the streets. God how this place had changed! Or maybe the place hadn't changed – maybe it was her. She was no longer that frightened teenager who'd run down the road with her daughter in her arms.

The buildings looked pretty much the same way they always had, but the West End had a whole different energy. Louder. Brighter. This London felt like it was lit with hope.

'This is incredible, Mum. You're so lucky you lived here.'

Maggie smiled seeing the excitement on Rose's face. Each step they took triggered a memory. This was where Luca had waved a handkerchief from the back of his Jaguar. This was the newsagent's where she'd bumped into DI Simons. That was the pub where she'd got arrested.

'See that pizza bar, Rose? That used to be a coffee shop – everyone used to hang out there.'

They crossed over Old Compton Street and she held her daughter's hand tightly when she saw the bakery on the corner, which had once been a cafe, until it was burned down in the protection wars.

'Maggie . . . Maggie?'

She heard her voice being called and she spun round, her eyes scanning the crowd.

'Maggie! It is you.'

'Oh my God . . . Davey! I can't believe it!'

She watched Davey push his way towards her, a huge grin on his face. 'Me neither! It's so good to see you.' He threw his arms around her and she returned the hug.

He let her go, blinking and not quite looking like he believed that he was seeing her in the flesh. 'I thought I'd never see you again – but here you are.'

'We came up for the Jubilee. This is my daughter . . . Rose.'

He stared at Rose, then smiled. 'Rose, you have no idea how good it is to see you.'

'Mum, who's this?'

'This is my friend Davey. He once did a very brave thing for me.' She smiled at him and they held each other's gaze for a moment.

'Come with me,' he said excitedly. 'I want to show you something. It won't take long, I promise.'

They followed him into Greek Street, then he stopped outside a pub and pointed. 'Look.'

She glanced up at the pub sign he was pointing at.

'*Maggie's!*' She turned to him. 'Oh my God, this pub isn't named after me, is it?'

Davey nodded. 'Come in, let me get you both a drink.'

'Can we, Mum, please?'

'Okay, two lemonades it is.' Maggie laughed and they made their way inside.

The entrance of the pub had old photographs on the walls,

black-and-white images of Soho in the early sixties. Maggie paused to study each one. The market on Berwick Street. The Windmill Theatre. A shot of the coffee shops on Old Compton Street. So many memories of how Soho used to be.

'These are great, Davey.'

'Yeah, things have changed so much. It's good to be reminded of how it used to be.'

They descended the narrow, blue-carpeted staircase, the sounds of the street behind them fading as they went.

Halfway down, they heard a voice call out from below.

'We'll be open in ten minutes.'

Maggie's hand clutched the banister, her legs suddenly unable to support her. She sank down onto the step, a cold wave washing through her body.

'Mum? Mum, are you all right?'

Maggie couldn't speak, but she nodded and gave a weak smile, then she glanced at Davey before turning her gaze in the direction of the voice.

'Is everything okay up there? Oh, Davey, I didn't know it was—' He broke off when he caught sight of Maggie. The right side of his face was marked with old burn scars, pulling at the corner of his eye and mouth. But Maggie would have known that face anywhere.

'Maggie,' Thomas whispered.

She couldn't see him through her tears. 'I . . . I thought you were dead.'

He took a step towards her. 'So did I.'

She frowned.

'Davey rescued me from the fire.' Thomas gestured with his hand. 'We own this place together. Me and Davey.' He glanced at Davey, who nodded at him.

403

She spun to look at Davey. 'Why didn't you tell me? Why didn't you tell me he was alive?'

Thomas walked up the stairs to her. He touched her face gently with his scarred hand. 'He couldn't, Maggie. You know what Rory and Malcolm were like. It was too risky . . . I'm sorry.'

Maggie nodded. She understood. But, at the same time, it hurt. All these years she'd lived with the pain of believing Thomas was dead. The grief had never gone away.

'I was in hospital for weeks . . . And when I got out you'd disappeared and nobody knew where you were.' He gave her a sad smile.

She looked into his green eyes, allowing herself for the first time in years to remember what it was like to love him. Then she shook herself out of her daze. 'Thomas, this is . . . Rose.'

Thomas stared at Maggie, and she could only manage to give the smallest of nods.

'She's . . .'

'Yes, Thomas.' Maggie's voice was hoarse with emotion. 'She is.' Maggie tapped the stair next to her for Thomas to come and sit down. She held on to his hand, and her daughter's. They sat down either side of her. She knew she needed to tell Rose who Thomas was, but that could come later.

'I thought I'd never see you again.' Thomas breathed the words, barely audible. 'I'm sorry, Maggie. I'm so sorry that I brought so many problems into your life and I couldn't protect you.' He glanced at Rose and gave the warmest smile. 'Either of you.'

'No, Thomas.' Maggie squeezed his hand. 'You were the only light I had back then. I've never regretted that you were in my life. I wouldn't change that for the world.' She wiped his tears away with her sleeve.

'So, no regret, Maggie?'

Maggie smiled again, a thousand memories, a thousand moments rushing through her. She leaned her head on Thomas's shoulder. 'No, Thomas, not a single one.'

RAISING READERS
Books Build Bright Futures

Dear Reader,

We'd love your attention for one more page to tell you about the crisis in children's reading, and what we can all do.

Studies have shown that reading for fun is the **single biggest predictor of a child's future life chances** – more than family circumstance, parents' educational background or income. It improves academic results, mental health, wealth, communication skills, ambition and happiness.[1]

The number of children reading for fun is in rapid decline. Young people have a lot of competition for their time. In 2024, 1 in 10 children and young people in the UK aged 5 to 18 did not own a single book at home.[2]

Hachette works extensively with schools, libraries and literacy charities, but here are some ways we can all raise more readers:

- Reading to children for just 10 minutes a day makes a difference
- Don't give up if children aren't regular readers – there will be books for them!
- Visit bookshops and libraries to get recommendations
- Encourage them to listen to audiobooks
- Support school libraries
- Give books as gifts

There's a lot more information about how to encourage children to read on our website: **www.RaisingReaders.co.uk**

Thank you for reading.

hachette
UK

1 OECD, '21st-Century Readers: Developing Literacy Skills in a Digital World', 2021, https://www.oecd.org/en/publications/21st-century-readers_a83d84cb-en.html
2 National Literacy Trust, 'Book Ownership in 2024', November 2024, https://literacytrust.org.uk/research-services/research-reports/book-ownership-in-2024